W9-CDX-683

"GRIPPING."

— The New York Times

"SUPERB."

— San Francisco Chronicle

"MASTERFUL."

— Entertainment Weekly

"PROVOCATIVE."

— The Wall Street Journal

"POWERFUL . . . MS. BROWN IS TENACIOUS IN HER EXAMINATION OF EACH MAJOR CHARACTER . . . THIS NOVEL, FOR ALL ITS PHILOSOPHICAL PROVOCATION AND LITERARY MERIT, IS ALSO AN UNABASHED, READ-UNTIL-DAWN PAGE-TURNER."
—*The New York Times Book Review*

High Praise for

BEFORE AND AFTER

the spectacular best seller by
ROSELLEN BROWN

"WONDERFULLY REAL AND DETAILED . . . A TERRIFIC PLOT, GREAT SUSPENSE AND PACING."
—*The Village Voice*

"A BRILLIANT EVOCATION . . . FEW CONTEMPORARY NOVELISTS CAN MATCH ROSELLEN BROWN'S SCRUPULOUS AND OFTEN BRILLIANT EXAMINATIONS OF DOMESTIC WOE."
—*The Atlanta Journal & Constitution*

"A STUNNING DRAMA . . . AN ABSORBING TALE OF A FAMILY'S STRUGGLE TO SURVIVE THE WORST EVENT OF THEIR COLLECTIVE LIVES . . . BROWN DOES AN AWE-INSPIRING JOB OF PUTTING THE READER INTO THE MIND OF EACH CHARACTER."
—*San Antonio Express-News*

"TABLOID HEADLINES ARE TURNED INTO POWERFUL FICTION IN THIS SHATTERING NOVEL ABOUT A 17-YEAR-OLD ACCUSED OF MURDERING HIS GIRLFRIEND."
—*New York*

Please turn the page for more extraordinary acclaim . . .

"CHILLING . . . BROWN WRITES BEAUTIFULLY AND BELIEVABLY, CAPTURING ANGER, DOUBT AND BEWILDERMENT."

—*People*

"BROWN IS BRAVE AND SUBTLE, NOT AFRAID OF COMPLEXITY AND LIFE'S MIXED FEELINGS . . . FEW WRITERS TODAY SHOW MORE CLEARLY THE KNIFE THAT CUTS EXISTENCE INTO TWO PARTS WHEN TRAGEDY STRIKES."

—*Chicago Sun-Times*

"*BEFORE AND AFTER* WORKS ON ONE LEVEL AS A SUSPENSE NOVEL—AND A SUPERB ONE—AND, ON ANOTHER, AS A POWERFUL STUDY OF ONE FAMILY."

—*San Francisco Chronicle*

"BEAUTIFULLY RENDERED . . . BY THE END OF THE BOOK, ONE IS TORN BETWEEN WANTING JUSTICE TO BE DONE AND CARING FOR A LIFE THAT IS IN DANGER OF BEING WASTED IN THE WAKE OF A PASSIONATE CRIME."

—*The Wall Street Journal*

"MASTERFUL . . . MAKES US REALIZE JUST HOW ENIGMATIC ORDINARY THINGS LIKE FAMILY LOVE AND LOYALTY ARE. WHAT MORE CAN WE ASK FROM A WORK OF FICTION?"

—*Entertainment Weekly*

"FIERCE, GRIPPING AND PAINFUL, *BEFORE AND AFTER* WILL BE ENJOYED AS A PSYCHOLOGICAL THRILLER. IT SHOULD ALSO BE APPRECIATED AS A SCRUPULOUSLY OBSERVED WORK OF LITERARY FICTION, ARGUABLY THE AMPLY GIFTED MS. BROWN'S FINEST WORK SO FAR."
—The New York Times

"READERS WILL REMAIN IMMERSED IN BROWN'S GRIPPING STORY. MESMERIZED BY THE QUESTIONS SHE RAISES AND BY THE BRAVE, INTELLIGENT, COMPASSIONATE MANNER IN WHICH SHE DEALS WITH THEM."
—Publishers Weekly

"RIVETING . . . WEDDING STUNNINGLY WROUGHT PROSE TO BRILLIANTLY OBSERVED DETAIL, BROWN TAKES US DEEPLY INSIDE HER CHARACTERS."
—The Miami Herald

"A REMARKABLE, NIGHTMARISH, OFTEN SHATTERING NOVEL."
—Kirkus Reviews

"COMPELLING . . . MS. BROWN'S WRITING REMINDS US OF THE POTENTIAL FOR PROXIMITY OF LANGUAGE AND EMOTION, AND DOES WHAT THE VERY BEST WRITING CAN, WHICH IS TO MAKE US FEEL."
—The Dallas Morning News

BEFORE AND AFTER

Rosellen Brown

A DELL BOOK

Published by
Dell Publishing
a division of
Bantam Doubleday Dell Publishing Group, Inc.
1540 Broadway
New York, New York 10036

If you purchased this book without a cover you should be aware that this book is stolen property. It was reported as "unsold and destroyed" to the publisher and neither the author nor the publisher has received any payment for this "stripped book."

Lyrics from "All the Things You Are" by Jerome Kern and Oscar Hammerstein, copyright © 1939, renewed by Polygram International Publishing, Inc., are reproduced by permission of Polygram International Publishing, Inc.

Copyright © 1992 by Rosellen Brown

All rights reserved. No part of this book may be reproduced or transmitted in any form or by any means, electronic or mechanical, including photocopying, recording, or by any information storage and retrieval system, without the written permission of the Publisher, except where permitted by law. For information address: Farrar Straus Giroux, New York, New York.

The trademark Dell® is registered in the U.S. Patent and Trademark Office.

ISBN: 0-440-21654-0

Reprinted by arrangement with Farrar Straus Giroux

Printed in the United States of America

Published simultaneously in Canada

September 1993

10 9 8 7 6 5 4 3 2 1

OPM

To my beloved New Hampshire friends,
who have kept a place for me
at their fires and at their tables

My thanks to the Ingram Merrill Foundation for their financial assistance and the trust that accompanied it.

I am grateful for the help of numerous prison officials in Westmoreland, Manchester, and Concord, New Hampshire, and Cambridge, Massachusetts, and for the assistance of L. Phillips Runyon, Susan Howard, Paul Schweizer, and Glenn Gotschall. I am especially indebted to Judge Mary Bacon of the 338th Criminal Court of Houston for more than technical advice: for a demonstration of judicial practice informed by humane ideals and a love of the complexities that fiction—the stories of a thousand strangers—can bring to the law.

When one does not love too much one does not love enough.

—*Pascal*

BEFORE
AND
AFTER

The little boy's smile is so wide, sun in his eyes, that he seems to be crying. He is fair-haired, not quite blond. Or it's the white light that douses his head and shoulders with pallor. Suddenly he flings his arms up, straight up, and catches a bar in his hands. He is six or seven—tall enough to catch the bar and hoist himself up and over, swinging like one of those little wooden monkeys who leap between two squeezed sticks and flip over and plummet down in a single fluid curve, the kind, no battery needed, that will repeat the trick without complaint as often as he is squeezed. But after two assaults on the bar the boy stands in the scuffed dirt before the camera, spreads his arms wide, grinning wildly, then clamps his arms around himself, hugging hard, his hands squeezing so tight you'd think it would hurt. He holds himself in a delighted embrace, his eyes a little crazed-on-purpose, as if to say, See me, I'll do anything! He is beaming.

* * *

She is about eight, all dressed up, her fair hair shining. She stands stiffly as if for a still photograph, then, grim-faced, salutes and abruptly vanishes. There is a lot of awkward focusing and unfocusing, crowds, shoulders, a fat boy turning to give the finger to the camera, amiably smiling. Even he, like the others, is wearing a suit; the girls flash by in festive dresses.

Finally, pitching and crooked in the frame, a graduation procession begins to shape up at the rear of the hall. Middle school, this must be, to judge by the half-fledged look of them, some of the boys still children, just as many of the girls fully in bloom. A flood of shiny red gowns pours down the aisle, a few accented with gold braid and a tassel at the end. This is for academic achievement; it is called the "dork ribbon" by the boys who don't have it, joined enthusiastically by those who do.

As he comes close, the boy, now fairly tall, his face victimized by blemishes cast across it like pebbles, smiles broadly, again that look that could be a wince, the way his cheeks draw back and wrinkle. Then he remembers himself and ducks his head, turning away.

There are no smooth fades between shots. Each refocusing is a wrench, subjects appear with the suddenness of a shout. The little girl is standing, who knows how long she's been patiently waiting there, with a paper cup in her hand. She is saying something—there is none of that intimate commentary of the wielder of the video camera who mutters like the broadcaster at a pro golf game—and gesturing toward the cup, making a vile face: sick, she seems to be saying. This stuff will make you sick. She is wearing her brother's dork ribbon, she raises its golden tassel to her face and moves it against her cheek like a little brush. She still doesn't smile, having obviously decided that gravity is more fun, more mysterious, in any event, than conviviality. Then her brother is there, suddenly, and she is brushing his cheek and he is defending himself with his elbows, he is pretending to strangle her. He pulls at the ribbon, disorganizes her hair. He looks very happy, in fact: sticks his tongue out, slaps his cheeks, hers, and then they perform a complicated set of maneuvers—only best friends or brothers and sisters have time to work out such rituals—with linked fingers, knuckles against heads, handclasps, and finally an elbow grip. They are falling over laughing. She disappears from sight entirely, apparently fallen to the floor under his feet.

Then, against a bulletin board, jostled and interrupted by the heads of passersby not thoughtful enough to stay out of the camera's way, a blond woman and a bearded man join the boy and girl, also smiling ceremonially and speaking unheard words.

The woman is not beautiful but she has the kind of attractiveness that comes of self-assurance, good, understated clothes, and possibly the sheen of money (long since overcome but evident, clinging like an old rumor). The man looks, in his dark, curly, red-tinged beard, to those who wish to see him that way, rabbinic. (There are, in fact, truck drivers, masons, and gas-station attendants who wear beards like this around here and no one would think such a thing about them.) He is not quite broad—certainly not heavy—but he gives the feeling of warmth and solidity, a good solid chest to nestle against and, evident here, the habit of making frequent small comforting movements around his children, smoothing, adjusting, resting his hand companionably on shoulder or arm. He and the woman turn to each other at one point, just after the large shadow of a passing family darkens them like a cloud, and, as if they were clasping hands, grin at each other above the heads of their clowning children.

PART 1

CAROLYN

She wasn't on ER, never was during the day when she had patients, but they called her in on it. She was feeling around Jennifer Foyle's neck and groin for tenderness, talking over the girl's curly head, speaking for some reason about smallpox, Jennifer's mother insisting that one of these days they'd all pay for discontinuing vaccinations—the mother rolled up her blue flowered blouse sleeve and showed off a large mark, very badly done. She speculated that AIDS might be the result of this generation's having missed their vaccinations. Maybe, Carolyn thought, she just wanted everyone else to have a crack at a scar like that, which was as large as the gold locket she wore around her neck, and pebbled.

Then Karen poked her head in without knocking and told her she was needed downstairs. "Really right away," she added with mock sternness, because she knew Carolyn's propensity for thoroughness, the fetish she made of finishing consultations neatly and carefully so that everything was understood, every question answered.

Grudgingly, Carolyn wrapped things up. "Okay, kid," she said direct to Jennifer, who giggled. "Nothing wrong that a little preventive antibiotic won't take care of." She wrote the prescription, smiled at the child and touched her sweet bare shoulder reassuringly, and hurried out the back way because the waiting room was full and the mothers there would, when they saw her heading out, either stop her for one quick question or simply be offended, in spite of reason, that she was running out on them. The only departure a group of mothers would countenance without muttering was that of an OB-GYN on the way to a delivery. "Make my apologies," she called to Karen as she went. "See if you can push everything back an hour."

She had listened so often to her own squishy footsteps along the corridors—the professional building was attached to the hospital, and all of it was paved with the same dark brown composition flooring—that sometimes she thought the sound of hurrying feet was the doctor's real heartbeat. There was snow outside, it had been falling all morning, so it was going to be a car wreck, some kid wrapped around a pole or plowed into, at the bottom of a long slide down a hill. She had a faint pang of anxiety about Jacob, out there after school, at large like all the others. (Judith would have been home by now, off the bus and straight into the warm kitchen.) But she had mostly learned to quash those: there's no way for a pediatrician to try out every catastrophe on her own children. Anyway, the statistics were with them, for what they were worth—were with anybody, one by one.

Teenagers in car wrecks, she thought, pushing through swinging doors. They were bad enough for anybody, of course—the unexpectedness, the terrible instant consequences—but they were worse for teenagers. Worst case, there'd be a death or a maiming so heartlessly premature.

But even if no one is hurt, even if it's just angry parents and a draw on the deductible, she had seen so much still-fresh confidence shattered that way, had seen such nasty psychological fallout. You might think it would be chastening, maybe get the boys especially to learn a little care and self-control. But an accident rarely seemed to yield more good than bad.

She thought this as she made the last turn to the emergency room, and already she could feel the anxiety rolling toward her in waves. She had passed two nurses and an orderly rushing the other way, and their nods had something in them of a familiar tension reserved for the awful days, the shocking injuries. This was a small town, a small hospital—everyone saw everything, or heard about it in a minute and a half. Not good, she thought. Distinctly not good.

The curtains were pulled around the far bed but she could see an unholy number of pants legs showing out underneath. Actually, the curtains weren't entirely closed —too late to bother protecting anyone's privacy; if anything, there was anger in the parting of the protective drapes, the sloppiness of a furious assertion: Look! See what we're dealing with in here! She saw an elbow, gesturing, protrude from the opening as she approached—Trygve Hanson's, it looked like, the oldest doctor on the staff, the one who had delivered and doctored three-quarters of the town before the OB-GYN newcomers and the cardiac and thoracic men and she and the other pediatricians moved in to split things between them.

Carolyn ducked in without disturbing the curtains. It was steamy inside the little tent and all of them were sweaty. But when she focused in, she understood that it wasn't the heat that was making them uncomfortable. Still on the gurney on which she'd been wheeled in was a girl with her skull stove in. It was bashed, collapsed like a beer can, one of the younger doctors indelicately put it.

Her hair was almost entirely bloody, one side of her face yellow to purple to brown—she was the kind of sight that renders a doctor an amateur, innocent of every hope of therapy or repair. She wished she could simply swoon and be carried out like any ordinary witness.

Carolyn took a deep disciplined breath. "Rape?" she asked, though the preferred phrase, borrowed from the law, would have been less loaded, softened by terror and anger to "sexual assault."

"Unlikely," said Tom McAnally. "She was fully dressed, just as you see her. In Tuttle's field—you know, over there where they keep the horses, behind that split-rail fence on Poor Farm Road?"

"No coat, no hat?"

"Looks like not." He cleared his throat like a reluctant boy asked to recite. "She was lying in the snow. Melted the snow down to the ground, they said."

Carolyn saw it obediently, a large pink circle, as if someone had spilled punch on ice. "You think this—happened—somewhere else."

Tom McAnally was looking at the girl's ankles. Her socks were drenched; he peeled them down delicately. "Clearly, somebody dumped her," he said sullenly to her feet. "But she died en route. Had a little pulse when they found her." The girl's jeans were bloody. It was only her head that had been mauled, though, and incidentally her neck, and her ear torn, but that was more than enough. A few suggestions were made of where to probe, what to look at. Tom said, standing, "Well, the coroner will have to go over her with a fine-toothed comb. We can't poke around under her fingernails to see if she scratched the bastard or anything." He glanced away as if the whole thing made him ashamed to look straight at them. He was a very large man with an impassive face; clearly his emotions caused him trouble he didn't like to talk about.

"Do we know who this is?" Carolyn asked, her voice almost gone.

"Martha Taverner," Tom said furiously, as if he might be challenged.

"Martha Taverner! I know—*you* know her, don't you?"

"Me, you mean?" Trygve asked, and cleared his throat. "I did a section on her mother for this one. Early, I remember, maybe thirty-five weeks. Don't remember why, but we had to. She was big as a full-term." He stared at a pleat in the no-color curtain. "God, was there cheering. They only had boys, generations of boys, the Taverners. They finally got their girl." He pulled in one long, shuddering breath. "Hell of a sight for me to see just before I retire." He said that softly. "Nobody ever taught us how to deal with barbarians, and forty years of medicine sure as hell never brought me any closer." He turned and pushed out into the room, as if he'd had enough of all of them.

Carolyn stood staring at the mess of the girl's head—here and there you could almost see, though you'd be guessing, that she was blond, that she was maybe sixteen or seventeen. She knew that because the girl had been in Jacob's class all the way along. When he gave a birthday party in first grade, still full of the flush of excitement at having a whole classful of new friends, he'd made them invite everybody, there must have been fifteen or twenty of them! And Martha had been there, still very blond, almost white-haired, and embarrassed to smile because she had so few teeth. They hadn't gone on being friends—class, or who knows what, had sent them in different directions. The Taverners didn't have it easy. Carolyn had last seen her packing ice-cream cones after school down at Jacey's. Her hair had darkened up a little but she was still a round-cheeked pretty girl, with an ironic look to her, as if she didn't take much at face value: Show me, her expression seemed to say. She had a cool, amused shrug.

Carolyn picked up her wrist, on which a fine-linked silver bracelet flopped. Her arm was already heavy with its absolute immobility. It was a small-boned wrist, frail as a cat's leg, entirely breakable, but unbroken. All of her was healthy, all eager, all wasted.

Someone had shown her.

She had to go back up to her office after that, though all she wanted was to sit down alone somewhere and grieve and be angry. "Doctors," she said to Tom as they started down the corridor, "are expected to be machines at times like this, going about our business without a dropped half hour for despair. Then we're criticized for not showing enough feeling in the hard moments."

"You're sure right there," Tom agreed. "They want you to stop on a dime, turn around, and suddenly you're the pastor with warm hands to lay on their foreheads."

Trygve had said he didn't know how to deal with barbarians. The thing, both good and bad, was that working in this town wouldn't prepare you for atrocities either—they had those car wrecks, they had occasional abusive live-in boyfriends who beat up on women and their women's children, but that was often subtle, rarely gross: the bruises were hidden and had to be probed for. Tractor accidents, falls from rooftops, every kind of bone break, and sometimes some sad, random, undisguisable maimings. But not murder—they didn't have murders in Hyland, population five thousand, give or take a few. Shopkeepers still walked down the street to the bank with their money visible in its canvas bag and no one had ever been hit on the head for it, as far as she knew. When burglaries took place, or car thefts—when bikes disappeared off lawns or mowers out of the work shed—they still tended to get blamed on outsiders, Massachusetts vandals passing through. Gossip, here, did the damage between antagonists that guns did in cities. It made doctors' ER duty tolerable and let them sleep most nights. But it left them, she thought this afternoon, more vulnerable, maybe, than they ought to be.

She looked for a broken bone on a very little boy then, barely able to make her usual friendly chatter with the child and the babysitter who'd brought him in, an older woman with pepper-and-salt hair, bowl-cut. The woman was in great distress over her responsibility for letting the child fall off a big round rock in his back yard, his favorite place to play. Ordinarily, Carolyn would have asked for a lot of detail to try to set the sitter's mind at ease, but now she felt, buzzing like a veil of bees around her head, the distraction of a dozen questions. Had they told Martha's parents yet? Who had done the telling? Probably the police, with their velvet touch. Ought she to have volunteered? Good God, they would want to see the girl. They would want to die at the sight of her—die or kill. She took refuge in examining the little boy's head and eyes for damage. He was very sweet, had stopped crying a long time ago and was looking around with an unquenchable stare at everything in the room. His eyes were so black they seemed all iris; she feared they might be dilated unnaturally. "We've been looking at his legs and his back," she explained to the sitter. "But he did fall a distance and there could be more subtle damage." The sitter's own eyes widened, alarmed. Carolyn reassured her; she had no reason to assume there were problems. "I'm just being careful," she said, staring into the child's marvelous face, his eyebrows frail as Oriental brushstrokes, getting him to track her light.

"Careful is what I guess I'm not," the sitter went on. She stood up and paced. Carolyn, less patient than she usually managed to be, told her to stop it. Her sternness was unpredictable, and when it emerged, it tended to surprise its object. Was it her blondness that seemed to promise softness (against her will), her perfectly modulated bedside manner with its slight hint of conscious control, the frequency of her laugh? She did think a pediatrician owed it to her patients to make visits to her office as stressless as possible. "It isn't good doctoring," she had said in public situations, "if the child puts up such a fuss about coming that it's easier to stay home."

But when she looked at the boy she saw how little it would take to mangle that strong square back, its vertebrae pushing through flesh like bent knuckles. She saw Martha Taverner as a young teenager, or not quite—eleven or twelve, maybe—in her own house. Carolyn was locally famous, had even been the subject of a story in *The New York Times* that she thought absurd for calling her heroic because she made house calls. RETURN OF OLD-TIME MEDICAL CARE, the story announced. "Dr. Reiser believes the multiple factors at work in the making of illness can only be discovered by attention to a patient's entire living circumstances, and that ideally includes where he lives." The girl's shirt was off, she remembered, her tiny breasts like tweaks of dough to cover the apples in a pie. They rose and fell on her narrow chest; she had pleurisy and might need to go to the hospital. Or was that her cousin (Donna? Denise?), who lived with them, who was always sick, her nose always running? It might not have been Martha at all . . . One way or another, she imagined a young girl just on the edge of what probably had brought her to this—a child with a body still pure, free of touch, free of wanting. Sentiment was such a dangerous draught, she rarely let herself have more than a drop of it. But today, now, the body that was her art and instrument seemed too frangible to be worth much. It was nothing but vulnerable, eaten from within or broken from without by some hostility that could as easily change directions like the wind and blow on elsewhere, leave a girl like this another sixty, seventy years to make a life. Or crumple it up, bones and lovely flesh and carefully tended hair, and fling it out, you could do that too. Someone had opened the door of a car and rolled out the remains of somebody's daughter.

"You can get him dressed now," she said to the babysitter, trying for softness. "Just keep an eye on him and call me if he complains of a headache, if he's nauseated, if he seems to be sleeping more than usual. Understand?"

The woman, looking deferential and relieved, picked up the boy's blue-checked cowboy shirt. It was so small, Carolyn thought, it would fit one of Judith's dolls.

BEN

I'M GOING TO TALK ABOUT THAT DAY. I'M GOING TO EASE THROUGH THE ordinary motions of the ordinary day, trying to remember: young winter in Hyland, the snow falling the way I like it best, so quietly, no wind, no noise like rain—you look out the window after long concentration, or, better, open the door, and there it is, everything changed, covered with softness, every angle forgiven, every eyesore pile of junk or ugly car fender hidden. And the smell of it —do you know snow smells sweet when it's falling? It's a little sweet, a little harsh, acid in the nostrils, but that's the cold and the damp, and your wet hat and gloves. The snow's like sugar.

All right—I'm coming toward it slowly. I can't rush up on the seam between before and after. (Not seam, no way. Excuse me. Chasm.) It's not fair to our whole long lives *before*. I didn't know *before* was over already. I didn't, and Carolyn didn't either.

I was bringing Mickey Tuohy into the house. We were huffing with the cold and the effort of dragging a load of wood from his uncle's lumberyard into the studio, and it only seemed decent to take him into the warm kitchen where the woodstove was on, and give him something in thanks. He didn't have to ride up here with his wood, that was a little extra because I give them so much business, so I was grateful.

Mickey has a sweet kind of shyness under his rough manners. Big, his eyes pale in a face that was red even without the cold, he stood there in his cap and overalls and his sloppy windbreaker with the insignia of his snowmobile club on the pocket: TRAILBUSTERS.

"Coffee? Tea?" I asked him, knowing he wanted a beer. "No, really. Something cold?" I held up a Heineken.

He was laconic; everyone in his family is, at least with me. "I wouldn't argue if I was to have one, Ben. Guess I'll let you twist my arm."

I handed him a damp bottle and took my own. "You've never been up here."

"Well, when it belonged to Landon and all them. You know. Way back." I had no idea how old Mickey was—I suspect he was grown up, compared to me and my friends, by the time he took his first job. "I was in here a lot as little kids. Chickie Landon and Albert—well, he was a lot older, he was grown almost—but we used to spend, oh, a whole hell of a lot of time together." He laughed, enjoying the memory, I think. "Horse-and-buggy days, nearly. Had that big double barn out there, burned down one summer. Hoosh, what a fire!"

"Yeah," I said. "Sometimes seems like everything up here burned one time or another, don't it? You wouldn't think anything old'd be left."

He nodded, moody, thinking about it, all the old town landmarks gone. "Or changed, if they didn't burn," he said. "All this looked different then." He took in all the carpentry I'd done, the rearranging, then murmured one of those "Ayups" you tend to think they only do on old-codger ads for Pepperidge Farm or wine coolers. He held up the beer. "You like them fancy foreign brands."

I suppose it was an accusation. I smiled, acknowledging a lot of space between us. "Drink up."

"Used to have cabinets over there where you got your window, just a little teensy window way up there, didn't let in no light, let alone *view*." Mickey made "view" sound like another fancy foreign brand. You can see a whole sweep of lawn out there now, way back to the paddock that we've given over to garden; there are apple trees, two peaches, and a pear. "You put in that picture window?"

"Yup. When we came, we renovated the whole—"

But he was lost to me. "It was kind of dark all the time, I remember, we'd be down—we had a game we called Covered Bridge, had a way of crawling through those chair legs, in and out. Jeezum, I can't see how we did that, can you?" He hulked his big shoulders up and back like a giant shrug. "Even when we were little! Chickie's mom was always on us to keep it down, hey, keep the noise down! She'd say 'Go on out with the chickens if you want to flap around!' I remember that." He chuckled intimately and shook his beer like a maraca, excited.

"I'll bet Chickie Landon never had one of these," I said, tapping my newest man, my shaman. The wood was so lovely, it was the color of a cello side, warmed with reds and golds. He stood in his own niche near the window.

Mickey came back with the smack of his bottle on the round table.

"No, I guess you're right about that." He looked a little shamefaced. "Well, Ben"—and he smiled slowly. "I don't know if I'm allowed to ask you what in the Sam Hill it's supposed to be." Mickey had this slightly too respectful quality I could have done without—it was a little too close to a servant's resentful shuffling. I don't think I put on much in the way of airs, but then, I can surely see how he might disagree.

I stood up in front of my sculpture. "That's okay, Mick. It's not bad manners to ask. I mean, you don't see one every day, I guess." I asked him what he thought it was.

"Me?!" I love this, when people get nonplussed, as if they might hurt your feelings because they can't guess your intentions. If you think art is only meant to be understood you could feel that, I suppose, no harm intended.

But he was game. "Gol-lee, Ben, I haven't a clue. Truly." He eyed it; he was wary. "Is it—a—like a monster, maybe? Something out of a bad dream?"

I thought that was pretty good. I pushed him a little, he resisted, we did a little dance, and finally he conceded that if what I was trying to build—but why in the *kitchen*, he wanted to know—was a shaman, a sort of medicine man/watcher/protector, and if a shaman was all that, why, then, it wasn't nearly half bad. "I don't know as I'd want him looking at me when I'm having my Wheaties, though," he admitted. "Don't he make you nervous, staring down your back like that?"

I said I found him reassuring. I thought it's like making a person, after the skin's on the bone you get to add everything you think he needs: give him an old buggy light like a jewel in his forehead, that glows in the lowest light, you fill his arms with everything portable, you polish him with your attention. Sort of like people with a metal plate in their knee, I told him, all their crockery, these metal rods and hunks of things I put on just because I liked them. Partly you add the things you want to because he's yours and he doesn't talk back. ("Yeah," Mickey said, laughing. "Not like your wife or your kids. Hey, I like that!") "My constructions were getting too grim, though. So now he's got a tape deck and the CB radio sitting in this little shelf in his stomach, see? Look, Mick, it's hard to see it but—" And I turned it on and got the slither of voices up and down the band, noise brighter than air. "Toggle to Jersey Jack" was signing off and going to Honolulu till winter was over. Mickey giggled.

I'm getting carried away. This doesn't matter right here. Carolyn calls me "the family narcissist." I am. I don't bring home a salary, I'm not a diplomate of the American Council of Pediatric Physicians and Surgeons, I don't have a brass nameplate on my door. I try not to be defensive and sometimes I succeed. Meanwhile, I think you'd agree I'd better have something.

Enough, then. I thanked Mickey for helping me in with the wood, I showed him to the door. More snow had fallen. "Careful going down the hill, Mickey. We've got a bad curve out there, it's hell when it's slick."

"Oh, don't I know it. I remember one time it was greasy, I sailed right off into that field crosst the way—" He was cheerful about his prospects.

When he left I stood in the doorway looking out, feeling warm and snug, the way you do when the lamps are on and the cold is right out there but your feet are dry. I was looking forward to the whole long evening: I'd picked up a video while I was in town, a movie about Van Gogh, and we were going to crowd into the den later and watch it together. I had to book time with the kids, which was getting harder and harder, especially with Jacob, who was always busy these days, on principle. (If he could substitute the flick for homework, of course, he might work up some enthusiasm.) There'd be a lot to talk about, I thought: Van Gogh's madness, his talent, whether it was necessary to suffer the way he did. And the good adolescent question: Who was responsible for his pain—himself, the world? Jacob and I loved to skirmish. Sometimes I think we'd choose sides just to have colors to fight under. He was getting sharp and fearless; Judith was still too young to mix it up, but she had promise. I felt like I had them in training, a luscious feeling to counter the snow-shocked, inarticulate friends they spent too much time with. (I loved Hyland for a hundred reasons, but the intellectual life of its high-school population was not one of them.)

I made dinner. This has always been part of our deal—Carolyn gets to put the house out of her head every day and go off into the clear fluorescent spaces of her office and the hospital. I get to answer to nobody, but in return I do the housewifely duties (which I like) and amuse the hell out of some of the guys I know downtown. They don't exactly say I'm pussywhipped—their word, not mine—but I'm pretty sure they tell it to each other. But what the hell. My best dish was red snapper Veracruzana—green olives, sauce a little spicy—and it could have been on a menu anywhere. In New Hampshire you can hardly eat ethnic, so you have to do it yourself, and I have conquered three or four cuisines tolerably. Jacob and Judith were game and Carolyn, I think, was relieved that I'd made a project out of duty and therefore took some pride in it. ("Your cooking is competitive," she says, implying that that's what you have to expect of a man in the kitchen. "You learn recipes and come up with methods as if you're climbing a mountain." I don't know if that's true or good or bad; it isn't something I have to argue.)

She came in while I was setting the table—the best placemats for Friday night, a little special something for the Sabbath we don't otherwise keep. She called out to me from the hall. "I'm going to have to speak to Jacob about how sloppy his parking is getting." She came into the kitchen pink-faced. The hair around her face was wet—it must have been dewed with snowflakes. She gave me a little hug of greeting. "His car is all over the garage, Ben, I swear I could hardly get in there at all."

"Ah, lady," I said, and caught hold of her. "Between thee and me let not mere circumstance intrude. Come bring thy body to the Sabbath bed, where we—"

"Ben! Are you crazy?"

I pretended to take offense. "What, then? Art thou affronted?"

She gave me a friendly little shove. "What are we eating, lovey? Something warm like stew, I hope, or soup?"

We really don't do too badly at that reversal, but every now and then, more in the presence of friends than when we're alone where we can take care of it, Carolyn seems a little self-conscious about expecting to be served like a husband. This is a small town with a lot of very traditional expectations, milk and cookies after school and guess who bakes them? But not today.

"Chili."

"Terrific." I got a kiss for that. "Is Judith upstairs?" She bent to pull her boots off. Even now, routine or not, I always find it provocative to see her calves, her lovely pale calves, suddenly unsheathed like that.

"We had a little set-to about her piano practicing. We're going to have to sit down with her and find out if she really wants to go on with her lessons."

She had gone to the cupboard where we keep the wine. "I need a little of this today." She poured generous glasses for both of us, though she hadn't asked and I hadn't answered. Then she told me about Martha Taverner. "I'm surprised you haven't heard all the wretched details on your CB."

"It hasn't been on," I said, and I was nearly dizzy with the shock of it, "except for a second when I was showing Mickey Tuohy the shaman." I knew Martha's father from slow-pitch softball. I didn't know him well, but he was more than a face to me—a smallish, wiry banty-man. Second baseman, his legs slightly bowed, his color and energy high. When we lost he got sullen and tried to fix the blame. But when we won he would get drunk on the joy of it. He was an infectious laugher. I couldn't say anything but "Jesus, Jesus," as if that might clear my head of the vision of his daughter dead.

Just then Judith called downstairs. I guess she had heard her mother.

"Where's the Boy?" Carolyn asked. I had to think for a second. She had said his car was in the garage, but I realized I hadn't seen him.

"Does he have those damn tapes turned up?" she asked. "I can't *hear* them."

"No, Judith was here when I got back, but he must be —well, I don't know. Maybe he's sleeping."

Teenagers sleep. They tell me it's normal. Sometimes I thought he went up there, lay down for an hour or so in the late-afternoon dark, and came downstairs two inches taller, with a doubled shoe size.

"Well, give him a little longer. This stuff needs to thicken. It hasn't reached its, mm—quintessence—yet." I looked under the lid; the steam of the chili came up and surrounded both our faces like a warm, sharp-sweet cloud.

Then the bell rang.

It rang into the ordinary noises of our day. It rasped so harshly that when I tried to go back to it, or just before, it sounded like the gong they ring at boxing matches, urgent, a rip through space and time, promising cruelty and pain.

I've heard about stories, how they're really just a finely strung architecture of *the way things were* and *the way things turned out,* held together—or divided, would be better—by the most terrible word, the word that lifts the roof off, lands the ax blow, curdles the milk. The blood. All the world's change, its doom, its fatality, is in it: *Then* . . . But that doesn't mean you know it when it comes.

Carolyn put her glass down on the round table I had begun to set. I remember finding it later and guzzling the last of her abandoned wine when I was beyond feeling anything, its heat, its cool, its flavor. By then, it was dregs left over from a century ago.

I figured it was someone who couldn't get up the hill.

We have to take our tow chain out when the weather's mean and yank our neighbors up; it happens a couple of times each winter.

"Fran," I heard her say, surprised. They were walking into the kitchen, she was laughing a little girlishly—he makes her nervous. "You haven't called me Dr. Reiser since we first moved here! What in the world does *that* mean?"

Fran Conklin came in behind her in his parka, his navy-blue wool hat to his eyes, his snowmobile boots leaving serious puddles, dirty ones, in his wake. He grabbed at the hat, pulled it off, and stood holding it like a scolded boy. "Ben," he said and shook my hand earnestly.

"Hey there, Chief. A visit out of uniform! Don't tell me they've got you collecting for the Policemen's Fund in the snow."

The police chief and I have had our moments. You have to understand that the police aren't viewed out here in the country—near-country, whatever you want to call it—quite as suspiciously as they are in the city. If there's any Establishment, it's not one that includes them, only the rich and the old families (which are usually the same). They're just local boys, not particularly violent, who have a steady necessary job; they have to buy their own guns, their uniforms. They have to plead with the town every time the department needs a new cruiser, and then get a used one someplace. But even at that the chief is a man to deal with, and we've had our hostilities. I put a sculpture up one time, for example, in the town park down near the falls—this was for the 4th of July celebration, and it was supposed to be the American Family, made of pickup parts, complete with a little wooden dog and cat on wheels. People loved it, kids climbed on it like it was a playground toy. It made them laugh. I was really tickled. For the first time I thought, Okay, I've crossed a line, they *get* it. But the chief didn't. He got Yahoo on me and pronounced it Refuse or Rubbish or something, I don't remember how he insulted it exactly, but he said I had to move it, dismantle it, it was an eyesore—unpainted wood with the detritus of the moment varnished into it, the non-biodegradables: McDonald's containers, one Adidas hightop, a hubcap, a button that said FREE LYNDON LAROUCHE. Fran won, all the power on his side, but not before the newspaper gave me their editorial blessing: "*Lighten up, Mr. Police Chief. Art these days is in the eye of the beholder*"—and he'd been made to feel like a heavy.

Nonetheless, we were not unfriendly. If he was overzealous in his line of work, I knew I was equally zealous in mine—we were both fanatics, so we had something in common, and by now we could laugh about it. But today, in our kitchen, standing in the sharp aura of chili and woodsmoke, he was not at ease.

"Keeping busy, you two? You've been working hard, Carolyn."

"Oh, I've got enough to do, I suppose." She smiled, a little bewildered, I could see that, around the eyes.

"Get you anything, Fran?" I asked. "A beer if you're not working?"

"No, that's okay, Ben. You managing to keep busy in this season? You must be snug in that workshop of yours."

"Right. Just bought a neat little stove—one of those kind of miniature Fishers with the deer and stuff on the side? Really nice piece of craftsmanship. Keeps the place so hot all I want to do is sleep." I realized, as I spoke, that when I talk to Fran or Mickey I start everything I say in the middle, casually discarding the "I" as if complete sentences were pretentious.

Anyway, Fran nodded perfunctorily, since it was clear he hadn't come up here in a snowstorm to find out how we were feeling. I saw him take a deep breath. "Jacob around?"

Oh. "Don't know, actually. We both just got in a little while ago—the car's here."

"Would you like me to see if he's here?" Carolyn volunteered. "I'll just have a look to see if he's up there asleep, Fran. You—need him for something?"

He pursed his lips a little, as if he was running something around in his mouth. "Why don't you do that, Carolyn," he said, rather too gently. He sounded like a man who was afraid he might break something.

I looked at him hard while Carolyn went upstairs. He hummed for a second or two, absurd, and kept his hands in his pockets. He was a broad-faced man with a forehead ruled like a music staff with creases. Just in the last year or two he'd started growing dewlaps.

Carolyn came back down looking troubled. "No, he hasn't been up there as far as I can see. Judith hasn't seen him. What is this, Fran? What's the matter?"

"I'm going to—" He stopped short. "He's—" And stopped again. The more he shuffled, the longer I went without breathing. If Jacob was hurt, Fran would be telling us, not looking for him. "All right." He looked resigned. "Something happened up on Poor Farm Road a little while ago. Something pretty bad." His face was bright red with the effort of this. "And we're trying to find some people to talk to about it."

"What? What happened?" We both said that. We both knew.

"Carolyn—" He turned to her. "A girl got herself killed."

"I know. I saw her." She didn't miss a beat.

Her abruptness seemed to take him by surprise. I could see his face harden. "You saw her."

"In ER. They had her in there—beyond saving, I mean." She was twisting her hands in a way I'd never seen. "It was awful. *You* know. But they called us all down."

Fran cleared his throat. At least he was very uncomfortable. "Then you have an idea— And you know who it was."

"But why do you want to talk to Jacob? What does—"

He looked away from us; he looked at the shaman in his corner, startled for a second, and then back. "I don't like to have to tell you this," he said simply. "I really don't. There are days I swear I wish I was back directing traffic instead of running this show." He put his hands together and cracked his knuckles. That always drives me berserk, I don't know why people think they have the right to make others listen. I restrained my anger but it wasn't easy. "Okay. Jacob was seen with this girl. He picked her up from work, she makes ice-cream cones at Jacey's after school." He flushed again. "Made. Even in winter—doesn't seem to slow anyone down." A small laugh. An attempt, to be generous, at shared humanity with the victims. "He came by with the car and they took off like they've been doing."

"They have?" I said, a little too vociferous. "Martha *Taverner?*"

Maybe he never mentioned it, Fran said. You know kids. And so on. But they'd been seen together by a lot of people, today and other days. And somebody called headquarters who'd seen the mess in front of Tuttle's fence, the smashed, the finished girl. And he needed to talk to Jacob. When the chief himself comes to your door, I suddenly realized, and I wondered where my head had been, you'd better believe you're in trouble. So I blew up at him.

"Look, Ben. I don't want to jump ahead, okay? Jacob's the last person I'd like to think about with a murder on my hands. This is a bludgeon death we've got here, a girl with her skull—well, I don't have to say. Carolyn, you saw it, dear. There isn't anybody I want to suspect of doing that, your son or anybody else's."

"Or someone passing through," I prompted him.

He was trying to be obliging. "Or someone passing through."

And then we went into second gear. I am making myself dredge all this up because, I suppose, it still has the little shreds of our innocence in it, the poor rags of our not-knowing. We struggled to stay dumb.

"And you don't know where he is," Fran said.

Carolyn frowned the way she does when she's studying something that won't yield. "The car's in the garage. I just—" She stopped because there was nothing else to say.

He wanted to see the car.

She moved to get her keys.

"No, wait," I said, so suddenly I didn't know it was coming. "You can't just do that."

"Do what?" Fran asked me, caught off-guard.

"I don't think you can just do that, go search somebody's car. You don't have a warrant."

Carolyn was aghast. She is a good girl sometimes, too often, maybe, under her take-charge cool. "*Ben*jamin," she said in a tone I didn't like. "This is *Fran*. We know him, he isn't just some cop in off the street."

I told her I knew who he was, thank you. I assured him I trusted him and knew he had a job to do. (Later, I thought, I will try to suggest that she doesn't have to speak that way to me in public, like I'm a little patient of hers who's been feeding his medicine to the cat.) "A warrant," I repeated. "Yes, a warrant, to come nosing around. What's so strange about that?"

I was trying to picture Jacob, my son, and I couldn't even see his face. I saw his body instead, the shiny blue jacket he has from the wrestling team—he wrestles at 120 pounds—his shoulders in a T-shirt broadening finally after years of being too small, too skinny. His Adam's apple that sticks out these days, exaggerated, like an erection. He's a nice-looking boy, not a knockout (just as well, I tell him, though of course he disagrees). But I couldn't conjure up his features, it was as if I hadn't seen him for months. The mystery of desperation, that seizing-up of the heart and brain. It just put a lock on memory. *Gone*, utterly gone. I needed to see him for myself, and fast.

Then I called Wendell, the only friend we have who's also a lawyer. (One of the many good things about Hyland is how few lawyers you have to know.) It was too late for the office, but he wasn't home either; only his inane machine gave out its syrup, which I blamed on Steph: "Wendell and Stephanie regret that they can't come to the phone now but they want you to know they *value* your call." Steph, breathless: she got it from church, he got it from est. I liked them anyway, but they sometimes strained at the edges of my patience, and one of these days, I thought, rather ungenerously, given that I needed Wendell right now, they're going to find themselves outside it. I told him to call me instantly when he got in.

Judith had come downstairs while I was on the phone. She took one look at us, her eyes widening, and went to her mother, who put an arm protectively around her shoulders. I wished she were young enough to be sent out of the room to be spared this scene. I wished we were all too young, at least by a day, so that we could be back on the other side of *Then*. But she is twelve. She's one of us.

We wrangled, Fran and I. He said he needed to have a look at the condition of Jacob's car. I told him it was my car and, as far as I could remember these things, he'd need a "show-cause order," something like that. He told me that playing hotshot lawyer would only make things (I suspect he meant feelings) harder, slow things down. "I know you're his father," he said soothingly. "You want to protect him. I've got kids, too, you know." But he had to ask me again. "Do you know where he might be? Did he have any special plans for today? Ben? Do you know anything you're not telling me?"

He looked at Judith. "Have you seen your brother, dear?"

Judith opened her mouth, but I yelled, "Hey, off-limits! Leave her out of this, okay? I'll tell you what I know that I'm not telling you. I know my son—"

"*Please,*" Carolyn said as if I was the crazy one here. "*Please,* Ben."

But the man was affronting my kitchen, my family, my day, my sight. He was suggesting something unimaginably insulting, and he was doing it in my own house. "I told you I haven't seen him since he went to school this morning, all right? We ate breakfast—Carolyn's gone already by the time we eat. Frozen waffles, right, Jude?" She nodded; she was still speechless, like someone who'd been kidnapped and wasn't sure it was all right to talk to her captors. "Real maple syrup, okay? Our own. Grade B, but good. Coffee for him. Or sugar, actually, with a little coffee in it. Tea for me. Hot chocolate for Judith. His lunch in a bag, I know because I packed it: tuna sandwich on rye, apple, very good chocolate-chip cookies. Some junk he chews, Sunbursts or something, he always throws those in—"

"Starbursts," Judith breathed softly.

"Starbursts. He says they keep him awake in class. That's it. That's what I know."

Carolyn, not helping, said, "Then what are you afraid of?"

"Who says I'm afraid of anything?" We were glaring at each other.

She wheedled at me a little. "What are you so angry at? I mean, why make an adversary out of poor Fran?" Somewhere along the way Fran had gotten poor. "I'm sure Jacob can explain why he wasn't with the girl. Maybe she got out of the car and walked away, maybe he dropped her somewhere, a thousand— Fran!" she suddenly said and put her hand to her mouth. It was a rough, much-used hand, I saw, focusing sharply, but she did the best she could with it, its neat nails, fingers modestly ringed. "How do we know *he's* all right? We haven't thought—

what if some madman did something to *both* of them! Maybe Jacob's hurt, or been kidnapped or—"

"Look," the chief said, ignoring her idea. "Can you think where he'd be—just—well, say it's an ordinary afternoon, what would he do?"

We looked at each other. "His friends," Judith offered. She may have been the calmest of us, as if having to sound adult pulled her up to a higher level, while the rest of us slipped backward with shocking speed. "Why don't you call Frodo and Jackie." She is a resourceful child, I thought gratefully, an oasis of cool. She had short fairish hair, cut like a Dutch boy's; she had the beginnings of a chest, but she was a dancer and a gymnast, a girl whose legs were always expressing a life of their own, turning and turning, the spokes of a lovely wheel, so the rest of her would probably stay like a washboard, flat but nicely inflected. "I'll call them if you want."

Fran's two-way radio gave out a sudden bleat. He listened to something so garbled it was like aggressive Chinese, and he muttered something back, and turned to go. "Please, Ben," he said to me at the door. "Please do your best not to obstruct this thing. Your son may have a perfect—there may be no problem at all. Chances are good. I'd be glad if he was out of it altogether, I don't know why you don't trust me. But don't put yourself in front of the law, okay? 'Cause it won't do anybody any good. Get your lawyer if you want, but don't block the law yourself, okay?"

"Of course," Carolyn assured him. Hostess to the bitter end. "He knows. He—"

"Also, do me a favor, both of you? Just think for one blessed minute about Terry and Mike Taverner over there in their kitchen. Well, you saw, Carolyn. I don't have to tell you. They had to put Terry under heavy sedation. Hostages to fortune, that's all we've got, our kids are—"

I wasn't feeling very tolerant. "What weekend criminal-justice course did you pick that up from?" It was less than decent of me. I deserved the look my wife shot me.

But Fran had dignity, along with chutzpah. "My priest, if you want to know. Just this past Sunday, he called his sermon 'Hostages to Fortune,' about how we're living dangerously when we love anybody, even ourselves, he said. Then he asked—"

"Weren't they looking for you back there on your beeper, Fran?" Maybe if he left we'd be back where we were.

I knew I'd regret my shortness with him somewhere down the line. But the way I understood it he came in out of the cold to announce that he suspected my son had murdered a girl and was hiding either here or somewhere else. Maybe here. Maybe he really believed we might have him upstairs, or down in the cellar crouched behind the furnace, so that while he talked with us he looked and listened very carefully, feeling the atmosphere, reading our body movements, trying to pick up the sound of creaking floorboards, weight shifting out of sight. It had been the most offensive and unreal half hour of my life—all I could do, finally, was open the door for him and banish him gratefully, without even the friendly pretense of a goodbye.

I still had the cold door latch in my hand—it was black hammered wrought iron, part of the colonial history we'd restored to the house, and it felt hard and elemental against my palm, like part of a shotgun. I stood there clutching it and looking at the old wood of the door, with its long, striated cracks no cold miraculously came through. I was thinking how totally implausible this was—in a funny way (or maybe not so funny, maybe dangerous), I don't think I believe in *reality* much. I mean this, even if it sounds demented. Events don't seem as real to me as imaginings. I live inside my head in a way Carolyn doesn't live in hers, and just as well, I suppose, for the agitated parents who call up when their baby's choking or screaming with pain and she has to decide what's wrong and how to fix it. I live for making things up. A real event, for me, is the good fit of two pieces of wood I have to glue, or finding two matched stones to set in for one of my creatures' eyes. So this was all doubly unreal to me. First, it was impossible to imagine Jacob on the run, Jacob even remotely in trouble, let alone guilty of—I don't have the words. An atrocity. When I last saw him he was in deep trouble with me for running up a couple of three-dollar overdue bills on his library books. I couldn't imagine him making real footsteps in the real world. I mean, I couldn't really believe anything any of us did made a *difference.* So this all felt like someone else's nightmare: I refused to believe it was mine, or, rather, ours. His.

But Carolyn disabused me of that. I made myself walk back into the kitchen and face her. Judith was standing in front of the woodstove holding up her hands as if she'd taken a chill.

"You should have let him look at the car," Carolyn said.

"The hell I should have. Not without a lawyer telling me I have to. And don't go telling me he's my friend, either. No police chief is my friend when he comes around on the goddamn job."

She came to me to put her arms around me, or maybe be taken into mine. One way or another, we fell together. "Please, Ben," she said into my chest. "Whatever this is, it's not a conspiracy." She put her ear against my breastbone, turning her head. "Sometimes your anxiety unhinges you."

I couldn't believe it. "It isn't anxiety, it's anger. Nobody ever gets murdered around here, so he's getting carried away. He thinks he's on *Hill Street Blues* or something."

Judith stirred where she was standing. "Maybe he's

covering up for one of those dumb friends of his, they're so weird. Maybe they ran away together."

We considered it—boys being boys together?—but it didn't make things much better. Anyway, he wasn't that kind of boy.

We stood like that, and then Judith came in with us, the three of us leaning against each other, until we had to *do* something. At least I did. I had no place to go, but that didn't mean I could stand still. I went to the desk where I kept my wallet and keys when I was in the house. The keys felt strange in my hand, my hand was strange to me. If you'd told me the molecules of the world had rearranged themselves, a little dance of basic structures all turned over and settled differently, I'd have believed it.

It gets dark shockingly early in January, although it had already turned a little on the cusp of the solstice. There was a moon and it was cruelly beautiful, I thought (at the same time that I thought how goddamn unoriginal, how melodramatic). But it was a taunt anyway, how it laid out a shimmering path, diamond dust, straight up to the garage that sat beside the workshop I'd made in the barn, a couple of hundred feet from the house.

The snow was lavender where the light came down on it, like the weird illumination you see in planetariums that changes every color and makes white electric blue. Jacob and I loved to go to the science museum in Boston—not that long ago he had been at that age when the noisy saga of whirling planets and inexplicable anti-gravitational feats, narrated by a man with a deep official-facts voice, was thrilling. He was easily, unstintingly thrilled, or used to be. Not now, though. Boys of seventeen aren't thrilled about much besides their muscles and their victories against everyone else's brains and bodies.

It was cold enough to collapse my nostrils, and damp, way below freezing. Carolyn's car tracks into the open garage were fresh, some new snow fallen into them but not enough to soften their edges much. I could see the tracks of Jacob's car were muted—they had taken a lot of snow, had long since lost their definition. Carolyn was right about the way he parked. The car, crooked, and half over the unmarked center line, didn't look aimed so much as abandoned.

Holy Jesus, what was the story? I put on the frail garage light and used my flashlight. The car was a roomy old brown Dodge, old-fashioned-feeling inside, like an empty rumpus room, too big ever to have been handsome. It was littered, as always—candy wrappers, a couple of pink and green mimeographed notices from school on the floor, a paperback about computers, in a mangled cover. If Fran had seen this, he'd have wondered what we were haggling about. I ran the flashlight up and down in stripes —some butts in the ashtray, stuck together with gum that was gray in this light. (He says he doesn't smoke. Right now I'd settle for a little disobedience, even a little flat-out lying.)

The backseat was rubble-strewn, too. Amazing, I was thinking, how the spirit of disorganization infects everything it touches, like the mildew that must be crawling under there. It was a triumph not to have sweat socks or wet towels to make it look even more like his room. His textbooks lay splayed on the seat, and a greasy bag with a crumpled napkin in it—doughnuts, probably. It smelled fried. I finished raking the seat with my little beam. Okay, Fran, I thought. Okay. You can have it.

At the last instant I thought I'd have a look at the trunk. I was beginning to feel relief wash over me like that moon-white air outside—a mystery, still, where he might be, but nothing suspicious. The trunk snapped open and rose with the slow deliberation of a drawbridge, and then I thought I'd fall over for lack of breath. Because I knew I was looking at blood. It wasn't red, or even brown—the world was a thousand grays out here, like a black-and-white movie. But I could see the shape of the splotches and worse, the little splatters that had flown off something. The something, I suspected, was the jack.

It was lying loose, out from under the cover that hides the spare and the tire-changing equipment; it had been flung, fast and sloppy, onto a mess of—I couldn't tell what, exactly. I thought I saw a beach towel, something like a Garfield cartoon, words and picture. I know I saw a backpack, and there might have been a T-shirt. I was wearing heavy gloves—I picked it up with my padded fingers. The screw part looked wet, maybe oil. (Impossible. Who oils a jack?) I held it out of the dark of the garage into the moonlight like something whose neck had been wrung. Then I took off one glove and held the glove in my teeth the way a dog would, and I touched the huge splashes of dark on the gnarled-up terry cloth, and in the valleys of the shiny nylon backpack. They were wet, undeniably, deeply wet, and when I rubbed hard the pads of my fingers came up rusty brown.

And when I turned, dry-mouthed, I saw that something was caught on the lip of the old battered ash can that stood in the corner. It was a woolen glove—not a kid's mitten, I mean large, gray, floppy-fingered. I recognized it before I even touched it, where it had snagged on the raggedy metal rim. *Please,* I prayed. *Please.*

But it was his, and it was dark with blood that had begun to freeze. I sniffed it—sour, that funny damp-wool, itchy smell you get used to in this weather where you're always spreading out your cap and gloves on the steaming radiator to stiffen up, drying. I knew he wore these gray ones, he kept saying "They don't match my jacket, they look dumb," but hadn't wanted to part with the money to buy new ones. (I wasn't buying, they were still good enough. If he cared that much, I told him, he knew what to do about it.) They stained my fingers. Down in the basket, on top of a mess of moist papers and an empty oil can, I found the other one and balled it up in my hand. So much, I thought, for saying *Please.*

Then I looked at the ground and saw where footprints, not mine, led away from the car. You couldn't hide anything with snow on the ground, it was like the deer tracks dogs can follow. It was what made winter such a cruel tracking season, why they gave out summonses to people who didn't keep their dogs tied up. The prints went out to the paddock, toward the open field. Slowly, as if I was stalking something myself, I followed them at a distance so I wouldn't confuse them with my own. They stopped at the fence—second thoughts here, maybe, about where he'd get to if he went into the woods. (*Nowhere* is where. The trees, thick in a lot of places, up hills and down, go for a few miles but eventually you're out on the blacktop, on Route 48. He would know that; he walked these woods, he skiied them, he had them in his head the way city kids know their block.) So they stopped at the fence; stymied, I suppose, they circled around and came back to the road, where they disappeared into a mess of tire marks and footprints. What the snow hadn't already obliterated, traffic took away, and my son with it.

Our lives are over, I thought, standing and looking down the road to where it disappeared into the bad curve. It was just like that: I thought it in words, like a sign, or like something I could read that was already printed out in black and white. It was a simple sentence —a *sentence*—and it felt final. Everything else was going to be detail, horrible, humiliating, maybe even justifying. But the fact, an act in the real world that believed in itself even if I didn't believe in it, was that our lives as just another family were done.

Later, when things got very bad, Carolyn accused me of airbrushing the truth away, of manufacturing miraculous salvation, of not accepting what I knew Jacob had done. No. I say that right here, early, totally. No. She didn't understand and that was one of the worst things. I had no illusions. But he was my son, and my love is not provisional upon his actions or his goodness.

All I said was that our lives as a family—no, our *life* as a family, our single life as an eight-legged graceful animal alive under a single pelt—was over.

CAROLYN

CAROLYN, AT THE KITCHEN SINK, WASHED HER HANDS UNDER THE HOTTEST water she could stand. Among doctors there were hand washers and *others*—she couldn't imagine touching a patient with dirty fingers. The water was so hot it was chilling. She stood blankly, letting the water drip down, until Judith said, "Mom?"

There was this child to be reassured, right here, wherever Jacob was. "Yes, darling. What?" She didn't mean to sound short but the syllables echoed back at her, separate as stones. She wiped her hands on her woolen skirt, wantonly. What difference did it make?

"Jacob was really mad this morning. He told me he might not go to school at all."

Carolyn put her hands on her daughter's narrow shoulders and pushed her gently into a chair. "Tell me what happened."

Judith raked her fingers through her hair anxiously; it

was the one mannerism she indulged without even realizing it, like a tic. Sometimes Carolyn wanted to shear all her hair off just to keep that hand still.

"Well, nothing happened, exactly. Only Jacob said Daddy was being stubborn about the prom. He said—"

But the phone rang. Then, once it started clamoring it wouldn't stop, an unstanched flow. The first call was her friend Annie Dineen, full of concern and sympathy. Word was out already, then. In this town, if you flushed your toilet three times in a row, everybody knew you were sick. Annie had begun "I just heard—" but Carolyn forgot to ask *how*.

The second was Karen, her nurse, to ask if she was going to take her on-call duty, or would Carolyn like her to find someone to cover for her. "Karen, what do you—what have you heard, and how?"

Karen, who was friendly but did not think of herself as a friend, considered her answer carefully. Considered the size of the gap between herself and her boss, to whom she was fiercely devoted, and opted for vagueness. It took her a minute. "It's around, Carolyn, that's all. I don't know where I first heard—I went to the A & P on the way home from work, I guess, and some people I knew were talking. I mean, this is only *suspicion*, right? There isn't anything at all—"

Carolyn pictured Karen pacing at her phone, earnest, a very thin woman only a little younger than herself, the dark hair that swung around her face like the perfect slick cap, in those TV ads, of the famous ice star who skates right up to the camera fast, her hair traveling at a slightly slower speed around her cheeks. Karen had that kind of warmth, cut with the same efficient briskness. "Everyone says she was pretty much of a flirt—or worse. You never know what they—"

"Karen." She was shocked. "Please. I don't want to hear this right now. I appreciate it, but it's too soon." It was too soon in so many ways you couldn't even begin to name them all—too soon to accept, let alone talk about, her child in the disembodied way of gossips. Even, she wanted to say to Karen, the well-intentioned ones. She hadn't lived with this sickening possibility an hour yet. What was the matter with people? "Some people I knew were talking"—talking, in the plural, before the poor girl's blood was dry! They were far out in front, then, those people; they were already enjoying the excitement of the chase. She murmured her thanks and when she'd hung up she found she was shivering as if the fire had gone out.

"Do you want some of this chili, Jude?" she asked, so listlessly that she was surprised when Judith answered yes. She scooped out a bowl for her. The smell of it, so luscious only a little while ago, made her nauseous.

The thing was that there were such different kinds of problems, even insoluble ones. Solving them was how she got through her day; she sometimes thought she could have been a mathematician. Some were your own fault, they were difficult or impossible simply because you didn't know enough—if you'd seen enough babies with neonatal distress, you deserved an opinion of which maternal illnesses could cross the placenta, or had to be genetic, or constituted only a passing danger. If you understood the chemicals stimulated by a particular medication, you could guess which other drugs would be contraindicated. Good doctors not only saw more, they paid attention to what they needed to and synthesized it and used it. Those were puzzles she didn't mind, though she preferred the kind for which she had all the pieces and simply hadn't figured out yet where they fit.

But this. The image of Jacob knocked the breath out of her. He had sat at the dinner table last night in his leather cap that was like Che's all these years later (the cap he never took off except for the same one in black felt, a sort of squashed beret), instructing them in the precise difference between two rock groups—Fears Without Tears, or Fears for Tears or something like that, and another—

though she could remember a thousand things she needed to, she had already forgotten this thing she didn't really care about. He had looked intense and slightly condescending; he had looked the way a teenage boy deserved to look when he talked to his illiterate parents. On this subject, at least, he and Judith were conspiratorial, which she liked. But now—if you didn't even know where he was, all the rest was out of your control, beyond even the haziest speculation. She closed her eyes to think. Why was his car safely back here, stashed in its rightful place? Even if you granted the wild possibility that he'd had anything to do with this crime—why would the car be up there, solid as a wall? None of it—his voice, his vocabulary—computed. The pieces wouldn't line up for arranging.

She put a pencil behind her ear as if she might need it to jot down details, and forced herself to the phone. Frodo's little brother was the only one at his house. Monosyllables. Jackie wasn't home, his mother said. Could she give him a message. She sounded appropriately surprised when Carolyn identified herself, and brought forth detail, friendly but wary—clearly she hadn't heard anything yet. Carolyn didn't know her; kids could be very friendly in Hyland and yet not come home with each other. They met elsewhere to do—whatever it was they did. He was at track, had been there since school let out. Carolyn could hear her politely suppressing curiosity. She thanked her and let her go. Wasn't there a bumper sticker, meant to be guilt-provoking, that asked DO YOU KNOW WHERE YOUR KID IS RIGHT NOW?

"D'you want to see if the radio has anything?" Judith asked. She had begun to look at her mother with an odd solicitiousness. Her slight smile was fixed exactly the way it used to be, Carolyn thought, when she talked to her dolls, a slightly exaggerated kindness and patience. A delicacy of approach.

"Why not."

Judith turned through music and random deejay talk to the local station, which was playing Muzak. They were nowhere near news time. Carolyn laughed glumly. "You can't expect to tune right in to a bulletin about what's on your mind," she said.

"They do it all the time in the movies," Judith objected. "And then they always listen to half of it and get mad and turn it off." She scooped the dark chili out of the blue bowl as if the excitement had only increased her appetite. Carolyn watched her, slightly hypnotized. She felt disembodied. With no way to enter the problem, she sat now, elbows on the table—barred outside, blank, confused. This was an unfamiliar way to feel, as if she'd taken a blow to the head, or was struggling to wake up early in the morning, while it was still dark out.

Then Ben was in the kitchen door.

"What?" she asked, bolting up. "Where is—"

He was shaking his head no. No, I don't have him? No, this is terrible? No, it's all untrue? But his eyes were alarming.

"I don't believe this." Carolyn steadied herself. "What's wrong? Why are you standing there that way?"

He paused to yank open his parka. His gloves were off, crammed into his pockets. "Oh, Jesus, Carolyn, he used the jack."

"What do you mean he used the jack? What are you talking about?"

"All right, *somebody* did. The jack's in the trunk, it's where it's supposed to be, next to the spare. But it's sort of—thrown back in, it's wet and there was a lot of melted snow in the trunk and—"

She had taken a step backward. "Where is it?"

He shook his head as if he was clearing lake water from his ears. "You don't have to see it. Believe me."

"For God's sake, Benny, what are you protecting me from? I've seen every—"

"Please. And Judith."

Judith, as if summoned, moved to her mother's side, her hand grasping for Carolyn's.

"Then tell me why you think he used it for—what you saw on it."

"Blood."

She stared at him. "Blood." She let it enter her mind slowly, carefully. "Are you sure it's not grease or something? Why are you so sure what you're seeing?"

He closed his eyes as if he could see it better that way. "I looked at it as carefully as I had to. In the opening, the big screw part in there. It's been wiped away on the outside, but he couldn't get it to—"

"Could it be wet? Ben? If it was out in the snow it could just be wet. He must have had a flat or had to get the wheels up out of the snow, maybe he got stuck." She hated the way he bent to the task, as if he'd get something out of proving he was right: he had taken charge of her instruction.

"There's hair in the bolts, caught in there. Long and pale. Blond. Isn't she blond?" His voice trembled.

She swayed as if she had been pushed, then steadied herself against the table.

"And a towel. A ripped-up shirt. That old blue backpack, remember he got a new one because the buckle broke? They were all in there and—they had stains on them. They were still wet."

"How did you know to look in there." She felt defeated.

"I don't know. I was already coming back down, I was so sure there was nothing in the car, and there wasn't. I just thought—let me be able to tell Fran the whole car's clean, you know? Slob's paradise but—you know, *unimplicated.* So I just opened the trunk to be thorough. God—well, it's a good thing I did, isn't it."

She stared at him angrily.

"Don't, Carolyn. You look like you think I'm glad about this."

"You look positively triumphant at your sleuthing powers." He was solving the puzzles, that was why. At least he felt he was doing something.

"Oh, please." He went to the sink and began to scrub his hands attentively. "When I think I was all ready to call Fran and tell him to take the car, I was so—"

"This is all wild speculation." She stared at the still life on the table but kept her distance. "You don't have the slightest idea what you're looking at."

"There's blood in the car, Carolyn," he began evenly, without turning toward her. "He must have thrown the jack in and taken off and I can't tell if there's anything in the carpet itself, it's—" He shook his head, speechless.

"But why is the car here, if he did something like that? It's here but he's not? Oh God, I know somebody's got him, nothing else makes sense. They made him drive home, I don't know why, and—you can't think he's involved with this jack, Ben. You can't."

Ben came back to the table. "I took it to my workshop. The fabric stuff I burned, it's done with, but the jack I took apart." Judith made a little noise of disbelief.

Carolyn was empty-handed, standing in the middle of the room. "What do you mean?"

"I mean, they don't need to see this. It won't help anything. You can't bury it out there—unless the snow stops, I mean, it'd have to melt faster than it does at 20—what is it, 20 or so?" He looked out the window at the round thermometer nailed to the tree. "The whole damn thermometer face is covered in snow. I could just have washed the prints off but—"

"Ben, you're babbling. I don't know what you're talking about. Come back." She ran her hand in front of his eyes as if she suspected his sanity. "Slow down."

He looked impatient. "I put it in my pile of old tools and stuff—like, disassembled and just thrown in, you know, it's full of dust and hunks of old appliances and shit. Nobody would ever think to look, or if they did, they could never connect it. You know. There are other old wood-chopping gloves and wedges and stuff under the rubble."

Carolyn flicked a quick look at Judith. "But you're an accomplice if you do that." She hated it when the children heard her tell even the smallest social white lie: "So sorry we can't come, we're already busy that night." Now Judith was hearing her father planning, freely admitting, a criminal act. She was seeing him compound everything. Carolyn wanted to stand between them, her arms held out to the sides to make a wall. Judith kept her face down, staring into the smudged bottom of her bowl. "*Ben.* Have you thought about what you're doing? Stop a minute, please—let's decide what—"

"What do we have to decide?" He stared at her coolly. "What, exactly, is the question?"

She couldn't do this. It was impossible even to begin to think about it. It was happening to someone else, she was dizzy with the unreality of it. How did he know he hadn't destroyed something that would lead them to wherever Jacob was hidden? Hiding? Held? How did he know? "And you won't let me see it. Any of it."

He looked at her with what would have been tenderness at another time; right now it only seemed patronizing. "Correct. It's been taken care of."

She stamped her foot; she felt like a child deprived of candy. "Taken care of."

Ben looked around wildly. He was a bulky man. He could be menacing if he wanted to, beard and shoulders, solid legs, woodcutter's chest. But though he used his voice all too fiercely, Carolyn thought, he never took advantage of his strength, never made so much as a move. Now he bent beside the stove and picked up the wrought-iron tongs that sat on top of the wood box. He looked at them a long time, frowning. They were a lattice of meshing metal, the way they folded open and shut like the little gate she'd used to keep the babies from tumbling down the stairs. She watched him raise the black tongs up, over his head, and swing them down in front of him like an ax. "Oh, but no. Wait. Better yet." He turned then and swung from the side like a batter going for a line drive. "Like that."

She covered her face with her hands.

"Daddy," Judith shouted. "That's terrible, what you're doing! Don't *do* that!" The tears had frozen on her lids, stopped there by disgust.

But Ben looked equally disgusted. He threw the tongs down and pulled the kitchen towel off its rack and wiped his sweaty face with it.

"Ben, listen." Carolyn stood with her hands on her opposite forearms, trying to warm up. "There are so many possibilities, I think we're being overdramatic here." She was going to force logic on it even while it slithered out of her grasp. "He got stuck and needed something out of the trunk to give him traction. Or to lift the car up. I don't know. He used the jack and he hurt himself with it. Maybe she was under the car, trying to help and it fell on her?" The casualness with which she put forth this suggestion sickened her. And even as she said it, she knew it didn't jibe with what she had seen: that was not a girl crushed by a car, it was a girl bludgeoned by someone who, at least at that moment, had hated her. But why assume it was Jacob who had done it? Why was he so sure of the worst thing, and the most unlikely? "I do know the facts are usually stranger than they look on the face of it. Look—" She cast around for something. "Last week a very hysterical mother brought in her little girl with her hands and wrists all blue, did I tell you this? It's wonderful." Her laugh rose up as wildly as flame would rise, taking paper out of her hand. "And she said she had scrubbed and scrubbed and it wasn't coming off, so obviously the stuff was internal and she was—"

"For Christ's sake," Ben said, and stamped down hard as if he were squashing her underfoot. "For Christ's *sake!*" He threw the smudged towel down on the counter. "Tell me, would you know his gloves if you saw them? The gray woolen ones? Would you recognize them if they were soaked with blood?" She gasped as if he'd held them up to her face. "I'm sorry," he whispered, and turned away from her so that he wouldn't have to see what he had done. "Sweetheart, I didn't want to tell you that part. I put them in the woodstove, okay? I—what else can I call it?—I destroyed them. Bloody fingers, Carolyn."

But she kept shaking her head against it. Slowly, side to side, she said no. She remembered to speak. "No," she said. "You were mistaken. There are a lot of gloves that are—"

"Call me," he said quietly, "when you're ready to consider reality." He disappeared into the living room and she heard his feet on the stairs.

"Judith," Carolyn said to her daughter, who was still at the table, her face gone sick-white. It had taken her a long time to find any voice at all. "If I even thought I understood your father, why he's so eager—"

"Don't, Mama. Please don't say." Judith scratched in the bottom of her empty bowl with her soup spoon. She was telling Carolyn not to be so selfish. She was telling her this was unnecessary. "Please don't argue. It's bad enough."

BEN

WENDELL SHOWED UP FINALLY THAT NIGHT. THIS WAS WENDELL BYE, KING of the yuppie lawyers, whose careful guardianship of his fellow townsfolks' modest assets has by now bought him a Jacuzzi, a 32-foot boat, and a neat camp in the woods where he murders deer but does it sentimentally, like a religious ritual, with his father's rifle.

He came in shaking the snow off his shoes with the delicacy of a cat; big men do that. His wife, Steph, came with him; this was closer than business. We shook hands with a certain ceremony, as if we were agreeing on something. When the women fell together, I could hear Steph's soft consoling voice, the one she gave her boys when they fell down. Wendell is a large presence, usually a comforting one; he was a linebacker at Dartmouth and everything about him, his long eyes beginning to droop at the sides, his chin, shoulders, wrists as wide as his arms, all of him reminds me of the loose, generous fleshiness of a St. Bernard. "You haven't heard anything?" he came in asking.

Carolyn spoke out of Steph's arms. "Wendell, we don't even know if *he's* all right, it's not impossible that he's in trouble somewhere."

He nodded. "Though you'd think a girl would make a better hostage for most people—"

"But who knows what happened first. Maybe they ran off because—" The possibilities passed before us like photographs in a batch, combinations of likely numbers, sexes, types. I assume we all saw them in the same disarray.

"True," he said reluctantly. "Too true, too true. We'd better put on full speed to find him, then."

"We?"

"They, I should say. They."

I had the sudden terrible feeling that he was going to be no help at all.

And I was right. When Carolyn suggested to him that he scold me for "being difficult" with Fran, I got my warning. He was a good Boy Scout.

Wendell sighed before he began, as if I was the object of some petty exasperation. Meanwhile, my son's life was hanging out there over a precipice. But I understood: somehow it was all too serious to arouse the proper seriousness in us—I could forgive him that, the way I had to forgive myself.

"Ben. A guy kicks his friend the chief of police in the gut, word's going to spread. What do you expect?" He turned dutifully to Carolyn and said what she wanted him to say. "See, Carolyn, I know Ben loves this place because it's so small. I mean, everybody's got his nose in everybody else's armpit and Ben thinks it's quaint."

"How about healthy?" I suggested. "What if Ben thinks it's healthy for people to take care of each other the way nobody does in New York City anymore. Could that be it?" I was thinking of how this town is a braid, so many people, so many experiences, bound up together, criss-crossing, tight. I didn't know yet what a noose that could be.

He shrugged. "Whatever. All I know is word travels faster than rain falls up here and you can't separate them at your convenience. That's what goes along with caring. You can't—"

"Wendell," I said as patiently as I could, which was not very. "I brought you up here to advise us, not to give me a lesson in village sociology."

He didn't look rebuked. "Can you show me the car, hotshot?"

I just looked at him. I wasn't being fresh, I was figuring the odds on whether I could trust him absolutely, and in the end I didn't like them.

"Look, Ben, you can't do that with me. First off, I'm your friend. And I love Jacob, Jesus, I've been through every damn class play of his, I gave him fifty bucks for the bike-a-thon last year. I don't just give that kind of money to anybody's kid, you know." I was supposed to smile with him. "But, second, you know you can't go getting into this hunted-animal posture with everybody who's going to want to help you. You don't want to be in this thing alone, the two of you, believe me. You'll go crazy, and you'll tear each other to bits, and Jacob, too, when you get him home. Don't keep the truth a secret. You've got little enough to be parceling out a drop here and a drop there."

Just when you need subtlety and intuition, you get canned speeches. Where could I find somebody whose judgment was steadier than mine but not so damned sentimental? Of course I got overexcited, that was my trademark. But I knew what I wanted, a wise adviser who could stop my mouth with logic and discretion.

I thought I'd better give him something. "I tried to find some footprints, but the snow—"

"Right," Wendell said innocently. "The goddamn

snow." And of course he looked at Carolyn, who opened her mouth to speak.

"Some of the—" she began. She was going to tell him about the jack.

"Hey—" It cost me something, but I raised one finger in warning.

And got what I expected. "What is that? What are you daring to say to me, Ben Reiser?" She stared at my finger, even when I took it down, with the look many women reserve for their husbands just after they've been struck. "Now you're going to presume to tell me when I can speak and when I have to be quiet?"

I could see out of the corner of my eye how Steph had drawn closer to Wendell in solidarity; in exclusion.

Carolyn's eyes had narrowed and I thought she might come at me with her nails, though I needn't bother to say that isn't the way she fights. "You can hold your own tongue if you want to, but you'd just better leave mine alone." Her voice was thin with rage.

The phone rang and released me. Carolyn had it in a dash. We waited a long time to see if it was news. "Who is this?" she said dully, then repeated it. I could see a vein in her cheek begin to throb in irregular bursts. "Well, whoever you are, I hope you sleep well tonight, you're a person of true compassion. Our first well-wisher, yes, aren't you proud? You haven't got much of a brain, but you've got mighty quick reflexes." When she put the phone down, her cheeks were wet.

"It's cold," Judith said abruptly. I don't know if she meant it or if she was trying to distract her mother—there were any number of things, I told myself, that people simply said in the course of talk; I didn't need to analyze every motive.

"Well, then." Carolyn put on a resolved look and went to scoop up a lot of newspaper from the wood box we keep it in. "Look, Wendell, we've absolutely given up on kindling, do you do this? The Cape Cod roll?" She counted out eight or nine sheets and began to roll the pile in from the corner.

"Eight seems to be the ideal, from empirical tests done right here. Reiser Labs, Limited. They have to be big ones, though—see, people who read tabloids don't deserve to get warm. Oh, is that terrible to say?" She giggled. "It isn't very PC, is it?" She covered her mouth with her hand. "But, see, this is the perfect end for *The New York Times*. Multipurpose, from reading it with your coffee to mulching the garden, Ben must use up a couple of trees just to do the garden, all the way to this generous offering of its whole body, imagine that, to make us warm and snug! See—then you twist it, it's just a big bow, paper—well, maybe four, I don't know why I keep making it so precise —it depends, and a lot of oxygen—" She was pulling the long ends through and making the rough knots as tight as she could. They looked like big white birds with pointed wings.

Steph, casting a long, pained look at me, took Carolyn by the shoulders gently. "Carolyn. Honey." She pressed her to her ample chest. "Take it easy now. Just try to relax."

Carolyn laughed and pulled away. "Leave it to me to be giving instructions even as they lead me away!" She wiped her face with the back of her hand, an unlikely gesture for her, a little crude, or maybe only a little child-like: I remember the babies beginning to wipe their eyes with balled fists when they were getting tired; they'd cross a line and suddenly their gestures were different. Such tenderness washed over me—for her, for them, for *then*—I don't know—that I was exhausted by it. I'd have given everything I owned just then to go somewhere alone, not to have to answer, explain, justify. But if I couldn't think about my life, what would I think about? I don't concentrate on wood in a vacuum, or shapes out in the empty air. There are always watchers. Those trees that make no noise when they fall in an empty forest, those are my sculptures in a space with no eyes in it.

Wendell had said it would take a little legal finagling for Fran to get his warrant. He had to go down and type up some papers and then find the judge to sign them—we were too far from a D.A. to need one—and then they'd have a right to the car and everything in it. I got him and Steph out as quick as I could and then I took off running. I swallowed a cup of black coffee like a runner tanking up on Gatorade for strength in the kick. Carolyn was on the phone with her friend Celene, murmuring little half sentences, her voice soft, like a pigeon's. All her authority was gone. Celene wasn't someone she needed to entertain with ceremony and she let herself go helpless before her, slack and tired and bewildered. "There is no way, no way in the world, what I saw . . . there's some mystery here, Celene," I heard her say, gathering up some energy and exhausting it in little waves. I wondered what in the world Celene was finding to say back.

I also wondered if we should be leaving the phone free in case somebody called with news, with word of something we'd have to produce to get him back again. Ransom. Bail.

All the way up to the garage my mouth stayed warm from the coffee, and bitter. I closed the garage doors. They didn't really close and I worried that, even though it was late evening by now, the neighbors riding up the road would wonder, since they'd never seen them shut before, and maybe come poke their heads into the opening between them. But no one looked in, at least no one I saw. Earlier I had lifted the backpack, the T-shirt, the towel out with extraordinary care, cradling them like precious objects, and had delivered them to the sweet little workshop stove I'd described to Fran; it was still plenty hot from before. The mess of it ignited—I kept the bag out, I cut that to ribbons with my long shears and dumped it in the pile of scraps I glued and embedded and buried in my creatures—and all of it was down to ash in no time; I stirred the ashes to be sure. Now, in the garage, I held my camping lantern to the carpet of the trunk, but I didn't see any blood on it—all that wretched adolescent junk of Jacob's had made a pretty firm nest, by the grace of—whatever. I wasn't ready to invite God in yet.

But the memory of the stains hung there like a ghost, as if they had a voice that whispered "I was here" even in their absence. If there was any blood in there, a single ghost of a single spatter, that could be the end of both of us. Christ.

Well, the car was such a mess it didn't seem farfetched that it might not even have carpeting in the trunk. It was a gamble worth taking. I hauled it up—it looked okay to me, but what do I know about blood-sniffing dogs, blood-sniffing chemicals? What if there was some Forensics King who could find the hundredth part of nothing? I went into my workshop with it, awkwardly, careful not to let it drag on the ground, an arrow to the spot. Carpet would make a stinking fire—I attacked it with a matte knife, and when I had strips and hunks, uneven, angular, I took them to my scrap corner and fed them to it as if it were the compost pile. I stirred the mound of leavings, turned it all over, flung it up and around as if to let it breathe. Pieces of cloth-of-gold shimmered out at me, wonderful stuff from the Lucky You Resale Shop that had benefited the Methodist church—somebody's real robe, I think it was, the kind of garment that Judith used to appropriate for her dress-up trunk, impressed that someone had bought it once in earnest. I liked to cut it up when I needed some shine in a collage; I would purify it, rip it safely out of context, not tacky lingerie anymore but gold, luscious shafts of light, abstract. That was the principle on which I built: a second chance for all those shapes and colors and textures freed of their purpose; the dun-colored pieces looked no more peculiar than most of it, the box of yellow zippers, the batting, the chintz drapes out of which, just last week, I had scissored gross pink flowers with leaves like lily pads. My heart beat so hard I was sure I could see it, thumping in and out like a frog's throat. What a sick joke, I thought, slicing the carpet into triangles and strips: deconstructing reality. May heaven help me.

My fabric pile was twin to the wood-and-tool pile that had eaten up the jack in pieces. There was one soft mound and one hard, out of which I pulled my creatures bit by bit. I suspected it would be pretty off-putting to most sane people, but I made myself stop spinning and *look* at it. Could I have it wrong, could it possibly be an invitation to plow right in and have a careful look? There was broken crockery enough to keep Julian Schnabel happy for a year, and deeply rusted garden tools, and the stripped fins of an old fan splayed out like a circle of fish bones . . . I'll tell you, I wasn't ready for deeper questions like Do I dare? *Should* I dare? All I thought was, Fran Conklin will never put his hand in there. This madman's garbage pile, he'd think—repulsive, organic, beginning to stink of decomposition. The mess would look to him like the inside of my head and he was not the man to do an inventory of the contents. I was betting our lives on it.

Back in the garage, diversion, again, seemed the only refuge. In the other car I carried another jack, a terrific little contraption I picked up last year at a yard sale. It was called Jack-in-the-Box and that's what it was, a collapsible little lever meant for one wheel at a time, much smaller than a full-fledged jack, and it sat in stray pieces in need of on-the-spot assembly, nestled in a red metal box about the size and shape of a first-aid kit. It was about the least lethal object imaginable, and it was shiny clean. I wasn't sure how it would serve exactly, but I didn't think it would hurt. I laid it neatly beside the crowbar and all the rest of the tire-changing stuff (which I wiped clean and sullied as much as I could with my own hands, to imply that I was the only one who ever changed a tire around here). I dumped a lot of grease around on the bare metal trunk floor, and other evidences of a general sloppiness no one would have trouble believing of me (though it was, in fact, excessive). Then I threw in some wood chunks coated, like something breaded, with sawdust and added a few truncated 4 × 4's, some oil-rank rags and tools, and other detritus of my trade. Anyone who built things, which was just about everyone—every man—in Hyland, would understand, though most were fanatically neat and would be morally repulsed by such wanton disorder. As unmasked secrets went, though, I could live with it.

Satisfied with the mess I had constructed, I opened the garage doors on the moon-splashed snow, and just in time. There came Fran with his warrant to look at the car inside and out. I let him look, I kept my distance. He pretended to be glad I had "decided to be reasonable"; I said I didn't think I had a choice, up against a piece of paper. "Paper covers rock. Scissors cut paper," I said, but I don't think he got it.

He went in with two silent helpers sent by the county, a couple of goony young guys with very short hair—I couldn't tell if he was assisting them or vice versa, they all muttered in an alien language, heads bent together—and they lifted a lot of fingerprints from inside and outside. Or tried—I couldn't decide whether to clean up the junk on the seats and had finally decided to leave it in its native jumble. But, just for the pleasure of defiance, I said I wished I could have washed the exterior of the car, and waxed it for him.

"Thanks for the thought, Ben," Fran said to me, eyeing the car roof suspiciously to see how clean it really was. "Don't worry about any beauty contests—we've got a couple of more important things on our minds." He sighed like a man who felt oppressed. "I see you're still doing your best."

I smiled, satisfied.

He was not going to pretend to be friendly. "Don't think I'm not taking note of your attitude, Ben. This kind of obstruction gets people sentences for tampering, if you don't know it."

"Tampering? What tampering? You got a whole bagful of disgusting high-school junk out of that car, I haven't touched a thing in there!" This was true. I felt safe and honest.

"Well, then, what the hell are you doing in here?"

I went wide-eyed. "I'm having a look at the car you want to see so badly. Don't I have a right to check it out myself?"

"How long have you been up here?"

I wasn't sure he had a right to ask me that kind of thing but I felt shaky. Who knows anything about the law, really? It was like the body, I thought, helpless. If I asked where your pancreas is, would you really know? So I didn't take a chance. "I just got up here a little while ago. All I did was look around and I sure don't see anything the matter."

"What have you been doing all this time?"

This is how you get embroiled. Every question comes at you from a different angle. One tiny misstep and you can fall and break your neck and maybe not even know how you put your foot down wrong. "Phone calls." (Could they check and see if we'd been on the phone? Well, Carolyn had been tying it up some—surely they wouldn't know which of us was talking.) "Comforting my wife and daughter, who didn't find it very—"

He'd been poking in the trunk while we talked, and bending to inspect the snowy floor. "And this trunk?"

"What about 'this trunk'? The trunk is full of my junk, so—?"

He smiled at me bitterly. "And the floor around it,

where did that sawdust come from? The little hunks of wood, those toothpicks of new wood stuck there on the snow? Ben, you're looking for trouble. You're not thinking clear about all this, I hope you recognize that."

There were bits of sawdust we'd walked into the snow-splotched concrete, he was right, shreds, and I'd better admit it. "Okay, I looked in the trunk. Do you blame me? I told you, I had a look. So some of this drifted out. So? Does that make me guilty of something?"

"And all that junk in there?"

"I have to use the car! Fran, I've got supplies to move around, I can't put this junk in Carolyn's car, believe me. She has a fit."

He looked disgusted. "Your attitude isn't exactly what I'd like to see in the father of somebody who is possibly guilty of a capital crime. There's levity here that I don't much like the sound of." He looked at me hard, studying me, apparently reappraising. "It's not a decent attitude, Ben. I must say I'm surprised to hear a man like you treating this like some kind of little—inconvenience." They were taking pictures. They were making a mold of the tire tread. This wasn't easy in the murky light. One of them went to their car and dragged out a huge lamp, like something a photographer would use.

I nodded toward the socket. "I'm not sure this place is wired for your big guns," I said, to be helpful, before I turned back to Fran. "Then you don't know the difference between anger and levity," I told him. I kicked the tire and felt stupid. I suppose I thought I'd better stay consistent in my defense of our rights, stay casual, even though I'd passed out of that first stage of angry surprise. Sometimes I get in over my head. Sometimes after I've let myself go I don't know how to recoup. May it not go down as a mark against Jacob.

Fran made a note in his book, underlined it. The goony guys nodded; they pointed; they dug their nails into the tread and peered under them to see what they had dislodged. "All right, Ben. I'm having this car moved now. This car is officially impounded. It's going to be evidence, if it comes to that." He kept shaking his head as if he'd never encountered a specimen like me. "I just want to tell you, if it turns out your kid's in trouble, then you're in trouble, too." He delivered a little click with his teeth, as if he was about to spit but thought better of it. "Got that?"

What could I say. But there was still an "if" in there. "Got it."

"And now," he said to me with too much satisfaction, "we've got a warrant for the house."

I stared. Why did it surprise me? They were *after* him. When I ought to have been anticipating the next assault I was like a ship with each passageway sealed off from the others to keep it from sinking at shipwreck time. I'd better learn to envision what was coming at us next.

"Not the whole house. Just Jacob's room. Do you want to see the piece of paper?"

I did not.

"Try to understand, Ben." The man did look concerned, I'll give him that. His broad features were tight, everything that could wrinkle wrinkled. He could pull off a good deep frown. I think he meant it, too—out of uniform he was a decent man. "We had to go to the judge to get this, and he had to agree that we had probable cause. You know what that is, it's a reasonable expectation that we might find something. And he thought we did. Simple enough."

"You're going fishing," I said.

"We're not going fishing. We have a well-established legal right to search the premises where there is reasonable suspicion that the occupant might have left evidence pertaining to a crime. No one says we have to know if it's a weapon or a note or a trail of blood." He looked at me with disappointment. "Now I promise you we will not touch the rest of the house. Only Jacob's room."

I ought to have stepped aside easily—I didn't think they'd find anything and the prospect of Fran's trying to make sense of that pit Jacob lived in was actually wonderful to contemplate—but principle kept fogging up (or was it clarifying?) the picture. I opened my mouth on one last objection, but Fran had begun to extract the papers from the inside pocket of his uniform. I was going to have to hear another speech. "Okay, come on. You'll be lucky if you can find his bed, let alone anything incriminating."

We turned to go and I had a sudden flash of the footprints I'd made from the garage to my workshop: busy me, so carefully clutching the jack, the carpet, the whole mess, to my chest, nothing scraping the ground, but my boots chewing up a trail of my own that could hang me. But nobody turned in that direction. They were too eager to get to pay dirt.

We walked down to the house single-file and the heat of the kitchen stove broke on us like a flash of bright sunlight, as if we had walked outside into daylight, not in. As if it weren't the middle of the night. Fran put the papers, with their seals and fancy cursive headings, on the table and smoothed out their sharp folds. They were the first of the state's official weapons against us; none of us came close enough to look at them.

There's a tin sign on Jacob's door that he lifted from the dump when they got a new one with half a dozen directions painted on it for GLASS (CLEAR BROWN GREEN), CANS, PAPER, and so on into the balkanized territories of recycling. It simply said TRASH, that outmoded concept, above an emphatic arrow. (The dump isn't what it used to be, tended by a little old guy, dirty and silent in the tattered lawn chair he'd retrieved from the edge of the pit, holding a pitchfork like the keeper of hell. Now there was a Refuse Administrator.) But I still called Jacob the Boss Dumpman.

Fran stood on the threshold and whistled. Then he and

his sidekicks tore into it. This was the only laughable thing that had happened in twenty-four hours—they lifted Jacob's socks to peer earnestly beneath them, they opened his closet without relish and unenthusiastically fingered his pockets. There seemed to be chewing gum everywhere, not necessarily chewed but melted in its wrapper. One of the short-hairs looked at every tape in the stack of plastic boxes, as if he might come upon one neatly labeled PLAN FOR MARTHA TAVERNER MURDER. He found a couple of Jacob's earrings lying loose and made a face. I stood in the hall smiling faintly, but Carolyn was having a hard time with the sight of these grown men lifting the blanket to stare at his sheets, and shaking out his sneakers, and turning the pages of his notebooks. "It's *stupid,*" she hissed at me. "Thoroughly useless and offensive and a—violation of everything." Fran was lifting underwear out of his drawer where, clean though it was, it lay strangled up tight.

I put my arm around her shoulder. If I had any equanimity about the obscenity of all this, that was only because I'd been there first. "So maybe you can see why I haven't just fallen into line," I said as gently as I could. "Now you see."

She lowered her head to my shoulder, defeated. "The occupant," she muttered. "The *premises.*"

"Tell me something," Fran said; he was obviously discouraged. "Have you noticed anything missing? Sometimes we need to be looking for what's *not* there, instead of what *is.*"

We were innocent this time—even with the best will in the world, which I did not have, I couldn't think what might be gone. I didn't come up here that often, and Carolyn, who was probably suffering some housewifely embarrassment as well as all else, had decided a long time ago never to set foot in here to clean it or even—worse!—to straighten the piles.

They were conferring about whether to lift fingerprints.

"Now or never," Fran was murmuring. "Once that little window of opportunity closes, it's shuttered up forever." But the crime, if it was Jacob's, had taken place elsewhere; they were finished with us for the moment.

Then we heard a noise of gratitude and discovery. One of the shorthairs, fingering the casual piles of pocket junk in a dish on Jacob's dresser, had come upon a key chain with a little cylinder at the end of it, plastic, that held a picture. When you pushed the bottom it lit up. I remember when he kept a photo of our old dog Glory in it, coming out of the lake shaking herself. I remember the way the sun hit the drops and the camera had accidentally caught them, little silver dazzles hanging in the air like ice chips.

"Hmm," the detective said and handed it to Fran.

"Oh-ho," Fran said. "Well, now."

He gave it to us in silence, as if the case had just been clinched. I grabbed it, held it to my eye, and pushed. It was Martha—I suppose it might have been, it was some blond teenager, anyway. But her head was turned, so that you could only catch a corner of her smile. She was standing with her back to the camera in a slightly too skimpy bikini bottom, white polka dots on blue, the cheeks of her pert rear high and young, and she was obviously holding the top to her breasts in front. From behind, all you saw was pure bare back, with faint pale strips where she wasn't tanned, and the strings of the suit dangling out to the sides. It was half innocent—if it had been a Norman Rockwell painting of a younger girl, a dog like Glory would have been leaping happily for the bikini ties—and half provocative, I guess—a moment of sexy fun. A homemade *Playboy* centerfold. She was laughing. Her body was new and lovely and I was pierced deep with the hope that it was someone else's, who would still get to use it. "So?"

"So," Fran said. "A link, wouldn't you say?"

I didn't have to say anything without Wendell there. But

really. "Fran, nobody's pretending they didn't know each other," I told him, instantly at the boil. "If that's her at all."

"That's her."

"I repeat, so?"

He threw it in the green plastic bag that held a few other irrelevancies: some handwriting, an invitation to a party, a tape called *Death-throes* by a group I've never heard of. (Thank God he wasn't a journal keeper, they'd have gobbled that up in a minute.) No gun, though, no drugs or drug paraphernalia, not so much as a penknife or a condom in silver foil.

"That's it," Fran said matter-of-factly. "We apologize for the inconvenience."

"Thanks for nothing, you mean."

Carolyn gave me one of those warning looks again, right out of the middle of her anger and hurt. *I don't understand you,* I said back with my eyes. *Why won't you help?*

"If the rest of your case is like this, Fran," I said and shook my head. "Pathetic haul you've got there, for all your official documents."

He ignored me. "My kid kept his room like that," he was saying to his geeks as they followed each other down the stairs, "I'd have sent him to military school, he'd be saluting before he said good morning."

We showed them the door in silence. I realized we smelled of cigarettes from standing around in there. We were sour with the smell of the cigarettes Jacob hadn't smoked when we could see him.

It was 10:30. More than once I picked up the phone to make sure it was working. I don't know why I kept checking the clock—the shock, I guess, of how little time it took to turn you upside down and shake your whole life out of your pockets. Four hours, I thought, that's all. Four hours.

Well, it only takes a second to die. Four hours, in comparison, is a slow leak.

It was the first night in my life I didn't sleep a single minute, or even want to close my eyes. Once I stayed up forever riding the subways with a girl I'd just met—we went from one line to another, every place they connected—BMT to IND to the shuttle at Grand Central and the IRT uptown and down, drunk on hopeful lust and maybe a little something out of a bottle. And when my father died I sat up for about thirty-six hours, wanting but not daring to close my eyes.

But this was the only time I went to bed washed, teeth brushed, as if it was an ordinary night, and then lay there for many hours staring up as if the dark were dirt and I was buried under it. Out where they lived on Birch Row, the Taverners were in worse shape than we were, and that didn't make it any better. They had some wondering to do but it wouldn't really change anything important for them when the mystery was solved. They had virtue—well, innocence, at least—and certainty. In the blank dark of our bedroom we had guilt—probable guilt—and hope, or confusion. But I agreed with Carolyn, or tried to agree with her, fought with myself to agree with her, that whatever we had, it was much too early—six hours, eight, ten, twelve hours—for despair.

BEN

Dear Folks,

Took a long time to get to Boston, so much snow they closed Deer Mountain (I love that, closing a mountain! Power!) so we had to go the long long way around. But we made it, slip-sliding all the way. Passed someone x-country skiing on the highway (in the slow lane).

I counted the highways out of Boston—there are 12. And sky routes everywhere.

I know you don't pray, but pray now.

J.

I TOOK IT OUT OF THE MAILBOX WITH AN AD FOR A NEW HARDWARE STORE downtown, a bank statement, and two bills. At first, before I got the photograph into focus and discovered that it was the Swan Boats in Boston Common, I thought it was a card from my brother Stuie, who had gone to Hawaii with his family over Christmas break. I suppose I'd been expecting some sea-and-rocky shore. But there were boats with graceful necks, gray-white like the granite of monuments, and the grass an impossible acid green beneath a sky that never was. So I turned it over with some curiosity. I was walking back from the mailbox across the little stretch of roughly plowed driveway and I stopped and read it and the world turned over and stopped dead.

No one had heard a thing, no one had had a clue. Of course, the police had put an alarm out—I had never before quite appreciated how graphic it was to call it an "all-points bulletin" but that was the scattershot we needed, everywhere, near, far, the whole sweep of the compass. We called them endlessly to prod them in the search. I didn't have the feeling it hurried them by a single second—they move as they will move, according to their Procedures. After a week, Mary, the police station receptionist, began to answer us—"No news"—as if we were cranks calling to see if they'd gotten a new shipment of, I don't know what, jelly beans. Finally she said to Carolyn, "Mrs. Reiser, do you really think you're the only ones who want to find your son?" And she was right, but who could blame us—just as we thought they'd forgotten our urgency to find him, I suppose we'd forgotten theirs. It was too punishing to remember why.

There was all kinds of speculation, all useless. Wendell told us people were calling him and coming by on the dimmest of pretexts—gossip was no inconsiderable purpose in Hyland. Everyone knew he was our lawyer; might he not happen to drop a crumb of information? (He was so wondrously upright he would not; he was offended at the very suggestion.) The police called for a list of Jacob's friends, for his hobbies and his habits: "places he might hang out." I tried to imagine him at the pizza parlor in Howe, at the electronic games in the movie-theater lobby.

And on the CB I heard outrage, I could sit in my

kitchen and monitor the speed with which "wanted for questioning" became much worse, more damning and final. Conversations about roadwork, changes of appointment times, bad weather approaching, all the matter-of-fact miscellany I loved about this place, the way voices crackled, low-tech, out of the box—into every conversation there seemed to break at least one comment about the "Taverner thing." What a stewpot, everybody's business made public with the zeal of civic duty. Once when my brother was visiting he borrowed my car and parked it on a deserted road to go running. And the next day when I was buying my newspaper at the Central, somebody said to me, tickled half to death, "Seen your car parked up on Ridge Road there, Ben. Taking an afternoon nap, were you?" Stuie said it was impossible, no one had driven past all the time he'd been running. "What do they have," he asked, a little flustered, "helicopters?" That was the way news spread; even non-news. We heard there was a meeting of "concerned citizens" that had gathered in the Taverners' living room. No one could tell me—would, I mean—what they had talked about. I heard something about pressure on the police to move faster, harder, involve the F.B.I. I could understand it, a roomful of furious fathers, even if it made my neck itch. What would I be doing if I were Mike Taverner, who deserved his rage, deserved his impatience? I'd have been up here, I suspected, with a noose in my quivering hand.

Carolyn, however, concentrated on kidnap. Whatever horrible history I had dragged in with the jack and the gloves she dismissed—she needed to see Jacob alive. What if he was being tortured? What if he was being raped? Locked in a closet? Covered with leaves in the woods? Left for dead. *Dead.* They trained Patty Hearst to use a rifle and do their dirty work, what if they forced him to rob armored trucks, commit atrocities. Steal. Steal girls. Steal boys. She went on like that, rabid imaginings and half of it I'm sure she couldn't utter, with her fist in her mouth. The rest, she said, guilt, innocence, whatever, we could worry about later. I stopped arguing, what did I want to argue for? I thought, I'd rather he robbed a Brink's truck than murdered his girlfriend.

Two witnesses had come forward, as yet unnamed. One had seen Jacob and Martha together, braked at the stop sign on the corner of Poor Farm Road and MacNeece Street about an hour, maybe more, before the other came upon them standing outside the car, in the snow, in front of Tuttle's fence. The second one had asked if they needed help. Jacob had waved him off. The police "crime squad"—a unit apparently born for the occasion—was making a strong appeal to witnesses. The quarry was Jacob or Martha or both, or "anything suspicious," which seemed to me dangerously vague. Jacob had not been seen leaving town, but what did that mean? That it was dark, or nearly. That he'd been hunched in a back seat in someone's car, his hat pulled down. Either an accomplice's car or an abductor's or a stranger's, or, or, or . . . I don't know why he didn't take his own—too traceable, maybe.

Everybody had a theory, from group riot to kidnap to drug frenzy. None of the theories seemed to have much to do with Jacob. We ourselves were without a single thought except Dear Lord—Lord if there is one, Lord if there isn't—bring him home to us and let us run our hands over him to see if he's really alive and ours. Let him come home somehow before they shoot him dead. I suppose if you'd pushed me I, too, would have declared for abduction—imagine trying to choose the least rotten fate for your child—because, though endangered, it left him guiltless. Mostly we were walking around the kitchen stunned and listening for the phone, and we heard the nasty speculation begin to waft in on us right through the walls, and—as he himself was now daring to suggest to us in an odd voice, unprecedented by any devotion in his life; quite the contrary, in fact—we prayed.

When I read his initial beneath the exhortation to pray, I was so stunned that I dropped the card in the snow and some of the letters ran as if they'd been cried on. But you could still read them.

When I gave the card to Carolyn she read it and reread it so fiercely I thought she would put it in her mouth and chew it up and swallow it to understand it better.

"He's *alive,*" I said, with a huge exhalation of relief. The sheer stupid fact of it was about as reassuring as saying he's blind, deaf, dumb, drawn and quartered, but he's breathing.

"He's alive and he's crazy," she said back to me without gratitude. She stared at the card again, shook it impatiently as if she might coax more speech out of it, turned it over and back again to the paint-by-numbers picture. "If this is his idea of communication . . ."

We had to go the long way: who were we supposed to picture? He was alive but was he *safe?* Could the card be like the phone call you make with a kidnapper's gun to your temple? It was postmarked yesterday: fairly new news. He wanted us to know where he was. Did he want anything else?

"What are we going to do with this?" Carolyn asked.

It took me a minute. "I guess we're not going to do anything."

"Don't you think we need to show this to someone? To Wendell?"

"Why show it to Wendell? What would you like him to do with the information?"

She bit her nail. "I don't know. But it seems to me we've got to do something with it." She sighed. She had announced a little while earlier that this would be her last day away from her office; she was not made for sitting idle. Nor for being a victim, either, though I wondered if she appreciated what she might find at work.

"Would you tell Fran where he is? Do you want to help get him caught?"

Carolyn sat down—we were still in the kitchen, we were always in the kitchen when we weren't working, especially in winter. The hot heart of the house was partly the woodstove and partly, I suppose, the primitive sacrament of eating that took place in there. Cooking and eating: keeping the body stoked as if it were another stove. "Why 'caught'?" she asked me from the center of a fury I hadn't seen gathering. "Why do you keep assuming he's got to be caught? Maybe it's *rescued.* Why do you think—"

I shook the card at her. "Doesn't it calmly describe that drive as some kind of an adventure? Doesn't it promise escape?"

"It's cryptic," she said. "That's all. Why should you read that as escape?"

So I asked the question neutrally: "Do you want to see him found?" I said we'd been pleading with them to find him, only find him. But this was a harder question than I had realized—do you want him found? *Do you want to help find him?* It was like some ultimate philosophical head-breaking first question about the order of the universe, the kind of balance they made stage tragedies out of, only couched in the terms of an ordinary-looking morning, sun on snow, cloudless, sharp. What I really mean is, this was the morning of Martha Taverner's funeral.

I made myself see it. I made myself. The girl would be in a closed casket at LeMois's Funeral Home, wearing her best dress invisibly, a white rose in her hands (I was guessing, just to make it harder on myself), and three-quarters of the town would be there, serious in suits, with Kleenexes balled in their fists, and, appallingly, we could not show our faces. We were sitting here in hostile quarantine and Jacob, apparently, was somewhere in Boston a couple of hours away, planning a life in exile but thinking of us thinking of him. I considered going off into the woods to scream—it was the one and only thing I needed to do, the one thing in the world if I couldn't stand face to face just then with Jacob, and there was no place to do it without attracting just the kind of attention I needed to scream about.

Carolyn got up and brought to the table the pad of paper that sits beside the telephone for messages. She thought hard for a while and then began to scribble in her impossible doctor's hand.

"What are you doing, writing back?"

She stopped and looked past me. "It's a list. Of possibilities."

"Such as? I didn't know we had enough choices to have a list."

"Oh, Ben, come on." This was a scientist; I forgot. "We can give the card to Wendell or to Fran and talk about how to help the Boston police find him. We can sit on it and do nothing. We can *go* to Boston and—"

"Find a needle in a haystack. Sure."

She ignored me. "We can—"

"Carolyn, 'we can' absolutely nothing. We can just sit still for a while and let things take their course without thinking we can help push them along, that's what we can. No list necessary."

A look of terrible pain crossed her face—I expected her to cry out, because it creased her features so profoundly, like an electric flash, that I was sure it must have hurt searingly, deep inside her head. But all she said, just above a whisper, was "It's time for Judith's lunch." She turned and went in search of our daughter, who, I knew but she didn't, had chosen not to get out of bed this morning, who lay in her nightgown, the one with red hearts on it, like a sick child, listening to Prince and Kenny G. and staring at the ceiling.

* * *

Tony and Celene Berger had arrived with their hands full of casseroles, as if someone had died, and I tried to be grateful and couldn't, though I think I faked it pretty well. It was so perverse not to be grateful that I don't think anybody suspected—then again, Tony's a pretty perverse type himself and might have sympathized. This was Celene's doing: "The point," she said, experienced at funerals—she has a family of about fifty, in all the towns that surround us here—"is to keep your energy free for other things."

"That's what I'm trying not to do," Carolyn said from the embrace in which her friend held her tight, but she was trying, too. "You're right," she answered Celene, grateful to be loved even if the price was having to eat a covered dish fit for a church supper. "Now if you could bring us a potful of *what* to think." For that, Celene held her a second or two longer: not that it wasn't sincere, but we learned pretty quickly that humility goes a long way toward disarming disgust and fear. When Celene saw that she was crying, she wouldn't let her go.

Then Annie Dineen came, alternate leader of the Friends' Brigade. Oh, bless them. As if we'd had a death.

She took up a lot of the kitchen: she is tall, broad, curly-headed, and rarely quiet. The children loved her. Everything about her has always seemed slightly larger than life; she always brought goodies, unlikely ones like metal crickets you could hide in your hand and hangers bent into shapes that could make square bubbles, and she took away things that needed fixing. She did them a hell of a lot better than I did, too. When Judith was little, I'm sure she thought of Annie as a fairy-tale character, the kind who helps the princess, in the dark of the night, sew a pile of golden garments out of straw. Once she presented Annie with her doll that had been lost all year in the field up at the top of the garden; had weathered a whole winter there, its pretty features bleached, its hair gone white, its clothes rotted away—the snow, the rain, the mud had bled it blank. She'd held it out to Annie, wordless and tearful, one of those wrenching moments that're only archetypal to you, not to your kid who's five and desperate—and Annie gave us a long look over her shoulder. "This is Lisa, right?" she asked, and Judith gave her a big-eyed nod. "Well, have you thought of naming her Lazarus?" But she took the denuded Lisa from her and the next week brought her back whole, healed, more beautiful than she had ever been. She had even, I remember, made little crimson slippers for Lisa's toeless feet. She was one of those people, Carolyn said, who touch things into bloom.

In fact, that was her business: she had been a social worker in another life, and had abandoned her dry-as-dust husband and, finally, men in general, for women and perennials. By now she'd landscaped every new and renovated building in town, except for the ones whose owners couldn't stand her. "Flowers are nicer. Bushes. I prefer a cactus, even, to a landlord. They don't abuse children. They don't beat each other up, or lie, or lock their grandmother in the closet." She had just had a client who did that, for the old lady's social-security check, which she was made to endorse through the half-opened door. That was her last atrocity. She bore too many grudges to be a social servant.

Now she stood in the middle of our kitchen in a bright fuchsia down jacket that looked, I swear, like a freshly opened rose above the long stalk of her legs. "I'm not prepared to hear this," she said simply. She looked from Carolyn's eyes to mine, hard. "You are telling me true."

"Too true," Carolyn said. "This would be a hell of a thing to joke about."

"But what are you actually telling me?"

I sighed. "Don't know."

"But he is not violent," Carolyn said sternly. "I know that. He does not inflict anything—physical—on anyone. Yelling maybe. A little adolescent stubbornness. Benign."

Annie let air out very slowly and noisily. "Your boy has a temper."

Carolyn closed her eyes against that. "No diagnoses, Annie. Where is he is our only question right now."

"You said you called Wendell. Is he going to be able to handle this?"

"Too soon, too soon." I said that, angrily. "Who says there's anything to handle? We're not giving him up to this yet."

Annie, whose energy level was higher, even, than mine —Carolyn calls us the Ritalin Twins—cracked her knuckles impatiently, the way I don't let my kids crack theirs. She paced. Her color was high with anger or with the heat of the woodstove. "Your son," she said specifically to Carolyn, "is your husband under a bushel, I hope you know that." She unzipped her jacket in a swoop. "God, I'm steaming!" She fanned herself with her bare hand. "No, really. He's his father with a gag on. A capped volcano. Bad news."

"Gee, Annie," I said, "thanks a bunch. I didn't know how much you loved me."

"No secret, is it, darlin'?"

"Did you come up here to be helpful?" I asked. "Or do you have to do a bloody psychiatric intake review before we can talk?"

She quieted herself grudgingly. "I'm sorry, dear. There's no sense speculating, is there? What can I do to help you?" She gave herself the look of a rebuked child. "Carolyn?"

Carolyn looked angry at both of us. She hugged herself, as if nobody else could do it satisfactorily—true enough just then. "Nothing." She thought hard. "Sometimes you could restrain yourself a little, Ann. For the sake of the rest of us." She closed her hands against her sweatered upper arms and squeezed hard. It was probably comfortable to hold handfuls of herself like that, as tight as if she were someone else. "Nothing," she said again. "I'm sorry. Ben? Don't you agree? Nothing? Nothing? Nothing?"

I went into the woods then, if not to scream at least to get free of the dead air and the out-of-synch vibes between me and Carolyn. I don't like to talk about vibes, that's adolescent, and outdated at that. But sometimes that's what you feel—the close fit, on a good day, between word and need feels literal, physical, an alignment of thought waves. Or the clangor in the air when everything you say grates on the other, and the bad fit seems to start down deep, in the cut of your primary cells, nothing congruent, nothing easy.

I put my skis on. First I went through the whole long tedious waxing, for once not impatient but grateful for something truly brainless, so automatic and basic that I could do it without the slightest engagement of the higher brain. I rubbed on the wax in deep thrusts—this is old-fashioned, in the day of non-wax skis, but I'm both poor and conservative when it comes to my sensual pleasures—and then I lit the torch to melt in the wax and held it close and heard the little sigh of the propane flame—oh God, to be alive like the flame, it wasn't fair, it wasn't possible they were taking that lovely girl and sealing up that box that held her and putting it in the hold under the cemetery, the winter vault, to wait until the thaw to lower her into the earth, and my flesh, my blood, had made it happen? I refused. I simply refused. The torch singed the outer edge of the left ski—I shook the wood and saw it had just blackened the fine knife-edge where it begins its forward curve, seared it rough, and I told myself to pay attention before I set my house on fire.

I carried them through the back door, out of balance the way they always are, tipping and knocking against the door frames, and clamped them on, and then I took off, too desperate, pushing too hard, to move out of myself into speed, into air. Of course it soothed me finally. When

I got onto the good path through the flat, the tiny branches, shiny with ice, whipping at my face from the bushes on both sides, I went almost joyfully around the curves and down the one singing long hill, my poles up, the skis knifing into new snow with a hiss. Of course I felt free of it for a couple of blessed minutes. But then I was at the bottom of the long hill, where the ash trees cluster like a pack of gossips in a ring.

Just beyond them there is a beech—more than one, actually, two wound around each other, neither dominant, neither dwarfed, bare-skinned the way beeches are, like a couple writhing in sexual agony. I've always thought that, anyway; have taken their photograph like a voyeur, from inside their weird embrace, from outside and all around their snaking, bound-together limbs. They stood there now as if I had sought them, a silver-gray shining with moisture that looked like a fine sweat. I don't think it was self-pity that made me lay my cheek against their bark, it was pity for Martha, for Mike and Terry Taverner who were having to give her up so soon, for Jacob, my small son who had grown—maybe, maybe not—into a terrifying stranger, a scourge who had done an unthinkable thing, for Judith and Carolyn and for myself too, why not for myself, but mostly for Jacob. It was all that pity for all those separate selves. What could I do with it all but plant my skis in a wide awkward V around the huge double trunk and lean my cheek against the tree, and wait and wait to be comforted.

CAROLYN

WAS HE WALKING AROUND HARVARD SQUARE LOOKING LIKE ANOTHER HIP kid? It was like a slightly thinned-out Calcutta there, a claustrophobic bazaar of the affluent, the crowds pressing anonymously around you, people handing you fliers for jazz clubs, nails shops, self-defense classes, half the kids still and forever scruffy, in khakis and hair that called attention to itself by extreme length or shortness or color or wild and monstrous shape. Maybe he was there passing as a Harvard kid or a hanger-on. Or walking in the Combat Zone, peering into the sex clubs, at the photos of the naked girls with their eyes blacked out. Everyone in that part of town looked hunted.

Partly it was being a mother, partly it was being a doctor who lived for, put all her sentiment into, the welfare of children—every moment of her life, it seemed, was devoted to making children comfortable, lessening their pain or keeping it from happening in the first place. She sat staring across the plants on the wide windowsill of the kitchen, fixed on the bird feeder that sagged from the little sycamore. They didn't bother, in fact they didn't dare, to fill it anymore, because Snappy the cat went up and dragged out the birds, and then they discovered the squirrels that patrolled and menaced, digging the fallen seeds out of the snow, walking upside down on the electric wire and leaping onto the branch, any old way to get to the feeder: they weren't buying seed to keep the squirrels fed. Then the cat brought in a squirrel carcass, opened, pink inside like a skinned chicken breast. Red in tooth and claw, everywhere you looked. She refused to think of him little, being soothed, powdered, patted. She saw him pulling on his current ski jacket—he had a sharp black one with red and yellow stripes in which she could see he felt expansive, mysterious, a little sinister. Last summer, diving off a rock at Skaggs Pond, his stomach concave, his elbows sharp. Boy. Boy at the ragged edge of manhood. She saw him trying to be fierce, to see if he could actually be cruel, and to stop herself from remembering him helpless and tiny.

Motherhood didn't keep. Why didn't more people admit it, that each phase was succeeded so totally by the next (if you were concentrating as hard as you had to) that sometimes she had trouble believing she'd *been* there. Their infancy was a rumor, distant, prodded by photographs and a few tapes—Judith had a lisp, Jacob giggled incessantly, gulping breath; he hiccuped a lot, she used to worry about him, because he took in so much air. She was astonished to hear them talking to each other on the tapes, singing their songs: these were the voices of someone else's children.

And then there were the videos, literal and abrupt, but they missed all the early years. And Jacob was better documented than Judith—the first, and they were somehow less busy then—but neither was sufficiently whole in her own unaided memory. It was a cheat. And she had begun to realize recently, especially as she watched her parents arrive in their seventies and eighties, that her whole life would fade the same way: a distant image, no more immediate than a good—at *best* a good—movie. If she concentrated as hard as she could, she might see something like snapshots. But memory, blood-memory, was overrated; in books it was too sharp, too clear and continuous. In fact, everything was shadow. The past was only an abstract idea broken into by little shards of clear image no longer than TV sound bites. *Cheat, cheat, cheat.*

She had been appalled when she was a teenager to watch how her cat failed to recognize her own kittens when they passed a certain age, or feel for them. The cat was a beautiful black longhair named Scumbles, and her mothering was so natural, her devotion so profound and complex, that Carolyn had been rapt with admiration. Watching the new mother moving her kittens, jerking them up by their damp scruffs and delivering them squealing to fresh hiding places for reasons no human could fathom, she was happy to think of herself as an animal, too. It was ennobling to be even distantly related to this loving, warming, protective little creature who, uninstructed, huddled around her five babies who were as small as thumbs, and licked them till they glistened.

But it was only a few months before she'd discovered Scumbles hissing viciously at her own half-grown babies like a stranger; she had grown territorial, and selfish about her food. Unsentimental! Carolyn had protested. How could she not feel the connection forever? How could she not know their smell and love it? Well, maybe if she saw him she could recover that connection. Maybe if she put her arms around him and remembered. But the boy she'd held against her, had scooped up off the ground and balanced on her hip, had carried in his sleep, was gone anyway; that wasn't the one she'd have if he stood in the doorway right now. The cat she'd have was a grown one who scented his fur with after-shave, deodorant, and mousse to disguise the smell his mother might claim as hers. A cat who did what he wanted to. A Tom.

She put her head on her folded arms and wept.

JUDITH

SOMETIMES THEY WERE A GOOD TEAM; THERE WAS A LOT BETWEEN THEM. When their father got harsh, or did some of the humiliating things he did—clowning too much at school when he was painting that mural with the kids, or arguing at town meeting so that everybody's parents laughed at him, or writing to the newspaper—or when their mother got tense and nasty, or too tired to pay attention—those were the times they got together and helped each other out. They had certain looks they exchanged that reminded them they knew what was going on, and trusted that it would pass; they had little routines, murmurings, and reminders of the day they this and the night they that. No one but family could share those things; they were too insignificant even to mention to friends, or expect that they'd understand.

There were other things, too. Once Judith let Jacob hide some money in her room that his friend Jackie wasn't supposed to have. He said, "You're good at not asking any questions, right?" and she was so flattered she said yes, sure, even though she knew something was wrong. She never told a lot of little things she happened to know, how Jacob wasn't always exactly where he said he was going to be, or with the people he said he'd be with. Maybe she knew more than she should, but he was her major fascination and always had been, and she made it a hobby—something more than a hobby—to follow him with her eyes and ears, to sleuth around and then memorize and swallow what she found.

And there was one more thing, or used to be. Sometimes she thought it was terrible and other times it was perfectly natural because he was her brother, a part of her life from her very first minute, but she wasn't admitting it to anyone, so no one could give her an opinion. One night when their parents went out and left them home, Jacob in charge—this must have been when she was about eight or nine and he was maybe thirteen, maybe a little less—and she had gone to take a bath, somehow he had come into the bathroom while she was getting her nightgown on. He had looked a little shy about it but he had asked her some questions about her body: what exactly, up close, certain places looked like, and they had prodded with very earnest curiosity at each other's hidden parts. She didn't mind his inspection of her—she was clean from the bath, the air was fogged with baby powder—and her parents had both told her endlessly, even tediously, how natural and beautiful "the body" was—funny formal word for the plain skin she walked around in.

Jacob had seemed very respectful of what he found; he didn't touch her at all, only asked, with the scientific gravity of their mother-the-doctor, if she'd show him what she looked like *inside.* She had never thought of herself as mysterious, but she supposed if you didn't have any experience being a girl you wouldn't even quite know how many holes they had, and where, and why. (Why she wasn't clear about herself. She wasn't exactly sure which one a baby came out of either, though she had a hunch.)

And then, part of the deal, she got to look at him. She had peed squatting next to Mickey Geyer when she was four, and had discovered he had an advantage in the matter and didn't get his shoes wet. She had sort of seen what he peed out of, and had caught various glimpses of her brother through the years—it was easier to see what boys had than girls—but a close-up view was a wonder. She found it off-putting, this odd protuberance that was a different color and a different texture than the rest of him. It was essentially silly, like a small pink animal, or something you'd find at the aquarium curled up on a sea rock, with a single off-center eye. "Don't touch," Jacob had warned her, "or it'll scare you."

"What do you mean?" She fixed her deepest concentration on it.

"I'll show you next time," her brother said. "It can do a trick." He had glanced, all through these investigations, at the door; had clearly been listening for the premature return of their parents.

"Why do you keep looking out there?" she asked. "They wouldn't get mad if they saw us."

"Want to bet?" Jacob asked, and he pulled up his jeans and buttoned and zipped them contemplatively, as if he was still thinking about what he had seen. He was such a contradiction even then, half polite and thoughtful, and half a little crazy with energy and flippancy. He called the hidden thing "Batman."

"They always say your body is good and nothing about it is dirty." Anyway, it couldn't be dirty after a bath, she thought gratefully.

"Yeah," he said. "But we're really not supposed to show each other, people who are related are like—it's not decent."

"Well, I don't know why." She wondered why he hadn't

gone to someone else then, a friend or a girl in his class. Of course, it made more sense to come to her; she didn't believe a stranger would have been better. She didn't know what was wrong and she couldn't wait to see his trick.

Their parents didn't leave them home again for a few weeks; Judith was tormented with curiosity. What could a soft rubbery thing do for a trick? Maybe he could pull it inside altogether, into that thin fluff of dark hair at the top, the way turtles could hide their heads. Maybe it had to do with those jiggly little bags in the back that were covered with gooseflesh as if they were cold. She was distracted and impatient and took to staring at the boys in her class when she could do it unobtrusively. They all carried that mystery hidden there in darkness. This movable mushroom that lolled its head this way and that, invisible, was much more peculiar than what she had that didn't actually *do* anything.

Batman emerged into light one night when their parents had driven into Howe to see a visiting ballet company. It was a snowy night and she was afraid they might not go; both of them stood at the front hall window watching the lights of the car poke through the cold mist and wondered how long they ought to wait, just to be sure their mother hadn't forgotten the tickets or her purse or something . . .

Then Jacob took his pants off altogether, signaling that they would not be rushed or anxious this time. He left his blue Michael Jackson T-shirt on, belling out at the waist like a tent. Then, in its shadow, he took her hand and closed it around himself. His eyes were odd—excited but strangely distant, as if he wasn't here with her but was somewhere else, seeing someone, or maybe no one, but not Judith, not his little sister. He closed his hand over hers tightly, the way her teacher used to do in penmanship, and moved it up and down, hard, and faster and faster, and Judith, alarmed, felt something live inside her grip. It flailed like their guinea pig when he was out of his cage and frightened. It was trying to escape. Once he opened her hand so that she could see and she understood the trick—Batman had been changed into something else entirely, a different shape and size, a different color. A magician's egg.

Finally, when she had had about enough of this urgent friction, Jacob shouted and bucked as if he was trying to get away and his head fell back alarmingly. He bared his teeth and his braces glinted in the small light of his bedroom lamp. He was in pain, she had hurt him without meaning to, and she was about to apologize when she saw that she was in possession of a handful of phlegm, and that was when she ran out of his room, close to gagging. She ran, waving her hand wildly to get it off her, down the stairs and out the front door, as if the house were on fire. He did not follow her. She went out onto the front path in her sock feet, and the bottom of her nightgown got sopping wet blotting up the snow. She stayed outside until it got too cold, and then she came in and went directly to her room and closed the door. She had rubbed her hand in the fresh snow the way she'd scrape her shoe when she'd picked up dog-do, but she could still see an odd filmy web, like leftover egg white, dried into the lifelines on her palm.

For a week Judith thought her brother too gross to be approached without averting her eyes. Compared to boys, she was grateful to be inanimate and unchanging. It took her a very long time to face him—not to forgive him exactly, because she couldn't decide whether to pity or to hate him for his disgusting trick—but when she settled it in her mind it was only because it was easier to spread the blame for the whole bizarre episode than to hold him responsible. She had to assume every boy could do this; maybe they grew out of it. But now she could understand why he worried that their parents would discover them. The boy who ate his breakfast at the table beside her, and read his biology essay out loud *(The Venus-Flytrap and Other Carnivorous Plants),* and seemed to harbor no visible agitation in his lap when they sat side by side in the back seat of the car—it was impossible that he so calmly possessed Batman and kept him in check, but it had to be true, unless it had all been a bad dream brought on by her parents' absence on a dangerous evening of cold and snow. She was not, however, inclined to such dreams.

It wasn't long afterwards that her mother told her about babies, in an explanation that wasn't easy to convert to images—people loving each other and then lying down on each other, she had seen that sort of thing in movies—but she wasn't eager to think Jacob's magic was a part of that. Did that mean she could have started a baby doing what they did? Did it hurt to do what her mother was suggesting everybody did? She remembered her brother's voice, his eyes, his helpless moan, her flight into the snow. She did not tell anyone, not even her best friend, Celeste, who had only sisters. Celeste had a wicked crush on Jacob, but if she heard about this she would never be able to look him in the eye again.

But he had been different in the last year or so. Sometimes she found it hard to believe they had ever played together those incessant stranded hours of country children: had made snow forts, bonfires, five-minute dramas in full ridiculous costume, Jacob bossing; throwing their brown-and-white Frisbee that looked like an Oreo. Jacob had characters with crazy voices like the Ancient Mariner, an old creep who kept grabbing you when he wanted to talk and then running off at the mouth about boring complicated movie plots that never were. If you could pinch him, his voice would disappear. There was Mr. Q., who was the exact opposite of Mr. T., a little wimp who made Woody Allen look like Superhulk. He always talked about his adventures getting sand kicked in his face, having his girl stolen away by surfer dudes. Judith thought Jacob should make movies or write books when he grew up—the best he would promise was that he'd never get a job where he had to wear a suit and tie. "Not even a basketball coach?" she asked him. "That," he allowed, "I'd have to think about."

But he had begun to develop what she called Dragon's Breath. Actually, what she thought of when he turned it on her were the scenes in *The Invasion of the Body Snatchers* when the people who have been taken—they still look normal but they are working for "the other side" —stare at their victims, open their mouths, and out comes a roar like fire, not a voice really but a gruesome hollow sucking sound: wind through the tunnel to hell.

The first time she heard it he had roared so loud he woke her out of a sound sleep. She heard his outraged voice all the way up the stairs, and heard her father's matching shout. They were in the kitchen. She stood on the stairs in the living room, bent over toward them, trying to discover what the argument was about. His hours again. It was two or three in the morning. Jacob's hours out with his friends, and maybe what they did while they were out together; between what she couldn't hear and what she couldn't comprehend she missed the gist of it, but they sounded as if they might come to blows.

But they didn't. She saw their exhausted faces when they trooped past her up to bed, first her mother's (who had hardly been heard from, or else had spoken in a voice too quiet to carry a room away), white and silent; then her father's, still red, sweat standing out on his beard like snowflakes, his chest heaving; finally Jacob, the victim and cause of the conflagration. He had passed over into another phase by now: he was wearing his coolest, most impassive face. He looked to Judith, standing aside to let them pass, like a blind man. He looked as if he had seen nothing, heard nothing, had been involved only accidentally in some great passion that didn't affect him, not really. She admired the suavity of that look, its remove, its superiority to the moment (though hadn't she just heard him shouting so fiercely his voice broke like a child's?). But he had stopped as if he'd kicked into a different phase; his rage had turned serene. When he came up to her (now she had fled to the top of the stairs), he put out his hand and tweaked her in the stomach without cracking a smile. How she loved him—his control, his conviction of his innocence. Her father looked foolish beside him, like a man who had run after a bus, shouting at it, banging on its door, left standing, finally, on the empty curb.

After a few minutes she went to Jacob's room to congratulate him, but she stopped short. He was smashing at his closet door with his bare hand, brutally, grunting as if each blow he landed were injuring someone. His Led Zeppelin poster was deeply gouged, its margin in shreds. Blood from his knuckles blossomed onto its white ground. She stood behind the door where he couldn't see her. Finally he stopped and cradled one elbow with his other hand, so that he could rock on his heels and suck on his mutilated fist. She saw in his tear-distorted face how much that yelling and then that control, that blind man's remove, had cost him. His own blood ran down his fingers to his wrist. What had he been doing all night that had been worth this?

Now she lay in her bed, warm in her nightgown though it was noon, trying to comprehend what was happening. He was gone and maybe they would catch him and shoot him down. She watched him running right past his breakfast, making for the school bus. She was always standing calmly beside the mailbox when he came charging out of the house just as the yellow bus peeked over the top of the hill. Or he'd get there when Nat was already closing the doors and jump on and give Nat a high-five, laughing. A lot of her recent memories of Jacob were accompanied by the choking smell of exhaust and the huge exhalation of breath of the closing bus door, that pneumatic releaser that Nat held in his big gloved hand. "You're shavin' it closer every time, Jake," Nat would say, amused, not angry. "One of these days you're gonna have to catch hold of the rear bumper."

But that was before he could drive. She wished he had never learned. They argued over the car the most: "If you want your own car that much, get a job. Save for it." That was their father's refrain, even though, as Jacob loved to point out, you wouldn't think an artist would be more of a tight-ass than those regular dads who worship the Chamber of Commerce. "A lot of good it does us that he has all these crazies in his head," Jacob would mutter. "He's the biggest capitalist on wheels." Their mother took a softer line; she didn't care about money. "What's ours is yours, I don't have to tell you that," she always said consolingly. Maybe that was because her mother and father were rich—it just didn't matter to her. Over their father's objections she bought him the old Dodge, cheap, when a custodian at the hospital died—Jacob called it the Curse for the first few months. He had to buy his own insurance, his gas, pay for repairs.

Once their mother caught him with some of her money—twenties right out of her purse. There was another one of those family rages that time, but Jacob was taking a new tack: instead of shrieking back, he doused his Dragon Breath first thing and went right into that silence. Judith watched him blown backward in the rush of their father's fury, like someone standing in the invisible wash of an airplane motor. But all he did was narrow his eyes in the wind. His defense now was to say nothing. His cheeks worked—a little insect of a vein batted against his skin, trapped, trying to get out, but he wouldn't open his mouth to let it escape.

"Aren't you going to answer me?" their father shouted. Three twenty-dollar bills flapped in his grip. Judith, though she'd heard about his crime, was horrified to actually see them—he really had taken them out of his mother's wallet, had dared to reach uninvited into the intimacy of her bag that smelled of cinnamon sugarless and remove them like a pickpocket, a stranger!

Jacob was not going to answer, he was going to wait him out, but his father took him by the back of his corduroy shirt and held him there as if he was about to lift him right off the ground; he tried to catch his son's gaze. They waited in silence. Surely someone was going to get tired. It was Jacob, finally, who said in a bleached-sounding voice, "You've got the bills, you've got the evidence. What more do you want?" He kept his eyes on his mother, who somehow looked more guilty than he did.

Judith knew what her father wanted, what every father seemed to: an apology. You could get them off you if you didn't mind giving up your dignity. He wanted to know he was powerful and respected and even if you stopped respecting him for demanding it, the loss was apparently worth it. Even at twelve Judith knew that, though he tended to be a lot gentler with her. She loved her father, of course, but she was thrilled at Jacob's solidarity with his own needs.

His muffler was shot, he had told her, as if that justified everything. It was making so much noise Roger-the-cop had stopped him at the bottom of the hill and warned him he was giving him a ticket next time. "You're disturbing the peace," he had told him. "If you don't fix that in a week, your name's going in the paper in the Court Proceedings and you're putting twenty-five bucks in my pocket for pollution and another twenty-five for sounding like a DC-10." A ticket was such a waste of cash he was extra-careful never to speed, even though his friends called him chicken. "I'm going to die without ever getting a ticket," he boasted. "Let them laugh, *their* money's gonna line Roger's uniform pockets and I'm gonna get a good tape deck. Let's see who laughs then."

That was when he got a job, after school and weekends, at the Arbor Nursery. He wrestled trees with their roots in burlap and watered, pruned, and planted, as gentle with the seedlings as a vet with new kittens. He talked to them, sang them songs, especially slow ones, ballads. When Judith bicycled out to see him there once, he gave her a violet in a pot, a beautiful purple called Ballerina. "Are you sure it's okay to give this to me?" she asked him. There were pinks and whites, their leaves like fancy velvet, ranged under fluorescent lights. She thought she might start a collection in her window.

"There's a lot more gone from here than a three-inch violet, kiddo," he said to her, looking all around as he said it. His open level gaze, his competent hands and good manners, and especially the way he sang James Taylor over the moist flats, that sad song about sweet dreams and flying machines, guaranteed that no one suspected. He took the metal hanger off a fuchsia plant and attached it to the rim of the green pot that held her violet. She pedaled home trying to hum "Fire and Rain," with the little Ballerina dangling from her handlebars, waving in its fringes of purple, the ultimate never-before never-again bike ornament.

CAROLYN

She called the office. "What are you doing, Karen?"

Karen breathed out a little puff of surprise. "Doing? You mean, like, am I filing charts or doing my nails?"

"I mean, is there any—is anyone there? Are they canceling?"

Karen laughed bleakly. "Well. There's a kind of hush in the office, I'd say. Your appointments—a few people called. Most just didn't show. A couple came in yesterday and wanted to know where you were. News doesn't penetrate under every rock, I guess."

She felt foolish putting the question to Karen, but Karen was the one who was sitting, right now, in the seat of knowledge. "What do you think—what would—if I came in this afternoon, what do you think I'd find?"

Karen was silent a long time. "Oh, Carolyn." (She had never called Carolyn "Doctor." Carolyn appreciated that.) "Some folks have been very nice. I mean, they're sort of—haven't people been calling to give you their support?"

"A few. Yes, actually, a good number, I suppose. But those are friends, of course. And a few nasty ones mixed in."

"Well, I mean, people are mostly being decent here. They're giving a lot of 'benefit of the doubt.' But—God, I don't know. The *Bugler*'s out, did you see that?"

Carolyn closed her eyes. Wendell had brought the newspaper up to them. The lead story mentioned Jacob, careful to add that the police wanted him for questioning; it did not call him a suspect. On page 2, at the top of the obituaries for eighty-two-year-old farmers and ninety-three-year-old nursing home favorites was a picture of Martha in a white blouse, smiling like anyone's daughter. The picture was obviously a year or two old; she looked like a member of the church choir. That had knocked the wind out of Carolyn, the dumb mechanical neutrality of the camera that had no powers of prophecy, that showed the world as it had been, not as it would be. The obituary did an absurd dance around the facts: the girl "died Wednesday in Hyland," it said, but then it threw the ball back at the reader: "(See story, p. 1)." There was a picture, grainy to the point of unintelligibility, of the split-rail fence in front of Tuttle's field where she had been found. All you could see in the picture were shadows in the snow—scuff marks? Tire tracks? It was a stupid, meaningless photograph of the fenders of police cars and the festive ribbons they put up to quarantine crime sites, but Carolyn's stomach rose to her chest when Wendell shook out the paper and laid it in front of her.

"You saw it?" Karen asked again.

Carolyn closed her eyes. "The *Bugler* is not a court of law."

"Oh, I didn't mean it was," Karen answered hastily. "Only it—sort of spreads the air of suspicion around. Sort of." It was clear what she was trying to say. "I just don't want you to be out there where people can hurt your feelings, that's all. I mean—they're not always as thoughtful as they could be. And some people never learned any tact even if they're trying to be nice."

Someone had told Karen that morning that she'd be afraid to let Carolyn put her hands on her little boy. Why? Karen had asked her, and smiled as icily as she could. You think she's murdered anyone lately? The woman had given her a terrible look and rushed away, pushing her child ahead of her as if they were fleeing contagion. She said to Carolyn, "Maybe you just want to do a couple of hours and feel things out. There's a lot of weeding and sorting to do in the files, too, that I know you've been wanting to find time for."

When she told Ben she was going in, he said brusquely, as if it were a betrayal, "Your funeral." His face reddened. This was like being around the dying—you lost half your vocabulary.

"For one thing, it's an admission of guilt to stay in quarantine. Jacob is *missing.*"

He only looked at her, a little owl-eyed.

"Anyway"—she thought for a moment and then went on—"do we have no existence outside our son's behavior?"

Ben's eyes flashed at her. Again she thought of an owl she had encountered one early evening, walking in the woods in summer. The white ruff of his feathers had been so proud and plumped that he seemed aggressive doing nothing but sitting on a branch looking down. He had leveled a cold glare at her, slicing the air between them, all silver edge like a scimitar. "That's an astonishing thing for a grown-up, presumably sane and functioning person to say under these circumstances," he told her with an abashing coldness. He went on staring, as if some horrible secretion were flowing from her mouth, coursing down her chin. "Maybe it would be best to pretend you never said that."

Was she losing her bearings? What was so terrible about saying that she would not feel reduced to nothing by this "suspicion" the newspaper had not even spoken of? (For a few days running, Nat the schoolbus driver had been kind enough to honk for Judith when he didn't find her at her post beside the mailbox. Certainly he knew she wasn't home with the sniffles—Nat knew everything. Bless him, he was not assuming she'd taken cover.) She thought her decision to go to work showed great confidence in Jacob; some people, at least, would recognize and respect it. Or, meanwhile, all her knowledge—swellings, symptoms, her hands' capabilities, her diagnostic sensitivity—what was supposed to happen to it? If they needed her before, didn't they need her now? This all felt like an endless snow day, everything closed, obligations suspended, while they watched the world suffocated under a chill white down comforter. They had had crises when, because the pump was electric and the wires were sunk under heavy snow, they couldn't even flush the toilets, let alone turn on the lights. The house had begun to feel like that by now: the air was turning rancid and they were out of conversation. She sat looking at Ben, who sat looking at nothing, poking at his absoluteness, turning over his anger, formulating, finally, her own plans. She was still Dr. Reiser, damn him. She loved her child and she loved her town, but she was still a person with some value and some function and she would not cut it off in the shadow of this innuendo. Damn them all.

She had to drive through town to get to the hospital. From up the hill, the roofs, still dusted with snow, were like cakes under a sifting of confectioner's sugar. This view always stopped her cold, it was so idyllic and yet so protective of its own: the picture-postcard village, best seen at Christmas, everyone inside and the streets silent. There were such nineteenth-century postcards, in fact, in the Historical Society, etchings of snug houses behind their fences, lacy carpenter's gothic hung from the eaves, wreaths on the doors.

Up close, Hyland was waking; it did that early, in the spirit of the farmers who used to milk their cows before dawn. There weren't many farms around anymore, only the Josses' tawny cows out Route 48—Joe Joss worked at the optical factory but he kept the farm and his wife ran the farmstand—and a herd of spotted Holsteins way at the far end of Camp Road, lolling and lowing among the stones of a lush green field. But those were a gentleman farmer's cattle, not the real thing. The townies always said, Cows like that, their shit don't smell. Those folks want to feed their petunias, they got to buy fertilizer in a bag just like the rest of us. They like a dirt road in spite of the mud and dust, 1789 over the doorway. They drink wine that looks like ginger ale, and they don't eat beef.

Still, there were folks up early, parked in front of Doreen's on Main Street, truckers, retailers who liked to open their stores before nine to get a jump on, and just plain Calvinists who believed you ought to turn out of bed before the sun came in the window. (Somehow their creed allowed them breakfast they had to pay for, and they didn't even mind leaving the tip.) They were sitting at the counter or spread out in the tall old wooden booths nobody would let Doreen replace with plastic, their heavy jackets hanging at the corners. Speculating, probably, laying odds: guilty/not guilty. Everyone liked Doreen's crullers and coffee sticks, but there were more of the Taverners' friends than theirs inside. *Dip and sip,* the sign said over the counter. Sometimes the lawyers came in, and the judge who worked out of the Town House across the street, dipping and sipping with everybody else.

Ben loved it down there, and sometimes he had a second breakfast with the same folks he played poker with: Rudy, who cleaned chimneys, and Sam, who sold insurance but liked art, liked Ben's sculptures. (Once he bought his wife a little vase he called "junk flowers" for her birthday, nuts and bolts and a couple of sprung springs.) Their straight-forwardness was what Ben loved; their good sense, their hatred of pretension. A deep-dyed thriftiness, a refusal to show off. The way their kids stayed around, lived in town forever. He hoped Jacob would stay around, too, go off to college but come back; he wanted Judith to settle up the road, when the time came, the way their neighbors' children did, and brought their babies around for daily loving.

Well, he was right. She didn't fancy the regulation life of the Boston suburbs, where every kitchen had the same sleek appliances and every yard the same Sunday garden. They liked the proportion of green to concrete here, and simple to elegant. Last bastion of . . . what? Not naïveté, not even decency, nobody had a corner on that. Responsibility? It was a place where what you did got credited to your account, good or bad. It stayed with you, on your record. Celene, of course, who grew up here, thought that was the worst thing going: you could get away with nothing. With less than you had done. Social determinism, she said. Save me! But she had gone away, met her big-city husband, and come back. I like to know the players on the scorecard, she said. I like my kids to know who to call if I ever leave them stranded. I don't want them afraid of strangers.

Carolyn hoped there was someone in Doreen's this morning to speak up for not knowing.

When she got out of her car, walking shakily across the ice-impacted parking lot, somebody waved from a distance. There, she thought, and then was horrified that since the last time she'd parked here she had been reduced to gratitude for an idle gesture.

A few mothers trickled in with their children. They tried to ignore the tension, like actors with little conviction trying to breathe life into a bad script. A few others came forth with sympathy that felt like condolence. She bobbed her head in acknowledgment, thanked them, and returned to the child at hand—she cut off a splint, did a throat culture, gave a newborn his shots and soothed his howling. She thought every mother looked at her with exaggerated attention, but she was probably wrong.

Nonetheless, by late afternoon she had a throbbing headache. A nurse she knew only slightly, a white-haired, sweet-faced woman recently returned from retirement, put her head around the door jamb just as Carolyn was passing—she must have been crouched, waiting—and said almost cheerfully and without preamble, "They ought to take a razor to his you-know-what, your son."

Carolyn stared, open-mouthed. The woman had vanished. She would have some response ready next time, she would have a shield to hold up, indifference or her own anger or just the inability to be surprised. She would not allow herself to be ambushed again.

Only Karen managed to strike the right note, or combination of notes. She was brisk and unsentimental on the one hand, and protective on the other, as if to question her instincts were to call into question the natural order. Carolyn heard her saying into the phone, with a perfect balance of unrancorous politeness and a strong suggestion of unofficial disappointment, "Well, thanks for calling, Mrs. Weber, and not just being a no-show. We can certainly use your appointment time." Though, of course, there was no one at all to use it. "I can understand you might be uncomfortable—yes—but I personally don't think you need to be. The doctor is going about her business here. Oh yes, certainly. Well, why not, after all?" A pause for incredulity. "Okay, thanks for your honesty, Mrs. Weber. Be well." She turned to Carolyn, who was plucking files from the carefully ordered shelves. "Hypocrites. Some of them are lovely, though, you've got to remember that. Don't think everybody's like that one. Some people have gone out of their way . . . And they have all kinds of little memories of things Jacob did for them. Myra Vance said she never would have gotten her little boy to step up on the school bus if Jacob hadn't protected him, this was years ago and she was still grateful. She said Jacob was the only boy in the lot who wasn't afraid to be kind."

As if he were dead. She hated the idea of being talked about, hated the necessity of pulling those memories up from the well of years. She smiled and nodded and took her files into her office, where she sank down on the corduroy couch and covered her mouth with her hand and pressed tight, for fear she'd be sick and humiliated on top of everything else.

One woman, a new patient, showed up with her eight-year-old, who had swimmer's ear. "Now, how," Carolyn asked, smiling, "has she managed to get swimmer's ear in January?"

The mother laughed. "Oh, we have an indoor pool. Not here, this is just our summer place and, you know, weekends. We live in Boston. Lexington, actually. We're just here to ski."

Carolyn took another look. The woman had a blond ponytail and wore high heels with her slacks; they had a wavy white stain line around the sole where the snow had lapped. Her sweater was a fabulous hand-knitted sphere of many colors, Italian, probably. An indoor pool. She wasn't up on local gossip much, then; she was here from Mars for the skiing.

"I'm so glad we could get an appointment at the last minute," she said and helped her daughter into her down jacket. "You're usually so busy. For a small town, I mean." Her daughter pulled her matching ponytail out of her collar. "But, whoo, it looks like a bomb hit your waiting room today. Well—lucky for us!" She folded her prescription down the middle emphatically and asked whether

her daughter's ear meant that the pool was contaminated.

Carolyn stared after her. This was the worst thing, she had seen it and read about it but never felt it, the way everything stands like a cut-out against a blank background. Shock, was it? How everything was blasted—voices echoed, tasteless and absurd, all platitude and hidden insult and devious judgment. Either the everyday world was unreal or she was. Or both.

> Seeing the world from 30,000 ft. There are more mountains in the US than my geography teacher ever told us. Someone said I could get tortillas made of *blue* corn out here! Dad, you could get into this kind of cooking. I mean "cuisine." "Cocina." Sleeping is hard.
>
> Missing you,
>
> J.

It was postmarked Albuquerque. When Carolyn came home from work, desperate for a drink, a bath, and the obliteration of an early bedtime, she found Ben sitting at the kitchen table staring at it. He had it propped up against a bottle of mayonnaise and he sat facing it like a man contemplating checkmate.

She read the card, then reached for the jar. "Why is this here?"

"I don't know. Tallest thing I could find to lean it against."

She snatched the jar away and took it to the refrigerator. "It's not good for it to be out of the refrigerator."

"Hey! Is that all you can do? What's the matter with you?" He waved the card at her. "This is Santa *Fe.*" It showed a long file of Indian women with their wares arranged on striped blankets against the front of a building, a sort of galleria, open-sided. Its arches were beautiful hard stone, while under them sat this neat row of soft-costumed women in long braids. "That's it? That's your whole reaction?"

"It is."

She was walking around the kitchen quickly, tight-lipped.

"Where do you think he got the money to—"

"He slaughters someone—all right, maybe, maybe not, that's too harsh. But he certainly knows what's going on here and he's writing cute notes about corn chips and cookery."

"Carolyn—"

"He is—this is a psychopathic response, do you realize that? The second one. That's what you're looking at, a serious form of insanity."

"No. Psychopathic? I don't even know what that is. I see somebody scared, haunted—look, he's not *sleeping.*"

She slapped a potholder down on the counter for no particular reason. "I should hope not. But it doesn't look like he's given up eating, does it?" The anger that crested behind her eyes was like no anger she had felt for the small things of her life. Was she supposed to worry that he wasn't sleeping? Somebody was sleeping, down there in the cemetery hold, once and for all. She realized how much comfort she'd been taking, cold but comfort nonetheless, imagining him the victim. Alive, of course alive, but desperate. Blameless.

She couldn't find a way to let it out; if the ground weren't thick with snow and the road still slick, she might go out and run for miles, then turn around and run back and maybe mercifully fall into bed with her brain burned out on cold and distance. She was going to explode. They had the whole rest of their lives to live, and nowhere to spend this fury, this movement, this frustration at not *knowing.* It had never occurred to her to think she was bad at "delay of gratification," that was a patronizing term you used for ghetto teenagers who robbed convenience stores to get enough money for gold chains and wild highs. She had to be doing something, though: working, cleaning up, touching something with her hands, her mind. Her unspent energy, in another minute, would smash against the wall and drip slowly down.

"I read the *Bugler* again," Ben said, coming toward her from another side.

"We all read it together."

"They're only saying they want to question him. That's important. There's nothing in there about suspicion or anything." He looked so complacent, sitting like a man waiting for his dinner. Nothing was cooking.

"Small favors. That doesn't mean he's not a suspect. It's just, I don't know, conservative journalism."

"But kind of them," he insisted. "They don't have to be kind. There's nothing incendiary in it."

"I guess. But people think what they want to think. The newspaper doesn't have much to do with it." She saw the quick flash and retreat of the sunny-faced nurse who wanted to take a razor to Jacob's privates. She would spare Ben for now, but she realized, as she tucked the abomination out of sight, that she had to face all that. She lived in an office crammed with the inflamed fantasies and vengeance of parents terrified in every conceivable way for their children, while Ben sat up here running his hands over the long, smooth limbs of his wooden figures. He walked around them studying them with the intentness she gave difficult diagnoses, and what he came up with was the need to plane another sixteenth of an inch off a forearm. He was as protected as a child—they didn't cut him with their eyes, his statues, or whisper about him, or threaten violence. Then again, he was the one who had warned her not to go: she had to grant him good instincts. She sighed and looked around. "Where's Judith?"

"She went over to Kerry's. I think she's ready to go back to school." He hadn't asked about her day and she wasn't volunteering. She had an image of Jacob sitting in a restaurant right on the square in Santa Fe, behind bright half curtains, dipping blue chips into chili. He nibbled a chip and gazed out on the square, where people were crossing back and forth in the cold winter sun in a restless traffic. She was afraid of the look on his face, neither frightened nor worried nor crazed. It was his ordinary everyday expression, which, if she could see it, she knew, would bring her to her knees. "No, she's not ready to go back," Carolyn said. "Unless it's different with children. But I suspect it would only be worse." She thought of her empty office, the blond woman and her daughter who said the waiting room looked like a bomb had hit it. Judith's face showed every blow, it was still new and soft and undamaged. She had the broad sweet forehead of an untested saint. "Believe me."

BEN

Passing through.

I never thought it had anything to do with St. Louis but here it is, real. This is hanging in the airport but I remember we saw it once at the Smithsonian so what's going on? Somebody's got a fake on their hands! I also never thought I'd ever be in Missouri. Not that I know the reason now.

Love,
J.

THE SPIRIT OF ST. LOUIS DANGLED LIKE A COLOSSAL INSECT OVER THE airport lobby, casting shadows. The card had an old-fashioned look to it, a matte, badly registered photo straight out of the forties, or earlier, maybe; its edges were deckled like the photos in my parents' albums, where everyone's young and the men wear bathing suits that cover their chests.

Carolyn had gone to get the mail. We weren't saying a whole lot to each other, we were sitting in the house feeling blunted as if we'd both had a swig of carbon monoxide, the way it steals up on you and you don't know it but you're about to pass out. At least that's how I felt. She didn't look too keen either, but she kept trying to read novels, pretending it was wonderful that she finally had a chance to relax a little. (Frankly, I thought it was slightly obscene even to fake satisfaction just now. You'd think she had a bad cold that was keeping her in bed for a few days, long enough to get a couple of Agatha Christies under her belt. But she doesn't know how to waste time, not even mourning time. She can't sit still. *O Lord,* I kept remembering, *teach us to sit still. Teach us, teach us, if it isn't too late.)*

God, I remember when I was a kid and my parents, because they were Orthodox, wouldn't answer the phone on *Shabbos.* That particular prohibition used to drive me completely berserk; questions of what you could or couldn't eat didn't intrude much—I ate what my mother put in front of me. And when I was young enough I didn't mind praying or even studying—my impatience with those came later, when I needed conscious conviction, a sense of the center of it all, and couldn't find it. But this was different: the sun would set on Friday night and until it went down again the next night I was expected to accept that the world simply didn't exist. There it was, you could walk through it, it could knock you down if you weren't careful crossing the street, other people did their shopping or they went to the movies in it, while we sat pretending everything was at rest. But in fact all that would happen to me was that, instead of calm, a gigantic tension would mount up inside my chest; it defeated all my father's intentions. The phone would ring and ring and go on ringing and I'd sit there with my hands under me and I'd twitch with the tension of being there and *not* being there. It was like being an ostrich.

So one day, on a morning when my father was in *shul* and for some reason I was home—I probably had a sniffle and my mother was making a preemptive strike against pneumonia—the phone had been ringing and ringing and I had terrible fantasies about something. Probably something worthy, knowing me at that age: my grandfather was in the nursing home by then, very old and frail, and I was sure they were calling to tell us he was dying, that he'd died, and we'd missed it while we were touching the Torah with our prayer books and kissing them. I was sure I could see them sitting there at the desk at the nursing home ringing us, wondering where in the hell we were. (It was *Shabbos;* of course they'd know. But matters of life and death take precedence.) So I lunged for the phone and I answered it.

Lord, Lord. It was a wrong number, and for that I'd sinned. "Hello, ees José there?" A shaggy-dog story. But later, when I was old enough to think about it and to walk away from so much else, I made some use of the moment, I thought: all our lives are a shaggy-dog story. All that urgency and there's nobody at the other end; or it's somebody looking for someone else. I suppose my father was actually very wise, if I choose to think of it that way: he knew he wasn't missing as much as he was getting, going down deep inside his silence, just angling for a little peace. He knew he wasn't indispensable, and neither was the world.

Now I saw myself waiting for the phone to ring, waiting for the world to wash Jacob back to me, and all we got were pushy reporters with new questions to ask (new only because they were too stupid for anyone to have bothered asking sooner), anguished friends, and the peculiar intrusions of those poor innocents who happened to call about other things—Would you like to contribute to the college centennial fund, to donate to your senator's campaign "to stay alive in the next election," and worse: Tim and Julia Novotny—he's a printmaker, she does the world's most beautiful silver—called to say they were driving on through from Binghamton to visit their son Scotty at Bates, where he's a freshman. (He and Jacob used to squash frogs together, I remember that from a summer when they were about nine or ten. They were big and little, fair and dark, Scotty a heavy pillowy-soft boy with invisible red-blond eyebrows and freckles. Together they looked like Boy Pals arranged by Central Casting.) "We're in Howe, half an hour maybe, sorry we didn't give you any warning, we don't have to stay over, but it would be lovely." And so on. The world is always out there still, come *Shabbos,* come murder, come madness.

We didn't meet them at the door with it, we sat them down, served them a drink, talked about Scotty. It seemed unfair, somehow, to spring it on people who cared about us, like some gratuitous cruelty we were doing them. It made us stupid with apologies. "But what can we do?" Julia demanded of us, the worst, flat-out and final. "You don't know where he *is.*" She covered her mouth with her hand as if the very idea were shameful, not to be uttered.

"Or if he's really—you know—if he's done anything terrible," Carolyn said with awful aplomb.

"Why hasn't this been in the papers?" Tim wanted to know, as if he'd been cheated of the chance to discover it himself and save us all this embarrassment. (Or no: that's ungenerous. How do I know why he asked? Maybe he thought it was a sign of media decency—unprecedented if it was—or a harbinger of Jacob's innocence.)

"It has, I think, here and there," I assured him. "But it's not quite sensational. Not yet. There's no—you know"—Carolyn and I seemed to say a lot of that, even though nobody knew at all—"no smoking gun."

"They only suspect," Tim offered me. When I took the offering like a gift and nodded, my eyes filled. There were a lot of reactions I had given up trying to control.

Carolyn left the room at that. We had had it out about talking too much, about wanting to mention the bloody jack as if she owed it to everybody who happened to be driving by to hand them our souls. "You don't have the right to tell everybody what you know," I told her. "You only owe it to Jacob to keep his secrets. If that's what they are. It might even come in handy later to have held our peace. Just—discretion. Reticence. What does it hurt you?"

It hurt her in direct proportion to the value of her friendships. "I like to be honest if I can, Benny. What are your friends for if you manipulate them like that, a little truth here, a little lie there? I have friends so I can be myself with them; otherwise, why bother?"

I loved that in her. She was honest the way children are honest, without calculation, without motive. But before Tim and Julia piled out of their car I held my finger to my lips. "Do Jacob a favor," I said as gently and undemandingly as I could. "You never know what people will make of something innocent. And once it's out, it's hard to call anything back."

I asked them about Scotty, who was starring in *Heartbreak House* that weekend, preparing to wear a waistcoat and muttonchops. Julia looked overcome. I wanted to tell her it was nice of her, but vaguely insulting, that she felt she couldn't say a single good thing about her own son, as if ours were finished, done for, and the comparison would kill us outright. We talked a lot about the state of lithography, and the dwindling market for good silver jewelry in a tight economy. Of course we'd have talked about all that anyway but the context was strange; altered. Every subject except Jacob felt like an evasion; the not-knowing hung in the room like smoke and made it hard to breathe. They didn't stay the night and we didn't insist.

I visited my workshop once every day, experimentally, but everything in there looked stupid, useless, self-indulgent. If this were the movies, I thought, I'd pick up an ax and torture some wood. Throw my favorite piece out the window or set it afire—it's damned unphotogenic, how an artist crashes and burns. I couldn't build anything or draw or even read the secondhand art books I'd been hoarding for a quiet day. The sketches push-pinned to the wall looked surpassingly trivial. Who needed all this, except for me? What good was this roomful of junk except on a cloudless morning, nothing owing a single soul? Somebody—Proust, I think—said that any artist who exchanges an hour of work for an hour with friends and talk, social life, has given that hour to something which is nonexistent. Now, looking at the row of hasty sketches, impulses waiting to catch fire, and the lists of addresses where I could scout out my throw-away clutter—hubcaps, bobbins, kitchen whisks!—to call the work itself nonexistent was a kindness it didn't deserve.

I had been trying to let my work lead me, I'd begun to listen to some of my critics when they said I manipulate my creatures too much, push them around, graft onto them too many bright ideas. Why must I take the beautiful wood and fiddle with it? Undermine it? Somebody told me my work was not funny, it was cynical, whereas I liked to call it ambivalent, a love-hate relationship with everything: America, the texture of my materials, the natural and the manufactured, all the things of this world. I hadn't begun to settle the question, but whoever was right, the sketches looked incomparably stupid right now. A luxury, all of it. Embarrassing that a grown man should spend his time approximately the way he did in kindergarten, pasting purple macaroni on a cigar box . . .

I picked up the newspaper or watched the seven o'clock news, put one down, turned the other one off. Armies were cutting swaths across borders, leaders were rising, falling—outside my line of vision, all of it. I was beginning to get a corner, at least, of an understanding of how people can commit suicide—not why but how: what it might feel like approaching. Nothing. Everything has the taste of nothing, it holds no attraction. (No savor, you've heard that. "Things lost their savor." What a thing to fall from, the constant taste of life on the tongue . . . and then nothing at all. I wasn't thinking of suicide, believe me. I only mean it was the first time since I was a teenager, when I felt things too much, not too little, that I could imagine it.) The only thing that felt good through the waiting were the walks, long walks into the woods on snowshoes. I didn't go up the road, I didn't want to run into neighbors, only sloughed away onto our own trail and into the monochrome of leafless trees and shadowy animal tracks and indentations where ice had dripped and melted the snow in craters. The cold air was sharp as a paper cut—it was about all I could feel. I welcomed it.

Carolyn came back with an armful of mail, most of it junk: ads, bills, pleas on behalf of the rain forest, the rights of political prisoners in Turkey and Korea, democrats right here in the U.S. of A. who dared to call themselves liberal. A sort of sympathy note, kindly and ominous, from a psychiatrist I used to go to who had seen something about Jacob in a Philadelphia paper: he assured me I was strong enough to handle "whatever happens." And an ad, in Jacob's name, for Macho-Mail: see-through undies—bull's-eyes, X marks the spot—Jockey shorts decorated with photos of stupendous apparatus, aphrodisiacs, "sexual aids for swingers." (He swore he was on their mailing list courtesy of his Tape-of-the-Month club.) Then she handed me an envelope from the government arts agency to which I had applied for a grant. For years I'd prayed for some solace from them, for years I'd gotten the thin letter of rejection. This was a fat white manila envelope full of forms to be filled out. Twenty thousand dollars' worth—no one, I suppose, could mind filling them out for the price. My chest turned over; I had drowned already and here came the life preserver. Oh, thanks, fellas, I thought dimly. Lawyers' fees. I didn't even tell Carolyn.

Stuck between an ad for the A & P and a renewal notice for *The New Republic* was the card from St. Louis. By now you'd think we'd have been expecting it, we should have been guessing where he'd light down next, but each one caught us like a surprise blow to the solar plexus. We couldn't quite manage the vision of Jacob winging around the country like a kid crossing Europe on a pass, sending frivolous messages from airports . . . Carolyn gasped when she pulled it out. She read it, turning it over, read it again, and handed it to me with the contorted look she had when she carried a dead pigeon off the porch, one of Snappy's gifts.

"There's something funny about these," I said to her. "I don't know what."

"They don't sound like him." My God, she looked so tired, so flat. Blondes fade like no one else.

I ran my finger along the fuzzy serrated edge of the card. "Not that we know what he sounds like in letters. When has he written to us since—I don't know, since he was ten and went to your parents' for a couple of weeks that summer?"

"Then what?"

I couldn't say. These didn't sound like a kid. There was something weirdly—ventriloquially—adult about them. Posturing? Trying to sound like an equal, like an adult among adults? It was disquieting. "He sounds like an impersonator. And—I don't know, it feels like he's"—I had to cast all around for the word—"it feels like he's playing with us. *Toying,* somehow. Provoking. Doesn't it?"

Carolyn was frowning. "It's the psyche of—you're right. He sounds like a stranger, somehow. I suppose nothing—what's the phrase?—nothing concentrates the mind better than—" She couldn't say it. I was hoarding the card so she just stood there empty-handed, her face crumpling.

* * *

It was about an hour after the message came that a woman called asking for either of us. Carolyn was the one who leaped for the phone each time, still waiting for ransom instructions. The caller wouldn't give her name. She sounded older, Carolyn said. (Older than what?) "I work down at the post office"—said very quietly—"and I just want you to know, if you don't already, we've got an order on to report your mail." Carolyn choked; she said she didn't even know what to ask. ("All the important moments in your life keep happening for the first time!") "I think they ought to tell you when they do that," the woman went on. "Everything that comes, they know it. So I'm just letting you know." That was all. Gently, she hung up. That was the feeling Carolyn had—gently. Considerately. If it was a warning, there was nothing we could do about it. A point of information. It meant they were trying to track the cards, so we shared that point with the police in St. Louis, in Boston, in Albuquerque and Santa Fe. If they were letters, sealed, would they open them? Was it Big Brother time when the heat was on?

I went down to the post office and looked around. The stamp line was stopped dead while the attendant behind the counter helped a very white-haired lady seal and address a package that should have been done up at home. He was as patient as a father, bent over the box almost reverently, half in light and half in shadow, like someone in a Renaissance painting. (Wouldn't he be amused, the Georges de La Tour of Hyland, New Hampshire, or maybe the Vermeer.) This is, I had to concede, a hard place to hate the bureaucracy.

There were at least three women behind him sorting mail, lifting canvas baskets, express, priority, foreign. None of them looked "older." I thanked them all, though I kept it to myself. The cards would keep coming, or stop, without their help or ours.

* * *

One night when I couldn't sleep I came downstairs for some warm milk, and in the vague, reflected blue-white of the kitchen my shaman sat brooding. His round, smooth shoulders gave off sharp little stabs of light. "Talk to me, pal," I muttered out loud. He sat there impassive—no judgments, no suspicions, like the tree he'd been part of.

Then I remembered he *could* talk. I leaned into the bowl of darkness that was his belly and hit the tape recorder button: PLAY. It clicked at me, end of the reel. I rewound it, standing there dumbly as if I were watching the damn thing think. And then, oh God, it was worse than spooky—the Grateful Dead, and then a little boy's voice doing an imitation of a ball-game announcer, it was Jacob doing the Sox with all the right inflections: "A swing and a miss and Boggs goes down swinging. That's two down in the bottom of the sixth and in the ondeck circle . . ." The voice was his and not-his, all complicated by the ventriloquism of the game. (Hadn't I already thought the word *ventriloquism* once today, his unearthly message from St. Louis?) "Pitcher doesn't like the catcher's sign, shakes it off, asks for another." Eight or nine, maybe. We went so often, splintery old Fenway that never changed, just sagged a little more with every season, three hours driving, round trip, and then sometimes three hours parking, just to watch the shadows come down on the outfield and the hotdog rolls disappearing down his throat, always eating, bird with an open mouth. The shock of the green when you came in, the heat of the city steaming up. Jacob made anguished cries every time somebody muffed the ball; with the Sox there was lots of anguish.

Sentimental Dad, All-American Dad. I sat in a stupor of nostalgia. Then the boy-voice disappeared and "No, peppers and mushrooms. Right. Not pepperoni, I said peppers. Okay. Like—is fifteen minutes enough?" And then I did my wise-guy stuff: "Enough?" he echoed. "Enough?

Enough? Enough? Enough?" And the Stones. "You can't always get what you want to." Then a mix, heady, self-indulgent, sound effects. Spike Jones. Judith laughing and laughing, glass breaking, the cat—yeow—Judith apologizing, "He knocked over some books, Daddy, it's okay, nothing broke," and Jacob again, conspiratorial, talking softly to someone on the phone, "No, never, I promise, listen, I really do. N-e-v-e-r. Believe me." Jesus, to Martha, maybe. It was appalling. The hairs stood up along my arms. All of it over. I stole it, shouldn't have had it in the first place, but there it was. There and gone. Present tense is all there is, I thought. The here-and-now.

I sat in the dark breathing hard and then I realized there was another sound in the room with me, the CB breathing out nothing, dead air but that little live charge in it when someone forgets to turn it off, an occasional hitch of random static. Pure present tense, waiting. A garble of sound splattered out for a second, it sounded like "Josie, where's the tacks?" but it probably wasn't. He could be out there somewhere. I was hearing cold night air pouring in, empty. The CB is so strange, like a hole in the air, a rip you can put your ear to. But there was nothing to hear on the other side. Then the tape in the shaman's belly ended with a whoop of joy from both my children out of the grave of their childhood. Enough, enough. A click at the tape's end, a gun being cocked.

So I dragged up to bed and lay down to hide in sleep.

Friends came by but, try though they might to be cheerful, the visits were like condolence calls. We feigned interest in their lives. Tony Berger and Celene brought news from the entire school district: he taught band at the high school, jazz especially, swinging arrangements, well conducted, always stiff—Tony, who left to his own devices put his chin all the way down to the keyboard and tore out the notes, it always seemed, with his mouth, a Thelonious Monk kind of hardslap funk, but kept it zipped where the kids could hear him. Celene had ladylike curls she got at the beauty parlor, but dangerously red; she drove from school to school to coax out little melodies from the chorus and taught every instrument from glockenspiel to tuba. The teachers in the teachers' room told her what they thought of our situation—they were never shy—and it wasn't good. The way they talked about us you'd think we were the Rockefellers, the Kennedys. "They'll never find him" seemed to be the consensus. "He's being protected." The implication was that we could (and would) pay anything. "God, Celene," I said, "I don't want to put you on the spot, but do you say anything?"

She has wonderful eyes—triangular, I once decided, with the apexes at the top, which made them large and innocent, and she used them to good effect, especially when she wanted to look affronted. "Of course I do. 'Don't you remember Ben when he got the middle-school kids together for that mural, that fabulous wallful of life, how can you say that? Rich? All the time he put in and he got paid in postage stamps.' "

"And?"

"And somehow, I hate to say it, they think that just proves you can afford it. 'We could never work for that little money!' Such gratitude. Oh, honey, you know how they are about artists up here. I'm barely tolerable, schlepping around" (she learned that from her husband) "masquerading as a regular gal. A parent asked me last week, 'Why do you teach them all these funny songs?' Her kid's in the marimba quartet. I said, 'What funny songs?' and she says, 'Those foreign ones. Aren't there enough good American songs without'—I don't remember what we did. Israeli. Japanese. I don't know. Hungarian." She likes to run her fingers through her hair—she tousled it up to unlock it, I think, from its neat school-day compliance.

"Same for Tonyburger. They love it when he takes the

jazz band to State and they win first for 'Tuxedo Junction' or something, but nobody really likes to think much about where that comes from. Not the jazz, not the jazz-man. He wears a jacket to school, remember that. No tie, I mean, that would be hypocrisy, but he pays—well, he pays maybe half his dues." I enjoyed considering how Celene got the way she is—a local girl with spirit and sophistication who met Tony in New York, in a smoky club, just the way girls dream it when they leave the little towns, and brought him back home to impersonate a WASP schoolteacher.

The Bergers were our best friends, all of us (except Celene) a little marginal, forever really New Yorkers, however decent we might be. (Nobody knew how much a sculptor earned; it was possible that I was actually making *money* on the dang-fool things I did, and that probably added to our mystery.) As for Annie, she was over the edge because her lovers were named Jane and Eda and, recently, Lord, Anneliese-who-couldn't-speak-English-so-we-know-they're-not-*talking*. It was never quite clear whether the true Hylanders wished they'd been able to slam the door before or after we moved in.

Wendell came, then began calling, since we had nothing to say to him. I needed to talk to somebody but it had better be someone with the imagination to misbehave. Tony sat at the table with me and I looked hard at him and considered. He was good with miscreants in the band room at school (and the band room attracted them) because he had enough of their spirit left, or remembered it fondly. His tall wiry body, his long, straight brown hair that fell in his eyes, were more youthful than Wendell had been in his teens. Hey, Tony, I wanted to say, hey, what if it turns out Jacob's innocent—let's just say—and *I'm* the only damn fool here who's guilty of anything! We had talked, over the years, about existential moments, choices, moral distinctions we could lay out carefully, like surgeons' instruments. All that had as much to do with this, now, as—I don't know—the cheerful instructions a stewardess gives you for exiting a burning plane. I didn't have time to think, Tony! I don't know if I helped him or damned him, trashing the jack, the gloves, the whole damn carpet from the back of the car. Maybe I slammed the jail-house door on him. They don't give you time to reason it out and choose your exit. But I did what prudent Wendell suggested early on: I kept my mouth shut and my options open.

My dreams were dry—that's the only word for them. I slept a lot, sometimes on the couch, like someone who'd been felled by illness or early retirement, and I never dreamed about what was happening, I just saw stretches of desert, cactus, faded blue mountains. A trolley ran into what I think they call a box canyon, the kind of sheer face that rises on all sides of a trail. I don't know who was on the trolley, it just carried a lot of people into a cul-de-sac with beautiful pale pink and blue striations in the rock. I don't know why: a life bleached of everything? Once I woke up just as I tipped forward into a little oasis pond in which I'd been studying my reflection. Narcissus? He didn't seem exactly apropos.

Except, except—I was a kid in the dreams, whenever I was in them at all. However you know those things, I was around Jacob's age. I was wearing my old black leather jacket, in which I had, once upon a time, tried to look fierce and angry, an artist with a grievance. One year I did nothing but curse, nobody could talk to me, I terrified my parents and affronted the relatives who hung out in our tiled kitchen, my pious aunts, my hardworking cousins. (I had an aunt who fasted once a week, twice sometimes, to mortify her soul for God—believe me, I had a lot to fall from.) I think I even scared my friends. Nothing like Jacob. I was so angry, had so much to break with, my father's and grandfather's dusty old religion, the suffocation of a houseful of love with no *mind*, I called it, still under the impression that mind was all that mattered, that it was reprehensible that our little apartment held no intellect, no art, only eating and keeping clean, eating and praying, praying and being polite. The ugly words that fell (or were pushed) from my mouth were better than sex, they were the forbidden release, the dam of "Thou shalt nots" breaking into tiny shards, and me stomping on them as viciously as I could.

But I never hurt anybody, at least not physically. My mother, of course, acted as if she'd been knifed, time and again. When I had the Catholic girlfriend who used to call and conduct incitements to orgasm on the phone. When I refused to apply to college until I'd painted for a couple of years and drove a cab to support myself. And so on. *Epater les parents.* I was hardly the first to discover the technique; then again, my lack of originality wasn't much comfort to them. I'm sure I hurt them as badly as they thought they could be hurt. But really they were flesh wounds. Little psychic nicks. I never raised a hand.

Just come back so we can talk to you. So we can *ask* you. I woke crying in my sleep one time, panting, huffing hard as if I was trying to dislodge something that was choking me. Carolyn, stretched next to me, took my head inside her arms and held my face against her bare breasts and patted my back the way you soothe a colicky baby. I had been dreaming of the Catholic Girlfriend and I was jacking up the couch on which we were sitting. That was all. I pushed up and down on the jack, faster and faster, not very mysteriously like sex, and the couch rose and it was levitated above water finally, like something in a floating temple garden, something Indian. Tranced, with a little black shadow under it that lay on the water like an ink spot. The girl pulled up her legs the way you would if you were taking wing on a flying carpet. But again, leaning forward, I fell in, head first, I kept doing that. I was hell-bent on drowning, apparently. "Benny, Benny," Carolyn was nearly singing, but she couldn't say, There, there, it'll be all right, because she'd be lying and she never lied. I kept on crying and finally, just at the point where you either stop, bored with your tears, and subside into ragged breathing, or fall asleep exhausted, I heard myself whispering, gulping, "Jacob!" Then she joined me and we cried together.

PART 2

BEN

I FINALLY FOUND SOMETHING TO DO WITH MY HANDS: I WAS MAKING fetishes. Praying, I suppose, as instructed. They were small enough to hold in my hand—clothespins with feathers. With buttons. Whittling a little. One I found myself assembling had breasts and a dark Brillo triangle. It scared hell out of me. I opened the woodstove door and threw it into the perfect center of the heat and watched it flare for a long second, hissing, a wild brilliance. I have to say that as it disappeared down to gray ash I felt a little quiver of its power, tiny as it was, and crude.

Maybe it was coming back to me, the feel of the image, realer than real. I went downtown to buy thumbtacks, red, white, and blue ones, and to do that, I had to swallow hard and walk myself into the Central, where everybody bought their newspapers, their birthday cards, their pens. It was an old store, nineteenth-century, spiffed up but not past a certain allowable point—its heavy door was ancient, slow-swinging. Everybody hated the electronic posts we had to walk through, recently installed, conspicuously late-twentieth-century, that shrieked—I suppose they shrieked, though I'd never heard them, they had their intended chilling effect—if a thief tried to get out with a little extra something. They stood there like a pair of watchdogs who didn't get to bark much.

I had my hand on the brass bar to open the door when I saw—I saw and I swear for a second I didn't understand—a photograph of Jacob, 8½ × 11, grainy Xerox but clear enough, taped inside the window just where everybody's eye must fall. I have entered this store every day, give or take a few, for the eleven years we've lived here, and that was why my first reflex was surprise, it was like catching my own face in a store window on Main Street: *Wait, I know this person!* Indeed I do, and above his name, in black bold caps, they had spelled out WANTED PERSON.

When all this finally penetrated, my knees went slack. I put out a hand to catch myself, my palm splayed there on the cold glass right across his face, Jacob in a dark T-shirt squinting in the sun a little, smiling as if he were wincing. Wrestling practice—it was his uniform shirt. Shadow gave him a second nose pointed off to the left, like a Picasso. A Cubist WANTED sign. A first. The damn thing was in the best possible place—I used to run a film series and that was where I taped the schedule for best effect. By sundown everyone would have seen it, that fine, avid, half child's face caught unawares, his father's palm print grotesquely stamped across it like a seal.

I walked back to the car, quaking, I know, like an old man. How do they *know?* For all I think I can guess of his guilt, how can they deal with him like some armed robber who had his picture snapped by a bank camera? Jacob, Jacob, wanted person, do we do our lives to ourselves or does chance leap out at us, randomly hungry, like one of those watchdogs?

Flesh of my flesh, no fetish in the world will keep their dogs off him now.

At about eleven the next morning Corey Weisbach called and I leaped from my stupor on the couch to full focused attention. His daughter had seen Jacob in Cambridge, walking along the river.

Julie was a classmate of his, had just been in *A Winter's Tale* with him, and knew him well enough not to be mistaken. "Did she speak to him?" I asked. I was ready to welcome any detail; I swear if she'd said he was chained to a tree or sleeping under a bridge I'd have been grateful.

"No," he said, sounding affronted, censorious, almost, "of course she didn't talk to him. She has natural presence of mind, she always has had. If she'd announced herself, don't you think he'd have been gone before she closed her mouth?"

I said I supposed so. *Santa Fe, St. Louis* flashed in my mind, those bright scenes burned into my sight like advertising logos. "Along the river?" I asked stupidly.

"On the footpath, not that far from Boylston Street, if you know Cambridge. She was walking with her cousin, he lives in one of those houses along there, those dormitories? There were very few people out, it's so cold. She said she got a good look." Jacob in his dark wool cap, his smooth black jacket with the hot stripes, eyes straight ahead, puffing steam. As if he'd read my thoughts, Corey Weisbach added, for confirmation: "She knew his jacket. She said she saw the jacket first and there he was."

Corey sold cars; he was from an old car-selling family, so successful that they stood just under the best Hyland families that didn't have to do anything for a living. They were the capitalist-aristocrats, with the Ford lot here in town, another, a huge one, in Howe. He had an assurance about him, a public man's solidity, a good voice for accepting awards from Kiwanis and Rotary. Such people are rarely caught off-guard, especially by odd lots and broken sizes like me. "Just strolling, looking normal as apple pie," he went on in that slightly offended tone that asked *How dare he?* A knock on the head, I thought, a hard smash by the murderer that's taken all his memory away. Far stranger things have happened.

I began to stammer out my gratitude, my fear that we might never have seen him again. I told him what a kind and sensitive thing he'd done by tipping us off, what a humane gesture it had been. Certainly we could get ourselves down there—two hours, tops, by the time we organized ourselves and pulled up on Memorial Drive. Just knowing where he was, more or less, though it still might not be easy . . .

"Mr. Reiser," Corey Weisbach said—we didn't really know each other, quite, only he was prominent enough so that he was *known*, a different matter. "You need to know we've called the authorities. It's altogether possible that they've picked him up already. In fact, I think I'd count on it."

I don't know what I said. I must have bleated something like "Of course, of *course.*" I tried to cover my tracks, humiliated to be caught thinking he'd saved us, only us; why, after all, would he have done that? My face was damp with every kind of emanation, sweat, tears, it was hot in here, after my parched dreams it seemed to be raining the moisture of relief. "Naturally you did what you had to."

"Well," Corey Weisbach said slowly, across a huge divide that it was not his fault lay between us. I don't know if he bought my assurance that I'd understood the whole time that we were not the first to learn Jacob's whereabouts. "You have to remember, Mr. Reiser, that while Julie is a classmate of your son's, she is also a classmate —or was, should I say—of the Taverner girl. So." To his credit, he sounded almost apologetic. "However." He paused rather dramatically. "It hasn't turned out to be so simple."

I said nothing, just waited for it to unwind however it would.

As it happened, Julie Weisbach, her famous presence of mind intact in spite of her astonishment and fear, had gone straight to a policeman who was standing in the brick plaza of the Kennedy School just across the street from where Jacob was strolling. "She assumed, as anyone would, that he would take care of it." I winced at that: the "it" he invoked, like an incursion of vermin or the spill of a noxious gas, was my son. But there was nothing the policeman could do: a possible suspect from another state—well, he was sorry to tell the girl, good intentions or not, that it was none of his business, technically speaking. If the kid committed a crime here, that was another thing. Or if they had some kind of a piece of paper from the New Hampshire police. A warrant. But you can't just pick somebody up because someone points a finger at him. He didn't phone in to check, he didn't listen when she insisted that a murder was important enough so that there *must* be a warrant somewhere. So, her father said, she had to stand there and watch Jacob just disappear around the bend. When she saw him last he was headed toward Stillman Infirmary, up near Mount Auburn, where the trackless trolley runs. And gone. (Gone! I thought. Thank God, gone!) It was very frustrating, Corey Weisbach told me as if he expected me to agree. I could imagine what he might have said about the Constitution just then; I wouldn't want to have heard it.

"So we've alerted the authorities here, since that seems to be the thing to do"—authorities, that ridiculous word, its all-purpose assertion of power and control—"and I assume they'll figure out how to proceed." I expected him to add the inevitable "After all, isn't that what we pay them for?" But instead he stopped for a minute and then he began again. He cleared his throat, almost decorously. "I'm very sorry."

I went to tell Carolyn, who was sitting placidly, infuriatingly, in an armchair in the living room, reading in golden light. She listened without saying anything, but her face lost ten years as I spoke. "So," she said quietly, as if that was that.

She came into my arms and we held between us, tightly, the possibility that we might see him soon. "How could we possibly find him?" I asked; I wanted to be reassured. "That is one big goddamn city."

"But you know the way you run into people, Ben—we can't go down there without seeing somebody from another life." It was true; the concentration of certain kinds of people around the Square was sometimes astonishing. It usually left you convinced there were only fifteen people in the world and you knew twelve of them. Then again, it was not outdoors weather; in January they put their heads down and walked to their destinations in a straight line, without loitering. The silver-jewelry salesmen and Ecuadorian-sweater peddlers weren't out, the musicians were blowing their horns, tuning their guitars, in warm living rooms.

"We're going," I said, nonetheless. "There is no way he's in Cambridge and we're not out trying to find him."

What a look she had on her face just then—not for me, mind you. It sailed right past me, winged past my ear and out the window: distant, almost—ironic, I guess. As if she had stepped back from all of it, stubbornly alone on her own side of the room. I think she was picturing us walking around Cambridge, peeking down alleys, knocking on strangers' doors, skulking around theater lobbies like obsessed lovers waiting for a glimpse of our beloved. She looked as if she was going to be embarrassed by such a search. "Carolyn, how can we not do this, even if it's impossible."

"How will I be able to live with myself," she answered

in a flat voice. "Right? Isn't that the sentence that comes next?"

Where in the hell was she going? Had she gone, I mean —clearly the damage was already done.

"Correct," I said with not one ounce of reserve or that goddamn irony that put everything at a far remove. "Correct. How could you live with yourself?"

She sighed, long and hard. "And if we find him—?"

"Yes? If we find him? What's the question?"

"Don't be dense, Ben. What do you do with him? Bring him back? Give him your credit card and drive him to the airport and say, Beat it? Go lose yourself?"

I didn't know. I probably would. *Santa Fe. St. Louis. A dozen other airports, Portland, Chicago, Los Angeles.* I suspected I would. But I didn't know. "You'd put him in leg chains and bring him home?"

She only looked at me. Her eyes darkened as she did; tears, I suppose. I wanted to shake her dry. "This is your son we're talking about." I said it as nastily as I could; being nice to her wasn't the point. "If you've forgotten. This is *Jacob.*"

"If I've forgotten." She kept on staring, dumbly, and his name hung in the air like something that had been struck with a mallet, the way it did the very first time we said it to his small dark head, still wet from its birth. It echoed. Finally she shook her head and the tears brimmed over and down. "I don't know either. That's why I don't want to be the one to find him." She tried to draw the tears back with a ragged breath. "Just—let whatever has to happen *happen.*"

That was enough for me. "I didn't know you were so goddamn passive," I said, thinking of the way she fought for her patients, how she insisted that too many things were allowed to run their course when intervention might have changed the balance. "Passive," I think, was her least favorite word.

I went into the kitchen, moving ungently to get my coat

and gloves. My sneakers would do; there wouldn't be enough snow in Boston for boots. Crust, maybe, slush, archipelagoes of ice on the sidewalks, gray stony mountains at the curb. Now that Corey Weisbach had alerted the authorities, everyone in Cambridge would be studying his face; they weren't going to let him slip through again. I picked up my coffee mug, which had been sitting cooling on the counter. It was a National Public Radio mug, heavy and dark, signed in white by a dozen composers. Chic. All I could think to do (though *think* is hardly the word) was to throw it against a surface that would stop it dead. I flung it at the farthest cupboard door like a pitch to the plate, and it disintegrated. Coffee ran like shitty water down the pale wood, and pieces of those signatures, Bach to Philip Glass, flew around the room as if I had detonated something with wires in it, and powder.

CAROLYN

THIS, SHE THOUGHT, WATCHING BEN FISHTAIL DOWN THE ROAD TOWARD Boston, is where judgment either kicks in or it doesn't. He truly believed—he had the ego to believe—he would show up, walk around town a little, and run smack into Jacob. He said he believed it based on the clear fact that when there's someone you unequivocally don't want to meet you will surely pass him, shoulder to shoulder, on the same side of the street. A good joke.

She had gone upstairs to Judith last night, to tuck her in, and had remembered a dropped stitch. "You started saying something that first night about how mad Jacob was the morning he—disappeared. But the phone rang."

Judith shrugged. "I don't know if it has to do with anything. I mean, you get in bad moods all the time and you don't go out and—" She sighed deeply and went around it. "He was just mad because Daddy told him he had to pay for the whole senior prom himself, whatever it cost.

Jacob wants to—wanted, I mean—to rent a stretch limo, you know the way they do, he and his friends and their girls and all, and, like, ride around in it all night? And Daddy just said, So where are you going to get the money for *that?*" She looked abashed, somehow, embarrassed, probably for her father; surely not for Jacob.

Carolyn steadied herself. "Were they yelling at each other?"

"Oh—" Judith looked trapped where she didn't want to be. "You know how they yell and then it just sort of passes. Jacob thinks Daddy's, like, secretly, you know, like, really *conservative?* Only he hides it, and that's worse. That's a hypocrite. *Jacob* says."

But Judith was right: could it matter that he'd started the day piqued at his father? Martha was the one he'd have sat with in the back of the limo, drinking who-knows-what, watching TV, feeling rich. If anything, Martha, you'd think, would have comforted him, ballasted him—whatever it took—against his ball-breaker dad.

She didn't worry about his hypocrisy. But for all his earnestness about his art, she sometimes wondered, very far down where she didn't like to go, if Ben was a sufficiently serious person. She wasn't quite sure what she meant by that, she only knew she had a hunch that in the really tight spots like the one they were in, he would carry on, perform, make people laugh; be strong, even, the way he'd hidden the bloody evidence without shame or even hesitation. With Ben, things—what he called principles, anyway—were open and shut. Something—humility? indecision? openness to grief, to ambiguity?—in spite of his artist's claim to complexity, like the claim he made to Jacob that money didn't matter when in fact it did—something was missing. He was so *resolved.* Was it something male that demanded assertiveness? Was it a habit born of presenting a solid front to his skeptical parents, who had wanted him to be an engineer, an accountant?

He had fought so hard for his independence; it was a tic now.

One of the intriguing things about Ben, when they'd met, was the fierceness of his commitment to things she, with all her valedictorian's confidence, couldn't see. She had come to a gallery with some friends not for the art, really, but for the wine and cheese, and the unfamiliar feeling in the air, the colorfully dressed women, the men with their unruly beards and their capacious clothes, the army jackets, the weathered leather vests and Moroccan bags, the paint-stained affectation of their jeans, stereotypes all and she knew it. She needed a change of scenery, though: in medical school, deep in the hard part, she'd needed a good place to waste time before she forgot how. Or at least a place to spend unregimented hours looking at something besides anatomy splayed out on a table. And there was Ben, who believed so forcefully in the necessity of his art. ("Mine. Not this stuff here tonight. I came for the wine and cheese.") He really believed it saved you, redeemed mere life from its "everydayness." You'll save lives, he said, but what for? What's a life? Any animal can have health, it's a minimal expectation. But then?

So he'd take her by the hand and lead her to the side of some mysterious canvas, some taut banner of color hanging suspended, hinting at a glory without a name. He made her stare at a Rothko, pink and orange, yellow shimmering like a sunset in a dream, even a medical student was entitled to a dream like that, until it became liquid, till it poured all around like blissful breaking light in the room. Yes, she said, yes, he was right, it was an experience as real as waking. She would leave the lists she was learning, parts of the shin and ankle, galaxies of ribs, alternative functions of organs, and go with him to see Michelangelo drypoints, or the stunning elegance of a Papuan mahogany paddle standing upright against a pure white wall, more sophisticated than anything a

Dansk designer could imagine. She watched him work and wondered what he saw; he covered half the canvas with his hand so that he could judge it, turned it on its side and upside down, and he said, Look, Doctor, what do you see? (A canvas standing on its head?) Then he'd attack a corner that was clearly—*he* said clearly—deficient. If she could see bacteria in a lens, he could see empty corners of canvas that shouted for attention. He would disappear inside a Bonnard and come out beaming.

And he was loving, so loving, in the details, and better than she was, in the whole. Not abstracted like so many men whose lives at work are the sole point of it all, with a little border of family for decoration. He was not hidden, he was not emotionally constipated. He honored all things that deserved honor: his children at play, in pain, in sleep. Her thoroughly equal need to do her work, even when the children were home sick. He was more vigorous than she was, and far more daring. They weren't talking enough right now, but he could talk, usually he could talk without this new defensiveness, and he'd never let her go to bed angry. He hugged too hard, but she'd always thought, So what, so what? It was the cost of his vitality.

She couldn't name the missing part. Since she subscribed to the ambiguity of just about everything, she didn't really want to. But the suspicion fell like a stone in her gut. Fell with the kind of deadly certainty she imagined overtaking people when they found the first symptom of their undoing: felt the lump, saw the blood, discovered that the little mole was expanding, its ragged edges reaching out. She loved Ben and respected him, but his enthusiasms and his panics sometimes had their way with him. In a pinch—in a vise like this one—she was plenty sure of his passion but not the least sure of his judgment.

* * *

For once the phone wasn't ringing—the helpful weren't clamoring to help nor the threateners threatening. She and Judith had a quick cold meal and sat down to watch the kind of junk the kids couldn't get enough of, beginning with the exception-that-proves-the-rule perfection of Bill Cosby's pretend house, kids, marriage: He's in the kitchen making a mess but trying; his beautiful lawyer-wife is laughing indulgently, ready to come to the rescue without the slightest trace of rancor, only a patronizing embrace when the chocolate pudding emerges looking like a cowflop. Given the relaxed state of her household, this woman must have made partner a long time ago.

Judith knew her mother never watched this sort of thing with her, she was a Public Television Mom who called the rest of this stuff "peanuts"—fattening but not filling. And once you start you can't stop. But she was happy to have her there, the two of them slender enough to fit into the same fat-lapped chair. And Carolyn needed her warmth: mothers, she had been known to say with the kind of authority only parents can have, and only when their young children are still pre-critical, have as many needs as children, but they've tucked most of them out of sight.

When they got up between shows to make cocoa, Judith began telling her mother about a girl in school who was a liar. She called her "pathological" so often Carolyn saw that she liked the professional sound of the word. "She said she was born in Borneo. Hey, born in Borneo!—maybe that's where she got that—and she lived on every continent and swam in every ocean. But then one time we were having geography and Mrs. Berney asked her to name the continents and she only got three. So then everybody could tell she was a pathological liar." Judith swept the hair behind her ears triumphantly and asked Carolyn why somebody would do that.

The answer, it seemed, always turned out to be the same, no matter what the infraction, Carolyn realized it even as she said it: "Insecurity. She must not think she's interesting enough, somehow, on her own. So she just improves on herself."

"I daydream like that," Judith said matter-of-factly. "I think of myself as, you know, like, a prima ballerina, or for a while I was the one who got picked to play Annie, I thought that would be the best thing. With a voice you could hear across the street, and I wouldn't have to go to school, I'd have *tutors.*" But, she meant, I'm not *crazy.* I'm not *pathological.*

"Mom."

"What, hon?" Carolyn got down two mugs and two marshmallows. What an all-American scene, she thought, the women at home being chummy in a pretty kitchen, talking daydreams. The father absent and the son not mentioned. The pathological son.

Judith was just where she was. "Do you think Jacob—"

Carolyn waited. Nothing. "What? Do I think Jacob what?"

"Was 'secure' or 'insecure'? *Is,* I mean. Sometimes I get very mixed up about people who are pushy or nasty actually being scared, and all. I mean, aren't there people who are just plain not nice? Not the opposite but, like—the way they act is the way they really are? Couldn't that be?"

Judith was tired of, she resisted, the relativity of judgment, the blight of knowing too much, or thinking you do. Dr. Freud's gift to the world: absolution by weakness, by prior pain. Carolyn couldn't blame her. She would try to answer but she had some questions to ask first. "Well, Jude, you know your brother. What do you think?"

"No, I don't. I don't think I know him. He does—funny things sometimes."

Carolyn let her go on. She stirred the pinkish cocoa carefully, scraping the grit from the bottom of the pan with the edge of her spoon.

"One time he was stoning a dog." Judith wasn't looking at her, she was tracing her finger on the table in a vortex as if she were stirring, too. "I didn't want to tell you. I mean—he made me promise." She stole a quick look at Carolyn. "Up in the meadow, he had this little yellow dog, I never saw it before, and he had it, like, on a rope attached to a tree? And one day—it was a Saturday, Celeste and I were going up in the woods, we had a picnic?" Her tentative eighties-speak monitored her listener endlessly: Get it? Understand? You following? She was not getting it. "He was throwing rocks at it, and it was howling, it was, like, hurling itself around the trunk of the tree and it kept getting stuck, like, in the rope, and dirtying itself and then stepping in it. Its fur was all—yuck, it was torn up, it was bleeding in these little patches, you know, like it looked like mange, sort of, but it wasn't a mangy dog, I don't think, it looked like a nice plain cute dog that probably belonged to somebody." She paused for a minute. "He wasn't trying to kill it or anything," she said as if to exonerate him a degree or two. "I don't know what he was trying to do. And then he got so mad at us for seeing him he threw a couple of rocks at us, and we ran away. It wasn't our fault we saw him, I told him that, we just came along, we were going out to the big rock. But, like—"

Carolyn was too stunned to pursue the details. Did he have another life? This couldn't be Jacob. He was never cruel! He was acerbic, ungrateful, sometimes devious perhaps, but she had never seen him cruel.

"Then he's so nice. Like that same night he offered to fix my bike? So I said, 'Oh, Jake, you're just being nice so I won't tell.' And he really got his feelings hurt, he said, 'They don't have anything to do with each other. You're my sister and your brakes are loose and this isn't, like, blackmail or anything.' "

Carolyn reached behind her like a blind woman to find a chair. How did she know him? How do you think you know your son? Up to a certain age, everything he does is visible to you. And gradually he walks away. She cried, she remembered, when she put his first tiny shoes on his feet, shoes no bigger than leaves—partly because they trammeled him so, they cropped his toes and held them caught. That was the end of the Garden of Eden for him, when she laced on that white scuffy leather with its million folds where his foot would scratch its lines of movement. And then because she could see already, at two months or whatever it was, three because she put it off so long and it was summer, that he would walk away someday. Everyone thought her tears were ridiculous, an overreaction, but she had been right, no one else cared enough to follow it through logically: those shoes were patterned to take him away from her. When she gave him over to others, to his sitters and the day-care center and then to school, the shadow began to fall across her gaze —of course she gave him over, of course she yielded him up, and gladly, naturally. She wasn't pathological.

Then she knew him by the spoor his actions left—those bike brakes he fixed for his sister, the way he answered the phone, the games they played in the backseat of the car, how he spoke to strangers, the way he wore his heels down on one side so badly that the shoemaker shook his head in despair, the way he toed in slightly, not enough to have to undergo that bar they gave severely pigeon-toed infants, but just enough to pull his shoes into an unmistakable curve. His soiled gym clothes, his sheets stiff with the evidence of his coming-of-age, the letters he wrote his grandparents, his love of math, the way he liked to buy gifts for people, his fear of airplanes overcome by the pilot's friendliness that time, his trip to the cockpit. His passion for raspberries, which he went to pick in season, even if it meant turning out of bed at dawn. What did she know, what did she not know? *Stoning a dog up in the meadow?* She had no breath for it. Judith circled her, saying, "Mom, are you all right? I shouldn't have told you." She had the stricken eyes of someone in trouble.

"No, I'm not all right, Jude." She closed her eyes. "It's good that you told me. It isn't your fault, love. But how can I be all right?" Seventeen years of infinite painstaking attention, intimate, consuming, slacking off as it had to around when? Eighth grade or so—a spotty dedication to the details after that. Not wanting to crowd him. Not asking more questions than she had to. Not saying "Don't do this or that" with girls, only saying "Don't come home too late. Call us if you're going to be very delayed. Drive carefully." *Stoning a dog. Watching its fur bead up with blood. Hearing it howl for release.*

What is impossible in this world?

Is there anything that cannot happen?

BEN

I WAS RELIEVED TO BE OUT OF THE NUMBING GRIP OF THE HOUSE. THE narrow road to Cambridge ran between high banks of plowed snow pocked black with automobile scum like stubble. It had gotten warm; there was fog. I drove carefully, twenty in school zones though the kids were safe inside, braking in the little towns that straddle the New Hampshire-Massachusetts border. Even at this speed, meant to incite no officers of the law, as if I could heal things by my care, I felt a little out-of-control—not quite, but nearly. I realized suddenly, if anything happened to one of my tires I'd have no jack. That made me laugh again, the laugh bubbling up like vomit. "Officer, what can I tell you, I have a thing about jacks. I even have one hidden in a pile of junk in my workshop. Confiscated, for the safety of the neighborhood." I was getting giddy, too alone with it, I wished Carolyn, at least, were with me, going where I was going. I kept forgetting what this was about. *I, I, I.*

The idea of murder, too, had become like a word you say too many times, didn't you do this when you were a kid, till it had no shape, no start or finish, had dumped its contents on the cold hard ground: Murder. An amusing-sounding word. *Murdermurdermurdermur.* The fog took me in as if I were heading into smoke, into a burning house, bent on rescue. I turned on the radio and shouted while the angriest heavy metal banged behind me, drums like something falling down the stairs, and shrieking guitars and words not meant to be understood. It was the kind of music you loved if you were sixteen, seventeen—murder music, make no mistake.

And I walked as if I were the one who was hunted. Across the Yard, mostly deserted in late afternoon, its bare little trees brittle, the criss-crossing cement paths that are so idyllic in spring nothing but brown-gray now, snow melting around them, wetting them down. Purposeful students passed me on their way to the silence of the library. The lights were on inside; they'd have to be, it was that kind of scene, me out here, all joy sealed up in there, deliciously warm. Of course, of course, like a scene in a fucking movie. It was extremely quiet, though if I listened hard the traffic gritted behind me on Mass. Avenue. Mostly it was boots squishing by, a squirrel clicking across the path and onto crusted snow. *Melancholy* is too literary a word. *Sorrowful* is too final. All I did was itch—I burned with impatience and exhaustion and bewilderment, and I couldn't scratch it. It made me drunk, so that I had the impulse to do insane things that might feel good, piss behind a tree, roll down the steps of Widener Library, assault the most innocent face I could see. And I saw plenty, these safe, unracked, unsuspect children with their green book bags, their long, bright scarves. What were their worst crimes, these comfortable, half-arrived

Harvard kids? Cheating on tests? Disloyalty to their roommates, the stealing of girlfriends, boyfriends? Vomiting up their ice-cream sundaes to stay thin? Unbridled masturbation? When I was that age—I think the first sculptures I made were actually all sublimated versions of fuckable women. It wasn't Rodin I was copying, they were all Henry Moores, those zaftig women with monstrous thighs and huge holes in the middle. Who'd have guessed you could get it off, metaphorically speaking, in the Sculpture Garden at the Museum of Modern Art? Well, that was probably what Moore intended. *Dermurdermur.* I saw a boy Jacob's exact height and build, but his jacket was wrong, it was navy, hooded, plain, and I was looking for sinister black, a little vain, with stripes. Maybe he ditched it, he's hiding in lamb's clothing—but Julie Weisbach had known him by his colors, and that was only a few hours ago. The boy in navy disappeared around a corner.

I walked until my feet were so cold I could hardly stand. It had been warm earlier but dark was seeping down and the air was thick with dampness, and icy, the sky pink with snow that was going to fall before morning. In front of the Coop the inevitable fliers were being pressed into passing hands. They aren't political anymore—I took a discount coupon for a new Indian vegetarian restaurant called Baba's, and a salmon-colored ad for a channeler who was coming to town to reunite us with our old selves; better ones, I hoped. Tickets were twelve bucks—would it be worth that to discover I was really Attila the Hun or a Carmelite nun? I stuffed them in a garbage can and thought, Maybe I need to print up a thousand likenesses of his face before the police do it, and put out a plea: HAVE YOU SEEN THIS PERSON? I wouldn't have to say why—just another missing kid, a runaway. I could staple them to lampposts, the way people did for strayed animals. Answers to Jacob. If seen, call collect.

I was standing at the corner, ready to cross the street, when I heard a cheerful voice shout "*Ben*jamin!" There was only one person who loved to call me that and I was right: it was Pearl Hedrick, who ran the gallery on Newbury Street where I showed a couple of years ago. She gave me the necessary hug, the cheek-to-cheek air kiss. She was svelte as a model, her mouth red as a joke, her short dark hair slicked back like a World War I German officer's. It always amazed me that she could be as serious about art as she was, looking like that—my prejudice, I guess. In fact, she simply treated herself like another work, shaped and painted with great precision.

"It's been so long, Ben, don't you get down here from your Eden anymore?" She pretended personal hurt. Beside her stood a young man, younger than she, who must have been her catch-of-the-day. He could only have taught at Harvard, or maybe even studied there, given the sweater and wool jacket (open to the freezing afternoon—who says intellectuals aren't macho?) and the untrammeled tufts of hair over his ears. "Ben Reiser, Marshall Biedenstein. Marshall"—she beamed at me, with a funny screwing-up of her face that came as close to a wink as someone like Pearl would allow herself—"has just learned that he's this year's Yale Younger Poet."

He didn't study his feet or shuffle uncomfortably. He looked straight at me, unsmiling, not at her, and amended her PR. "Next year's, technically."

I congratulated him as heartily as I could. I knew a poet pretty well once who threshed every ounce of his experience into careful lines; once he was thrown off a subway platform by a drunk and I remember thinking, after my gratitude that he hadn't hit the third rail or been mowed down by a D train, Oh my God, we'll never hear the end of this. And we didn't; he did a whole series, in a dozen voices. Now, looking at the swarthy-faced young poet, whose eyes were critical and a little too weary for his years unless he'd had one hell of a life, I wondered, Lord, what would he make of us? What effusion about the impossibility of knowing an Other, or about the unpredictability of the fates. How many types of ambiguity could he summon in Jacob's name and mine? All of them deserved, mind you, but off to the side just now, slightly ridiculous. No wonder Carolyn despises what I do with my life—the thought flashed up like a nasty fin out of the water. Which matters most, Benny, a temperature of 104 or a lovely pegged seam (Look, Ma, no nails!). Or the discoveries Pearl was always making with breathy enthusiasm, the Lithuanians and Inuits who made paintings on broken glass or sculptures out of human bone. Once she gave over her whole gallery to a mock-up of a dentist's office, in painted plaster. Well, I should talk—I was her flavor-of-the-month once, me and my bonded junk, and grateful for it. You couldn't compare a Michelangelo to a 104 fever either . . . Marshall Biedenstein would have been amused to know what invisible armies swarmed, snarling, across his face and sweatered chest.

I stared at them both out of my haze, amazed, simply, that we spoke a shared language. I suppose I'd really drifted, as if I were not the hunter but the quarry. But I must have been coherent, insofar as I spoke (I remember asking *her* nothing), because she didn't pass her hand before my eyes to check my state of mind, nor did she even seem to regard me oddly. She asked many eager ordinary questions about the family, one by one. When she got to Jacob I said, "Fine, fine," and then madly, just on a hunch, "You haven't seen him, by any chance? Out here today?" As if she wouldn't have mentioned it if she had. (Someone had told me his picture'd been in the *Globe:* on the lam. Apparently she didn't read those pages.)

"Lost him?" She shook her head sympathetically. "Try the record store, I think that's where they congregate at his age."

"Well, if you see him—" But I trailed off. If, then? as Carolyn might put it. If Pearl told him, Hey, Jacob, I just ran into your father on that corner, what would he do?

We weren't the only ones, Carolyn and I, who were staggered by unanswerables.

I turned down her invitation to go in someplace to warm up over a drink and celebrate Marshall's good luck. "I really need to find him and get home before it snows," I said, and clapped her too hard on the arm, the way I might have slammed a racquetball opponent a shade too heartily for his victory. "Marshall," I said firmly, as if I were his uncle or one of those friends of the Graduate's family who suggested that his future lay in plastics. "Good luck with it. I hope they make a movie of your book." He didn't smile. I found a shred of polite curiosity and asked what it was called.

"*The Delights of Death,*" he told me, smiling finally, beginning to turn away.

The delights of death. Well, it was his baby. I guess it sounded good to him. I wanted to say, "Hey, watch that, mister, you've got power under your hands with a title like that." My grandmother would have said, more simply, "Darling, you shouldn't know from it."

"Give my best to the crew!" Pearl shouted and, turning her boyish head, crossed the street with her arm firmly tucked into her lover's, a solidarity that looked nearly spiteful. I stood where I was, across a swollen river of traffic. My fingers were so sweaty inside my gloves that I pulled them out into the knifing cold and discovered they were shaking. Oh, the delights of death! We were all like little children reaching after experience we couldn't —shouldn't—have. Wasn't reality terrible enough without our carefully consided reputations with their perfectly mitered corners, their clever line breaks? Yes, my love, I thought, a 104 fever-and-rising is worse, counts for more, kicks the globe out of alignment on its axis. And death is no delight: not a fruit, not a flower, not a metaphor for anything else on earth.

* * *

I called someone I thought I remembered he knew, one of the few Hyland High graduates who'd made it to Harvard. He'd been a Westinghouse Science Search finalist with a good experiment on nutrition in—something. Not mice. Well, close enough. His roommate answered. No, Larry Tournier wasn't there; neither was anyone else. Ridiculous to think he might be there. I didn't know another soul he knew. I went into a coffee shop, drank from a cup so hot it made my eyes tear when I bent my head over it. I picked a fight with the waitress because they charged for a second cup; after that, she made a wide berth around me. I put my head down on the Formica table and tried to sleep, looking, I'm sure, like a drunk who'd happened to get his hands on fifty cents for coffee and not a penny more, and even though I was too exhausted for honorable wakefulness I couldn't even drift away. I heard the buzz and shamble of the despised beautiful children arguing, flirting, discussing Kierkegaard or the Celtics or whatever the hell they do when they sit around at dinner. If the waitress only knew, I thought melodramatically, why I'm so tired, who I've been looking for and why—Martha Taverner packing cones at Jacey's looked a little like this girl, healthy and blond and a blend of slyness and innocence appropriate to her age—she'd be out the door with two more hours still left on her shift. All the dangers were past for me, I thought, give or take a couple of forms of annihilation (I was sure that if I went outside I'd fall into the path of a car or crack my spine slipping on an icy patch). Hey, kid, I told myself, my cheek sticky against the tabletop, now you can go be an existentialist hero. Enlist in Nicaragua, in El Salvador, what do you have to lose? I felt a peculiar light-headed exultation. Jacob, no question, would be feeling the same thing, whatever else it might bring with it —ties cut, obligations canceled, the criminal is free, the free man is a criminal, when you have no place to lay your head it all comes to the same thing in the end.

* * *

I had a place to lay my head, of course, only it was an hour and a half away. I spent the night in the parking lot of a mini-mall in Concord. Just as I headed north out of Cambridge it had started to snow, and between the scrim of flakes that was coming down like heavy fog and the bleariness of my own exhaustion once I'd passed that moment of self-dramatization—the free man is a criminal!—I knew I couldn't hold on to the car, it was going to spin out on me. I only hoped the police wouldn't come shining their lights in the window. I curled up on the backseat and prayed not to dream. When the light came in to me in the morning, the sky and the ground were exactly the same glowing white—I felt as if I was trapped inside a pearl.

When I got home Carolyn was on the phone giving a consultation about the dosage of a baby's medication. All I heard was "Not before three months. No, never. Please, when I say never I mean absolutely *never.*" But she was gesturing wildly. I didn't understand.

Finally she took the pad and wrote in big letters: THEY FOUND HIM!

Judith came running in while I was washing the night off my face at the kitchen sink. "Daddy! You didn't see him? He's in Cambridge right where you were! But I don't understand about all the postcards."

I hugged her hard. "You can ask him yourself, sweet-face. Do you know anything else? He's okay?"

She kept on holding my hand, gleeful, as if this was the end of it and everything was going to be all right. "Oh, it's so complicated. He was staying with somebody, we don't know him. Someone he met, I guess. And he was, like, in some kind of trouble, they were arresting him, I think he was mad at somebody and he stole all his stuff, his stereo and his clothes and all, it was about drugs—"

"Wait, wait. Jacob did?"

"No, this *other* guy—" She gave me a look that said this

should all be self-evident. "So, they just found him there. Jacob. Like—I think it was, like, a complete coincidence." She hugged me again. "I don't exactly understand. But Mommy says we have to go down there, so you have to get right back in the car. My poor daddy!" She hopped around, the way I remembered the two of them, very little, when we suggested a movie, a day at the amusement park. "Daddy, aren't you glad?"

I didn't know. I thought he might have been safer on the run. But maybe not. Hiding out with a druggie, a stranger with a temper, a taste for vengeance—I don't suppose that's what a sane man would call freedom.

"It's snowing real bad, Judith."

"But we've got to go! How can we not go? He's in jail, but Wendell said we can see him if we go right now."

I was afraid, and not of the drive. I didn't want her to see me terrified, so I only repeated it. "Coming home I slid around a lot, and it's getting worse fast."

She said "*Dad*dy!" with the exasperated superior look she's learned from Carolyn: "When I say *never* . . ." "He's in *jail* and he *needs* us. *I'm* going to go if I have to *walk!*" Judith knew that people used to do that. I read it in the town history: nineteenth-century students who went to school near Boston routinely walked eighty miles home, eighty miles back, up mountains, across valleys, for their holidays. They seemed to make nothing of it. I wondered what their soles were made of. Superior soles, superior souls. *They had Jacob:* I kept seeing the blue-white glare of a cop car's lights flashing on, flashing off, sweeping across his face, his body, all the way to his toes where his feet turn in a little. On for danger, off for safety, exposed, hidden, exposed, hidden, urgently blinking, showing him to us for an instant, then taking him away. I stood at the window and watched the world being obliterated, minute by minute losing ground to the color of nothing.

CAROLYN

THEY WERE GOING TO LEAVE JUDITH AT HOME; SHE SWORE SHE WOULD never forgive them. It had suddenly occurred to Carolyn that they couldn't bring a child, however loving and concerned, to a jail-house confrontation—it was worse than a visit to the ICU, not only inappropriate but probably illegal.

"We'll take you to the Rapaports'," she said, forming the idea even as she spoke. They had a good number of friends in and around Boston, but the Rapaports' daughter was Judith's age. "We're going to stay over, so you can come with us and just—play with Clarissa when we go to see him."

"Thanks," Judith answered frigidly. "I don't 'play with' anyone anymore, in case you haven't noticed." She was pale with anger. "And normal people are in school, anyway."

She didn't like the sound of that "normal." "Well,

maybe you can go along with her, wouldn't that be interesting, to see another school?"

Judith answered, but Carolyn wasn't listening. She had realized that there were a lot of things she needed to say to Ben about Jacob that she somehow didn't want her daughter to hear. It was odd—this was the same reluctance that had kept her from ever acknowledging within Judith's hearing that she had had an abortion once, very soon, too soon, after Judith's birth; some delicacy made her hesitate for fear Judith would generalize to herself: If you could so easily cast off a child, why then, it could as easily have been me! She thought this a ridiculous qualm, especially since she had had no second thoughts about the abortion beyond regret, the necessary sadness. She herself had generalized, actually: had stood over Judith's crib the evening after the "procedure" and mourned for the little clump of cells never to become a soul in exact proportion to how much she loved this whole and complex and *achieved* little person sleeping in the shadows of the night-light.

But she worried a lot about the distortions in children's minds, the connections between events that load them with mistaken responsibility or make them accidental, unintended victims—she saw it among her patients, the children traumatized by rotten luck from which they can never untangle their own character; the children with tics and twitches, the ones who bump into sharp objects and fall too often, who think themselves wicked.

She stopped herself then. A lot of good it's done, that protectiveness, she thought bitterly. Given the outcome, probably everything they'd done ought to be stood on its head. But that was futile and extreme, and far too self-pitying. She went to pack some clothes. "Put out some food for Snap," she called over her shoulder to Judith. "Enough dry food for a couple of days."

"Are we leaving the heat on, so she won't freeze?"

Judith was still speaking stiffly, to punish her. "Last time her water bowl froze over."

"The heat? Oh, Jude, really. Cats don't freeze indoors, whatever the temperature." Even if they did, she was thinking, *enough* protectiveness. Enough trying to guess exactly what everybody needs. What is given doesn't correlate with what's received. If she can't figure out how to keep herself warm, then let her freeze.

It didn't quite feel like a jail. She wasn't sure what she'd been expecting—that somehow, because she didn't like to watch cop movies on television, and read mystery stories only because they were like chess games, regretting the gratuitousness of the bloodshed it took to get them started, reality should have rearranged itself—gentled itself—into something less raw. She had never understood why people needed guns and chases and fists splintering jaws to feel stimulated. If it was some primal fantasy wish-fulfillment, then there was more anger out there than she'd like to acknowledge, held under by main force. Or else most lives were simply too boring—that was plausible. She had daily mysteries, life-and-death choices (though not as many as people might think); maybe she couldn't imagine how dull the average routine could be.

The Cambridge jail was up high, like a penthouse, at the top of the court building. Except for the man who searched your bag and the electrical apparatus hulked at the entrance as if you were about to board a plane, it was distinctly unlurid; it could have been any kind of office building—Universal Bathroom Tiles on 3, Pharmaceuticals Inc. on 10. There was a lively foot traffic (lawyers? clerks?) and the cheerful back-and-forth of hallway acquaintanceship conducted in flat-voweled Bostonian. When you pushed the seventeenth-floor button, of course, you gave yourself away as something other than a courthouse functionary. But even then, Carolyn thought, I must look like a lawyer, not a mother. Except for the set of her face, her mouth rigid almost to the point of distortion, she did look like some assistant D.A. with a mission.

But Ben did the talking. He looked grim and a little angry, as if, provoked, he would be relieved to blame this whole thing on the police. They were met, from behind glass, with the emotionless attention of a round, mustachioed clerk dressed in police blue, a flag on his sleeve. Back where he sat, there were counters and old desks and a phone that rang incessantly; the only time it wasn't jangling was when someone was speaking into it.

They filled out, "subscribed under the penalties of perjury"—the grammar didn't seem quite right—green forms bristling with the supposition that they might have things to hide but would confess them here to buy their way in for a visit: Their true name. Their own previous felonies. Whether they were on furlough from another Correctional Institution. She was overwhelmed with this forced glimpse of just who was out there, who was in here, how they were related. Jesus, the perfumed garden she lived in . . . Name of Inmate (the word shocked her there in print, as if he had already been convicted of something). Relationship. They pushed the forms through a window on a sliding tray.

They declared they had no weapons—it was clearly time to stop being astonished or affronted by anything. Reluctantly, Carolyn hung her purse in a locker. (Patients desperately hated to give up their things—she remembered, from her internship, how women who had to take off their wedding rings before they were rolled into the operating room would cry and argue: Not then, of all times, to be stripped of their familiar identifying tokens, not when they were about to be stripped of everything, including consciousness! She felt the leap of anger as she hung her shoulder bag from a hook and watched Ben empty his pockets of all his petty jangling treasure. They were right, it was humiliating and, separated from her familiar props, she felt herself giving up defenses she didn't know she had.)

They passed through a red door—cheerful except for the sign that repeated yet again NO FIREARMS PAST THIS POINT—so thick it was like entering a safe. Then they were in the long, uninflected room where they would face their Inmate through glass, absurdly near him, close enough to see his pores, his every eyelash. But brown telephones, ordinary-looking except that like lobby phones they had no dial, hung beside each chair.

You faced rabbits through a cage, you faced parrots and canaries and guinea pigs. You did not face your son. The glass was impermeably thick. She could see fingerprints, cloudy as scummy water, where the fluorescence flashed against it. You would have to sit next to other visitors? Share conversations about—well, about anything: this was all you had of each other. Bail or regret or revenge or—whatever? "I don't think anybody stays in here very long, it's not really a *prison*," Ben said quietly, as if they were surrounded by listeners. "It's mostly pretrial, so I'll bet people don't stay around forever."

Carolyn looked around, dispirited. This was not one of those spaces like hospital waiting rooms that had been furnished with kindness to keep spirits up—it had a scuffed, plain-wood, businesslike look, no visual euphemisms here for bad luck, bad judgment, bad karma. The attitude, she thought, looked like: You got yourself into this, bud, and we're not obliged to keep you happy. Or your family, either. If that makes you feel sad or guilty, fine.

They sat for a long time, silent. There was nothing to say. Carolyn leaned on her elbow, her hand over her eyes—the fluorescence, buzzing slightly, was giving her a headache, and, she thought angrily, there was nothing to look at, anyway. For whatever reason, no one else was visiting yet; a quiet time, a lull. The longer they waited, the closer she drifted toward sleep—she felt like someone on a boat bobbing without sound or movement. A mercy just now, this suspension. There was no before in it, there was no after. There was no now.

Finally, someone joined them. A very small woman, quite young, with curlers under a red-and-yellow flowered kerchief, had entered the room and, apparently accustomed to the routine, had taken a seat a few berths down from theirs. She did not look upset to be there; she chewed gum vociferously. She looked as if she might be Italian, or Portuguese, maybe, given where they were. She paid them no attention. After a few minutes' wait, during which she assiduously picked the polish off the nails of her left hand, blowing little flakes of pink into the air, a very thin, wiry young man in baggy gray came out of the lockup to sit down before her. She began to speak into her telephone, without preliminaries, in the tone someone would use who was entirely exhausted by argument. Oh my, oh my, Carolyn thought. Here's someone who's been here too many times, sister or sweetheart; here's someone who's giving more than she's getting. They never did hear the young man's voice but through the glass they watched him suffer the harangue; he looked exactly as he would have at home in his own room, bored, hostile, eager to be free of her but not quite willing to cut her loose.

Jacob was not wearing his own clothes either; real jail or holding cell, they doled out their shapeless institutional gray; and he was pale. His hair was tamped down as if he'd just removed his hat. She tried to read his face but found it scrupulously blank.

She started to rise and so did Ben, but Jacob's jailers had arranged things as awkwardly as they could to prevent any unseemly shows of affection. It was a sealed border. They gawked across the distance like accusers and accused. To reach for him was impossible. But there he was, alive, whole, familiar.

"Cruel bastards," Ben muttered. They were spared, at least, having to confront the question of whether, if he could have, Jacob would have reached forward to fall into their arms. He stood utterly still, utterly blank. Carolyn raked his face for a sign—terror suppressed, or relief, or the beginning of a grief-stricken crumbling—but she saw a blankness so pure she had to restrain herself from thrusting herself through the window and shaking him. He was very young, she thought fleetingly, to have such absolute control of himself. It was hard to believe this was the moment they'd been praying for.

Ben was the one who was crumbling. Tears stood out on his cheeks, huge and copious, and he couldn't seem to stop reaching toward the dead surface of the glass; he so much needed to touch Jacob, his hands twitched with balked energy. "Jacob," he said urgently, then said it again, and then again, to the air. No one had touched the phone.

Jacob was looking them over as if to decide whether he wanted to claim them.

Ben finally reached for the receiver, but the inhumaneness of speaking through an instrument to someone who sat right before his eyes was too disorienting to be borne. "Reach out and touch someone" played under Carolyn's breath; she didn't dare sing it aloud, but the cruelty of the joke broke on her like a sweat. Were they trying to induce madness, or only accidentally succeeding?

"Jake, we have to talk," Ben said in a conspiratorial whisper. "Talk to us." Jacob sat on the edge of the wooden chair. He did not move his chair in confidingly as his father did nor did he lift his receiver from its hook.

Carolyn was looking for a familiar sign in him and hadn't found one. It was as if someone had done an extraordinarily good job of making a model of Jacob but could not fake an animating spirit; she didn't recognize him.

Ben was gesturing to her to join them. She sat down,

hollow. Are you all right? was all she wanted to know, but as if they were in a phone booth, she would have to wait her turn. Was he mocking them, or was the absurdity of this setup too much for him to overcome? Ben gestured to him to pick up the telephone as if he might conceivably have failed to notice that it was there. The guard who stood against the wall on Jacob's side must have shouted something to him because Jacob turned to look at him sideways. He nodded almost imperceptibly, a flicker that barely registered, but he still didn't reach for the phone. Nor could they force him to. For someone who didn't want to be dragged into confrontation, it was a dream too good to be true.

So they stared. His silence was appropriate to the event, she thought; it was like a play by Beckett—they needed garbage cans to sit in, or blackness all around them. Their stupefied voices would hang out in space and flap like laundered nightclothes, meaningless. Meanwhile, in the real world, was he all right? Was he in control or had he sustained some shock, some damaging injury? "Could we ask them if we can get near him?" she asked Ben, feeling foolish. "If we tell them he won't use the phone?"

Overcome, Ben just shook his head hopelessly. Jacob was watching them from the far side, taking it all in. His eyes followed her as she walked back to the guard on their side and tried to explain.

"Contact visits are a different day," the guard replied in his officially flattened machine-voice. "An inmate has to be here two weeks before you can—"

She grasped at a straw bobbing past. "This is just a boy. He's seventeen. It's the first—"

"You got to talk to them out front, lady. Maybe the sheriff will let you, he's a juvenile." He looked supremely unconcerned. Other visitors had begun to crowd into the long, narrow room and he was keeping his eye on them.

A few who must have been regulars greeted him like an old friend.

Carolyn liked the way that sentence had come out: so the sheriff was a juvenile! She gestured to Ben that she was going out to follow up on the possibility. He had sunk back in his chair, reduced to exhaustion, and he and Jacob were staring at each other like animals, each waiting for the other to break and run. But they were engaged, she thought, desperate, as she made signs to the clerk to let her out so that she could find the child-sheriff and get his permission to touch her son. Wordless or not, Ben and Jacob were having something like a conversation, hostile but full of feeling.

When she brought back permission—they were to see him in a little room off to the side, an exception granted only in deference to his age—she felt triumphant. Any scrap or bone they threw you in a system like this was a miracle.

So they had to go out and come back in again. This time, for their "contact visit"—it sounded like a sport, maybe, or a sexual encounter—a woman, unsmiling, passed a metal detector over their bodies gravely and carefully, turned them as if she were assessing them for crooked hems, uneven pockets.

"Good Lord," Carolyn murmured, "do they really think we'd be going in there with a weapon?"

"Hmmp, you can laugh." The woman, unsmiling, continued to vacuum up the back of her skirt. "You be surprised what folks'll try to bring in there. Youn't believe it." She didn't smile or provide details. Carolyn was left to ponder: grenades? pet cats? nerve gas?

And it was worse. There was a wide table in the room and Jacob took hasty refuge on the far side and sat down barricaded safely behind it. As if it were a cloak he could wrap himself up in tight, proof, in his distance, against touch or feeling or a soaking in hot parental tears, he sat with two feet of Formica between them and gazed serenely, expectantly, into their faces.

Was the child in shock? Could this be some kind of dissociative reaction? Carolyn flipped through every possibility she could think of. His cool assessing glance was chilling. Carolyn ran ahead of him constructing explanations: a sufficiency of terror could do this, just seize up every emotion. Couldn't it? He seemed, even without the glass, to have a transparent shield around him. She had seen this in autistic children, a margin of safety, an aura of negative emotional ions, that turned back curiosity, killed feeling by seeming not to recognize it. Or tried to. It wasn't arrogance; it was incapacity.

"Jacob." Ben had restrained his impulse to seize him, lug him forcibly into an embrace. Temperately, he had sat down on his own side and now merely leaned forward; but he had the deadly sound of fatherly lecturer in his voice. "We're relieved to see you safe." No response. She wasn't surprised. "I don't know if you can imagine how much we've been worrying—" They were all disembodied. How could it be that he sounded so insincere about something so palpably, urgently true? Maybe the lights in this holding pen were sucking the life out of them, or the suspicion that they could be heard by strangers?

Ben was trying a new tack, High Jocularity. "Listen, your sister wanted us to ask you first off, Jacob—the postcards? How did you—were you *in* all those places? Did you come back here after you flew all around the country? Jake?"

They got a fine edge of a smile for that—he looked distantly amused. But he wasn't saying. Carolyn thought of the voice on the postcards, that unfamiliar adult chumminess. That ventriloquism. He had apparently thought better of it.

"You don't think you're going to be able to hold out like this forever, do you?" Ben was beginning to rise to it

—he knew he was being provoked, but knowing it and staying calm in the face of it were two separate things. "If you won't talk to us—"

"We've told the police nothing," Carolyn said evenly, to cut off the badgering. Ben glared at her. Probably he thought that was his to say; she couldn't quite claim it, given her abjectness with Fran. "Your father has—protected you." She wished there were some way to measure what was going on inside him, some internal seismograph, like a lie detector, she supposed, to show them what this silence was secretly costing him. Were they registering, somewhere deep behind his unchanging eyes? Amnesia? Or had he taken a blow to the head? That was absurd, but it had to be considered. "Jacob, look," she began again, trying for a different tone from Ben's. "Maybe you can begin by telling us what they've told you. Why you're here?"

He looked at her unblinking. She vowed not to jabber the way you do when someone doesn't hold up his end of the conversation. "Do you know why you're here?"

At this he cast his eyes to the ceiling as if to some mysterious force above, for relief. This was a gesture so familiar she breathed out hard in gratitude. At least he was functioning.

"Hey, Bartleby," Ben taunted. "You know *Bartleby the Scrivener,* did you ever read that in your English class? He's the guy who 'preferred not to.' Whatever anyone wanted from him, he just said the same damn thing over and over. 'I prefer not to. I prefer not to.' " *That,* Carolyn thought, will certainly not get us where we have to go. She was surprised and maybe a little bit hurt that Jacob didn't give his father the same fresh have-mercy look.

Ben, who had not even glanced at her, went on to repeat the obvious: that standing silent was not going to get Jacob out of this. Poor child, Carolyn was thinking, even while she wanted to grab him by the shoulders and shake the words out of him. Of course he knows that, but it's probably digging him in deeper. *Panic.* She had frozen, once, before a committee that was examining her—she was very young, this was for a scholarship to college. But she knew what it felt like, at a certain point it's like wanting to be buried deeper, deeper as long as you're already dead, to bury your shame. It had been one of the most terrifying moments of helplessness of her life—that dim comprehension, as if through a scrim, through alcohol or pain, that you were doing this to yourself. No one else was doing it to you. It was an animal response, deer freezing in headlights, raccoon stunned at the side of the road. "Jacob," she whispered with feeling. How could he not answer the pain in her voice?

Easy or difficult, he resisted. He looked down at the table where one of his hands lay. When he saw it, clean and chapped, a vulnerable part of himself on display, he pulled it into his lap. Then he raised his eyes again and looked at them both without interest, without need or concern. *Dead in the eyes,* she thought, weary. Passive resistance. "You understand that you have a hearing tomorrow?" she asked brusquely. "Have they told you that?" I sound like Ben, she thought. Maybe this would work better if they didn't seem so damned abject. "There's a warrant for you from New Hampshire. For your arrest. Which is why you're here." If things had been normal, he'd have said in a snide voice, "Aren't I arrested already?" But he persisted in his silence. "All they're going to do is determine that you're the person named in the warrant. Wendell says that's all they'll do."

"And you may have to say a word or two, Jake, I don't think they're going to want to talk with you but they may have to ask you who you are, something like that." This was Ben in a stricken voice. "I hope you're ready to say a little more to them, at least." He laughed briefly and bitterly. "I think they'll appoint a lawyer for you, you have to have somebody from here, state of Massachusetts. Just to make things complicated. And when you're back in Hyland we'll get you your real lawyer and they'll set bail." He looked hard at his son. "Bail. To get you out and home. But not tomorrow. I don't know how long that'll take. But—" There was a lot more to say but it didn't look as if Jacob was even listening. This was a powerful game; for the moment he was winning it.

Carolyn stood up, hoping Ben would follow without trying to overrule her. "Do some thinking overnight about what you plan to say to Wendell tomorrow, too. He's coming first thing in the morning. He'll be here for the hearing." She gave him a businesslike look. "Don't waste his time, Jacob."

That got a little flare out of him—was he affronted that she seemed to care more about Wendell's time than about his feelings? Good, then. Anger would be *something.*

Ben was coming, too. He had made the sign "I love you" with his fingers. He and the kids knew a little sign language; they enjoyed signaling to each other in infuriating silence and making her squirm. "You could learn if you wanted," they teased. "It's a free country, nobody's keeping you out." Now Ben waited an extra second to see if, caught off-guard, Jacob would reciprocate—anything to show a connection.

The guard had begun to come forward as soon as Carolyn pushed back her chair, and Jacob, apparently without a flicker of temptation to sign a message back to his father, I Love You, or even something noncommittal, had risen and turned to meet him. He looked as if he couldn't wait to leave them, to return to—God, was it an actual cell they had him in? Were there other men in there, too, sullen-looking boys like the one who was not looking at that young woman's face, criminals, drunk drivers, drug pushers? Whatever was back there, she thought, defeated, too discouraged even to be able to look at Ben, he seemed to prefer it to facing his parents.

* * *

Ben took her hand as they turned down the street in front of the jail. He made a noise against his teeth, a sort of sucking *tsk* as if he was getting ready to spit something out. He did that when he was perplexed; it was an intimate sound, his own wheels grinding.

Carolyn stopped at the corner and held up her hand as if she were only regathering her breath. She wasn't at all sure Ben would understand how she was embarrassed, just then, to be a parent. It was an absurdity, a millstone, the way Jacob's intransigence made them into heavies. She saw herself as thick-haunched, awkwardly dressed, trammeled by burdens—a classic out-of-it mother whose child looked past her ear, her conventional hairdo, her hopeful irrelevance, into the middle distance.

Sometimes, over the years, she had actually enjoyed the tension between the public role and her private sense of self, which must still somehow have been locked in unchanging girlhood and independence, traveling light.

Walking across the gym floor en route to the wooden risers from which she would watch the school band perform, Jacob in the rear with the bass drum, or cheering as the Memorial Day parade bore her Judith toward her, miniature, looming larger until she was full-sized and then away, dwindling again, to disappear down the street and around the corner, Judith staring dutifully front, no smile for her parents, her teeth gritted with the effort of supporting her half of the HYLAND ELEMENTARY SCHOOL flag, yellow on dark green satin. She would feel the flush of half-proud, half-embarrassed wonder, sometimes it would raise the hair on her neck, that she was here, that these children belonged to her, going through the funny, vulnerable paces of their own childhoods. Was it insane to feel so cut in half, so unwhole in the practice of motherhood? *You think too much,* her mother used to tell her. *Just do it* (whatever it was: polishing the silver, dressing for a party, learning to drive), *and stop saying, Isn't it funny to—* Her mentor in high-school biology had said the same thing: Carolyn, don't think about it, pith the damn frog and be done with it. He isn't *blaming* you, and you don't have to ask what he's feeling just now. Ditto her college mentor. By medical school she had it under control but that didn't mean she couldn't still be ambushed, when she wasn't expecting it, by astonishment at where she sometimes found herself: that she had money in her wallet, big bills, not the quarters she'd saved from her allowance! That she lay naked on a bed with this swarthy man lowering his head, groaning with pleasure, to her full-grown breasts! That she could look at a child and say, "This boy has a clear case of—" based on the confluence of three separate symptoms. "Now, here is what we will do." And get it right . . .

And now, who were these people (she was part of this awkward unit, hinged by a little distance her son did not bother to perceive) coercing this silent angry boy into speech. Trying to coerce, not even succeeding. She saw them reflected back in his eyes, generic parents—"God, my mom! My dad!"—she could hear it—and wanted to sit on the edge of the curb and weep ruin, weep defeat.

She walked beside Ben toward their car without a single word. Ben was the one who was weeping, he was so much better at that than she was, nearly silently, his face washed evenly with tears so thick she was afraid he would step off a curb into traffic, blinded. Why couldn't they come together in their grief and talk about it, she wondered. Why were they walking side by side alone?

She needed a cup of coffee to steady herself; they were, God knows, in no hurry. They drove until they began to recognize buildings, a modest comfort, as if, in the neighborhood of the jail, they had been lost in the woods. Around Putnam Square, Ben found a parking space. The musical chairs of commerce kept replacing shops and restaurants with fresh alternatives—this year's fashions in cuisine and apparel achieved their fifteen minutes of fortune, if not exactly fame. Every time they came down to Cambridge they discovered that an old hair salon had become an antiques shop or a hardware store had yielded to a bagel bakery. They headed toward something new called Café Olé. Their favorite jumbled army-navy store (where Carolyn remembered finding a canteen and a set of flares once for Jacob's Boy Scout trip) had become a wondrously green flower shop, a dash of tropical green that looked as if it should exude its steamy sweetness right out onto the frigid street. Carolyn idly took in the new arrangement. *Plus ça change,* she thought, slowing and turning for a moment to the window full of flowers for a resuscitating glimpse of softness and color; it was so thickly beaded with moisture she could barely make out shapes inside.

Had she not made that abortive turn from their relentless hike, she would not have seen CARTE BLANCHE next door. It was narrow and cluttered, with the dusty moted light of an old bookstore, not the new breed that features paperbacks at half price, but the real kind, whose air is thick with the lint of aging paper. In the window hung the famous funny etching of the Sutro Baths, all those men in their pastel one-piece bathing suits standing chatting on scaffolding above the blue-green pool. In the window, books were opened to old, formal pen-and-inks and etchings, and ranged before them in fan-shaped designs like full hands of playing cards lay dozens of postcards, picture side up. Carolyn slowed, bewildered, and looked again; Ben was moving on ahead as if he were alone.

VALENTINES. VICTORIANA. WORLD CAPITALS. U.S. CITIES.
PETS. FAMOUS FACES.
BLANK CARDS. QUAINT MESSAGES.
FOR COLLECTORS, FOR CORRESPONDENCE.
TIRED OF THE SAME OLD BOGEYS AND MONROES?
WE HAVE 18,000 CARDS. COLLECTION GROWING DAILY!!!!

She called out to Ben to stop. He turned to her from the entrance to Café Olé, annoyed. "Is this the time to go window shopping?"

She hurried to him and took his arm to drag him back. "You're so damn predictable," she said, not smiling, and realized her heart was beating as if it was trying to finish her off once and for all. "How about a picture of Al Jolson. Ginger Rogers? How about Burns and Allen? Clarence Darrow? Buenos Aires? Benny—" She made herself breathe slowly, deeply. "How about Santa Fe?"

When she called the Rapaports she was prepared to give a rudimentary explanation and invite themselves to stay in their friends' big Cambridge house for as long as it took. Discussing Jacob would be the necessary price of admission but, she thought, there'd be no solace in it.

The housekeeper answered, whose English was so bad that it hardly seemed worth leaving her name, let alone a message. She tried to get Sarah's and Michael's work numbers, without success. It may have been her anxiety of the moment, but she was furious with them for their fashionable mercies, the knee-jerk charity to the needy that drove them to a series of encounters (often comic, if you liked that sort of thing) with problematic employees. They seemed always to be forced to watch their yardmen confront New World machinery for the first time, turned loose upon many-horsepower engines at the edges of their lawn, or to try to explain the microwave (not to mention the house rules regarding child behavior) to women who had worn their babies in multicolored slings they'd woven themselves, who had cooked over pit fires in the mountains of Ecuador. They had almost sacrificed Dickie to one of them when he was tiny: she had left him alone in the bathtub and run to answer the urgent buzz of the dryer for fear it was getting ready to explode, and he had gone under for an alarming instant. Nice people all of them, and God knows desperate, but in sore need of acculturation. Today Carolyn had no patience with the shy, terrified woman who couldn't tell her how to reach the Rapaports at work, and she had no time to reason it out, chase them down department by department, Michael at Harvard, Sarah at Wellesley.

"We'll show up on their doorstep," she told Ben bitterly. "We'll be waifs in the night, with luggage, and hope they haven't promised the guest room to anybody else."

They arrived just as Sarah was raising her head from the trunk of her car, her arms laden with shopping bags. "Are you just passing by, you two?" she called to them cheerfully. Ben put his little overnight bag down beside a crusted remnant of snow and went to rescue her from her packages. "Don't I wish," he said, and Sarah, holding on to a paper bag from the posh little gourmet takeout around the corner as if he were trying to steal it from her, looked at him finally and said, with suitable alarm, "Benny, what's the matter?"

"Tell you inside," he mumbled. "Sarah, let me *help.*"

"I'm not used to gentlemen anymore." She laughed, and yielded it up. In spite of the cold, she was bareheaded. Her short dark hair was beginning to be striped with gray, as if someone had taken white ink to it with a ruler, but she still looked like a playful girl. "Just put your nose in there, isn't that divine?" Garlic rose up out of the depths of the bag as dizzying as Scotch on an empty stomach.

They followed her into the shade of late afternoon in a big old house, which contained the voices of children and television and the smell of cooking more or less accomplished by "Azula, who is a *wonderful* cook. A little narrow maybe"—Ben and Carolyn threw each other a look—"but she makes some stews you've never dreamed of."

"I don't doubt it," Carolyn said, smiling. The sight of the tulips in the center of the dining-room table, a still point, innocent, purple, cool, was an insult to their own disorder. The whole house, in fact, infuriated her today, though she had always loved it. Michael was a Japanese scholar, an expert on a dynasty in some century—tenth? twelfth? She could never remember; it was as real to him as—well, maybe, Carolyn thought, World War II—an event he had just missed participating in by a few unlucky years. Having failed to be there in the flesh, he had collected as many artifacts of the time as they could afford, and had blended them unsettlingly into the old Cambridge house with its heavy dark-wood cornices and long, old-fashioned, deep-silled windows. The walls were hung with brass gongs and delicately traced triptychs of mist and mountains; pastel paper screens lopped off corners, and a luscious dark blue-and-hyacinth silk kimono was stretched glistening like something wet on the dining-room wall, its arms outstretched. Today Carolyn eyed it with irritation—how strange to hang an empty garment that way, spread-eagled like an invisible Christ on an invisible cross.

At the last minute, faced with spending a few days with a pretty good but not intimate friend here in this peculiar one-down situation, Judith had asked to be left at Celeste's house in Hyland. "At least," she had said angrily, turning from their proffered kisses, "I don't have to explain anything."

Preparing to explain it to Sarah as she unpacked her groceries, made requests of her son, answered her daughter's phone call from school, where soccer practice was running late, started a salad, stirred Azula's mystery stew with a perplexed expression—"Where does she get the *ingredients?*" she asked the pot aloud—they understood Judith's reluctance.

"Maybe we should wait till Michael's home, so we don't have to go through things twice," Ben began. This was a very ascetic kitchen, pure white, always clean, its decorations beautifully controlled. In this room the children's best drawings were neatly framed, with an air of permanence that honored kindergarten art as an absolute. In it, Carolyn thought, Ben looked hot and sweaty. He looked like an emotional desperado. He looked like a Jew among the British.

"Won't have to go through *what* twice?" Sarah stopped stirring. "Are you sick? Are you here for tests? *What?*"

Their glances at each other crested, this time, together. However distant they might feel from moment to moment, the world kept flinging them back against each other, hard. "Jacob's in some trouble," Ben began carefully, and Carolyn closed her eyes so that she could hear his familiar welcome voice and not have to see the first wash of comprehension across her friend's face, or notice whether she took a step backward, literally or figuratively, before politeness and concern propelled her toward them to seize them in her arms, whispering empty comfort.

She was good, though. She commiserated without gush, and inquired without pushing. Sarah was a professional responder. She was a dean at Wellesley, a job she routinely defined as "full-time role model." Carolyn was always a little bemused by the idea of the contentlessness of such a position—she had imagined that role models actually had to do something of their own besides offer generic inspiration. (She had, for example, spoken before enough groups to know that she was, for young women, an irresistible representative of the Medical Profession.) But apparently that was an outmoded prerequisite.

Sarah, without asking if they wanted any, brought them glass mugs of steaming cider, spiked, and handed it around with a look that said, Anything you think you need is fully justified. But she was not sentimental about it. The only time she flinched was when Carolyn told her about their trip to see Jacob in the lockup. "Literally, not one word!" she repeated, ready for outrage. Obviously, it was easier to picture teenage recalcitrance than bloody crime. Who could blame her.

"Not one word." Carolyn put her mug down fast and covered her wet eyes with her hands and Sarah hurried to put her arms around her.

"He'll come around, Car. He's got to. He'll need you something awful. Later. You'll see."

Against her rough cotton shoulder Carolyn could cry, surprised and relieved, as if, after much useless agitation, a stopper had come unstuck. She supposed she was free to relax here because Sarah had listened to them without seeming too thoroughly appalled. The more astonished and effusive people were, the further they were from understanding. No one who gawked at them, however sympathetically, could remember they were still connected, in spite of it all, human. Maybe it was distance—maybe down here Sarah was just far enough away from Hyland so that the only community she cared about was Ben and Carolyn together. Or maybe it was her profession as neutral listener, full-time waterproof shoulder. Somehow, Ben might put it, she had the moves.

When Michael came home they watched him shuck his suit, his tie, his shirt, his shoes, and thrust his bare pink toes, showing out under his cuffs like little shrimp, into paper slippers. This was ritual; he looked oppressed before he had himself in place for his evening. Then he sat stupefied in the wake of their news.

But not for long. Michael was made for taking people and situations in hand; he organized and improved them, he saved people from the folly of their own arrangements and made connections. He traded up. "We've got to get you a better lawyer than the court-appointed nonentity they're going to give you."

"But they said it didn't matter for this," Ben protested. "This isn't his real lawyer, Mike, this is pure procedure, tomorrow. Is he Jacob Reiser, that's all they need to know. Is he the person named in the warrant. Does he waive an extradition hearing. A notary could do it, if they'd let him."

Michael looked at him shrewdly. "Never believe a petty official, I mean a time-server bureaucrat who talks to you in a public building, about anything that matters. I wouldn't trust them if I had a traffic ticket, and look what you're facing here. Ben. Please." He usually knew best, somehow, and at a certain point people tended to yield to his judgment. The cost was that they also tended to feel themselves a little careless in the light of his care, a little unreasonable under the soothing balm of his logic. Ben sometimes resented having things taken out of his hands, but Carolyn recognized, now, by the way she felt herself, how exhausted he was, far out beyond the reach of pride. How grateful. Michael furrowed his very handsome brow—his face was actually getting better-looking as time took the prettiness out of his features and replaced it with perfected concentration, seasoned earnest concern—and thought about what they needed.

They went up to bed fairly early. Depression, Sarah certainly understood, was fatiguing. She followed them up the long polished-wood stairway carrying a bowl of fruit, fetched them towels, and finally brought them the little television set that usually sat surrounded by clutter in Dickie's room. "School night," she said. "He surely doesn't need this." She put it on the painted oak dresser and plugged it in. "Watch Letterman or something stupid," she advised. "You could probably use a chicken that can jump through a hoop or an interview with Tiny Tim." Then, probably because she recognized that she was treating them like will-less children, she backed off. "Last thing, I promise. Do you need an alarm clock? Actually, the general mayhem around here in the morning would wake the dead."

Thank God, Carolyn thought, she didn't blush at that. People did, as if all of death were theirs to feel responsible for. "We're fine," she said. "Relax, Sarah. We'll be okay. Really." Sarah came forward to give her a brief kiss on the cheek. Oh, the helplessness of friends, it was another burden for which she felt guilty. "I'm sorry to have just—dumped this on your doorstep," she said. "You didn't need this."

"Ha!" Sarah smoothed the hair off Carolyn's forehead. "Well, I don't suppose you did either, did you? I tell my kids life is what happens when you've made other plans. But look, we're all caught in a net together, you know. And I never like to regret that. I just wish we could do more to help."

Carolyn shooed her out the door. "At least let me not feel responsible for having you fall asleep at work tomorrow."

"Oh, what a lovely idea. My head down on my desk, my shoes off, dozing. I'd thank you if you could arrange it."

Ben had turned on the television, on which some diaphanous fabric was sweeping across the faces of the MTV dancers, a sea of swirling pastel waves, like the movement of clouds blown by a high wind, the music rising and falling with them. It looked like a pageant some arty third-grade teacher might assemble in which dozens of hapless obedient children dragged across the stage flowing sheets their mothers had tie-dyed.

Carolyn let down her skirt, pulled off her sweater, and stood in a kind of bewilderment in the center of the room. Occasionally she found herself forgetting what was happening, what had brought about all this effort, this nimbus of pain that surrounded everything. Objectless depression, the sense, merely, that things were not as they ought to be—it could become its own habit. Sometimes she passed into a merciful blankness, like standing sleep.

When she returned, refocused, she saw Ben staring at her, naked, from the side of the bed. He hadn't looked at her that way since all this began; they had not made love once since the day Jacob disappeared. She had thought, many an evening, that it would be a mercy to lie comforted in each other's arms; it would be a promise of continuing life. But they were dry as sun-parched bones, and faintly disgusted at the thought of damp and dark and pleasurable touch. Swamp was what she saw when she thought of sex these days. Provocation. Danger. She saw that blond head defiled, however indirectly, by sex. Without a word of testimony, she was sure of it.

That may have been why there was something almost angry in Ben's eyes right now, something more like lust than the sweet invitation she was accustomed to. Lust always had a little blame in it, she thought; a little sense of helpless entrapment. She turned away embarrassed.

But the MTV was off and he was beside her, and the way he turned her to him did not promise gentleness. His hands were everywhere on her, every part of him awake and anxious. He didn't say a word.

She didn't resist. Confused, not sure whether this was a violation or his reading of a need of hers more secret than even she could acknowledge, she let him chafe her skin pink under his rough carpenter's hands and lay her back across the edge of the bed, where he pinned her desperately to the pink-and-green garlands on the sheets. He took no time with her, so that he had to rip his way in, and he howled when he came. He sounded like a man felled from behind by surprise. Far, far from herself she felt nothing but wonder at their animal selves. His. Hers, just now, was all too human, too conscious, and when she heard the distant laughter and elated voices of the television set on the other side of the wall, or maybe downstairs in the den—wherever it was, it testified to how sound traveled even in this well-built old house—she was mortified. Little Dickie lying in his bed, bereft of his television set, wondering if someone—someone else—was being murdered in the room next door. The rest of them not daring to look at each other, forced to listen.

She moved herself angrily to dislodge the weight of Ben's body from hers. She glared at him. "What a performance," she said.

"What?" Sweat stood everywhere on him, his head, his shoulders drenched.

"Well, they certainly know you're still alive and functioning."

Ben breathed in hard as if she'd slapped him. "I don't know why it would have occurred to them I'm not. Anyway, what the hell do I care what they think?"

"I don't know, you tell me. But since Michael makes everybody feel sort of like a helpless kid, I suppose you had to assert a little—I mean, that wasn't exactly private."

"Oh Jesus." He took her hand and held it, and hung his head down over his furred chest. "You think that, hunh?" He closed his eyes and swayed a little like a man at prayer. "Won't anything ever be the same again? Carolyn? This will sound sentimental, I know, but—we're here in this—this normal house. I see these two people who can get into bed together at the end of the day like ordinary people and enjoy each other, make love like—friends, whatever you want to call it—and then turn over and go to sleep and not have dreams with battered heads in them and see the straps of electric chairs and—last night, I didn't tell you, I saw Jacob's ashes on an altar." He looked away, squinting at the memory. "It was the bimah in the little synagogue where my father used to take me, and everybody was bending over this towel with—I know it was Jacob—the way we bent over him at his *bris.*" He spoke without looking at her. He kneaded her fingers hard. "Not everybody has to go to bed to that. So I looked at the two of them, those two fucking lucky people, and I thought, That's what they're going to do when they go to bed tonight, they're going to think about us, poor schmucks who are in such trouble, and they're going to reach out for each other and celebrate their good luck. So I reached for you. So. I'm sorry."

He lay down and turned his back to her. She sat with her arms around herself because it had gotten cold; they must have turned the thermostat down before they went to bed. She put her hand out and touched his back, but he hadn't cooled down yet. Under the field of wildflowers on the comforter he was burning like a man delirious with fever.

JUDITH

Celeste was in love with Jacob and she made it clear to Judith that "this thing" that had happened (*if,* in fact, it really had; she had her doubts) was hardly enough to change her mind about him. If anything, it seemed to make him a hero in her eyes. Her light blue gaze drifted a little when she talked about him, the way it did when she thought up dopey stories in which she bumped into rock stars in unlikely places, was instantly recognized as the hidden princess of their dreams, and packed off with them to an endless island honeymoon. Her stories ended with tearful scenes when they had to return to the world to attend to their careers—she was good at threatening, at having them choose her over ten-city tours. When the New Kids on the Block challenged the Cure for her love, it was like a glorious gang fight. Celeste, a little pudgy, her no-color hair soft and curly as a baby's, her bust fast developing too large a life of its own, dreamed up these tales like a fortune-teller gazing into a cloudy 26-inch full-color crystal ball.

If she wanted to go on with this love nonsense, Judith thought, that was her business. But when Celeste's parents dropped them on line at the movies in Howe, she didn't appreciate Celeste's stage whisper to some boys from school who were a few spaces ahead, "Hey, you know Judith, don't you? Her brother is *Jacob Reiser.*" Because Celeste was so stupidly sincere, this was meant as the highest recommendation, as if Judith was the real celebrity here. But one of the boys looked sick and made a gesture as if he was going to let go of his dinner, and after a rude once-over, a large, heavy, red-eared kid named Rex said evenly, "My dad says they ought to do something to them to make that sicko give himself up."

Judith was confused by all those theys and thems—who was supposed to be doing what to whom? And why would "that sicko" give himself up because of it?

Celeste only looked irritated. "Rex!" She stamped her sneaker as if she were flirting. Judith moved behind her and turned her head away. Celeste thought she was doing her a favor, acting natural (if you could call it that). After the movie, Judith was going to have a talk with her.

She couldn't pay attention to what was on the screen, she only heard the grate and clamor of overexcited voices and occasionally the self-congratulatory clangor of cars exploding into each other. Instead, she saw her brother, very small, being yanked around violently in handcuffs, she saw him surrounded by crowds who were taunting him like a cornered animal, poking him with sticks. She tried to think of other things, the way she did when she went to the dentist, but nothing came. She saw Brian, the boy she liked just then, but he wouldn't look at her. She picked through the clothes on the rack at the Open Trunk as if she were pulling them aside one by one, turning up their price tags. What she saw was Martha Taverner, who worked next door to the Open Trunk at

Jacey's, leaning over the ice-cream pails. Saw what everyone was thinking, Martha somewhere in bed or in the backseat of the Dodge with no clothes on, and Jacob looking like the brother who had shocked her years ago with his naked body, and he was approaching Martha shrieking with that jack in his hands. Everyone, the last few weeks, had been picturing her brother stark-naked—they were all working on the same humiliating story. Probably the details differed, but the story was the two of them doing what they weren't supposed to be doing and then fighting, somehow. Then she saw Martha lying in the ground with dirt on her eyes, turning to bones, her dress and her shoes all falling away, everything falling away, and Jacob still out there somewhere. Under *The Spirit of St. Louis*, against a pillar in Santa Fe. She refused to see him crying in her mother's arms right now, retching, facing what he'd done. She coughed once, twice, to keep herself from whimpering out loud.

Celeste was shoving popcorn at her. "No, it's okay," she said. "Thanks." She'd have choked. She wished she had no body, either to eat or dress or take to the bathroom. She knew she would never let a boy touch her. There were no Jewish nuns, but maybe she could begin a —it was called holy orders, wasn't it? You could do good for people but you wouldn't have to get married, and no one could try to get near you. That would be the closest thing to having no body. She didn't like having breasts, they hurt all the time, and although they weren't big enough to be cumbersome yet and might never be—it was strange not to know what you'd be shaped like forever—she watched Celeste trying to figure out how to lie on hers comfortably, and failing.

The boys she knew sat with their hammy legs wide apart all the time, hogging space. Or else they were skinny little nerds who looked like they were still in third grade. The big ones belched and sweated as if they were enjoying stomping across the world—why wouldn't they be, no one discouraged them from it. And it wasn't just the farm kids either, the ones who did chores before class and came in smelling of manure. It was all the boys, or mostly. (Not Brian.) The idea of one of them going inside her was too creepy even to think about, it was too totally disgusting. This had nothing to do with her brother, it was her independent thought and she had begun on it quite a while before this mess. Anyway, Jacob was at least somewhat delicate compared to most of them, he seemed light-boned and clear-faced next to boys like that Rex, the beefy and flatulent kind. Jacob didn't think farting was especially funny or that it proved his unique skill; when he stood in front of her he didn't block the light.

Whatever hostile brain waves Judith was sending out during the endless chaos of the movie, Rex didn't receive them. When she and Celeste had walked up to the top of the aisle, he was waiting there with his crew. "Hey, you want us to drive you home?" he asked neutrally, as if he didn't really care what answer they gave.

"My parents are picking us up," Celeste answered. "They went to eat and they're coming back to get us." She actually sounded regretful.

"We'll take you for pizza." Rex put on a hopeful look that made Judith queasy. "Tell them we'll bring you right home. We'll just stop at Midtown for some slices."

Celeste gave Judith a rhapsodic stare. This was why she had put blue shadow around her eyes. She seemed to be saying the New Kids on the Block are birds in the bush but here are some real boys in the hand. Or almost. Or planning to be. "We'll talk about it," Celeste offered. "Wait a minute." She pushed Judith against the wall under the glassed-in fire extinguisher. "Don't you want to?" Her question was a statement, nearly an order.

"*Celeste*, those boys are gross. That Rex looks like a—ham." She had wanted a more disgusting and original word, but you could never find one when you needed one. His hands seemed to be attached to his arms, the widest part, without any wrist in between. His neck was wrinkled like a fat old man's. He probably had a spare tire, white and freckled. He reminded her of lard.

"They're okay. What are you, scared?"

She was, a little. Old warnings bobbed to the surface of her memory, cautions against getting into cars, going with strangers, letting boys get close enough to touch. Well, they had gone off to Cambridge without her, so a lot they cared. Anyway, who said these characters would get to touch?

"Why should I be scared?" The fire extinguisher stood out for her like an object in a museum; she stared at it. FOR EMERGENCY USE ONLY. Her father could use it, make something funny out of that nozzle. Its wound hose was like some flat coiled living thing. "Lester, I really don't feel good. I'd rather go home."

Celeste shook her by the arm. "*Jude.* We'll just pick up some"—she used Rex's word as if it were her own—"slices."

Judith remembered that she was a guest, and not in a good position to argue. She followed listlessly. Out in front, Celeste dismissed her parents, who seemed to think it was cute that these boys, real ones, not daydreams, were showing an interest. Celeste's mother, she suspected, already feared for her daughter's social life: she was always on her to lose what she called her "chubbies," learn to dance, take an interest in makeup. Her own mother had a fit when she put on makeup. "There's time enough," she always said, implying there was time enough for a lot of things.

One of the boys had a car. What was a sixteen-year-old doing out with these eighth-grade turkeys? She suppressed the question. The back of the car, where she sat sullenly between three of them, squashed between down jackets, was thick with smoke and sweat. The driver, named Kenner or Canner or something close, was gunning his motor at the stoplight on the highway. Before it had finished turning, he took off so fast her insides rattled. Celeste was chattering away, but no one seemed to be listening; they conducted their own stop-start but non-stop-dumb conversation right over her. This is what it's going to be, Judith thought, hunching around her anger. Everyone she knew was going to arrange their lives to make room for creeps like these just because they wore pants. Her brother had once said, "Well, kid, you can't understand that until you really like someone—I mean *really* like someone. Then everything that looks stupid makes sense. You'll be surprised." He always had a girl around to like, either up close or from afar; he'd been having crushes as far back as she could remember.

Maybe she was a slow learner. Or there was something wrong with her. She knew that some girls like other girls *that way*—Dana Parry and a strange mutant who called herself C. Sharp, who looked like neither a girl nor a boy, were found once in the same gym shower and dragged off to a very public suspension. She couldn't figure out just what they did with each other; they didn't seem properly equipped to do much. And she'd heard about it, of course, on television. But she didn't like girls like that. She thought about Celeste trying to kiss her or hold her close in any way more intimate than their old chumminess that gave them a lot of reasons to hug, and it disgusted her. But boys, made for poking and preening, disgusted her even more. She didn't like anyone like that. If that made her abnormal, she could live with it.

They were driving past Derby Lake, slow going behind a long line of cautious drivers; much more rocking and gliding around those curves, S after S, and she'd be sick. But then they were turning up the hill road away from the lake that, farther on, ran past the grand estates. Very Old Money lived up here, mostly in the summer, and psychiatrists who must charge a lot to pay for their stables, and people who owned factories. A newspaper editor who had something called a villa had once bought one of her father's sculptures and put it out in his garden. When her dad went to visit it after about a year the man was very apologetic because it was covered solid with bird droppings.

She sat up and looked out anxiously. Rex was puffing ostentatiously on what he kept calling a reefer. "You want some?" He held it under her nose; it smelled like burning hay. Her brother did that sometimes—he once sprayed room freshener all over his clothes to get the smell out before their parents came home, so then he smelled like lilies of the valley. "Get that away from me!" Judith shook her head more to dislodge the heavy smell than to refuse it. She turned so hard she heard her neck snap like a popped joint. They were passing huge dark houses fast, rushing past tennis courts—she couldn't see them but she knew—and triple garages and shapely little artificial ponds. The moon was barely showing on the horizon, lazily making its appearance, and there wasn't much light on the snow in the outstretched fields.

She ought to have been complaining—this wasn't the way to Midtown Pizza, for sure. But she felt weighed down by loneliness and talking seemed a great effort. Her parents were hours away. Her brother was not with them, not yet. Her strange, harsh, delicate brother, part of every day of her life, and he might have killed someone. He might have wanted to hurt her, someone he really liked. And he might have to die for it. She had to go over this again and again, and every time it ended up with Martha's face, insofar as she remembered it, and little handfuls of dirt on her eyelids. Maybe if she let herself see that often enough she'd get bored with it and let it go. She wasn't bored yet. She wanted more than anything to open the door and roll out of the car into the snow. But the door was next to Celeste, who was giggling strangely. She had puffed on that stupid reefer, or she wouldn't be sounding so dumb and out of control. She was talking about whether Madonna looked better blond or brunette, as if anyone could care.

Judith closed her eyes and felt like something hurtling through space, a falling star, a comet getting faster and faster. Her body was very far away. She didn't ever want to stop. They spun out once, she could feel the wheels lock and the car do a huge slow helpless circle on the ice while everyone just said "Oooooh!" as if they were at an amusement park. "Do it again!" Rex shouted. "Go back and jam the brakes, man!"

The driver ignored him. Celeste sighed. Judith had just seen *Dr. Zhivago* on video and this was like flying across the steppes in a carriage, only warmer. (If she said that, Celeste would squeal, "Omar Sha*rif*, those eyes!") They hurried on a little farther and then she felt the car turning, this time on purpose, into a driveway that seemed to go on for a mile. When they lurched to a stop she opened her eyes, saw nothing but the bulk of a huge dark house, wished she could close them again and sleep. "Get out," Rex said to her roughly and pushed her arm with his knee. "You're so dumb you're up shit's creek and you don't even know it."

No one had a key to the house, but Canner went around to the back, and after a long wait in a hard wet cold that ate at her toes, he opened the front door for them from inside. "Enter my palace," he said grandly, with a sweep. "The master is at home."

The boys and Celeste walked respectfully around the ground floor of the house, their boots and sneakers dropping pools of dirty water on the carpets. Judith stood slumped near the door, not even curious. She had seen beautiful houses before; at the moment Chinese bowls and claw-footed sideboards did not interest her. What were they doing here? Were these gawking boys, who were fingering everything they could get their hands on, going to begin fingering her and Celeste next? One part of her was terrified and sickened at the thought; but the larger, stronger part was very far away, quite calmly watching herself and them, and the miniature cannon they were playing with, handing around as if they were trying to decide whether to buy it.

"You *live* here?" Celeste asked, her eyes goggling.

"Yeah," Rex said from across the long room. "We live here and I'm the King of England."

Whose house was this? She was not going to ask. She wasn't going to say a single word. Canner was staring wide-eyed as a small child into a grandfather clock as if it were a shop window. "When's the hour, dammit?" he asked. "I want to hear this mother say something."

They moved around the room impatiently, laying their hands on everything just because no one could tell them not to. Finally Rex said, "Okay, where do you think they keep the fuckin phone?"

Celeste stopped short. She was holding a huge glass apple too lightly in her hands. "What do you want the phone for? Are you calling in our order?"

This made all of them laugh, but Judith knew Celeste hadn't been kidding. One of the boys, a blond so fair he seemed to have no lashes—she thought of her white guinea pig—stood by so quietly she could see he didn't want to participate any more than she did. "Just how're you gonna do this?" he asked Rex anxiously. He was a follower, that was clear. A weak sister, Rex probably thought.

"Simple," Rex answered. "Cinch, okay? We just call and say she's been kidnapped, is all. We say 'Get the word out,' like, on the TV news and all, and tell him if he turns himself in they get her back. Otherwise, we keep her." He cast her a long look. "And who knows what we do to her." His jacket was open on a dusty blue T-shirt; all she could read of it said "yours too." He shrugged. "El cincho."

"And we don't want money. Remember that," Canner added earnestly. "We're just the vigilantes here." He was a tall skinny boy with short hair that stood up like the metal filings in a magnet game she used to have. You could take a little stick and organize piles of black dots under the screen; she used to pave heads with straight up-and-down hair. Judith knew she ought to be alarmed, but she seemed to be seeing them through the wrong end of a telescope. This was all so stupid she stayed very calm; she felt a vast condescending superiority before these self-important fools. They wanted to be criminals obviously, but they weren't very smart. And they seemed to be making up the script as they went along. If they didn't use their muscle on her, she could surely manage them. She wondered if she ought to tell them first that Jacob was in custody already or let them make their phone call and get themselves in trouble.

"Y'know," the blond boy was saying, wetting his lips nervously. Judith wondered if he was officially an albino. When he spoke, his whole face was as red as shredded flesh. It looked like it must hurt. "Y'know, you get the death penalty for kidnapping."

"Yeah, well, this is in the line of duty, isn't it? We're helping the cops with this thing, since they seem to be fucking up, as usual. It's not just, like, *kidnapping.* You know what I mean? It's for a *cause.*" Canner stared at the blond boy as if to frighten him into agreement.

"I don't know," he was saying. A bit of a whiner. She was on his side in this, but she could see how annoying he might be. "This is—"

Judith couldn't believe her own voice. "You can save your trouble, dummies. My brother's already in jail, if you want to know." She wanted to tell them they weren't up to a life of crime, but she decided they'd figure that out soon enough themselves.

"Where? How come we never heard?" They turned on her, all of them.

Rex refused to believe her. Canner said, "Why should we believe you? You just want to get out of here."

"Well, then," she said, smiling, "go ahead and call. I don't have anything to lose if they laugh at you down there. Go ahead." She ran her hand along the smooth back of a brocade chair. It was cool and solid. "Get yourself in trouble. Fine with me." All she wanted to do was go lie down somewhere, and feel the nothing she had discovered in the speeding car. She wondered distantly if this was the kind of nothing that led people to commit suicide. Were you trying to make that nothing permanent? Was that all it was?

Maybe, she thought, they would trash the house, since they had no other reason to be here now. It was disappointing, really. They didn't seem inclined to do anything. Whoever the house belonged to, they acted like invited guests, except that Rex pocketed the miniature cannon and the blond boy accidentally knocked an egg —it was one of those expensive permanent Easter eggs, crisscrossed with fabric and gold paint—off an end table and watched it shatter at his feet. His poor dead-white face colored again, an extraordinary throbbing red like food coloring rising up a paper towel, spreading evenly through it. She felt protective toward him because he could hide nothing, and with these creeps who were his friends that was like walking around naked.

But they didn't frighten her anymore. She went to Canner, who had the keys. "You better drive us home now," she said, planting herself right in front of him, limb for limb, praying she wouldn't blush or sound like she was begging. "Or you're going to get in a lot of trouble."

He didn't even argue, just rounded them up with a single sweep of his arm.

So they went home, morose and silent. She knew they wouldn't try anything else with her, she had made them look so pathetic. Celeste, who had never quite decided whether to be angry or scared or one of the girls, muttered to Judith her disappointment at missing out on those pizza slices. (God, Judith thought, she's ruined. She will *never* be thin.) Celeste thanked them when they stopped to let the two of them out at the foot of her driveway, the motor racing, Canner's foot twitching heavily on the gas even while they idled. Judith said nothing. She felt vaguely triumphant—the only words she had uttered had been the news of her brother's capture, her opinion of the stupidity of their little adventure, and the order to take them home. She walked away from the car as fast as she could.

She was ready to erase the failed gangsters from her mind, but this was going to put a crimp in her friendship with Celeste, there was no ignoring it. Celeste wanted to be one of those girls who—she had heard her mother use the phrase and she liked it—would lie down in front of a regiment. That was such a funny, terrible thing to imagine. She saw Celeste on her back in a dusty field, all flesh like a slug without its shell, her quivery thighs and new doughy breasts in the harsh light, and a huge crowd of boys in khaki, a whole platoon with the short hair of new recruits, comes marching right across her, carrying the flag. They don't even stop to do her harm.

The hard part, Judith thought when they had gone to bed in silence, pretending to be quiet because of the sleeping household, was that she knew she wouldn't even tell her parents what had happened. Or hadn't. What might have. They were having enough trouble with what really had, and worse yet, with what was going to. Anyway, she thought, except for the first minute or two, she hadn't even been frightened. But it was strange. (The pillow was so soft under her head she felt as if she were sinking backward into the bed. It reminded her she wasn't home.) Crime used to be a television word, or something you met in games or in the movies. You watched murderers and raspy-voiced detectives instead of the fairies she remembered from kids' books. Cars flying through space took the place of flying carpets and witches on broomsticks—fantasy land! But that wasn't real crime . . . Now it was as if one awful act led to another, or brought it on, even if this stupid prank wasn't anything but boys pretending. There was something contagious about it, and she knew it wouldn't end until her brother had been hurt, and badly. (Or someone else, if they were lucky. She knocked on the wood beside the bed, she always did that, just in case, when she was wishing. You never know.) But someone would pay: A crime for a crime.

She had sometimes wanted to be an only child, like Celeste.

She was altogether alone, and even when they all came home, she knew, bringing him or not bringing him, it didn't matter, she would be more alone still.

Why were they all hooked together so that no one could get free? Why couldn't you just say, "I don't know anything about that, don't look at me"?

He was a special boy. A high-quality, sensitive, handsome, complicated boy. She thought of sloppy Rex and Canner, shifty and unhealthy-looking, and that blond guinea pig, and saw beside them the slender, fine-featured, well-shaped, smart-mouthed Jacob she loved. She had to jam her knuckles in her mouth to keep from crying out, cursing him.

BEN

CATS, I THOUGHT—THERE WAS ALL TOO MUCH TIME FOR THOUGHT—have it best: pure pleasure, pure distress. No rumination, no regrets. Snappy the cat was my idol of the moment. When she rolls over on her back, the way horses do, only far more gracefully, a little wave peaking and curling over itself, she is the most joyful thing alive. When I do something nasty to her, yank her head back to jam a pill between those sharp teeth or grab an illegal chicken wing out of her mouth and cuff her across her narrow little behind for being a thief, she registers no memory of it, and keeps none.

By which I mean, I was beginning to have serious doubts about my part in all this, and I couldn't afford to.

Carolyn told me how angry Jacob had been about the prom, when I'd tried to get him to recognize unnecessary self-indulgence, if only he'd let himself look at it honestly.

Her take on it was not that I was wrong to be appalled—limos, drinking-and-driving, the whole bit that leaves kids maimed, dead, and at the very least impoverished—but that I ought somehow to have taught him better by now, other ways: "Coming down hard on him now—decent end, indecent means, not only ineffective but, you know, counterproductive." And more. "It never worked, your rage with him. Some kids can take it, Jacob never could. He'd fix on the anger, not on the cause of it. Just shut down. And you'd go on."

"Why didn't he learn from me what matters, then? What's worth that kind of money, and that reckless endangerment? Why hasn't he had the pride to want to buy his own gas all this time, his clothes, his records? Why did he have to make me into a shrieking capitalist heavy?"

"*Make* you?"

"Make me, yes. Who are the fathers whose sons grow up understanding their family's values, anyway?" He said I was worse than the dads who wore plaid pants and played golf and went to Rotary meetings. He hated the way that was at odds with the figures I put out in the garden to scare the marauders, the Junk Patrol that clattered like no wind chimes you ever heard, to keep the birds and raccoons away. My tin men with their noisy armor flapping. "What does one thing have to do with the other?" I'd ask him. "I just want you to pay your own way. Nobody paid mine."

"Think about that," he'd say. We went through this a couple of dozen times over the years, livid and sputtering, until he stopped responding and just stood like one of my statues and tuned it out. "Think about it, you're not hang-loose. That's just a pose. You're Grandpa all over again. You just think you're liberated. Hip. Funky. Under the jazz and the wet paint and the Do Your Own Thing, you're a goddamn patriarch."

The curse word of the age. The conversation stopper. Am I? Was I? I wanted them to grow up independent.

They're supposed to want to be independent. Why should my son be crippled by privilege? Even modest middle-class privilege sucks the juices, blunts the will—I don't want him taking anything for granted because we made it too easy. So we'd talk about hypocrisy. "How about you?" I'd ask him. "How about wanting everything done for you, paid for, but you get to call all the shots." At which point Carolyn would point out from the sidelines that he's still a child, Ben, how can we not support him, he's in high school. "But he wants the privileges of an adult," I'd insist, and have to feel petulant when I knew I wasn't the hypocrite here. It was embarrassing to be caught in the claws of such an old conflict. But I wanted him strong; I wanted his own muscle to hold him up. Does that make me a reactionary?

I asked Tony Berger if he thought I was a throwback. He laughed and said, "Oh, Ben, you know real patriarchs don't bake quiche."

I told him I was serious. I think of myself as nurturant, loving. I thought I was giving them encouragement, structure, and a minimum of rules, so they won't grow up soft. "It's a narcissistic generation out there, I don't want one of those I-me mall-babies."

"I know, I teach plenty of them," Tony said. "Even up here. Designer brains. But you've got a style of excess," he told me, "that's the thing. A heavy hand. Sometimes he doesn't know where the power's coming from, it's like a hard wind blowing. You know that."

I didn't. I knew they sometimes hated it, but I didn't think they hated me.

"I love you anyway, pal, and you're no worse than the rest of us inconsistent bastards, but . . ." *But* was the last word he used.

I took to my bed that day. I had no breath, I felt like I'd fallen. "Winded," we called it when I was a kid and seemed to spend half my time getting tripped. Tripping myself. I lay in bed under the china-blue quilt and saw one scene after another in deadening three-in-the-morning kitchen light. I studied my son's face, the way it closed up on me, shuttered, shaded, blinded, all my hopes and intentions misheard. Mis-said? I feel like my last word to the world, like Tony's to me, will only be confusion: *But.*

Every time we had to do something new and intolerable I said to myself, "They had to shop for a coffin." "They had to tell her grandparents." This was a good corrective for self-pity. I had to resort to that, the whole set of those, when we went looking for the bail we were going to need.

Jacob has a trust fund, modest, from his grandparents. Carolyn's side, obviously. But it's very hard to get to it, it's one of those things you don't just call up on your instant-teller bank card. A second mortgage on the house, the same thing. Who has $100,000, $200,000 lying around? And who, even if he's lucky enough to get it within sight, can produce it in cash?

Who's ever paid much attention to bail? I know the signs for bondsmen sprout like dandelions on the streets around every big city courthouse, the way monument carvers bunch up on the road to the cemetery. Makes sense. But that's where my familiarity ends. And so, I suspect, does yours. Even if we called her parents, they wouldn't have it at home in a sock. I guess they'd call their broker and tell him to sell something. A couple of things.

"What do they expect of us, Wendell?" I asked him this angrily.

"Bailwise, you mean?"

"Bailwise." Jesus.

"It's hard to answer that, buddy," Wendell had said. "Depending on the evidence, the prosecution might, probably would, allege that it was a capital crime, in which case we could just about kiss bail goodbye. Capital crimes involve robberies, rape. Kidnapping. Killing a cop." It was hard to say those words to us, I think, but he did, though he swaddled them as much as he could. "I wouldn't be surprised if they thought kidnapping was a distinct possibility here. It wouldn't be unexpected."

Nothing is real, I told myself. And nothing lasts.

"And if by some miracle," Carolyn began, "it's not a capital crime? If it's just—what's the opposite?—just a garden-variety crime? What? Vanilla?"

"Not so fast there. Before the bond, first there's the matter of his status." By which he meant, were we going to opt to have him tried as a juvenile (which he was) or an adult (which, if we chose wrong, he just might conceivably not ever get to be)? "Small chance, small chance," Wendell told us there in the Rapaports' gorgeous living room. "None really. They would never execute. *No* way. Not this boy."

The word was a black hole: our lives, both, all of them, collapsed inward, imploded, disappeared at the sound of it. Somehow I hadn't expected him to say it. *Execute?* Taste would prohibit saying it, or concern for our feelings. It was like the worst diagnosis Carolyn could make of a patient's chances, and I knew she'd only deliver it to parents she judged could deal with it. Why did Wendell think we could deal so casually with *execute?* He didn't care, was the truth, of course; we had to deal with it whether we could or not. As, eventually, did the parents of dying children. I was embarrassed at my own naïveté. I had not passed yet into some stage, I saw, in which I accepted that the wheels of this court, this system, were going to roll on whatever we understood, Carolyn and me, or liked to pretend we could control.

I recovered first. "Why do you say no way?" *I,* at least, didn't have to say the word.

"First off, you're in New Hampshire, Ben. This isn't Texas, one of those wild and crazy Southern states that love to pull the lever. Or injection, actually, it's not electric anymore."

"Thanks," we both said. A comforting distinction.

"And class. Let's be honest here. Look at him." By which he meant, I suppose, too clean, too white, too middle class, too—"All the things you are," Wendell said, a song, a bloody love song, I thought without gratitude. You are the precious touch of springtime. What kind of correlations could you make, then—no one was executed in the last calendar year whose parents have butcher-block kitchen counters? Who eat sun-dried tomatoes and fresh pasta in cream sauce? Who listen to Bach on good equipment? I'd always understood that, of course; everyone understood it.

Carolyn said, "That's terrible, you know."

"Yeah, it is. Sure it is." He shouldn't comb his hair down like that, like an aging Beatle or a Down syndrome boy with too high a forehead. I wished I could tell him. He looked saddened. "It *is* terrible for the folks at the other end, and it's probably a good argument against the death penalty, but this isn't the time to waste any energy bleeding for them, to be perfectly frank. You've got enough to deal with."

"All the things we are, Car," I said to her. "If only we could bottle it and sell it. Buy the right wines and keep your kids safe from execution! Assure your little felons their future as short-termers!" We joined hands. I raised her knuckles to my lips and kissed them and closed my eyes.

Hey, Mom and Dad, how's tricks on Hilton Head? You got your fifteen minutes of winter yet? That pretty, pretty land. Anyone flushed a toilet down there lately? Anyone dropped a candy-bar wrapper on the grass and gone to jail for it?

Funny I should mention jail. Let's see, that reminds me.

Remember your grandson, Jacob? Our oldest, right, and older than you know. Well, see—I say—what if—

How much do you love him? Let me ask you that, first off. Or us, Carolyn and me, how much do you love us, that's what it comes down to if you strip it clean. How thick is blood compared to water? And another generation down, is it still pretty viscous, do you think? Holding firm, the color recognizable, your own?

Because we had a nice boy here, he—

"Good God," she said to me. "You're not in any condition to call my parents. Ben, for pity's sake." She took the telephone gently from my hand. We were in the still, indirectly lit reaches of the Rapaports' kitchen, where the white telephone hung surrounded by an assortment of note-taking paraphernalia that was no help to Azula. All the pads had departmental insignias on them; doodling, you had your choice of Wellesley or Harvard. Michael and Sarah were at work. Azula was in charge, in her fashion; she had cleared the counters of breakfast plates and crumbs, stacked the dishwasher, tidied the morning newspapers behind which the family had taken its coffee and orange juice. "This is not a sociable time for us," Sarah told us apologetically, knowing how relieved we'd all be.

We had managed, so far, to tell very little to Carolyn's parents. This had entailed wholesale lying of a kind she'd never before indulged in, and though she hardly confided everything in them—when had she stopped? she asked me as if I knew. Twelve? Sixteen? It was actually something she ought to think about, she said, and try to remember. (I never did confide in mine, so I had no yardstick to extend to her.) It was a strain, the magnitude of oversight her ordinary tone had represented for three weeks now. They were her parents and they didn't need to know; she hadn't wanted to panic them. Jacob has run away, she'd told them. We don't know where he is, but we've heard from him by postcard, we know he's okay . . . No lies there, right? Only omissions necessary for everyone's peace of mind.

But being able to get away with it, not being accountable—I could see how it was another loss for her. Meanwhile, she prayed no national newspaper would seize on the case, or one of those Murder-of-the-Week television programs. The chances that they were reading the back pages of *The New York Times* these days were slim. (The Boston papers were wild with it: MURDER SUSPECT NETTED IN CAMBRIDGE DRUG BUST. True, they admitted he was not implicated in the drug bust; true, he wasn't exactly a slavering butcher with a knife in his hand. But headline writers don't write for the reassurance of grandparents.) We said, Well, so many boys light out for the territories. You know. So many come home. Protecting them, we felt like we were protecting our children. Mostly Bea and Ira seemed to be playing bridge and tending their perennials these days. They were taking a class in Bulbs and Tubers and another called New Varieties of Religious Experience, taught by a Presbyterian who played the guitar. I called it their WASP Afterlife.

The issue was a lot simpler for me because my mother, in the Hebrew Home for the Aged, had given no signs of understanding a human sentence, simple or complex, for many years. She had become for me—I've finally killed the pain and learned to allow myself to think it—a geological phenomenon whose stunned state reminded me more of a natural outcropping or a calcified extrusion, a barnacle perhaps, than of the woman I had, with whatever misgivings, loved. She was a set of memories I cherished, but the woman I visited, poor hairless toothless wordless thing, had no relation to those. I had wished I could go to my father's grave and talk to him there, ask for advice, emotional only, to put to use the late-dawning respect and sympathy I had developed in his last years. But that was a luxury: before I could commune about ultimate responses I had to—the phrase had not stopped making me cringe—find bail, fast, an impossible amount of it.

There are all kinds of impenetrable bond arrangements out there that made me sick to my stomach to try to understand—Carolyn does the taxes. Ten percent of $100,000 (not that we had it). I thought about the future and I quailed. You don't use one of those guys out on the street, I had learned, if you're not desperate. If you're not and you do, they'll introduce you to the desperation you've been missing. You could give them ten, twenty thousand just for the loan of their money. You could worry, too, about getting your legs broken if your boy skipped to St. Louis again, or Santa Fe. It seemed like a bad deal.

"I'll do it, Benny. Let me. I can handle them." She was all pale and beige today, head to foot, as if she were in a state of semi-erasure.

I didn't argue. I went into the dining room, where I could half hear her half of the conversation in the silent house, and sat down. The empty kimono hung on the wall, flat as a cast-off skin. Random phrases broke over me: "could be a person but . . . the evidence will . . . and the lawyer . . . not reason to . . . all right." Her voice was horribly steady, unrecognizably controlled. She was holding on for all of us. Jacob would have been proud.

She is the Good Daughter, that's the thing. She has a younger sister, Nina, who had put them through so much that Carolyn, not inclined to be difficult in the first place, had been cast, irrevocably, as the one who does no wrong, and they expected her to live up to it. And she was giving up the title. One child, I've long since realized, has to be the one to give pain, the other to spare it, soothe, smooth it over, never offend. Household economy; the Grimm Brothers understood it. (So now Judith could be stuck with that—it was probably bound to be her lot anyhow, if that was any consolation.)

To complicate matters, they were not actually her parents. I mean that only biologically. Water's been turned to blood there, though, in a kind of alchemy they've worked hard at. They were given the gift of her at a week and a half, after they had despaired of having their own natural child; and in a little more than a year, to the accompaniment of the laughter of the gods, Bea was pregnant with Nina. (They say that's not as common, statistically, as it seems to be. Maybe it's just such a stunning coincidence that every instance you hear about seems to count double?)

Somehow they never seemed defensive about the adoption, so that Carolyn, during the phase in which she maundered around dreaming of her "real" (thus superior) parents, never had to feel guilty or secretive. And the curiosity passed—it had been a "private" adoption; she was told by the doctor, who was a friend of Bea and Ira's, who "took care of it," that her parents were young, healthy, he a pharmacy student, she a nurse—how wonderful, she thought when she decided to become a doctor: fulfilling the family pattern, maybe even its genetic heritage!

But her own parents were good enough for her. In the end, the sufficiency of their affection—its daily sufficiency—seemed to satisfy her more than it did Nina, who, I've always been convinced, never forgave the interloper—not even related by blood!—for getting there first. Getting where? Into her parents' concentration, their affections? Surely they loved Nina at least as well. If loving-kindness is a mystery, I swear so is unassuageable anger, the refusal to be happy.

Nina's a marvelous woman, by the way, from certain angles, the easy ones: she's the kids' favorite, for all the reasons she's hard for us to get along with—she's unpredictable (unreliable), openhanded (careless), she sends them crazy gifts from wherever she lights down in her quest for "authenticity"—they have a set of shrunken heads, a box of mother-of-pearl dominoes, a gold-plated lute—none of which she can afford, though she doesn't scruple to ask her parents for money. She never shows the teeth of her anger and disappointment to the children, the sense that she's been fundamentally cheated and the world owes her reparations. But Carolyn gets silence and defensive accusations. I tell her she's lazy, I tell her she's never worked as hard as Carolyn works in a single day—you can imagine how popular I am with her—and she tells me I'm prejudiced. Well, of course I am; it's Carolyn I love. She makes me feel like a Republican bridge player, all self-righteous condemnation, rigid goal-setting. (For that, I've always wanted to say, the pure thing, you should meet my brother, Stuie. Who's actually a terrific, generous, warmhearted guy in his plodding way—he's a CPA, successful enough for a place with a cathedral ceiling and a pool, "a small one, a junior," he told me in an attempt, I thought, and I found it poignant, not to touch off envy in his older brother. His way isn't mine, but we manage to recognize the boundaries and keep away from the dangerous spots. Also he lives in San Jose, just far enough so that it doesn't matter that much what kind of music he plays, what kind of house I live in. Mostly we have to come to terms over our mother; mostly there isn't much left to come to terms with. I haven't told him about Jacob because we don't speak more than maybe four times a year and it would be strange if I called up to inform him. Funny, that. It would matter to him, and yet to announce it out of the sheer blue spaces of our distance would seem almost—I don't know, almost a form of boasting: Look what I'm into now, my ordinary brother. High crimes and misdemeanors. Not even junior-sized.)

I loved Carolyn's parents because they were steady and unflappable. My mother was wildly superstitious, everything she did and believed seemed tinged with the smell of the Old Country: she called my in-laws Yankees. That amused the hell out of them, because, after all, they were only one generation more "American." My father's considerable wisdom was all about the arduousness of being a Jew and an immigrant—the difficulty of a decency prompted by faith. He had been schooled in religious matters in Kiev, but here he was in "clucks and suits," a cutter with a sharp eye and a sharp knife who only came to life on the Sabbath. Whereas Ira Miller, Carolyn's father (a Dad, where Herschl Reiser was a Papa), was a perfume and cologne importer, more successful than such things ought to make you, value for value. He gave away a handsome bit of it to charity but, though he disdained ostentation, he also gave his daughters lovely wardrobes and expensive educations.

And Bea. She had champagne hair when I first met her and it has stayed exactly as it was, not a single bubble of a curl gone flat in all these years. She's a lot sadder than she was years ago, what with all Nina's miseries, the abuse of substances her parents had never even heard of, but Bea is still openhearted to us, and perfect to the children. Possibly she smiles too much, like the President's wife, and attempts to gloss over the bad patches unconvincingly, but that's always seemed more brave to me than blind. The only thing wrong with the two of them, we'd decided, is that they had gratefully retired to this stage set by the sea, where they were indisputably happy: they'd bought the illusion, there, of the perfectable landscape that is all wealthy, white, and golf-addicted. It is not *political,* Ira has said. The right to be safe and comfortable is nobody's business but our own. Ah, well. Carolyn told me I shouldn't be so damn superior about it—happy parents, she says, are nothing to look in the mouth—and of course she's right.

But now I found myself wondering, pressing the heels of my hands to my eyes that were as exhausted as if I'd been driving cross-country in bad light. Now whom would they blame for this little bombshell? I the deviant one, the immigrant's boy, the one with the bristly beard who stole their blond daughter? Or some kind of wayward gene in Carolyn's background that no one had had to account for, or ever could? Would they turn on me and admit to suspicions they've kept on the leash all these years, I the nonprofit one, the tumultuous, argumentative one with the New York accent and the leftist politics who seemed to enjoy making them squirm over every choice they made? Would they exempt their Golden Girl, their Good Witch of the East, from responsibility?

Oh stop, I thought. Oh stop, *oh stop.* How do I manage to intrude myself on everything? She was talking to her parents who were loving if genteel, forgiving if abused. Why the hell did I have to think about their regard of *me?* And why did I have to suspect it? I pictured them in their long, low sunny house in its clump of carefully spared trees on the old South Carolina plantation that had become a haven for retired couples of Unimpeachable Taste and Unimaginable Means.

They were trying to understand what their daughter was telling them about why she needed to hand over an extraordinary sum just to promise that Jacob would not skip out of our line of vision again. Their grandson had not, last time they'd seen him, had a bizarre hairdo in a primary color, he did not cut school or, as far as they knew (but that was fast disappearing as a criterion), deal drugs like others' unwise, unlucky grandsons. (Their neighbors the Pursleys had a boy, once their best A-1 adorable grandson, in jail for crack, using it or selling it they could never remember, but it probably didn't make much difference. For this the grandparents now had to suffer the word *poor* before their names as reliably as a prefix.)

My in-laws were on both extensions of the phone, separated from each other by many Oriental hall runners. Carolyn's father would be stock-still in the mauve Queen Anne chair in the corner of the living room near the long windows. Three kinds of birds would be playing hopscotch on the other side of the glass where he dutifully put out seed and her mother wondered if he was spoiling them. He would call out to his wife, if not yet, then soon, "Bea, my nitro, can you bring me my nitro, please? I'm afraid to go get it myself."

Carolyn, her cheeks bright pink as if she'd been hit, sweat at her hairline, would be clutching and unclutching the fist that wasn't holding the phone, pleading silently, "Daddy, don't die, don't die of this!" Out loud she said in a calm, pinched voice, "Listen, Ben has won a grant, yes, isn't that nice? From the government, yes, for his work." She didn't say *finally*. "But we don't get that money for a few months, that's the problem, or we wouldn't have to—yes, well, I hate to have to ask, since we *will* have it, or some of it, I mean, it's just inconveniently timed." Also, inconveniently, a good deal less than this was going to cost us. Why hadn't Jacob thought of that, I wondered. Why couldn't he have waited like a thoughtful boy until my check came from Uncle Sam—God, my mind in its desperation was a disgusting thing! It was as if it housed a worm that crawled away from me into the most bizarre places. I came in and put my hands on Carolyn's shoulders; surprised, she jumped under my touch. Oh Christ, Ira, I thought, laying my cheek on her hair, which smelled vaguely of raspberries, don't you die, too. I could hear her mother's tiny faraway voice pleading with her that it not be true, it not be true. *They make mistakes, darling,* she was insisting. *The police are notorious for needing suspects! Except that he—seems to have run off—do you have any reason to think he* did *this thing?*

Azula came down the stairs carrying a full yellow plastic basket of dirty wash. She stopped, bowed a little, like an Oriental woman, with her eyes fixed on us as she had probably been instructed. She hefted the basket to her hip and headed for the basement stairs. "Chov a nice day!" she said enthusiastically, with a terrific Hebrew guttural, showing her very white teeth. She had probably been practicing as she approached, saying it over and over until it sounded like a single word. Her glossy black hair hung in braids over her shoulders, straight and slender as asparagus spears.

We stared at her. Carolyn put her hand over the receiver as if she were going to say something, then smiled earnestly, nodding.

"You too," I said, showing my teeth back. "Have a good one."

Wendell rang the bell and through the narrow margins of glass beside the door I could see how patiently he stood on the front step waiting to be admitted. Probably, I thought, your best lawyer would be pacing around out there all bound-up energy, puma-like. We had wondered if we were going to get a small-town defense out of him. Was Michael right, should we go for the best available heavyweight? He had offered to buy us one. We had, for the moment at least, declined. Because, of course, Wendell was not going to be our defender, he didn't want to take on a case as heavy as this, nor (though he didn't say so) would he so alienate his neighbors. Bad enough he was advising us now. He might help out, if it came to that, but even he insisted we needed a defense from outside, an experienced hardball player. Has anyone noticed what it costs—disgusting how money kept intruding—$100,000 maybe, right out in front, probably double, depending—to be defended? Has anyone noticed that it's a specialty that takes manic devotion, specific experience, and a clear desk, and lawyers like Wendell Bye have one out of three if we're lucky?

No, I had never noticed. I had not had occasion to interest myself in the subject. There's a state team, a homicide defense squad or something, he had told us reassuringly. It sounded like a club the neighborhood kids had made up. "If you can't go out and hire yourself a big name, they pretty much give you somebody who only does this. It's like a defense pool, it's service. Vastly underpaid. It keeps the game at least a little even." He smiled wanly.

"Underpaid."

"Well, compared to the Louis Nizers and the Melvin Bellis. A *little.*"

Even when he wasn't working, Wendell wore a tie, not the offhand kitschy kind I've got, flamingos or heavenly babies in raucous colors, but something striped and collegiate. (Stephanie, I realized, though I'd never thought about it before, wore stockings, too, on every occasion but a picnic.) Their rectitude was bizarre and, I thought, terrifying.

He came in gravely and looked around. "These folks have a little something stashed away, I guess," he ventured.

That wouldn't have been the first thing I'd have noticed. He stood staring at the high-colored warriors' shields over the mantel; he seemed to be considering a witticism but apparently thought better of it. Just as well; if it didn't have to do with the Seven Samurai, I didn't want to hear it.

Carolyn came in from the kitchen and gave him a desultory peck on the cheek. "You've seen him?"

Wendell Bye tends to have the look of a man whose glasses have fogged up suddenly. He stood now blinking very solemnly behind them. "I've seen him, yes." He sat down on one of the white end chairs and balanced his attaché case on his knees. But when it was open he stared into it for a minute and then, as if he didn't much like what he saw in there, slowly closed it again. "You could say I've seen him, but I haven't heard him." He laughed. "Hey, that's the definition of a perfect child, isn't it?"

Oh Christ. I was on my feet shouting. Carolyn tried to quiet me by raising her hands and patting the air. "Some perfect child! We warned him, Wendell, we told him you were coming and he'd better not waste your time."

"I'm sorry," Carolyn said to him quietly. "I really am, Wendell. Did he just—sit there?"

Wendell sighed. "He didn't look angry. You know what he's like. We get exercised and he manages to stay as calm and detached as the Buddha."

I couldn't stop walking around the room, I suppose it was the energy I'd have used to wallop Jacob if he'd tried a performance like that in my presence. (Nonsense, I knew I hadn't been able to do anything with him when we visited. But that was in public. That was a jail, for God's sake.) "Does he really think he can keep up this way?" I wanted to know. "If he ignores us, we'll just go away? Wendell, does he know what he's up against, do you think? That this isn't a little game?"

Wendell shrugged. "I'm no psychologist, Ben. I don't know what he thinks he's doing. I told him, I think pretty accurately, what our alternatives are." He took his glasses off and rubbed the little red ditches on the sides of his nose; he looked as relieved as someone who'd removed his shoes. "But I can't tell you what he heard because he didn't ask me anything, he didn't make me repeat anything or clarify it or any of the kind of things people do a lot of when they're with lawyers. *You* know."

When it came to the need for clarification, yes, I sure as hell did know.

"I tried to reassure him that he might have plenty to say in his own defense, that depending on what he has to tell, there might possibly be no case at all." He looked at me with a hopeless grin. "If that impressed him, he wasn't saying."

I flared at him. "Is that true? What do you mean?"

Wendell looked at me with the opposite of compassion. I think he knew, or at least suspected, that, though I liked him well enough, I was not particularly impressed with his intelligence; he felt vaguely patronized, and that was true enough, I guess. Because the law uses words, I've always made the haphazard and quite incorrect assumption that the people who practice it value literacy, and might even go so far as to read a little. Not so. Wendell and Stephanie have the largest TV screen I've seen in a private house, and they have a hot tub, a very good car and a fully equipped van. But if there are any books in their house they're catalogues of creature comforts just waiting to be purchased. I think they've actually invested in a series of classics with gold-tooled covers, but those are never intended for reading, after all. They're to fill the random shelf or two with something tasteful.

When he talks about law, though, he loves to use phrases like "terms of art" which basically means "Do me a favor and lay off, Ben. This is my bailiwick." As someone who has her own private vocabulary, Carolyn is sympathetic. Apparently she recognizes a fellow craftsman. I was being cruel, as far as she was concerned; this was a bit of unbecoming contemptuousness, the snobbery of an artist just as narrowly invested in his own jargon but who has to maintain the myth of his absolute openness. She insisted that Wendell loved his profession, and those moments of swelling pride that I found toad-like and defensive she was pleased to understand. He had a job to do and he did it well. What he read or didn't read afterhours was his own business: Do you ask your doctor what he reads? I couldn't argue. And why he was our friend was something I could worry about another time.

"Listen, Ben," he said slowly and clearly. Whatever was going to happen, he must have felt good about this role reversal, anyway. "I told Jacob they've got a couple of eyewitnesses, you know that, and I suppose they do. But it's not clear exactly what they saw, and at worst that's circumstantial, anyway. They aren't saying—at least they haven't said—they've got somebody who saw the murder. Or saw him dumping—no, pardon me, let me rephrase that—saw the body being dumped. The other forensic stuff—we'll have to see. They might have the softest case in the world, for all we know."

He seemed to be pleading with me; these must have been the words he used with my son that had got him nowhere. His earnestness was endearing, and it would go over well in a courtroom, where he looked like everyone's good scout. But I understood, watching and listening to him, in his blue rep tie with the little red and gold crowns on it, and his trustworthy square shoulder pads vaguely reminiscent of highschool football gear, his reasonable voice, how Jacob saw only an assistant principal or one of those short-sleeved Mormons who come to the door with free literature about salvation. He would never volunteer a word to such a man. (If I wanted to argue that I was more his kind of man in my sloppy shirt, with my less than regular demeanor, I'm also his father and there could be no bigger disqualification than that.) Maybe style plays too large a part in teenage life, but we're not about to change that. At least not in time.

"If he'd talk we might be able to establish some alternatives. Where he was, whether they split up along the way—"

"Wendell," Carolyn said. She was being very circumspect, looking at him hard, narrowing her eyes. "Are you talking about what you believe or what you think we can establish?"

He licked his lips quickly, which signaled that he was about to give a little lecture. I think she had asked something very naïve. "Carolyn, what do you think the law is." He didn't wait for an answer. "Isn't it just a matter of who can establish what most effectively? By which I mean most convincingly."

"What—" She seemed to dig around with her toe.

Then she sighed and began again. "What about the truth of what happened? Don't you ever ask?"

He looked at her, that navy rep look of his, for a long time. Behind his eyes I could see little warning flares going off: No, no, don't complicate things this way! In that split second he understood that we knew things it would make him unhappy to hear. He would probably get over his unhappiness, he's good at that, but would that knowledge hamper the vigor of his defense? This moment must change hands all the time, I thought, between client and lawyer. What a business, to devote yourself to such expediency. To build the house of your work on evasion, illusion, intimidation, all for hire to strangers. He will have to ask us now, will have to know what we know, for fear it can be used against us.

Wendell drew away from us an inch or two. "The truth," he said, not just to Carolyn, "sometimes enters in. You can't always expect to keep it out. But the truth isn't always simple, Carolyn. And it's up to the prosecution to prove what they can prove. If they can't, well"—and he looked all around as if we were a whole roomful of listeners—"then they've failed in their mandate. It's a fair fight." I thought he was too simple a man to really relish perverting the truth, playing the angles. No wonder he was not the lawyer for us, who would need to.

CAROLYN

It was too ridiculous. She couldn't believe they did it *literally.* Wendell told them the Massachusetts "authorities" would escort Jacob to the state line and hand him—like a piece of goods, a package or a sheaf of stapled papers!—to the New Hampshire "authorities." He had some trouble understanding why the prospect caused his clients such bitter amusement. They laughed and laughed, until he saw the tears of rage in Carolyn's eyes.

"Can we watch?" she asked, and wiped them away angrily with the back of her hand. "Can we see the great habeas-corpus exchange?"

He hesitated. Really, they made things hard for themselves.

"I mean, that wouldn't be illegal, would it? We could just ride behind the police car—at a decent distance—and when they stop there—"

"At the barbed wire on the frontier—" Ben added eagerly.

"We'll just get out—we wouldn't crowd them or anything, they don't even have to know we're there! And we'll just watch."

"Right." Ben again. "We wouldn't dream of saying anything, or interfering. We'd just see him in the act of being extradited. I've always wanted to see an act of extradition, what it looks like, how—"

"Okay," Wendell said, maybe a little too harshly. "All right, I hear you." One of Steph's phrases. "I truthfully don't know if you can do that or not, I never knew anybody who wanted to."

Carolyn was seething—some of Ben's anger seemed to be spreading through her like a stain. "I can't imagine why not. It's not every day you get to see your kid get—what's the word?—manumitted? Or was that just for slaves? I don't remember, but it sounds like 'handed over.' "

"Carolyn," Wendell said.

"*Remanded.* That's it, remanded. It had 'man' in it, I knew that was the thing. From 'hand,' though, certainly not from 'man,' don't you think?" She looked momentarily satisfied.

He reached out his own hand to touch her arm but pulled it back at the last minute; it didn't seem a terribly good idea. "Wouldn't it just be easier if you went on home and then met us in court? I'd let you know as soon as the arraignment's set. There just isn't any need—"

Reason not the need, kept going through her head. Oh, reason not the need, but let the deed be done. Shakespeare, was it? *Lear,* maybe. What was all this archaic business cluttering up her head, the manumission of slaves, the well-turned Elizabethan sentence? At this rate she'd start beginning her sentences with "Whereas . . ." Is this what happened when you got involved with the formal system of the law and all their stiff and fancy language?

"We'll be there," she told him firmly. She was trying to imagine whether the police car would screech to a halt right beside the little black-and-white vertical marker between the states, or else a little farther on, the big blue-and-gold sign that said BIENVENUE A NEW HAMPSHIRE—WELCOME TO NEW HAMPSHIRE, while the traffic roared past on Route 3. The shoulder was full of pocked and crusted snow these days, sealed with ice that kept melting and refreezing. TWO HIT BY CAR DURING PRISONER RETURN. HORRIFIED PARENTS WATCH, HELPLESS. Or would they pull off and drive into the safety of some gas station or Dunkin' Donuts near the highway, give him over (in handcuffs?) and go in and have a cup of something hot and a frosted donut while Jacob sat locked in the car looking out, his mouth watering? "We'll be there," she said again firmly to Wendell, who looked faintly disgusted. "Nobody has to understand this but us."

Wendell was wrong. New Hampshire sent a sheriff down, sparing a cruiser for a few hours, and he took Jacob away before they even got to the jail. Abducted by the law.

When they inquired at the desk about the transfer, the clerk with the mustache looked at them from behind the glass and said coolly, "Don't get angry at *me*, sir. Tell your lawyer he's out of date. We used to do that, but not anymore."

Ben was prepared to object.

"Truth is," said the cop, shaking his head in what must have been admiration, "those sheriffs like to get away for a couple hours, you know? It's a nice drive, like half a day off . . ." He winked. "Taxpayers' expense."

Walking into the Town House wasn't easy, nor was crossing, as casually as possible, the creaky wooden floor to the courtroom. She smiled and nodded to the half-dozen people she saw, whether she knew them or not—the town clerk, whose heels clicked importantly, sharp little hammers (she would be on the phone in her office as soon as she could get there, to spread the word of Jacob's arrival), a few men in work clothes who were renovating the ground-floor bathroom, an assortment of anonymous others going about their business. Everyone knew why they were there.

And they were here, she conceded, hardly a moment too soon. Celene had information, courtesy of a chain of gossips the length of a city block, that if Jacob hadn't been found and returned to Hyland, the Taverners were planning on leading a vigil, and soon—candles, black ribbons—to protest the inefficiency or indifference of the police. Jacob's picture mounted on their picket signs like a head on a pike? Martha's beside his? Could anyone have watched such a thing and not thought about a lynching?

And now, how many people had seen Jacob being unloaded from the country sheriff's car, his hands helpless in their cuffs, his face and the sheriff's wholly impassive, looking neither way? What did they mean when they talked about secrecy for juveniles? Oh, to have done this in the dark! Celene had offered to come, to be with them; school was over for the day (which only increased the number of curious observers in front of the Town House). "It's okay," Carolyn had told her. "I'm filing away every nice suggestion like that, though. I'm making a list for the heavenly accountant, and I promise I'll make sure he sees it." As long as no one else could live it for her, there didn't seem to be any reason to involve another soul. She wished she could thank her friends more convincingly, but the gap between them loomed deep and dangerous and could not be acknowledged. It was as if a lake that had an invisible floor had sprung up between her house and the houses of her friends, yet every day they came outside and walked across it toward her as casually as if it were a field of milkweed and yarrow and blowing grasses. They seemed to get across; she lived at the bottom, where there was no air, no light . . .

When she and Ben came in through the heavy swinging courtroom door, Jacob turned and looked at them. Something in his gaze, Carolyn thought instantly, was a little different from that jail-house stare. It seemed more—permeable. Penetrable. He seemed to recognize them.

But it was unnatural to keep coming upon him in these alien places—after his disappearance, it was the next profound disconnection. A weaning, she thought. What an irony, for a mother to be weaned, as suddenly as those who fling a child off the breast violently, without remorse. One morning he is your son, and then he's a boy you keep encountering distantly in public rooms; whenever you see him now he's lit harshly by fluorescence, and his custodians hover barely out of sight. He was back in familiar clothing at least, his blue-and-green striped sweater, his worn jeans with one fashionably torn and flapping knee. He was seated in the first row of benches, alone. Wendell stood to the side of the judge's bench talking to Tom Grady, the judge, who was holding his robe in his hands casually, as if it were his raincoat. Wendell put up his hand when he saw them, as if to say, Hang on there, don't go!

Ben went ahead of her, straight to Jacob. He sat down beside him, touched his arm, and then—Carolyn was astonished—put his head roughly, affectionately, on his son's shoulder. He was beyond reunion: skip the welcoming embrace. It was as if he was saying, *There, then. That's over. Thank God.* It was like a deep, half-laughing sigh of relief. Joking, almost: simply a meeting after too long a separation. "I'm going on the theory that he's terrified," Ben had said at breakfast. "I'm giving him the benefit of the doubt—I think he's frozen with fear." Maybe, she thought. "And maybe if I act on that I'll get some results."

Jacob didn't turn to him now to reciprocate, but he didn't throw him off either.

Carolyn approached slowly. She was aware of a huge anger that had replaced her relief at seeing him alive in that jail, closed into that safe behind the bright red door. She didn't like game playing except in its time—game time—and, frightened or not, he was manipulating them, even now. "Jacob," she said. (How could you lean against someone who didn't want to lean against *you?*)

Jacob looked at her as if it were an ordinary day and she had found him in the little grandstand at the ball field. What is the matter with you? she was desperate to ask him, and mean it literally. Have you taken leave of your senses? Are you *psychotic?* Her heart pounded so hard it nearly knocked her off-balance. But how could anyone answer such a question usefully? What were those syllogisms—*All men lie. I am a man. I lie.* Why dishonor your own sanity by asking?

Tom Grady had ducked out long enough to squirm into his batwinged black robe, which looked strangely dramatic in the deserted courtroom. He was followed by Della Fort, the court clerk, a woman of such anonymous figure and feature that Carolyn thought it a wonder that she could summon up her name at all. Della had owned the house, years ago, that was rented to Judith's day-care center; so were acquaintanceships layered in Hyland—everyone played at least two roles, usually more, in the dramas of each other's lives. She also had a daughter who'd had scoliosis, whom Carolyn had helped. She baked phenomenal prize-winning cakes, decorated in blue and purple, with silver shot like mercury embedded in them, and dustings of rainbow sugar and other inedible-looking designs that suggested a wild, suppressed imagination. She came to the door doggedly, year after year, to collect for the Cancer Society. She looked stern and met no one's eye in the courtroom—apparently that came with her job. But Carolyn was suffused with gratitude that she was the only outsider there besides the judge; she seemed, suddenly, such a familiar. I have lived some of my life with you, Della Fort, she thought. I have spent the last eleven years right here under the same weather, seeing the same hills. Surely that ought to buy us a little sympathy?

Tom Grady was a lawyer who served as district court judge a couple of days a week, hearing drunk-driving and petty-theft charges, mostly. Today, for this special hearing, he had simply walked down the hill from his office toward the Town House, instead of up toward his neat Victorian clapboard, where his wife was waiting supper. He was a heavy, hard-sweating red-blond man who looked as if he might drive an eighteen-wheeler. (In fact, from what Carolyn knew of him, for all he suggested a sixteenth-century executioner, he was a man of fairly delicate sensibilities.)

He gestured to Jacob to come forward to sit at one of the tables closer to his bench.

"May we come, too, sir?" Ben asked in a tone so respectful, or terrified, it nearly made Carolyn smile.

"If you like, Mr. Reiser. But that's usually reserved for counsel." The judge had a husky consoling voice; he sounded like Mel Tormé.

All of them got up and moved. Ben sat to Jacob's left, but Carolyn moved one chair over on his right, so that Wendell could be beside him. She thought of all the movies she'd seen—where else do you ever get to observe courtrooms?—and the newspaper sketches, in which the head of the accused is inclined in the direction of his lawyer, who's giving directions. Jacob's head did not incline. It looked alert and independent and even, perhaps, relaxed. When Wendell wanted to say something to him, he was the one who leaned over to speak quietly in Jacob's ear, which did not so much as twitch. Jacob's hair was slightly shaggy over his collar line, but not extremely so. He'd been wearing that blue-and-green sweater for a long time now. The boy was about to be placed under a murder indictment, and his mother, otherwise blank, was faintly amused to recognize that she was worrying about clean underwear.

Fran Conklin had entered silently, alone. This was not going to be a public circus—she was getting to be grateful for small favors. He sat down at the other table. His uniform was cumbersome, the hardware on his belt clacked against his chair and his gun in its holster was pushed up at such an awkward angle that it looked ready to tumble out onto the floor. It looked dangerous. MURDER SUSPECT SHOT AT ARRAIGNMENT BY POLICE CHIEF'S REVOLVER. Carolyn could hardly get herself to look at Fran. She was surprised at the resentment she harbored toward him—it was illogical and she didn't like to indulge illogic, it was undignified and counterproductive. Ben leaned forward anxiously, clasping and unclasping his hands. She sat perfectly still, forcing herself to breathe regularly, the way she did when she couldn't sleep, to even out her heartbeat. If they reacted this way to the arraignment, which was nothing—pro forma, more or less, the judge a known quantity, close to home—how were they going to act during the trial?

The judge's voice ground into use as if it was a rusty thing that needed to be practiced in the open air. He begged their indulgence for having, at this irregular hour, to dispense with certain formal rituals—he could declare court in session himself, and no one need stand at his approach. This was a special session but it was genuine and binding in the sight of the state and the nation whose flags flanked him. They nodded obediently. They seemed to be holding their breath.

Fran heaved himself up slowly to take his place to be sworn. He moved reluctantly, as if he were as heavy as Tom Grady. Tom asked Fran, Captain Conklin, what complaint he was bringing, and Fran, looking at no one, in a monotone as if he came to report a murder a day, named the accused, juvenile Jacob Reiser, a suspect in the homicide of one Martha Taverner of Hyland on January 14. He was asked if said Jacob Reiser was present; he looked at Jacob, at all of them for the first time, without a flicker of feeling, and said, "Yes, your honor. That's him."

Jacob shuddered, she was sure she could feel it all along her side, although it was Wendell she sat next to. He quivered like a piece of paper lifted by a light breeze. Then he subsided. Ben seemed to have been poked by Fran's pointed finger, so violently did he recoil. He put his arm over his son's shoulder and held on.

Carolyn saw the rest of the arraignment through a scrim as red and damp as blood. (For reasons not apparent to her, juvenile court demanded "true" or "not true," chargeable or not chargeable; guilt or non-guilt was not suggested, as if it might be too difficult a concept for children to comprehend. She would ask Wendell why; he wouldn't know.) Jacob went forward, stood stolidly, and said in a soft, awestruck voice that did not waver, "Not true" to the accusation.

But there were other parts which Wendell took charge of, suddenly authoritative compared to the rest of them, and thank God for that. He was enumerating all the potent reasons Jacob should be cheaply bailed, or, better yet, simply released in his parents' custody. His court voice was almost unrecognizable, except for the local flatness of his accent, as if he and Tom didn't play golf together, play bridge, drink beer, even, shoulder to shoulder, piss in the bushes—Wendell had told them this in a moment of boastful pride—when they were nearing the ninth hole, too far from the golf-course clubhouse to hike up there in times of need. Wendell stood up in his gray business suit, petitioning the court: The defendant's longtime residency in Hyland was a factor. His parents' attachment to the community. Their home ownership. His previously flawless character. And, finally, the fact that he was still at this moment a juvenile who could be supervised, for whom his parents could be responsible. (What an assumption, Carolyn thought. Wouldn't they be safer assuring the whereabouts of Snappy the cat?)

All the other words flew by now as they sat clenched, trying to understand: Adjudicatory. Adult. Juvenile. Certification. And money. Money they understood. Money came into it publicly: could they afford a lawyer, or would they turn to the state? They had nearly come to blows over this: of course her parents would buy them the best they could find. Of course Ben said no. "Ben, this is *Jacob.*"

"Thanks for reminding me." He stared into her eyes as if he thought she was crazy.

"Ben, you're not being consistent. I thought there was nothing you wouldn't do—"

"Not this. They've got plenty of respectable lawyers, Wendell said so. Experienced at homicide. That's all they do."

"You'll leave it to chance, to mercy? Is this the way you'd feel about buying a good surgeon if he needed an operation? Or would you take him to the charity hospital and throw him on their mercy, let any old doctor—it's nice that they have a squad of idealistic folks doing their pro bono obligation on the homicide patrol. But any old *stranger?*"

Ben had looked at her viciously. "Honey, they're all strangers, aren't they? Everybody's a stranger. Your son's a fucking stranger, when it comes to that."

She wasn't sure she could deal with such thoroughgoing bitterness. She sat quiet and waited. His face had closed over like a lake glazed with ice, shiny and malevolent. "Sometimes I forget you've always had choices," he said stonily. "Good schools, good clothes."

"Is this really the time—"

"You're right, it's not. But I'm not having your parents hock their goods," he said, hissing on the *s*'s, "so we can give it away to some headline grabber we import in here from Hollywood."

"But what if he—she—can do a better job? What if—"

"Carolyn, do you know what kind of money you're talking about? A decent defense in this country shouldn't cost like that. It shouldn't support some goddamn pop hero and his closetful of terrific suits."

She'd thought those old resentments had died. (Wouldn't the Taverners be surprised to hear how he saw himself as the poor boy, now and forever! What a crazy continuum they were on, all of them.) She appealed to Wendell for advice; he refused to step between them. "He can get a good defense from the state. He can get a good defense from a big name, with a lot of expenses attached because the guy's got to come in here with his whole team from who-knows-where. Sometimes it's just as well when people don't have a choice, if they clearly don't have the resources." He looked uncomfortable; he focused straight ahead and would not turn toward either of them. "Sometimes it's not."

"Ben, separate the issues," she had pleaded finally, beside him in bed. "Take your anger about class, take your disappointment that your kids didn't grow up needy, take all of it and put it away till this is over. Sort it out when we're finished. Meanwhile—"

"Think about Jacob."

"Think about Jacob."

"Okay," he had said, and pulled the covers up to his neck, "but understand, can you? It's hard to keep any self-respect the way things are going. I don't work anymore—"

"Neither do I."

"You may not have much of a practice left right now, but, honey, you know what you *know*. It's hard stuff, solid. It doesn't evaporate, it doesn't—self-destruct. I feel like my brain's being eaten out by termites. When I don't do it, I lose it. So it's going fast. And now we turn to your parents again and ask for some of your daddy's gold."

"We can get another mortgage, Benny. We can sell some art." She pulled him close. "You can do what you tell your son, darling. Somehow or other, you can pay your own way."

For the first time in her life Carolyn wished she had gone to law school, to protect herself—protect them—from this helplessness, so that she wouldn't feel this curtain of terror pulled across her eyes, through which she seemed to see only shadows. Ben was holding Jacob's hand; Jacob, who looked about twelve, was letting him.

"Your honor, we will have counsel," Wendell was saying. "We do not need to ask the state's assistance." She made herself move into his seat, which was still warm, and take Jacob's other hand. It was cold and damp, but not as rigid as her own.

"Now," said Tom Grady. "The question of bail." The judge sat for a moment or two in unabashed silence, communing with whatever legal and judicial muses informed the lower court of Grieves County. He was one of those hard-breathing men who kept a balled-up handkerchief at the ready and he applied it to his whole face lightly, as if for soothing, as he spoke. When he turned his head fast, drops flew from him, like an actor's spit. He even wiped his eyes like a mourner; all of him seemed damp.

The defendant was, by law, entitled to bail. However, the judge reminded the court, said defendant had just been returned from an absence from the state that had made his presence here today the result of nothing but good fortune. In addition to his demonstrated unreliability, and perhaps more significant, there was the matter of a community seriously concerned for its welfare and so anxious to bring the perpetrator of a terrible, an unthinkable, crime to justice that for the defendant's own safety, as well as for the reassurance of the court, there would be no bail. He leaned down a little to speak to them, as if the court reporter couldn't hear him that way. "I'm going to speak frankly to you, Mr. and Mrs. Reiser. Jacob. I'd like this town to cool off a little before you come back out." He waited to see if they understood; then he put back his official demeanor. "The matter will be raised again after he is, or is not, certified as an adult." He looked at Ben and Carolyn. "I'm sorry."

Carolyn sat stunned at the impact of what he had said to them—that Jacob was not safe here. What did he know that he wasn't saying? That the people out there, her neighbors, were earnest enough in their anger to do him harm? Vigilante justice, even in a state that wasn't wild and crazy and quick on the trigger? Justice against butcher-block kitchens, Wendell? Vengeance against subscriptions to *The New Yorker*, there's that, too. Celene's hostile reports from the teachers' room echoed in her head: the Taverners, like Celene, had relatives scattered in every town for miles around: aunts of every age; brothers-in-law with guns in their pickups; illegitimate cousins. Right now every inkblot on their family history made them more appealingly vulnerable, more familiar, more in need of protection—people would probably join up and ride with them, if it came to that. She could hear Jacob breathing, not hard but fast, as if he'd been running. She felt the blindness break up into separate tears, a steady flow of them that rolled breakneck right down her chin and off. They beaded up on her sweater and skirt as if she'd dropped a handful of sequins in her lap.

He was going up to Concord, then, for his own safety, to be held in the youth facility until the first of his many hearings could begin. They had gotten him back just to lose him again. Once he gave her hand a little tug—reassurance or a nervous quaver? Tom Grady banged his gavel, a ferocious crack as unexpected as gunshot. This was supposed to be the sound of the state speaking; it was harsh and inhuman, like a tree falling, as impersonal as it could manage to be. They sat in silence until Fran, who scowled to deny he was secretly pleased, filled in for the missing bailiff and came to take Jacob, not ungently, away.

JUDITH

IT WAS NO COINCIDENCE THAT SHE NEVER EVEN GOT TO SEE HIM. THEY could have taken her to Cambridge and they didn't; they could have brought her down to the trial—her father kept saying it wasn't a trial, it was "just an arraignment-which-is-nothing"—but they didn't. And when they came back from it they didn't look like it was nothing either, and good for them. They went to sleep. Or to bed anyway, as if the rest of the day didn't interest them. It got dark so early you could pretend it was nighttime, she supposed, if you had to. One way or another, they didn't say much to her; both of them looked like they'd been hit in the stomach, hard.

All of it went together; they had no respect for you if you were a child. They could forget about you or close the door on you, leave you out as if you weren't even in the family. But she knew Jacob would have liked to see her, that was the other thing. She understood some things no grownup even remembered, and he would have appreciated that.

She was so angry they caught her crying when they got home. She refused to talk to them or even ask the questions that were burning on her tongue: Did you find out about the postcards? Did he admit anything? Was he upset, or was he Good Ol' Mr. Cool? Was he downtown at the jail now? (One time, on a class trip, they got to see the lockup in the basement, and it was too gross for human beings—narrow little cells smaller than closets, featuring a toilet bowl and a bunk that was welded into the wall, in that order of appearance, so that the seatless bowl was mostly what you saw. People throw seats: everything was determined by whether it could become a weapon! What wasn't brick was black iron. This place could make a saint into an animal, she'd thought, though the cop who was showing them around—it was Troy James's older brother, so it was hard to take him seriously; he and Troy kept punching each other as if they were home—told them no one stayed there more than overnight. Mostly it was for drunks to sleep it off and then go upstairs to the courtroom and get fined and sent back out on the street. Frankly, he admitted, nobody much tried to make a weapon out of anything, they didn't have the energy, although people sometimes tried to harm themselves. Somebody once hung himself, Troy's brother didn't say how or why. She had wondered then if killing yourself in jail meant you were guilty or just ashamed. Either way, it was too horrible and lonely to imagine . . . She had liked thinking about those weapons, though: she had once taken what was called an "unusual uses" test at school to see if she should go into a special enrichment class: What would you do with a brick that no one else might think of? A gum wrapper? A snakeskin? After the trip to the lockup she was obsessed with what, besides making a club with it and trying to beat someone to the ground—boring—you could do with a toilet seat, a coat hook, a desk drawer.

She didn't have to ask where he was. "They're taking him to Concord," her mother had said first thing when she had hung up her coat. Her eyes were red, her cheeks pale. "It's a place that's all kids waiting for the same thing, you know, for trials and other legal business, so he'll have a lot of—company." She hesitated on the last word: Judith could see her revulsion at the kind of people he'd be living with. Maybe he'd come out knowing how to be a real criminal.

If he came out. And he was a criminal already. She could not remember that.

They thought she was crying for him. She wanted them to know she was angry at them, but that would have made her seem selfish. All she could do was stand there and feel the facts, and her parents' indifference to her, pelt down on her like cold rain. "Jude, we'll go up there as soon as they let us. Not today, it's too late and he's got to settle in."

Her father still hadn't said anything; he was a dangerous red, as if he might explode any minute. "Tomorrow, if you'd like to. He wants to see you."

Sure, she thought. She couldn't help herself: "How do you know that?"

Then she could tell her mother was lying, no one had even mentioned her. Her mother couldn't lie, it was one of her weaknesses. All she could do was bite on her lip until it got as red as her husband's face. Judith might as well be invisible, not even live here—not even live—for all anyone cared about her. She swooped down on Snappy, who had come in when her parents opened the door and was innocently, delicately, bobbing up and down over her dry food. She buried her wet face in the cat's coat. Cold. It was cold and vaguely damp and smelled like her blanket, woolly and nearly sweet. Snap went soft when she squeezed, and made a helpless noise down in her throat, pleasure and the hope that she'd hold on.

Then her parents dragged up to bed like old people, and Judith sat in the kitchen watching the sky turn from deep blue to purple to black, trying to catch the changes as they happened; failing.

Yes, they visited. She vowed to herself never to go back.

It was a bland, old-fashioned brick building, and he was up on the third floor behind a door they had to buzz until someone came to let them in. Judith couldn't decide whether the expressionless young woman who gestured much too quickly in each direction at day room and library and the "clients' " single rooms was an inmate or a staff member; she never said. *(Clients?* What a funny word for kids who got caught and put away.) Heavy in her brown boyish corduroys, her lank reddish hair a little ragged, the girl didn't look like she really wanted to be bothered with them—all their smiling didn't get her to smile back. She brought them into the dining room (aqua plastic chairs, paintings that looked as if the "clients" had done them for some class) and left them to go find Jacob.

Judith crashed up against him like a bird flying into a brick wall. Oh, he was handsome, his features clear and his eyes a penetrating gray-blue. The color of new jeans. She searched them for pain, for change at least, but couldn't find it there. He stood straight as a soldier as she said his name over and over, and looked at her with distaste as if she were some nervy stranger petitioning him sloppily with her love. He even took a step backward, relieved, when she lowered her arms from his neck.

She was never going to have him alone—it dawned on her as the smiling director (bouncing along in clean sneakers like a gym teacher in need of a whistle) showed them where they could sit. A brother is for whispering to, for arguing with about what show, what channel. When she was little he had fixed her dollhouse after two visiting cousins, Uncle Stuie's boys, knocked the second-floor ceiling down and demolished half the living-room furniture (and laughed and laughed about it). Ditto the hammock, which ripped under their weight when they threw themselves into it—porky little jerks they were, overfed boys with bangs—and Jacob had managed to get the complicated ropes braided back together the right way, which took incredible patience and more brains than she had. He made the best grilled-cheese sandwiches. He held Snappy down so she could slip a new flea collar on. He told ghost stories that really scared her. He gave her his track trophy to put up on her own shelf. Hit her in the arm, sang with her in the backseat of the car, dirtied up the lyrics of all the clean songs, so that once she laughed so hard she wet her pants. Told her secrets, though apparently not the important ones. Laughed outrageously at nothing. Mouthed off. None of that was it, though. It was hard to say what he was, but it was more than the separate good things he did. He was the backdrop, part of the natural world, that was all. Just was. Always was and had been, since the beginning. She had a school friend, Sandra Lee, whose brother was killed in a wreck on graduation night last year—it was horrible, but it wasn't the same: he was *gone.* Once and for all gone, and everyone was devastated; it made him a hero, almost. But she didn't have Jacob back. She didn't even have his shadow. Her parents did, they had what they needed, right? Had got him back, safe if not free. She didn't have anything.

This place felt like school, falsely cheerful and disinfected. There were no private corners. They had you flushed out into bright light. She sat at the far end of the table and heard the dim mumble of her parents' voices. Once or twice he said something. "Can I have my comic books?"

"The ones with the sexy women? All that cleavage, the

boots and clubs? *Jacob.*" Why couldn't her father keep his mouth shut?

That was when Jacob gave her a long, penetrating look: *You see?* She tried to send back a signal: *I do, I see exactly.* Anything he wanted.

Her mother was quiet. She ran her fingertip back and forth on the edge of the table until it got annoying. This small talk was getting to her, Judith could tell. Her mother had told her once that she could never just chat, it had been a problem when she was a teenager: she always had *purposes,* she said, even if they weren't important purposes. Her day was organized, it had a lot of work in it that she made for herself. Sure I had fun, she insisted —it just depends on what you call fun. She was already working after school in some kind of lab when she was sixteen. She bred flowers as a hobby, poking invisible pollen down into the reproductive organs of lilies and tulips. ("Sexy!" Jacob had waved his hand as if the idea was too hot to touch.) She wore matching sweater-and-skirt sets and stockings. No wonder she wasn't very good at the random gabble of teenagers. Judith wasn't so sure she'd have liked her. She saw her in homeroom, one of the geeks—the kind of girl somebody's always turning to in those old movies, and taking off her glasses, or pulling the pins out of her tightly wound hair, and whispering with surprise, "Why, you're—beautiful!"

Her father was talking so gleefully about this ADC place—they all thought that meant Adolescent Detention Center, which made sense, but it really meant Awaiting Disposition of the Court, which didn't sound so much like a name as a problem—that you'd think he was trying to sell Jacob on wanting to go there, like a college. So they had TV and phone privileges and someone would come in to do schoolwork with them. She could just imagine— she saw some of the others with their terrible skin and their shambling uncooperative walks, saw how they were *refusing,* just saying No! to all that, to all the reasonable plans for their vocational this and rehabilitation that. Just because they had gotten caught at something didn't mean they had to go soft and roll over. She wouldn't want to be their teacher, thank you. She was somewhere in between: could see how all the forced good cheer of strangers would just make Jacob angry (and he was the polite type). But she knew she'd always do what people wanted her to do and even find some pleasure in it; would be just enough, push came to shove, like her grim-faced mother. They were two good girls who listened to reason, which was soothing. Which could always be argued for. Who didn't like anger, or dumb resistance, or shows of force. *Geeks*, the kind who won medals at graduation from the American Legion. God, she thought. If I were somebody else, I wouldn't like me either.

She didn't bother to say another word to her brother. In the car her father chattered and then fell silent, and her mother looked bewitched as if by some pain she couldn't place, or by a complex problem she was trying to solve. When she was thinking, she just disappeared.

Judith herself had been wondering how they would go about buying a lawyer for her brother—that was what her father called it, as if he was trying to be irritating. It didn't make sense to do the cheap thing if you could afford to do the expensive one: her mother had taught her that about possessions—not that she threw money around, only that she believed quality showed. Her closet proved it—a small number of nice things that fit beautifully, with fine details on them.

In the middle of one of their arguments about it, Judith thought her father was going to strike her mother (though he had never done it). She had always been terrified, far far down below the words to say it, that sometime in one of his rages he would boil over and—without planning to, he would never dream of doing such a thing, but in the strange sleepwalking, anger-drunk state he passed into—he would whap her mother in the face.

Then *blackout.*

That would be the end of their marriage, right then and there. If her father had pride, her mother had it even worse.

She looked at them now as they pulled into the garage, and all she saw was distance, both of them someplace else, alone, brooding. That was all anyone did around here anymore. They could be cheerful sometimes but they never seemed to forget, they only forgave, which you couldn't trust because they kept a list of angers and they could whip it out in a second. She was used to a lot more of the noise of talk and laughing, with somebody's favorite music—Schubert or Hammer or the Dead—always floating in the background. Every time she had a question for them, she knew they'd look pained answering it. For parents, they seemed very confused. It was better to try to puzzle things out for herself.

The spot where Jacob's old car usually sat had been empty for a long time now. Creepy, as if his car was his spirit and they had vanished together.

When they got the woodstove going and took the chill off the room, her mother opened two cans of tomato soup and put a steaming bowl in front of Judith, with saltines and carrot sticks. "Not much of a dinner, honey. I'm sorry." As if this wasn't the way it had been for weeks now, catch-as-catch-can dinners and not much conversation at the table. The funeral food had stopped a long time ago, at their own request. But wouldn't it have stopped anyway, when the air of fresh emergency was over?

"It's okay, I'm not hungry."

"We may suffer a little in the food department if we have to keep driving to Concord."

"I said it's okay." It looked like a brimming bowl of blood to her, and it smelled sour, like her memories of the day-care center. She roiled her spoon around in it awhile as if she was trying, just to get her mother off her back, then went up to bed and undressed without turning on the lights. In the dark she imagined herself at that place Awaiting Disposition of the Court—she had thought disposition had to do with whether people were naturally nice or nasty—going to open the door for visiting parents. She would be kind to them because they'd all be grieving and she'd pay special attention to brothers and sisters, who'd be feeling lonely and scared. She would have a room with a lock on it, and she would make friends with older girls who had shoplifted what they wanted and stole cars maybe, but underneath they would be basically misunderstood and really very sweet, only with parents who never listened to them, or drank, or beat up on them, or worse. (Much worse could happen, though the idea of your father stealing into your room and making you do things was too sick to imagine. The first times she'd heard about it she was ready to say no, they're making that up, that never could happen. Your *father* who used to change your diapers!)

She fell asleep imagining herself the best worker in the dining room (where the kids served and cleaned up and weren't allowed to complain). She would have the most energy and the best attitude. Disposition. She would be a criminal—she never did figure out why she was there—and a star at the same time, the director's favorite, the earner of every privilege they had: late nights, free candy bars from the machine. And her parents would weep when they came to see her, and take her hands and kiss them and not let go through the whole visit.

There were no secrets, not in this town.

Celeste met her the next morning where the bus dropped her off behind the middle school. She was hissing with excitement, breathing fog, gray-blue like her cap and scarf, color of cigarette smoke. "Did you know she was *pregnant?*"

"What?" Judith asked. "Who?" Her science book open on her lap on the bus, she had been trying to picture an amoeba.

"Martha." Celeste had made Martha Taverner into a star in the movie of her life. "The *au*topsy report. My father heard it, he was at the Oddfellows and he's not supposed to know, but they're all talking about it, so he said it wasn't any secret. They found out she was having a baby."

Her glee pushed Judith back a step. Oh God, she thought, oh God, it was all true then, her vision of her brother naked on the slim thighs of that innocent-looking girl. Batman at work, as evil as she'd understood him to be, strange flesh that changed when it came near girls, and now the whole world imagining them thrashing and panting. All the Odd Fellows.

"Two things," Celeste went on heedlessly, all of it good news, and exhilarating. "She was pregnant *and*—there was this cabin they went to? Her friend, you know this girl Tina Guy, she says they always went there, like after school and all, and they used it that day. They found, like, all kinds of stuff, cigarettes and cups and stuff, and they're *sure.*"

Judith hugged her books to her chest as if they might block out sound. She was going to throw up, but she would fling herself under the bus wheels before she'd do it here. "Thanks a lot," she said and gave Celeste a long, summarizing look, and walked as quickly as she could across the blacktop that was striped with shiny patches like an iced cake, toward the woods behind the playground. They were shallow and thin but no one could see her a few feet in.

She balanced her books delicately on a dry rock, pulled her jacket clear, and bent over a little dip, a basin made by the drip of melting ice, behind a scrawny pine. All she could do was retch for a while, but she closed her eyes and tried, and finally her breakfast came up on her.

It was yesterday's soup—imagining it viscous, blood-red, with the thin scum of its chill across it in little wrinkles—that got her to heave up her Wheatena and cocoa. Let them set a bowl of blood in front of the killer prince, the *father* prince. Batman a father. And there was nowhere she could go to get away from him.

CAROLYN

Annie Dineen suggested she go shopping at the mall.

"Please, Annie! I wouldn't do that in the first place, so why should I do it in the second?"

"Take your mind off," Annie said. "I'd suggest—tree pruning? Or fly-tying? Fox hunting? Anything if I thought it would help."

It was Judith, Carolyn decided, who could use some distraction. The little girl—that's what she was, or used to be, before they were dragged into all this—was so depressed these days, and who could blame her—she seemed confused somewhere between wanting her parents to take note of that and at the same time to ignore it, to notice her and then leave her alone.

Well, nothing was as reliable for the purpose as the urgency of acquisition. The terms of the hunt were specific and finite: they went in search of a new hat-and-glove set because the one Judith had was "geeky"; they couldn't come home without a leotard, specifically in purple or teal blue, for the honor of the gymnastics team. And there was some kind of blouse she absolutely needed that she couldn't describe but would know when she saw it.

They started off gaily, fresh and untried. Ben and Jacob had sports to share, and all of them had certain family rituals, but shopping had recently become their coinage, somehow, as it had been hers and her mother's. (Her sister had noisily, contemptuously opted out every chance she got.) She could see a feeling of happy well-being envelop Judith, exactly the way her face could look deeply satisfied—I'm-in-my-seat-all's-right-with-the-world-and-I-even-have-a-giant-tub-of-popcorn-heavy-on-the-butter—as the coming attractions flashed past at the movies. You could probably brainwash the whole generation to do your bidding if only the Cineplex Odeon music preceded the command, or the AMC logo, AND NOW OUR FEATURE PRESENTATION!, bright shiny letters flying off the screen into the dark.

Carolyn suggested that Judith bring some tapes—the nearest mall was a long ride, far enough away to feel like an outing. What careened around them in the car was mostly rhythm. She asked dutiful questions: Why is Janet Jackson so popular? Was she finished with Michael, wasn't he passé? Were any of them heroes to her? ("Heroes?" Judith echoed blankly. It was too serious a question, an adult intrusion. "You mean, do I think of them, like, in *real* life?)"

The drive took three-quarters of an hour through green country and suburbanized farm towns whose huge colonial houses were fair game for commerce if they faced the road—INSURANCE and CARPETS and group practices. Judith chattered about school friends, a teacher who was about to be fired for being too mean, her new interest which just might lead her—"maybe, maybe," she said almost prayerfully—to ask for riding lessons. The more frivolous the conversation, the more Carolyn could feel her neck and shoulders relax. She told Judith stories about elementary school, and how—hadn't she ever heard this?—she took the train alone to Chicago when she was eleven and fell asleep and didn't wake up until they were in Denver.

The traffic began to bunch up near the mall, and by the time they maneuvered through the parking lot and found a space, they were ready for lunch. They went off giggling guiltily, swinging hands, to find some food. Judith was delighted. "We haven't even worked yet!" Carolyn was happy on the one hand, sad on the other, because this was exactly the kind of weightless pleasure she never had time for with her daughter. It was hard to be grim here, or to believe in things like actions and consequences. The first good thing she'd found to say about catastrophe was that she could take the day off and no one cared.

And it was intoxicating: lights reflecting in mirrors, a woman in a white coat like a doctor, coming at them with an atomizerful of something heavy and expensive and suggestively named—Carolyn waved her away as if she were a swarm of attacking flies, but Judith gratefully gave her a wrist and couldn't stop sniffing it as they rode up the escalator. The tables were piled with color, neatly folded, and music filled the air around them, gentle jazz to keep their pace up. She felt drunk walking through it all: irresponsible, obscurely stimulated, utterly unreal. "Hats," she said to Judith. "Business. Hats and gloves. Where would they be?"

"Oh, look, Mom! Wouldn't you look beautiful in this? This is so—*you!*" They stopped to consider a dark satin blouse with a deep red yoke. "It would be so nice with your hair. Ooh!"

Carolyn laughed. "You sound like you're in pain! Judith, what do I need dressing-up clothes for right now? Really—"

"Oh, Mom, *need!* Just try it on, oh please. I just want to see it on you. Isn't it—luscious?" Carolyn could hear her trying the word; she and Celeste probably had a whole new vocabulary for their vanity, their hopeful judgments, their desperations.

For Judith's sake, she pulled down the hanger and took it into the dressing room along with a pair of lounging slacks in the same dark satin, like a night sky not quite black yet. They were as thick and smooth as wet paint.

Judith sat on a stool admiring as Carolyn pulled her sweater off over her head. "You have such a nice neck." She seemed eager to be childlike, fawning. Anything you want, Carolyn thought. Sweet child, anything. "*I've* got these horrible collarbones." Judith made a gaunt face.

Gravely, they discussed bones and shoulder blades. "They'll fill out, Jude, I promise you. I was so scrawny you wouldn't believe it. Size three on top."

Judith, frowning, raised her shoulders to make her hollows even hollower. "And I'll never have—you know." She gestured at Carolyn. "Which is *fine.* Except my clothes look so empty!" Judith had only bought her first bra this year—her gymnast's body, its purity of line, its innocent asexual firmness, nearly brought tears to Carolyn's eyes. She could feel Judith studying her, wondering what it felt like to be so soft and rounded, to stand there in your lacy white full slip, then drop it and step into black satin and button it, turning more glamorous with every inch of flesh you covered up. "Nice," she said and reached out to pat it as if it were fur. "You look like a movie star. Are you going to get it?"

"Oh, Judith, what would I do with it? We're not going out to very many dinner parties, you know." (As if they ever dressed for them, anyway.) She turned and looked at the long line of her back. It was terrific, actually—surprisingly graceful, a costume out of someone else's life. Or would a little vanity, some care for herself, be good for her right now?

"I think you should get yourself something extravagantly beautiful!" Judith said rapturously and put her arms around her mother's waist. "I think you should put it on after supper and turn all the lights down and go in and surprise Daddy. He'll say, 'Who is this fabulous woman? Is she the one who's been so—' " That musky perfume Judith had acquired downstairs seemed to surround them both.

"Judith!" She was pleading, laughing. "Have mercy!" Who's been so—no need to finish it.

A gang of high-school girls swept into a couple of dressing rooms across the way, noisy, full of brazen exclamation. "Wait till he sees this, he will just lie down and roll over!"

"So will your mother. Jeez, Nicole, you'll never even get out of the house in that. They'll lock you up!"

"Oh, give me a break. Here, what happens if the zipper's down just a little. Look."

Judith tensed and pressed her head to her mother's shoulder. Carolyn watched her freeze, she could feel her skinny elbows sharp against her waist; Judith had a sickened look around her mouth. Fabulous women and fabulous girls, then, were not the same thing.

"That is *so* cool!" They exploded into self-satisfied laughter.

"Wait, wait," Nicole called out. "Look, when I roll the bottoms up. Hey, what a difference. Oh, wow!"

"Oh God, I ruined it!" Judith said against her mother's collarbone.

"What?" Carolyn pulled back and looked at her and then down at the front of her blouse.

"Tears on your shirt. Oh, look what I did. These splotches."

Dear God. "Not to worry, honey. We'll hang it up and it'll be fine." She smoothed her daughter's hair. "Nobody can trace tears." She pulled a handkerchief out of her purse. Judith wiped her face and handed it back to her.

She held the hanky to her own face and breathed once, twice, three times, slowly, restoratively, in the dark. Then she opened her eyes on the megawatt dazzle and willed it to take her back out of herself again.

BEN

He was from Manchester, an in-state boy, to assuage me. Wendell knew him well. "The best. Better than the best," he said, but the imperfection of my faith in Wendell's judgment was surely not discussable.

"He's one of these characters who're eaten up by their cases."

"Great. You think there'll be a bite or two left for the trial?"

"No, Ben, listen. With this guy, if there's any chance that there won't *be* a trial, you've got it. He's lost one case in his lifetime. This man is totally devoted to defense. He lives poor—he's one of these old-time types like a country doctor, you could imagine him living behind his office. I mean it. And the state won't give you any trouble over him."

"But he'll take the full amount anyway—"

"Well." Wendell straightened the knot in his tie. "But

you'll get more than your money's worth, I promise you. Look, go see him. Interview the hell out of him, make him prove he's worth his fee. He's right up the road in Manchester. Go on."

On the way we talked about the gossip. The little fucker couldn't keep his zipper up, I started out, but then I have to admit a single long look out from under Carolyn's eyebrows silenced me. The hypocrisy, all right. She didn't have to say it: How old was I when I found my first willing woman? How old when I was desperate and only lacked somebody who wanted me back? I was older than Jacob the first time, but not by much and not by choice. I could still imagine the rank gray sheets we made even ranker (the borrowed bed in the studio of my friend Maxie down on Wooster Street), a girl named Theda and me. I thought I'd die of it, I couldn't understand why half the world didn't suffer heart attacks at climax. Well, maybe they do, Theda had said, straightforward as she was in all things, including sex—she never promised what she wouldn't give. How would you know? We made up honest obituaries, I remember: Mr. Jones expired after three rounds of Miss Smith. Mr. Williams passed on when Mrs. Williams climbed on top of him and covered his face with her hair. John and Joan Johnson died simultaneously. Suicide, we laughed, and reached out for each other.

"It could be the motive," Carolyn said and didn't look at me.

"If you say motive, it means you believe it."

She gave a bitter half laugh, a sort of aborted bark. "Do you manage not to believe it? Since when?"

I would have had trouble saying what I thought: that whether he did it or whether, miraculously, he didn't, I had lost faith in knowing anything. How could it matter what I believed, I couldn't imagine what his head was full of. His memories, now, were his own—well, they always had been, of course, only it wasn't so visible—and his motives, too.

You start out thinking your child's life is in your hand, you can hold it all right there: he's with you all the time, that little baby. If he plays with friends you're there, you referee the squabbles. Carolyn and I took turns. (If anything, I took some of her turns.) You buy the toys, you close him in the yard where he'll be safe. And you think you know the whole cast of characters in his head, the scary parts, and the sweet dreams. Only, one night he has a nightmare. It rips his sleep in two, and yours as well. You rush in, pull him from his crib as if it's on fire and comfort him against your shoulder—and he can't tell you a thing. Or a word or two he gives you, a hint, a clue to where the monster came from—oh, that terrible movie, as if you need Walt Disney to make nightmares. It's huge and hairy and it was right behind him. Or he fell from a cliff onto the rocks below. Whatever. Where did he get that from? He doesn't watch violence on the tube. He's never had a trauma. Spontaneous combustion is what it is. The little microbes grow in the warmth of his head, that moist medium.

Then he matures a little out of eyeshot: down at the day care, where he has experiences you never hear about, little ones too insignificant to report. Ginny pushed him off the swing, Seth gave him his cupcake at lunch. Good, bad, invisible all of it.

The arrogance. The chutzpah. It's his life, even if it's small, and hedged by adult watchers. It's his life. But it's a long way from that to knocking up a woman, and a long way, I realized with a shock that was almost electric in its violence, between the young father I was and the grandfather he'd have made me. Would have, could have, except for Death Intervening: it rolled over me like a sheet pulled up over my face.

"It would help," I ventured, "if he'd talk to us a little. It really would."

"When he comes home," she said. "When we get him bailed. Maybe he'll be more himself at home. He looks like he's—blinded—in these places. Blinded by the lights."

"You mean figuratively."

She sighed. "Figuratively."

I thought about that girl pregnant, the carelessness. Idiots.

So he was upset by that, or guilty, or scared. A dozen *or*'s, interchangeable at this distance. I didn't even know what we'd tell the lawyer except *Please. Whatever it takes.*

If it hadn't been for his name, I'd have taken him for Jewish. Demaris, though: Panos. Manchester's very Greek. He was small, swarthy, quick, my age, maybe younger, with a lot of dark hair in what would have been a pompadour a generation ago. His pants were slightly belled—Jacob would laugh—a wimpy light blue you'd more likely find on a furniture salesman than on the best defense attorney in sight. Most of the lawyers were on Elm Street in the slick new buildings. He was in a house, not quite Victorian, on a side street near downtown. The house, he told us later, was in the family, at a distance; Greek families are nice to each other. He had a deal he couldn't have gotten for a better address. "If you keep your overhead down, you can take the work that needs taking," he said. "Why should I take it from you and kiss it while it goes by on its way to the landlord?"

Oh God, we were wary. His receptionist told us to have a seat in the tiny living room/waiting room, and we went sniffing around as if the man's magazines (a wide variety: *Golfer's Digest* to *Smithsonian* to some kind of hot-rod fanzine—for kids in trouble?) would tell us something profound. His plants were the kind that lived without a lot of attention, spiky unendearing things, and the walls were done in Greek Restaurant posters: the aching blue of the Aegean, the stone steps of island villages. White-domed chapel, white houses over the steep, rocky fields. Free from another relative, I'll bet. I watched Carolyn for a reaction; she was showing none. Curiosity, but so far nothing else. When she held judgment in abeyance there was an unnatural look to her, a quality of strained silence that was very noisy indeed. The scientist gathering evidence, being scrupulously neutral, before she dares a hypothesis. Fair enough. I was inclined to like him for the sheer perversity of his unstylish digs. But I had to watch that: you can be hung for a populist as easily as for an aristocrat. It depends on who's in power.

He came out himself, walking fast. "Panos Demaris," he said, and I could feel us being sucked up into his gaze, which was fiercer by far than mine or Carolyn's. His handshake was emphatic. I saw he even took corners at a slight tilt, as if they were banked, so he wouldn't have to slow down.

A deep silence overtook us, though, when we were all seated in his office; only the leather chairs squawked. It was a vastly populated place, black-and-white photos of historical figures, Manchester dignitaries and maybe national ones as well, and what had to be family everywhere, children, grandmothers, and dozens in between. He waited us out. All I could think of was my shrink saying nothing, with infuriating patience, the one who helped me through art school by hearing me take my family apart and put it back together a little differently. Demaris's family on the wall could have been mine, I thought, a little weary—all those people who love us too much and (because of that, I suppose; because they ask too much) whom we fail. I wondered if Greek families smothered their children. The question answered itself.

Finally Carolyn ventured forward, or we'd still be sitting there. "Wendell Bye told you about us."

He raised an eyebrow: not a contradiction.

"Our son—"

He wanted to hear what we'd say. He looked from her

to me. I had to say something, so I trusted my voice and added, "He's seventeen. A high-school junior."

"He's accused," Carolyn went on and pulled the Velcro tab on her shoulder bag so that it sounded like a bandage being torn from flesh, "of killing a girl. A classmate. A girlfriend." She pulled out a peach-colored tissue and held it tight, just in case. "We don't have the slightest idea if he did or not."

"God," I said, knowing it was stupid but wanting, I suppose, to establish something with this man, "did you ever used to read Donald Duck in the funnies? We sound like those nephews of his, you know, Huey, Louie and Dewey, who split up their speeches between the three of them?"

Carolyn looked at me astonished. I had no idea how to read Panos Demaris's face. The man spends a lot of time in front of juries.

Then we told him everything we knew—minus the parts I'd erased, it amounted to slightly more than nothing. He took notes but ventured no opinions. Which did not mean he didn't have them.

"Do you have to believe somebody's innocent to take his case?" There was Carolyn again with her naïve high-minded irrelevant question. I wasn't afraid she'd bolt and tell him about the jack, no way would she do that. I think she wanted to establish her eccentricity, which was not (like his) her style, but her purity and innocence. Her moral earnestness. I thought she looked silly at it.

He laughed quietly, maybe patronizingly, maybe with appreciation. He was not a noisy man, only an energetic one who had trouble sitting still. "I work with a lot of juveniles," he said, "who are in every kind of trouble you can think of. A lot of them haven't been innocent of any accusation you'd care to lay on them since they were four. But they still deserve a good defense."

How nice to be so resolved. "How do you know he'll talk to you?" I asked.

It was a cliché, I could have seen it in a movie at the

end of a scene just like this one—probably had seen it already—but I liked it in proportion to how much I needed to hear it. "He'll talk to me." He breathed out hard and beat a little tattoo on the desk with his index fingers, as if he were impatient to get started. "I can't promise you he'll tell me the truth, but he'll talk to me, if that's what's worrying you."

Carolyn drove home and I closed my eyes. I saw Panos Demaris and Carolyn and some old woman in black, a woman of Samos or Siphnos, or maybe Vilna or Minsk, who walked between them. They were strolling casually together in a field, not close together, walking down toward the sea. She was going away with him, that was clear, but I wasn't in the dream at all, except, I suppose, as the eyes that saw them getting smaller and smaller, like people in one of those posters. She was going to be his, but I didn't object. I didn't have to watch. I opened my eyes and saw Carolyn's tight face as she accelerated to pass a truck.

I guess I considered mastery and virility interchangeable. How about mastery and victory, though?

I wondered if he had other clothes to wear to court.

We seemed to be on the road all the time. We went to see Jacob apparently so I could try to small-talk about TV programs and the NBA, and came home furious and exhausted from the effort of confronting nothing. Judith refused to come, for reasons she kept obscure, and Carolyn, Jacob, and I killed time like three other people we'd never been properly introduced to. And after he'd been to visit the ADC facility, we went to Manchester to talk to Demaris. I wondered if they'd talked basketball.

"He's a smart boy," he told us, minus the details. "I like him. Do you mind if I eat while we talk?" It was three-thirty. He unwrapped a gyro sandwich from greasy white paper and bent low over it, shoulders practically to the desk to protect his shirt.

"Is this late lunch or early dinner?" Carolyn asked. It was clear he perplexed her—one of the things that make us very different is that she doesn't have a whole lot of tolerance for eccentricity unless it serves a purpose.

"Breakfast, I think. I had a pre-trial meeting and I never did stop." He seemed to be as committed as Wendell had promised: he didn't take vacations, he drove a disreputable car. ("Come now," he'd said when a New York cousin had suggested that his car was an embarrassment to a member of the professional community. "This is New Hampshire. I'd be embarrassed to drive anything better.") Still, he didn't hesitate to tell us we weren't what he had in mind when he took "needy" cases cheap. "Admit it, do yourselves and me the favor of a good hard look," he'd said very simply and maybe a little wearily. "No matter how you're hurting financially from all this, and I'm sure you are, look: I just finished a case for a kid who lives in the projects over there." He led us over there with his chin. I didn't know Manchester had projects. "A kid who sleeps in the living room on chairs. Every time he gets taller, they add another chair." Shrug. He knew when to shut up.

More small talk. Around now, my foot begins to bounce: *Well? Well? Well?*

"Okay. He's still not saying anything. I asked him if he understood what the situation looks like—you run away, you're going to look guilty of something—and he seems to. But he won't even try to talk his way out of it—I think he's probably just being a kid, you know, you see this. Hoping if he can hang tough long enough it'll all go away." The meat in his sandwich looked like dirty washcloth. He swallowed a big piece. "So I told him, look, I don't really want to have to write your story for you, but I will if I have to. If you don't help me out, I will. I can come up with some plausible enough stuff—there's not-guilty-by-reason-of-incapacity—you're drunk. You're high. You know. Insanity's no good up here, you don't want to use that with a New Hampshire jury if you have any other choice, they're not friendly to people who are too—too different from what they think they are." He laughed with a kind of awe. "Whatever they really are, of course. But up here you're supposed to have some control of yourself, more than most places, I think. It's not a real generous climate, you understand, if you claim you were crazy the way the courts want you to be crazy—it all looks too convenient, a category of impaired moral judgment but you don't look nuts, swing from the trees, whatever. You know—being clear about the difference between right and wrong—it's an unsatisfactory definition to everyone who uses it and everyone it's used against."

"A moral category," I said.

"With an odd pragmatic twist. They fight each other." He shrugged. "So then there's self-defense, there's—well, we've got a few more tricks in the bag. But we shouldn't have to be writing this for him, you know? We shouldn't have to use a crowbar to get his mouth open like this. And we have to know what we're up against. What are they going to find. What kind of material evidence do they have." These were statements, not questions. In that form they were especially terrifying. "He'd better give it some hard thought, you know? Because I can't do this myself." He swallowed the last of his sandwich with an audible gulp. "Let me ask you a couple of questions about Jacob, if I might. I have to get a bead on him, okay?" He got up and walked around a little, then suddenly bent to a crouch, bounced a few times on his haunches, hard, and came back up. "My circulation stops, I can feel it. My blood must be coagulating."

"Too much retsina," I suggested. "As long as your brain stays fluid, that's all we ask."

Panos laughed. But his change of pace was quick as a

snake's fang. "Do you think Jacob tends to level with you about most things?"

I began my answer before the question was out. "Do you mean, are we close?"

"No, that's not the same thing. I only mean factual things: does he tend to tell the truth?"

Carolyn looked at me. He didn't lie, did he? "Not particularly," she said. "I can't think—you mean, very little things? He says he's taken out the garbage but he hasn't? That kind of thing?"

Panos nodded. "Well, that's a teenager for you. I've got a couple, God help us. I mean maybe slightly larger things. Where he's going, where he's been. Where he gets his money, that kind of thing."

"He's about average, I think," I said.

"No, wait, Ben. Do you think everybody has these shouting matches at three in the morning? I wonder if he's not a little—"

"But that's not lying. It's just not, I don't know, it's not what you'd call good reporting. He doesn't see the need. I don't think most kids his age see it, not till they get to be parents themselves. Panos, he's a very ordinary boy."

"Ever steal anything that you know of? Even petty crimes?"

"He's a slob," I put in, thinking hard. "Sometimes he's too disorganized to get his act together. So he ends up with—oh, I remember once he told me—way later, he told me—that he never handed in his pledge money for a walkathon, he kept forgetting to bring it in to school. About seventy bucks, I think it was for multiple sclerosis. Or wait, no. Muscular dystrophy, I mean. The Jerry Lewis thing. Whatever. So he just kept the money. Venial sins."

I remembered the bills he'd taken from Carolyn's purse. It felt like a betrayal to say anything about them, though I didn't know why. She must have felt it, too—she kept her mouth shut.

But we told him a thousand inconsequential things

about Jacob, from his prowess with computers—a kid of his time—to his mediocre wrestling and his will to win at least one match this year. His allergy to peanuts, his volunteer work reading stories one summer at the Old Age Home. (He sounded unlikely, a paragon. I didn't quite recognize him.) I said he still had friends from grade school. Also new ones he never brought home, for what that meant, shyness, embarrassment, who could tell. I told him Jacob liked to help me in my workshop when he could, or used to, how we'd talk about everything, while we shaped and sanded and glued, from art to sports to other kids, even a little about girls. I never knew if he was open with me, how could I tell? I thought we were close. This was a while ago, though. Before he could drive. Maybe before he had secrets, I don't know. A couple of times I credited him when I showed my work: A Collaboration by Benjamin and Jacob Reiser.

Did we see ourselves as out of the ordinary?

"In general, you mean, or in Hyland?" I asked.

"Either. Both."

Carolyn and I looked at each other, uncertain. "In general it's hard to say," Carolyn began. "You know, you can't see yourself without a context. So—" She shrugged. "In New York, where we came from, no, we were about a dime a dozen."

"Nickel," I suggested.

"But here—Hyland. Well . . ."

"In Hyland," I went on, "we are and aren't unique. I mean, I have a poker game—had, I guess—with a real mixed crew, a guy who cleans chimneys, one who does insurance, and a jazz pianist who teaches band at the high school. So it depends on what you want to look at. We belong to the PTO, Carolyn sings in the chorus. We don't want to be out of the ordinary. We didn't come up here to stand out."

"On the other hand," Carolyn said a little stiffly, "I'm a physician and my husband is a sculptor, so . . . There's a certain complicated status in those. Hyland is a rural town going a little suburban, getting a little too classy for some people. But there have always been a lot of people with money who haven't had to work for it, sort of old Boston, and to them I suppose we're just—"

"Working stiffs," I said.

"So your status shifts all the time. Depending on who's doing what for whom. And who you're talking to. Just about everybody has some kind of authority."

"And the girl's family? The Taverners?"

We sighed. "Martha's father," Carolyn ventured, "is one of those men who've never quite—gotten themselves together, I think. He's had a drinking problem. He seems pleasant, I think he's funny, isn't he, Ben? He and some other men in town used to do, sort of, practical jokes. They once painted the street purple in front of the Town House. I don't remember why. And they hooked up some kind of record to the fire alarm that time, some song, and played it all around town?" She looked fairly helpless. "I don't really know Mrs. Taverner. But they have a lot of advocates in Hyland. You understand that. They grew up here, they have family here, they have the advantage of—"

"Belonging," I said. "Whatever their virtues or ours, Mr. Demaris, the town is a little more theirs than it is ours. I imagine you'd recognize the situation. Plus, you know, factor this in, that we're Jewish. Less than a minority."

"And has that caused problems?"

"Well, whatever they're saying among themselves, some people are very respectful, actually. I guess it's better than being completely godless. But somebody once told me," I said to him, and my mouth felt full of dust, "that if everything went well, we'd never hear about it. But if anything ever went wrong—"

Panos looked at us hard, without a flicker. I daresay he was wondering if we were snobs who couldn't admit it or true egalitarians with our ankles in a trap. Wondering if there was anybody left in Hyland to love us. He waited a few beats till everything settled.

"Okay," he said then. "Back to Jacob." It felt like a long way back. He tapped on his forehead with the eraser at the end of his pencil. "You're describing a pretty regular kid. As you say. Let me ask you—now try to take this as a neutral question, okay? It's not an accusation. Would you say Jacob has any particularly—any psychological problems that you've been at all concerned about?"

So we listened to Panos try to defuse the accusation (because, of course, there was an accusation, a vague one, hidden in his palm): "But anger," he said. "This is very important. Please listen. Does Jacob have any particularly severe problems with expressing anger? Does he tend to keep things bottled up? Does he ever explode? When a kid stays as—*quiet*—as he's staying . . ."

Carolyn reached for my arm and gently put her hand on it. Whether she thought she had to restrain me or comfort me, I don't know. Before we could say anything, Panos continued, not at all defensively but still in that conspiratorial don't-tell-the-children half whisper, "You really need to know something, Mr. and Mrs. Reiser." He smiled. "Mr. and Doctor?"

"Ben and Carolyn," she said.

"Ben and Carolyn, then. I have the preliminary police report, the medical examiner's report—these things they have to give us, of course—and you need to understand that whether whatever Jacob finally tells us is true or not true—hard for us to say, right, until we hear it? But you need to understand that this report describes a head wound to the girl that was not the result of a single blow. It reports a bludgeoning so severe and repeated that—" He sighed, a long, whistling sigh like that of a runner coming to rest. "The details don't—they'd only add to your distress unnecessarily. The point is, he hit her once and then apparently he hit her again and went on hitting her, thus, you see— Of course, that's usually how it is. If you hit somebody once, you tend to go on."

He had lifted his head for a minute; he'd delivered most of this matter-of-fact speech to the paper his sandwich came in, opened up there on his desk like a huge white sharp-petaled flower. I was listening, hungry for anything. If Jacob gave us some parts, even random bits, we could begin constructing something. But he glanced up and saw Carolyn dissolving as he spoke. She had her hands to her face, as if, eyes covered, she wouldn't have to hear it. "Oh, now—please, Dr. Reiser. Why have—"

Carolyn slapped at the air in front of her face. "You can't *do* that!" she cried out at him, and her face was awful, twisted the way I've never seen it, between disgust and—I don't know what it was. Horror at her own disgust, maybe. "You can't just guess what might have happened —what he isn't saying—like it's a bunch of ordinary everyday events like that! Jesus," she said, breathless, and she put one open hand over her eyes. "How do you expect us to *survive* this?"

Panos Demaris looked at me very quickly. If she saw it I know it only made her angrier—the man checking with the other man: Does this happen to her often?

She wasn't finished. "Just because you hear this kind of thing every day. You spend your time with horrible, violent people—" She stood up and her chair would have fallen over if I hadn't managed to steady it. "Please, Mr. Demaris. This is the first time we've had to hear this kind of thing."

He looked pained. "Is it? You're very lucky, then." He gave her a smile he'd have regretted had he known her better.

"Don't patronize me, sir. I see plenty of awful violence and pain. I'm a physician and there isn't a lot I haven't seen." She had the tissue balled in her fist, but she'd be damned if she'd use it and look like a lady dabbing her eyes at curtain call. "Ben, help me. How can I say this?"

Her voice threatened to give out on her. "This is my *son* you're talking about."

"You might be surprised, Doctor, to remember that it is always somebody's son. Or daughter. Even if he's been in trouble before. All this may be very sharp and fresh for you and that's one factor, I suppose, in the kind of pain it's giving you. It's hard to come to terms with the shock of it. But the mothers whose sons have been through everything already come in here so weary that they aren't actually much better protected than you are." He looked straight at her, intensely focused on her eyes. "They're like—well, I can imagine patients, maybe, who have no immune systems left, who've been weakened by all their previous assaults. So, if I might—I don't want to detract one iota from what you're feeling, but I have to say this—don't assume this is harder for you than it is for anyone else."

He was calling her on her self-righteousness. She closed her eyes. I don't know what she was telling herself.

"Are you asking me for a more—delicate—presentation of the possibilities? Or would you prefer different facts? Because he could give you those if he wanted to cooperate. But I'm not sure you'd like them much better."

She had her composure back. That would be the last *cri de coeur* he was going to hear from her.

"I'm not unsympathetic, please don't infer that from all this. This has nothing to do with sympathy. But, Dr. Reiser, I thought you told me you had seen the corpse."

"The corpse! It wasn't any corpse, it was a girl I knew. All right. Enough," Carolyn said. "God, I sometimes think *I'm* getting callous from seeing one too many—corpses."

Panos Demaris drained his can of diet soda. "These are the parameters that have to be sketched in before we can do anything else." He was going to keep his distance. I sympathized. "I'm sorry. I regret them. But they're unavoidable. Meanwhile, Jacob. He'll come around eventually, I can guarantee he'll get tired of this game. He's wasting time, and I wish—ah, well. Sometimes when they get away from the institutional setting, you know, that'll do it. There's something poisonous about being watched twenty-four hours a day, it doesn't exactly encourage spontaneity." He smothered his mouth and chin in a giant paper napkin. "Then there are some procedural matters, of course. I have a great deal of careful work to do and how you—I—we—feel about the case isn't going to matter very much, unfortunately." He ran his hand over his cheeks; they looked ready for a late-afternoon shave. I could see why Wendell had said he was like a country doctor—he was stern but not harsh. He had, I thought with some gratitude, no *side* to him.

On the way to the car I touched her arm as tenderly as I could get myself to.

"Because he sounded like a goddamn police report. Here's Jacob stock-still like a deer in the headlights, you know—just paralyzed—and I expect this guy to start talking any minute about the *alleged perpetrator*, the way they do. Where the hell were you, I'd like to know, you and your famous anger?"

That roughness didn't sound like her. She was the woman who had been so nice to Fran Conklin when he came as the messenger. I wasn't sure what it was about Panos that had bothered her so. "Oh, Carolyn. You were so busy being hostile and what I was hearing was somebody trying to understand. But you can't blame him for being exasperated—he's got a job to do and he isn't getting any help, let alone gratitude, from any quarter."

She ignored that. "I can see that the price of having this demon for the defense is that we're going to be condescended to endlessly about how much poorer other people are, and how much more they've suffered. Can't you see the man's got it in for people like us, Benny? We're useful just to float his business so that he can minister to the more deserving."

I told her that was a willful exaggeration.

"Forget it," she said, with the weariest look. "I wish he'd eaten before we got there. We're paying for his time and he's *dining*. All that greasy disgusting food dripping down."

"Try a little charity for a change," I suggested to my wife, who could look elegant even in despair. Only the rest of the world ate with its mouth full. "Do you think he'd do better by Jacob on an empty stomach?"

CAROLYN

THE FIRST NEWS STORY THAT MENTIONED JACOB BY NAME DECLARED HIM an adult. "Today you are a man" used to be the greeting on a boy's Bar Mitzvah day; lacking that semi-official optimism, Carolyn supposed only the boy himself, and his attentive parents, dare put a date on his coming-of-age. But for Jacob the court conferred maturity and it was a defeat, though not a surprise. Nothing good issued from it: all it meant was consequences more dire and long-lasting than they meted out to "juveniles," and far less leniency. Panos Demaris said it was inevitable and enjoined them from becoming depressed: a seventeen-year-old accused of murdering a girl, he said, sounds about as seasoned as they come. There is no court that would not have found that way.

It also meant that his anonymity was gone, though in a place like Hyland that had been a joke from day one. It felt like a good time to leave town. Her parents had suggested that Hilton Head was lovely even in this season, more temperate by far than New England in winter. "We have all your birds down here, dear!" her mother enticed her. "You'd recognize some of them."

Carolyn thanked her politely but told her she'd have to await a more promising time. "We have bail to deal with, Mom, and then, God, a grand jury. I'm not really sure what that'll mean, but I do know it means we're not going anywhere." How casual that sounded, how cheerfully routine.

They repulsed reporters, trying to be kindly; probably, after the third, failing. Carolyn especially resented the one who, camera in hand, threatened that if no one in the house consented to an interview, people would tend to draw their own conclusions. "Draw whatever you want to," she had said to him in a voice that felt sore with repressed fury. "You might try to remember the rudiments of law that say someone's innocent unless proven otherwise."

"Oh please," the young man had said, as if that one had gone out with the bunny hop. Very young. She was rooting, as she closed the door firmly on him, for his writing hand to wither and fall off.

She wished she worked downtown in an insurance office where the worst that could happen might be that someone would cut her dead as she handed over a policy, or behind the counter at the laundry, where people wouldn't feel themselves intimately contaminated by her hands.

Her patient load had dwindled to the point where she had to release Karen to find a job with a reliable payroll. "You'd think you had AIDS," Karen said to her furiously, in tears. "You'd think you could hurt their little precious by breathing on him. Oh, Carolyn, I don't *get* it!"

Carolyn made herself smile. "You've come to the wrong place if you think I can explain." Even the other doctors at the hospital were cool—civil but wary. She had heard that Tom McAnally was outraged that she had come down to look at Martha's body the day she was murdered. Did he think she knew something about Jacob's involvement, that he had come to her confessing, whereupon she'd gone coolly back to work behind a mask of innocence? Where was his good sense, not to mention his compassion? Apparently, doctors didn't have one whit more than civilians.

She held Karen to her, smoothed her already smooth hair. Karen had promised to come back when the cloud moved on. Carolyn didn't dare think about that: who would they all be when—if—the cloud moved on?

She could feel herself thickening intellectually like a sidelined athlete whose waist begins to soften. Desultory reading wasn't going to remove her from the scene, its weight of boredom and anxiety, but study might. She used to study best when she was depressed, the way some people ate and others drank. It meant a trip to Boston to find the texts she needed—no one at the little Hyland Community Hospital had a serious up-to-date library—and she walked in the shadow of the medical-center buildings, feeling her old awe at the power of comprehension they represented, the real nobility of effort and dedication. That was easy to lose at home, even under the best of circumstances; the intellectual limitations of day-in-day-out country doctoring were immense. Ben probably felt that when he came down to spend the day in the museum.

And it was a relief to be restored to anonymity again, to cross the street and enter the medical bookstore, that hush, in search of a monograph on blood gases in children. She even felt the gaze of a man in an overcoat (very urban, as far removed from her husband's country clothes as Harrods or Burberrys from Monte's Work Clothes—"Rough Goods for the Man Who Can Rough It"

—in Hyland). He looked at her appreciatively, while she kept her gaze scrupulously straight, picking up one book, riffling it, picking up another. God only knew what his suppositions about her might be like. God only knew that, no matter what they were, they were wrong. She had to smile at the thought of what she'd have to lay on him, as the kids would say, over a cup of coffee. Poor man!

She wanted to bring Judith something. She walked up Newbury Street past the gorgeous shops, their tasteful minimalism, but nothing had much savor. Worse, Judith would see the gesture for what it was. Even so, wasn't it better to bring home something than nothing? The little African basket cost a lot more than it ought to, and none of it was going back to Dakar either. Into it she slipped a necklace made of bananas, watermelon, and—what was that, kiwi? Absurd.

And Judith took it from her gravely, said thanks, bore it off to her room like a dog going to bury a bone. Carolyn would be surprised if she ever saw her daughter wearing it—all it would do was smell of tragedy for her forever. A bribe in return for a smile, and not even a smile to show for it. The most disquieting thing about Judith's depression was that she knew how responsible her daughter was, how hard she usually worked at causing her parents no pain. She was a hider, not an aggrandizer, this one. She sometimes seemed to have been born understanding what it felt like to be her own parent. So, her mother thought, she's beyond even that kind of control. It's a smart girl, she thought, who knows ruin when she sees it.

She dressed for the bail hearing the way she might for a funeral, heedlessly. This time Judith was coming; she seemed to be preparing herself with extraordinary care, as if her first public appearance in the Reiser entourage demanded it. For a girl a little too shy for glamour, it was an odd reaction—Carolyn thought she detected a touch of mascara on her fair lids; she certainly smelled tea roses. All of it without consultation: Judith, these days, dressed and did just about everything else behind closed doors. Independence was coming anyway, but Carolyn couldn't help resenting the suddenness of her hostility; she had little doubt Judith had not jumped but had been pushed. Or pulled.

They went in the other direction from Concord and Manchester, westward, in the direction of Vermont. How many official sites could they hit in a month, she wondered, public spaces that existed for the maintenance of order, flying flags. Grieves County Superior Court was a fine Victorian building in Howe, tall, narrow, brick, which had looked ugly for a few generations but was back in favor now, all its trim newly painted in authentic colors. It had a state-shaped plaque beside its door, filling in a little history. There was something smug about it, as if its enthusiastic renovation might make the harsh realities of justice more attractive as well. At least more picturesque.

So they were bringing Jacob over in a sheriff's car, the way they'd brought him back from Massachusetts. Taxpayers' expense again, thanks. All these collaborators in what used to be a private fate. A form of fame, she thought bitterly. Oh, Jacob, you could have spared us such acclaim. The headline in yesterday's *Bugler* read MURDER SUSPECT TO GET HOWE HEARING. Next week they would incite what they could: LOCAL SUSPECT BAILED; HOME. Something to feed those who enjoyed slavering. They had found a photograph, an informal one. (Which cooperative friend had volunteered snapshots?) It was Jacob laughing, handsome and unforgivably carefree. The murderer with his friends; Martha was probably just outside camera range. There was no way not to look callous if you were still alive—logical or not, this seemed to be a picture of his current happiness. Two reporters slouched outside the courtroom with their cameras hanging from their hands; she didn't recognize either of them.

But it was all emotionless. What was she expecting, she

asked herself sternly. Not a sensational scene. Probably something shapely as a movie, though, with all the dull parts cut. Close-ups of the principals. Jacob's eyes, Panos Demaris's busy little body—what a strutter he was, a rooster in gray gabardine, unglamorous but commanding, everywhere at once, and familiar to all. The judge, who looked as if he had indigestion—it was right after lunch, maybe he did—and kept his eyes on the long windows of his courtroom, which were gray with gathering rain. He looked like a man who was worried about his golf game. But it was February; probably he wondered if it would turn to snow and slow him down on his way home.

There was a lot of muttering out of earshot, up in front of the judge. It wasn't their business, much—they had supplied the suspect; now they had to sit tight. What it felt like, in fact, was a movie in the making, before the editor got to work. She'd seen one being made once, in a neighboring town that had been pushed back a century by the addition of copious sand in the streets, and a rearrangement of the general-store porch: more barrels and rakes, the ice machine gone, petunias everywhere. Much ado about less than nothing: stasis. Paralysis, nearly, while a hundred assistants ran around with clipboards and nothing happened for the cameras. Days had vanished before they got their takes. Endless, repetitive, wearying, with no climaxes; no hint, even, of what it was all about.

Judith sat sullenly and picked at a hangnail. Ben was somewhere else; he hummed under his breath (which aggravated her almost as much as the clipping of his nails with that little silver gizmo—she plotted divorce whenever she heard him at that. "Bite them!" she'd whisper to herself, knowing how irrational she'd seem if she ever brought her disgust out in the open). Now he sat and hummed as if he were happy.

The judge spoke suddenly, having said very little to anyone but the men who'd huddled at the bench. He made it sound routine: the seriousness of the crime, the nature of, the dangers of. Understood. A hundred thousand, just like that. The request—the order—seemed to come out of nowhere. Not that they weren't prepared for it, only that the purpose for it all had faded. They were going to ransom him for a bank check delivered by hand to the clerk's office downstairs, for a hundred thousand dollars. Carolyn forced herself to close her eyes and remember the blue-brown-purple of the girl's concave temple, her hair stiff in a hardened glue of blood, and the tissues of her skull. She saw Tom McAnally roll her socks down over her blue-white ankles, the skin mottled with cold. All right, she said to herself. It felt sordid, like masturbation, she was ashamed of it, having to stimulate herself to imagine the cruelest part, to remember what and why and to say "Okay, Ben. Do it," because he was the one with the check in his pocket. "Let's go." She said it, though, and rose to her feet. A hundred thousand, and all in one lump, was cheap for the breath of somebody's daughter.

None of them talked to the reporters, who raised their cameras and took those heartless courthouse-steps photographs the papers are always full of, the kind that make either friends or antagonists of those who confront them over their breakfast coffee. Unfriendly, that family, they would say. See, they won't even look at us.

Jacob sat beside his sister all the way home, exactly as he'd done all his boyhood, when he could fill endless hours giggling, making the occasional outcry, negotiating over territory, reading comics silently or aloud. The time, remember, Jacob, on a winding road, when Judith vomited all over you as you slept? She didn't ask him if he remembered. The frequency of his trips in the backseat had dwindled to just about nothing now that he could drive—where did they drive to that he wanted to go without coercion?

Carolyn could see how awkward Judith felt getting in beside him. He lurched through the door and sat down heavily and stared straight ahead. She went around quietly to the other side and got in rather more demurely than usual. Carolyn tried to imagine what all this felt like to him but his silence—not surly but absent—accomplished what he must have wanted it to: it made him nearly unrecognizable. Unclaimable. She couldn't get a handhold. Such self-removal, all his softness and vulnerability effaced along with the particulars of his personality. And it threw them all off. There was nothing they could say to each other that did not sound forced. He was like the twisted ankle, she thought, that pulled the entire body into misalignment. The trip from Howe took half an hour; Ben finally turned on the radio to cut the uncustomary silence. It made her heartsick that nobody argued about what kind of music to listen to.

She closed her eyes as they sped east. The rain that had worried the judge was finally falling but the air was warm and it did nothing worse than blacken the highway and cause the tires to sizzle. "Skunk!" Judith called out and wrinkled her nose. Once that would have brought an instant echo from her brother, who could never resist it—he'd hit her in the arm and shout "Double skunk!" back at her and they'd mock each other until long after the smell of the dead skunk subsided. Carolyn could see from Ben's eyes that he was high on the excitement of the trip. They seemed to dart like the pupils in REM sleep, registering everything fast, a little dance of consciousness there on the inside of the windshield. Occasionally he'd do some of that tuneless humming. She wondered finally, as they drove into the center of town and then out of it again, if anybody had seen them, had seen his, Jacob's, head sticking up unashamed there in the back of the car. A homecoming.

It wasn't late and the drive had not been particularly arduous, but his weight had exhausted them. His absence was heavy, torpid, aggressive—hauling him home was something like shouldering a feed sack. They put the sack down in the middle of the kitchen floor, where it stood refusing to make a move or acknowledge any recognition. "You can do whatever the hell you want to with your catatonic self," Ben said in a voice nearly inaudible with restrained fury, "but don't even think of opening that front door."

The rhythm of such exchanges demanded that Jacob counter, "What if I do?" But he said nothing, only stood looking as if he hadn't heard. Ben, perhaps in gratitude, denied himself his rhetorical "Do you understand?" Carolyn felt like applauding his restraint.

She was overwhelmed with the futility of standing up on her two feet. "I'm going to lie down for a few minutes," she said dimly. "Jacob, are you hungry?" She looked willing to cook him a meal. "Take your coat off." She arranged a smile. "Stay awhile."

Judith, foraging in the refrigerator, emerged with a small fluted cup of chocolate pudding, plucked the whipped-cream can from the door and ostentatiously circled it over the surface till she had spun a peak that glistened like shaving cream. Good girl, Carolyn thought. But her brother gave no sign of noticing. "My God," Judith said bravely. "He'll even pass up chocolate!" She breathed out a long sigh of ordinary exasperation, turned her back smartly like a marcher, and left the room.

Both of them took off their shoes and got under the quilt. They were careful not to touch.

The bed took her in, hard below, soft above, the quilt like a light warm body pressed against hers. "God, are we going to get wrinkled."

"You going somewhere?" Ben closed his eyes. "All right. Is he mad? Angry, I mean? Is he scared? I just wish I —just—*got* it."

"He's punishing us. I don't even know what I mean, but I feel it. He's—"

"He's sending death rays," Ben said. "Well, maybe this is what it takes."

"What takes?"

Ben turned on his side, away from her. "Living with what he's done." He sounded half asleep, he yawned as if he were comfortably lying down for a nap. How far they had come since that first night when it had all broken on them. They were accommodating its impossibility, like a chronic life-threatening illness. "Being who he is."

"Or keeping it out," she protested. But even as she said it she thought vaguely, Too abstract, too textbooky. Too neat. That's the way strangers think, not parents. But she didn't know how parents thought, generic parents. Pale late-afternoon light made emphatic squares high on the wall. She, too, was washing out in a wave that obliterated the horizon and turned her over and over and pulled her down. On Wednesday when the *Bugler* came out they'd be facing the camera with the long, dark shutters of the courthouse looming behind them. People would look at them and shake their heads at the way they masqueraded as an ordinary family.

In the kitchen Jacob, in his black parka scored with red and yellow stripes, was facing the broom closet, shivering so violently he put his arms around himself and held tight.

They woke a few hours later, the heavy weight gone as if they'd only suffered jet lag. Jacob was watching television, his jacket still zipped. Carolyn brought a bowl of potato soup into the den and set it in front of him on the little table. The room was dark except for the box of high-colored figures who ran and stopped and stood facing each other around a wooden bar so highly polished it gave off stars of light. The laugh track swelled and diminished like a wave cresting and breaking against a beach. *Cheers.*

How odd, she thought: the old blue light was gone, the unearthly glow that had risen in the days of black-and-white, filling every window with its phosphorescence as you walked down the street, peeking in. She put the spoon down beside the soup bowl. Her son's face was pink in the rainbow light. He was focused on an argument between a very tall woman and two men, one in a sweat suit, one in a raincoat—she was disconcerted by how hard he was concentrating, as if she'd caught him in an act he had claimed he could no longer perform. His attention was quite intact, thank you.

Alongside her anger, she felt a rising wave of desperation: she was going to die—she thought, literally die—of claustrophobia. There was no world anymore. He was all she was doomed to think about—would it be for months? For years, more likely. This fine face, the gentle dark curve of eyebrow, the firm and perfect nose, the hardening contours that were once so soft, she was going to be walled in with it, unresponsive, distant, unacknowledging. She had patients whose parents were similarly doomed—it was unspeakable to watch them see their child dwindle toward death or master pain or overcome paralysis. Maybe it was worse, someone else could say. But, worse or better, wasn't this different? His body had not overcome him in one of those genetic mishaps or dire accidents of matter; he had taken his fate, her fate—the fate of that poor dear girl—and twisted it like someone mutilating iron bars. ("Oh, Mom," she could hear him taunt, "what makes her 'dear' all of a sudden?") He had vehemently deformed them, then crawled through head-first, only it was a cage he'd crept into, not out of. And they all had to follow.

"You don't have to pretend not to be hungry," she said to him, trying for some kind of warmth. "You're going to have to give some signs of life—eat, go to the bathroom.

Whatever. Sleep." He didn't take his eyes off the screen. The California Raisins were leering and dancing in shades, to a funky beat. She was tempted to turn it off to see if, in his effrontery, his shamelessness, he would object. "Don't worry, we won't mistake them for signs of communication."

She was an impatient woman—her father had always told her that was what naturally came of being smart: no time for fools, for repetitiveness, for the imprecise or the sentimental. He always made it seem like the best way to be. (That her sister, Nina, was a vague and sentimental fool was the other, the implied, half of the message. Only in the last few years had Carolyn begun to realize she herself had been the bearer—innocent at first, then maybe all too willing—of that caustic opinion. At the moment Nina wasn't speaking to her, or, as far as she knew, to anyone else much either.)

Now, duly impatient, she wanted to fast-forward. Skip the details, bring them to the denouement. The process ought to have interested her but didn't. *What happens?* was all she wanted to know. Somewhere she had read, *"Our winter afternoons have been known at times to last a hundred years."* She felt as if they might be entering year 2.

A dinner party. Imagine: the mother of the accused entertains with a duck confit, game hens with persimmon, arugula salad, and lemon ice. They would put *her* in jail for such an obscenity.

The mother of the accused goes shopping, finds a Ralph Lauren at $19.99. She is lynched in her own front yard.

It is winter; she cannot garden. She cannot ride or hike. The victims get the attention, and the "perpetrators." But she had never thought about the forfeit of ordinary life for —what? fellow travelers?

She remembered her friend Carla, who said, in the middle of her chemotherapy, "I used to wish I'd have time for all these books. Watch out what you wish for—by the time you get it, you'll be too nauseous to enjoy it."

When she was last heard from, Nina was in Montana being dwarfed by the space, the scenery. (The space in her head, Carolyn had thought harshly, had finally met its match. Then she repented thinking so ungenerously. But she'd thought it and it stuck.) "It's great out here because you're *expected* to be insignificant. No one looms very large and every man-made creation looks pathetic. The houses look like glued-together toothpicks." It was such a good defense Carolyn imagined colonies of the self-hating and insecure huddled up in the long blue shadows of the mountains, where nothing mattered. (Hunters and homesteaders didn't lack confidence, though. Maybe there were two populations.)

Nina called late in the evening. It was strange. She had, unpredictably, been speaking to their parents; every now and then some mysterious impulse forced or invited her, it was hard to know which, to call them. "How is he, Car?" she asked flatly, either sedated or feeling coerced. Well, she wasn't gloating, anyway.

Carolyn swallowed what filled her throat like blood. "Bailed. We just brought him home and we're just—here. Nobody really knows yet. But he won't talk to us, Nina. I don't have the vaguest idea how he is."

Nina laughed. She had a husky voice, a voice that had been strafed by chemicals and smoke, endlessly, and repaired by silence. She knew this ploy. "Oh ho, Car, I'll bet that's one you really can't handle!" It made her merry; if there was a special skill entailed by self-annihilation, she was a past master. "Hey, put him on. I want to talk to him."

She tried to imagine Nina, sitting in a little wooden house, perhaps—she'd never rent a trailer, though she'd said there were a lot of them out there, nestled in the capacious arms of the foothills. It would be one of the ugly excrescences she had described in the ostentatious landscape, like a Popsicle construction in danger of flattening by falling rocks. "Story of my life," she would say if you pushed her.

"What's going on out there, Nina? Are you potting?"

"Potting or potted, sister dear? I don't know what I'm doing, exactly. A lot of meditation. Yoga. I'm learning some Blackfoot medicine, and a little Crow. It's okay. Though a lot you care."

"Oh please, Neen. Did you call to remind me of our first fifteen years? Do I really need that right now?"

Nina sighed. "Sorry. No, I distinctly did not." She sounded sincere. "I didn't—every time I think I've stopped being angry about—everything—I relax and forget myself. Look, is the kid there? I want to speak to him."

What the hell, Carolyn thought. She picked up the extension in the room where Jacob was sitting tranced, brought it to him, and said, "Your aunt Nina. She's calling you from outer space." She forced the phone at him; by reflex, he received it. Back in the kitchen, the receiver lay where she'd put it down, in front of the row of cookbooks. She took it from the counter with great delicacy and put it to her ear.

"Hey, minx," she heard her sister saying. "Seen any good flicks I need to know about?"

"An old one," Jacob said, his voice not even rusty. "Did you ever hear of this thing, *Casablanca?* I think it's real famous."

Nina laughed softly. "I've heard of it. I've even seen it ten or fifteen times. You liked it?"

"Mmm. Yeah, it was better than all the noise they're putting out now. It was, like—it felt like *history*. But it was funny, too."

"I always knew you had good taste. Have any new books for our list?" They had a record of unlikely all-time Bests that went back to when he was very little, books on how to make rockets and ice-cream sundaes, books about sled dogs and maharajas.

He hesitated. "No. I've been—like—busy."

Nina grunted acquiescence. "I heard." She waited.

"What did you hear?"

She sighed, very long and hard. "Heard you may have done something you can't take back."

The pauses were lengthening. "Right."

Judith was standing in the kitchen door watching her. Embarrassed, Carolyn turned away. On the wall were photographs of Judith and Jacob deep in the middle of their childhoods, smiling when they weren't eating. In one, Jacob was flying through the air with his feet tucked under him—he was kneeling in space!—above sunstruck water. His mouth was open on a shout of joy.

"What do you think about it, Jake?" Nina could talk as delicately as tweezers moved.

"What do I think? I think I might not come out of this alive."

"Meaning—"

Another impossible pause. "Meaning they'll get me or I'll get myself. Either one."

"Jacob."

"Mmm—"

"Jacob, you old minx. Don't help them out, please. Don't be cruel to yourself." Her words were tightening, coiling up with urgency. "If you need punishing, let them do it to you, they'll be only too glad to. Don't do it to yourself. You hear me?"

His voice was dwindling, he sounded as if he were being bawled out, not encouraged; the air on the line was thick with the tears he was fighting. "Yeah. I hear."

She told him his parents had her phone number if he needed it. She told him a funny story about a sheep that had gotten its muzzle frozen to her doorstep and how she had eased him free with her steaming tea kettle and made a friend who came inside now and slept, sometimes, beside her bed like a dog. "It's not a smell you'd really want to get to know, but he gives off a lot of warmth these days." She told him the mountains looked like painted backdrops for the kind of movies they don't make anymore, and the Indians drove a hundred miles from one town to the next, their engines steaming. She told him she only had electricity about half the time. "I wish you could see it out here," she said.

He gave a little snort for the absurdity of the wish. "Me too."

"I love you, fella," she said huskily, as if that were just another story. "You are my favoritest boy of all time."

Carolyn heard her end of the connection click off.

Judith stood with her hands on her hips, the seal of her negative judgment. "Would you do that to me, too? *God* . . ."

Carolyn laughed without pleasure. Her chest was quivering with tension. "Oh, Judith, don't be such a purist. There are *times*—"

"You and Daddy always tell us there are no exceptions: you don't steal, you don't cheat, and you don't *peek!* Or eavesdrop."

"Keep your voice down," she whispered. "Shhh . . ." She wanted Judith to go away so she could think about what she'd heard. Or not heard. The love in it, the disorder. He had admitted nothing. Only the danger he was in, not a word about guilt or circumstances. Leave it to Nina to manage to have the chance to open him up a little and to blow it on *feelings*.

As would Ben, perhaps. He would soothe rather than challenge. Either that, she realized with some surprise, or he'd annihilate him. There it was: either he'd take his son in his arms and stroke his terror away or he'd shout down the rafters and threaten mayhem. That was what you called being a loose cannon.

"I feel like telling Jacob!" Judith announced. "I think I will. I'll tell him, 'You're not the only criminal here!' " She must have been remembering how Jacob had been grounded once for listening to her phone conversation and then making fun of the nonsense he'd heard, she and Celeste dreaming about love, boys, haircuts. Justice was still an absolute for her.

Nina, Nina, Nina. Not a solid bone in her body, gone to the fat of self-contempt, and not a solid challenging thought in her head. Had she done that on purpose, generously concerned for how her nephew must be suffering, or did she just lose it, let it go by, the chance to push a little, find out the truth? Reality was a bad word to Nina. It was never good news, loaded rather with ill will and hard adjustments; it was packed with high-explosive facts that promised death to the status quo.

Once, when their mother fell on the ice and they were very young—eight, maybe, and six, or nine and seven—trailing her home from the store on a snowy day, her arms full of heavy paper bags, and her legs had leaped out from under her and she'd hit the sidewalk hard, Carolyn had insisted on knowing exactly what hurt. Here, her back? Or only her seat, this bone at the end of her tail? She had just learned in school that sometimes people shouldn't move when they've been hurt, and she was trying it out, grateful to have some way to help, and she had poked and prodded for the details. Nina, making little sounds like a crying gull—or maybe they were encouragements, you couldn't tell—whipped off her coat to cover her mother up, right to the chin. Even though she'd left her mittens home, she'd pounded the snow into a sumptuous mound and packed it under her mother's head for a pillow, and stroked her face while she arranged her on it. It had never occurred to Carolyn that her sister might be a better person than she was. For all her social ineptness, and her incapacity for joy, perhaps she was, profoundly, more decent, more loving. We should have been a single girl, she thought. Or a single woman. We would have been perfect, a blend of hard and soft, prod and soothe. Cure and nurture.

They would have been a hell of a lot less lonely, both of them, for sure.

JUDITH

"JAKE," SHE SAID FROM HIS DOORWAY THE NEXT AFTERNOON, A WHISPER. "I know you don't want to talk much but—please! Did you go anywhere, really?" She stood on one foot and then the other. "Just—like in twenty-five words or less? *Please?*"

He had been sitting with his back turned to his desk. He was looking at his room as if he had never seen it before, like someone judging a stranger's life by his surroundings, undecided what he thought of him. He sighed and closed his eyes. "Sure I went," he said quietly. "Every day I got up and went out to Logan—" That was the airport, way at the end of the T line. "I had a bunch of these postcards, you know? Like with all these cities on them. I got them at this crazy store? And I looked around and found a flight that was going where I wanted to go, and then I found someone who wouldn't mind mailing a card for me when they got there."

Judith stared. His eyes were still closed and he smiled, though not at her.

"And after I gave it to—whoever—nobody ever turned me down—I sat in one of those seats there in the waiting area, you know, near the ticket counter. Excuse me, podium, they like to call it podium, like, the most pretentious thing so you can't figure out what they're talking about. And I closed my eyes like this. And I went with them. I got there quicker. And cheaper. St. Louis and Albuquerque. See, you can't fly direct to Santa Fe on a big plane, you've got to go to Albuquerque. I went to all of them." She wondered if the same slow tears squeezed out of his eyes when he sat in the airport. He'd have been embarrassed. "But you won't tell, will you? Nobody would understand."

"Mm-mmmh, I won't," she promised. "I understand, though. I hope you had a good time." She didn't like pitying Jacob, it didn't feel normal. He talked about sentimental people as if they were ugly. She wished she could put her arms around him, but he'd never forgive her. She waited for a threat but he just turned his back on her and, this time, judged the view from his dusty window, dirty snow down in the driveway, stamped a hundred times by tire tread, and the distant hills turning purple with cold.

BEN

JACOB ONCE SAID THAT WE MADE A FETISH OUT OF THE DINNER TABLE. I never really thought much about it, I assumed that everybody everywhere got together once a day—probably Bedouins in the desert did it, and Ethiopians, who dipped that spongy bread into a single dish. It wasn't a self-conscious move to keep the family together, it was only natural: love, curiosity and concern for each other's day, plus the sheer need to eat—it was half a dozen things, all of them benign. But no, he said. He had a lot of friends who ate on the run. Even here, where big-city dissolution hadn't visibly set in, one-parent families, second-shift families. Families that didn't like each other. It was dazzling, the little window he opened on varieties of family habit. And he'd been studying some sociology in school, or maybe it was psychology. Whatever, it gave us a name—we were the nuclear family, and maybe we took too much for granted. Judith was alarmed. (This was a few years ago.) What, she wanted to know, did our family have to do with the atom bomb? We laughed, but she was right—didn't it make us sound dangerous, like something about to detonate?

Now, though. All of us arrived at the table by sheer force of expectation, at six o'clock. Jacob's first night home, I'd made Szechuan chicken, fried rice, incredibly overpriced out-of-season snow peas. (Every trip to the supermarket cost me a little boiled blood. Some people were matter-of-fact and said hello; others cut me, turned their baskets away. Even the polite ones, though, didn't want to talk—"So how are things?" was too ridiculous—and neither did I. But we had to eat, so I ran the gauntlet with an expressionless face.

Then again, last time, on my way home with the groceries, I stopped for gas—it's all full-service in this town, we need the jobs—and the kid who filled my tank, tall as a basketball player but a little too hunched, too slow, too heavy-boned, leaned in and said, "Hey, say hi to Jake for me. Tell him Freddy." "Okay, Freddy," I said, so pleased I was embarrassed. He was as neutral as the windshield he was wetting down. "Anything else?" "No, hi's good enough." He turned the squeegee over. "From Freddy.")

"I'll bet they didn't serve this at the—at Deer Creek," Carolyn went at him doggedly. That was what they called the youth facility, named, like a suburban street, by dreamers.

He smiled faintly and forked it up. Let me assume gratitude is an emotion too deep for words. He never touched Carolyn's soup that first night, but now he was eating, at least, as if they'd been starving him. His cheeks were drawn, his color terrible, but I hadn't attributed it to bad nutrition; there were enough reasons to look less than your best in the lockup.

The rest of us chattered about this and that. Judith told us they were casting *Working;* there were no appropriate parts for her; she thought she might work backstage, on lights or props. We were like a stereo set, an odd one, three speakers set up with enormous distance between them. Each voice came from somewhere else. And in the middle sat the Space.

Carolyn tried to address it more or less directly. "What were you eating, Jake? At Deer Creek."

He shrugged. "You know," he said into his fork. "The usual." His first words.

"The usual. Well, I've never had a meal in a place like that, so what's 'the usual'?"

He only shook his head as if the answer was too complex for his vocabulary.

I had to restrain myself—had to and did. So Judith leaped in again and tried to plug the hole. I was grateful to her, but it didn't solve the problem.

A *deus ex machina* did. We are not abandoned yet, I thought. There are still unfilled spaces for luck in the world, even if they are set in motion by sheer nastiness.

What happened was, the phone rang. We had, these days, no small quantity of ill-wishers who felt duty-bound to inform us that our son should be in a high-security prison awaiting his moment in the chair. We're the folks who had just yesterday received in our mailbox the subtle message that JEWS BLEED CHILDREN!, illustrated by a flattened stick figure, drops of blood flying off in all directions, the way children draw the rays of the sun. The first few times, as Carolyn had warned me, they really catch you in the solar plexus. But you can't go on letting yourself be injured, and so you don't. Callous or not, you just work out a routine and you play it like a tape. There's no "I-thou" with your harassers (who only think they're God), and I'd given up feeling guilty over it.

This gloater was a thin-voiced old man who took a while to get to it but finally advocated stoning. I had long thought that if this could only be a laughing matter, we'd have plenty to practice on. "Yessir, I see," I said with unforced calm. "That's very biblical. And you'd cast the first one, I take it?" Consternation on the wire. This was, I suppose, like foiling an exhibitionist by yawning at the show of his most precious possessions. So he said it again, only louder, and added that it figured that my boy would go wrong, I was such a wise guy.

Therefore, I closed with my usual. "Now I want you to listen carefully." I liked to say that confidentially, so he'd lean in and concentrate on a message just for him. "I want you to know, you good American, that my son is innocent. Until he is found guilty by a court of law, he is no more guilty than you are. And no one has done that yet. No, no," I said over his complaints. "You are going to have to live with that fact for a long time, and maybe even longer than that, because he is still, this minute, a free young man, legally here on bond, against whom nothing has been proven." I didn't pause to hear his reaction (which would undoubtedly have been something along the lines of "But you and I know"). I hung up and sat down again. My face still flushed with each performance.

Judith applauded. "Yay, Daddy, you are *so* cool!"

But Jacob was looking at me hard. "Do you believe that?"

His voice broke over me like a memory. "What do you mean? Do I believe everyone's innocent until proven guilty? Unless, I should say. Of course I believe that. Our system—"

"I don't mean our system. I mean, about me. Do you believe I'm not guilty?"

Ah, that was another story, wasn't it? I chewed my chicken very deliberately, I took a sip of water. "Jacob," I said, "I don't know. Now that you're here, we can talk about that. We've got plenty of time." I wanted to tell him what I'd done for him, guilty or not. I don't mean for credit, or to make him love me. I mean, so that he would feel safe. Would relax a little and trust us. "It doesn't matter," I told him instead—I meant it as a rough translation. "Whatever the truth is, we're standing here with you. Believe me, it doesn't matter."

"Not that. I don't mean that. That's all sentimental bullshit. I mean—"

"Hey," Carolyn said. "Hey, not so fast. Sentimental bullshit?"

"Oh, everybody's parents say stuff like that. That isn't—"

"Do they," she said coolly, and I was grateful. "Do they, indeed. And they hide the murder weapon and destroy some of the evidence? Do they really? You know that for a fact?" Her face was a dangerous white mottled with color as bright as welts.

He looked at both of us, one to the other and back again, as if to ask each of us if this was a joke. Honest to God, he really didn't get it. "What 'murder weapon'?" Said not with wonder, let alone gratitude, but with contempt, as if we were his accusers.

It was undignified to claim credit for what we—what I—had done. It was offensive to cite the parents of his friend Frodo, and God knows how many of the rest of his friends as well, who had made clear they would not so automatically "say stuff like that." This was no competition. So I asked him to tell us what had happened. As he spoke, I reminded myself that I'd despaired of ever hearing his voice again. Hearing it, I didn't have to like what it said. That was the point, wasn't it? This was our problem, not only his, and we would have to solve it together. That was both what caused and what came of those endless evening meals at this table that he liked to mock, the leisurely accounts, the transfer of information, the patient accretion of a thousand daily incidents of circumstance and character. The bad old Nuclear Family all in a huddle of particles around its nucleus, which was—I didn't know what. Once upon a time it might automatically have been the Father—Jacob's patriarch. But it surely was not so these days, nor did I want it to be.

In the middle of the table, the chicken glistened slick in its sauce. The vegetables around it were bright as ornaments. I had prepared the dinner as a sign of hope, to loosen tongues and remind us of other days. But we didn't have to recognize that for it to work on us. We only had to eat and feel reassured.

"How am I supposed to sit here over this chicken and talk about killing somebody?" He looked down at the hodgepodge on his plate, the brown and green and the red of the pepper, and back up at us where we sat still, afraid to utter a syllable. "If I'm going to be here with you—"

"You wouldn't talk to us when you were in Cambridge. You wouldn't talk at Deer Creek. You wouldn't talk *any*time. God only knows what that was all about. What are —how are we supposed to know what to think, let alone do?" This was me at my most rational. "Really, what would you have us do to help you?"

He looked cornered. But I saw his point: maybe this ordinary scene, this familiar family picture we had assembled as if nothing had changed, just made it all the more impossible. Did we need a cemetery at midnight, though, like some spooky gothic romance? Did we need the fogs of goddamn Transylvania?

I repeated myself carefully. "What would you have us do to help you if you won't—" I wanted to say *surrender.* "Stop running, Jacob," I pleaded instead. "You're home now. Can't you finally stop running?"

His voice was almost unrecognizably quiet. "If I tell you what happened—this wasn't *me.* It wasn't *me,* all right?" He pushed his plate away. Had the grace, I thought unkindly, to turn away from it. The possibilities were gone: flight, lying, silence, all of them were old, as he might put it. They dead-ended here. Home or trapped, I didn't know which he felt. I didn't try to guess for him anymore.

"Okay. If I can." He closed his eyes and kept them

closed a long time. Then he opened them but did not look at us. "We were—we were, like—we hung out together a lot this year. I know you didn't even know that. I didn't—it didn't seem like it was something you ought to know. You wouldn't have liked to know. Don't ask me why, that seems stupid now, but it didn't then. And it doesn't matter, I don't think. It wouldn't have changed anything anyway."

Judith put her elbows on the table and propped her head on her open hands. She looked like a student on the first day of school, prepared for anything that came her way. And my son went on talking. His face was pale when he began, but it reddened as he spoke, until, by the end, I was afraid for him. Did teenagers have strokes? Could a seventeen-year-old agitate himself into a broken blood vessel?

He told us they'd had a cabin they went to after school, many many times. It was a hunting camp, long disused, that had belonged to Martha's uncle, Harry Pipes, back off a logging road that came down near the junction of Poor Farm and Skittles Roads. "We'd leave the car and walk in when it was muddy or snowy. Otherwise, you could ride. The cabin didn't have much in it—a couple of pots and pans and lousy old dishes, a rusty stove. A dart board we used. A couch." I'll bet. "All of it was ratty, but it didn't matter, we could get away from everybody there, it was—like—enough." I passed no judgments. I saw Theda looking down on me from behind her hedge of dark hair, I saw our young unused bodies fitted together tight, and I thought, All right, so what? Good, in fact. Carolyn, the Virgin Queen, her eyes dark with reproach—or maybe simple sadness, let me not presume—did not look quite so forgiving. But that's another story.

On that day—when he called it that day his eyes opened wide as if he'd been slapped—they'd had a terrible argument. She had been going after him from the minute he'd picked her up at the ice-cream shop, at

Jacey's, very disdainful, clearly picking a fight. "So when we got to the cabin I tried to get her to tell me what was wrong and she finally told me, she said, 'You're not going to like this, but'—and it turns out she's pregnant. And I'm not who she's mad at really, she's mad at everyone and everything. God especially, for letting this happen. She was heavy into God sometimes, especially when she needed anything. I used to tell her God was her sugar daddy." He gave a snort of laughter. "Which, of course, she didn't like."

I nodded. "We knew that, Jacob. That she was pregnant. They—found it out. You know." I couldn't get myself to say the word *autopsy,* as if it might shock him.

"Okay. But it's more complicated, see. God, it's a fucking soap opera." He looked at Carolyn and Judith, who were shifting in their seats. "Excuse me." I wanted to say we've got more important things to worry about here than harsh language.

The complicated part was that she didn't think the baby was his. "Just like *As the World Turns.*" And that was when things really got nasty. She wouldn't say whose it might be, or how, let alone why. "Only, she had obviously been—you know. Getting around. And I never had a clue." He laughed at the delicacy of his impulse toward euphemism; he was embarrassed. "She figured it wasn't ours because we were"—he glanced very quickly at Judith, as if maybe she shouldn't be hearing these details; but he went on—"we were always pretty careful. I really wanted to be . . . I was trying to be *responsible,* you know? I didn't think there was anything wrong with what we were doing, but I didn't want her getting in any trouble like that." At this, the memory, I guess, of his concern —it must have been the tenderness of his care about her —he was swamped with tears. He got up and walked around the room slowly, shaking his head as if, rough enough with it, he could clear it of emotion.

"So then, I don't know," he said when he came back to

us, but he didn't sit down again, he stood and paced. "Then, I guess she's trying to make the break, you know, she starts insulting me and saying all kinds of—it was pretty stupid, it was, like, you're no good anyway, now I can tell you I never really liked you, that kind of thing. She says, like, you think you're so terrific and your parents are such big deals, you and that house with that lawn. The lawn really freaked her out, she always talked about it. I'd say, God, all that lawn is is a pain in the ass if you want to know, I have to mow it, but it was, like, you'd think it was a goddamn estate here or something with a drawbridge."

He cleared his throat. This was more talking than most boys his age do in a year. "And then, she's getting all wound up, she even blames me for, like, taking care with her. For using—only a wimp would, you know, think ahead like that, and—I don't know, it was all too—sort of, too controlled for her. You know what I mean? She made it seem like she only respected somebody who would—like, just force her. So I said, 'Are you looking for a caveman, you want some guy to yank you around by your hair? You like the idea some hairy ape knocks you up and doesn't even give a damn what he's doing?' And she goes, like, 'Yes. Yes, that's what I want, and that's sure not *you*.' Which ought to make me proud, I suppose, but, boy, not then. It made me feel like a turd right then." He rubbed his whole face hard with his open hand. "And, I mean, I don't even know if I *believe* all this shit. I mean, excuse me, this, like—anger. I kept feeling like she was very confused and just raging around at everybody, and she was trying to blame me for whatever part she could sort of pin on me, you know. Something my fault. So then—so then—" This he couldn't say. He stood for a while with his lips tightly closed. "She did some stuff that was—not so nice. To, like, provoke me. To get me to be like that, you know, that wild man." This was when his face began to redden so terribly I was afraid for him. He was teary and short of breath but, worse, he was redder than he'd been after the triathlon we ran in last year. "I don't want to talk about it, I don't—just—I couldn't be that. I couldn't do anything she wanted me to do. And I was—" He breathed out very hard.

"Ashamed?" I prompted.

"Ashamed and angry and disgusted and—like, so many different things I couldn't see straight. So I said, Let's go, that's all, this is the end of it, I'll take you home and you can have your baby or not have it, or stay with your caveman or not, I don't care. And we left."

And then and then? We sat in silence.

"And then, I don't know, we walked out to the road real far apart and got in the car, and just around when we got over toward Tuttle's, she says, 'Oh, Jacob, I didn't mean any of that, I'm sorry.' She's crying. She's just confused, is all. 'Pull over here,' she goes, 'I'll show you I don't mean any of it.' So I pull off—this is so stupid—we're in front of that fence and, you know, we sit for a while and we sort of make up. I'm still upset, because frankly I didn't like some of the things she said, I figure deep down she must really mean them, and I know I'm probably going to hear them again on a bad day. But we sit there awhile, we're like—very friendly. And it's beginning to get dark by now. So when I start up the car again we're stuck. We're deep in shit."

All this, I found, was easy to picture. It *was* Jacob, recognizably, humanly Jacob, who was telling this story. I know it's going to end terribly but at least he's real, he's warm and pulsing with blood, and I knew it, I knew it: he is no fiend. Either that's clear or it's not clear, how I could be in a state of near-euphoria because the voice that's telling us this is no stranger's.

And then it gets terrible again. They try a bunch of ways to get out of the rut, but anyone knows how you just dig yourself deeper. They rock it, she tries to back it up while he pushes, they put a mesh screen under the wheels, nothing helps. Finally she thinks of jacking up the car. He's not sure what that will do, but she says they can at least fill in the pit they've made by now under the wheels, so they can start again on smooth snow. So they do that, and when they let the car down gently it doesn't help. Recriminations. "She's ragging me and saying if I had some real shoulders I could have pushed harder. I mean, this is so dumb it's like—I could never say this in a court, they'd laugh at me, it's not—how could it end that way?" He kept shaking his head. "So I hand her the jack to put away since it didn't work, and she calls me something choice, I don't even remember, a turkey or something, a dweeb, some kind of a loser, I don't know, but it was, like, one thing too many and I lost it. I slapped her." He sighed. "I did, I slapped her, not hard. I just caught her on the side of her chin. I was so tired, and I wanted to get home and get her out of my sight. I called her some names I shouldn't have—you know. Not nice. You can guess." I *could* guess, shame and impatience and dishonor and sexual humiliation too, all closing down on him like the dark that was deepening full-speed by then. "And when I slapped her she grabbed me and hit me in the face, first with her hand, then, I suppose I was trying to get her off me, we were sort of fighting—about to fight —and she swung at me with the jack." He made a terrible sound then, as if he was being stabbed, his flesh torn —as if the words, each one embedded in his skin, were being removed from him by force. "Please," he said, "*please,* do I have to do this?"

We sat stock-still.

"You have to do it," I said.

He went over and put his hands out to my shaman, my pile of wood in the corner, sitting unlit and unlikely, and slid them gently over its fat curved shoulders the way a blind person or a baby feels something it's trying to learn by touch alone. For solace, oh my Jacob. To touch something hard and true under his hands. He stood there for a few minutes, weeping frankly, not fighting it. Carolyn got up and went and stood beside him, held him around the shoulders, firm. I realized I hadn't heard him cry for years. When he put that damn cap on, sign he was a true adolescent, vain and strong and all the rest, he went too adult to cry. "Okay," he said at last. "I can do it. Okay." Carolyn sat down.

His voice was frayed. I could barely hear him. "She swung and she just missed me and I just—grabbed it, she was screaming at me and I pulled it out of her hands and then—" He covered his face, not with his hands but with the crook of his arm, with the gray nubbled sleeve of his sweater. I hated to think what he was seeing in that prickly dark where he rested his eyes. It was a long time. Nobody said anything. Judith sniffled once and we sat tight. "The thing is," he finally said, "you say *murder*, you say *dead, bludgeoned to death*, and it sounds so—mysterious. And so huge. It sounds so—impossible to imagine. But it wasn't. It wasn't something I was trying to do, it wasn't something I thought about. Even after I did it—I mean after it *happened*—I couldn't believe I could have hurt her like that. No way. Unreal. It was like any accident—you know, if I'd have swung and missed like she did, just a couple of inches off, we'd be—everything would just—my biggest problem would be, like, do I say hello when I see her in the hall at school?"

He looked at us with all the bewilderment we'd been trapped with all these weeks, the amazement at how accident could become sickening reality. It made sense. It computed. I went to him where he stood, his eyes huge, swimming in tears again at his unspeakable luck, and I took him in my arms and felt him lean against me, no more resistance, no more refusals. "You'll be all right, Jacob," I whispered to him. "If you tell them exactly that—every word of it—you'll be fine." I could hear the words in the courtroom, I could see the wonder in his own eyes, the bewilderment that made him a victim, too.

He nodded against me, though he didn't in fact relax the stiffness of his shoulders, the tension that made him feel ready to flee. (Only later did I remember the jack—how could he ever explain its disappearance? It was too insane: somehow or other I'd have to convince him to lie for me!)

Out of the corner of my eye I could see Carolyn, her thin hands stretched in front of her on the table. Her fingers opened and closed, opened and closed, like an ecstatic cat's. She did that when she was troubled and thinking hard; it seemed to sop up her unspent energy. She looked pretty overwhelmed herself, but she was frowning. Her face was aloof with her own refusals, and my chest flipped over. Ambush. I couldn't imagine what she was thinking, but just then, no question, I felt as one with Jacob, and frightened of my wife. Why would she not be satisfied? We weren't out of the woods yet, I thought, and I clung as hard as I could. He would have to get this story heard, however he could. He would have to say it out in court, say it wherever he could get a hearing. An accident. Bad fortune. Anger all around, and the terrible means at hand.

CAROLYN

THEY WERE THE ONLY PEOPLE SHE KNEW WHO DIDN'T HAVE A dishwasher. Although in principle she believed you should never look a timesaving device in the mouth, she liked to swirl her hands around in warm water and think —it was a primitive satisfaction. She filled up the sink around the dinner dishes and felt the pleasure of plunging, all the way to the wrists, into the heat. Outside the kitchen window and across the black lawn, headlights flashed through the dark and vanished, like comets.

The trickle of doubt, a thin stream, worked slowly through her. She dragged her fingers through the soapy spirals, invoking whatever feelings would come, logical or not. It wasn't that she didn't believe his story, it seemed thoroughly plausible: not sensational, not an account of unrecognizable passion. Quite the contrary, it was as banal as real life, as unexceptional, one event leading to another, a confusion of emotions spreading outward until they stained everything. And his dissociation from its effects she had understood: Did *I* do that? How could this have happened, we were just . . . we were only . . . I didn't mean . . . As if he'd broken a vase. As if he'd let the cat out when they'd told him to keep her in. But that was where she stuck. You might do something accidentally, she'd seen people who had hit children in their cars; dogs, even. She'd seen them reduced to near-hysteria because they'd caused harm guiltlessly. Had broken something irreplaceable, not even by inattention. "She just ran out . . ." "He suddenly popped out from between two cars . . ." "He was chasing his ball and it was getting dark . . ." Oh God, they cried, oh God, forgive me!, the drivers no less in need of comfort than the parents.

He had mangled this girl—this woman—with whom he had shared the most intimate acts, and words, and feelings, hours and hours of them. He had just, by the side of Tuttle's split-rail fence, whispered in her ear, grazed his lips, probably, along her delicate neckbone where the short fair hairs curled. Then he had mauled her. Had felt the connection of the steel with that familiar fine blond hair, her breakable skull—and he had fled. *Hit-and-run*, she had gone to bed thinking that first night, her movements slower and slower, pulling off her sweater, slipping off her bra, wading as if through some heavy dreamtide toward bed. The most heinous cowards, she always thought when they brought the human road kill to the ER, were the hit-and-runs, who must have looked around to be sure they hadn't been seen, turned off their headlights if it was dark, and crept away fast. *Hit-and-run*. It was not the same crime, the blameless one, those others had wrought with their cars, the ones who came shrieking in with blood in their voices, blood now, forever, on their hands.

Road kill. Callous word that made animals sound like prey, the daily, expectable haul. But the girl—she stopped still, a plate like a wide flat stone between her hands. Jesus, the girl. She hadn't been hit once, almost accidentally, the way Jacob told it. The image crawled up unbidden out of her memory, finally. Oh Jesus, that mangled skull she had seen, that was the result of some huge anger, some colossal, unimaginable, tearing fury. If only his aim, he had said, had been as bad as hers. But no. No. It might have happened to him, the whole terrible scene that he didn't go looking for, but once in it, hadn't he smashed and smashed and gone on smashing? Self-defense? Ah, no way. And then he ran away. Never called for help, never flagged down a car or got himself to the nearest house or . . . The water, going dark, flecked with bits of that good dinner, swayed under her hands. She was going to be sick.

Carolyn turned away from the sink, hands dripping. He was only a child, terrified. Can you call a frightened boy a coward? And the slashing, smashing fury, she had seen that a lot over the years around here—it was habit with Ben. He had trashed his sculptures when they had betrayed him, when they refused to work. He had been so angry once she watched him put his whole arm through the composition board of his studio, almost ecstatic; then had seen him subside, satisfied, like a man at sex. (And Jacob had come with a Magic Marker and drawn an arrow—red—aimed at the spot, a long exclamation—a %#$&*!—coming out of it.) Once he'd made a bonfire and, though it took nearly an hour to catch, he'd consumed the piece he'd been wrestling with, and his face had held pure murderous rancor in it, hatred of the wood as if it had been some accursed flesh. He tried and failed and tried again to throttle that rage—what would he have been capable of with a piece of hard metal in his hands? How many times would *he* have hit her? She put her arms around herself, stamping dark wet handprints on her opposite sleeves like stenciled flowers, so cold, so cold beside the stove that was too hot to come near, that gave off waves of light-bending warmth like desert air that makes mirages on the horizon, and rocked herself. Her son was being torn from her for good, she could feel it. He had torn himself once and then, the closer she came to the truth, again and again and yet again. Her chest was gaping where he had been attached, if only by invisible threads, and the winter air blew in now, cold.

BEN

ONE NIGHT, A LITTLE STIR-CRAZY, WE WENT DOWN TO OUR FRIENDS MOCK and Harlie Frazier's. They had given up New Jersey and bought the Hyland Inn and Tavern not so long ago, right in the middle of town, a lovely old building with chipping paint and sagging porches that they pulled back from the brink of ruin by a huge application of love and money. Now that it was spick-and-span, the town had proudly reclaimed it. Mock found a spinning wheel for the front hall, an eighteenth-century secretary to tuck beside the registration desk to hold brochures for the local craft shops, and they moved in half a dozen canopy beds with a cloud cover of lace.

I loved sitting in the dark tavern in the great macho chairs—wood and leather, like something medieval. Hyland had looked like this once without self-consciousness. I came down here to be a curmudgeon and ride my hobbyhorses: In 1832, if you bought lumber of a certain specification, you got it, you didn't share a couple of inches with the mill. If you ate chickens, they were clean and healthy. There were no motorcycles. The long sign over the bar, genuine and mighty heavy, painted bunches of grapes at either end, greeted us:

ENTER WAYFARERS AND FRIENDS. 1828.

This was an oasis: real life went by in the street outside while the guests borrowed the rocking chairs and pondered life among the natives. It amused me to watch the men coming out of the dining room with their hands up against their jackets, patting down satiation, their wives flushed with a good heavy New England meal. (You can smell it at the door: always the fried scrod, always the bread pudding with its tinge of sweet burned molasses.) The fireplace worked assiduously behind us. In summer there'd be petunias in boxes on the porch, and blue lobelia, and a garden of greens to eat from. The place was charmed.

Mock came out from behind the bar when she saw us, and sat down at our booth. "So . . ." she said, noncommittal, turning a spoon in her large hands.

"So," Carolyn repeated. Mock and Harlie hadn't called or come by. "How's the season going, Mockie? Okay?"

She shrugged. She's an ample woman with a little-girl blunt haircut that makes her dark head seem small on her big body, and the long white apron she wore, authentic-looking, made her loom even larger. It was muslin, with lace at the bottom: Vermeer's women wore these, and German peasants. "Decent skiing," she said, "no artificial snow this year," and that was all. The room was busy, with a nice lamp glow like something you'd kindle by hand, and a buzz of conversation all around. If I were the proprietor I'd feel like a host giving a good, if sober, party. "You look like a mummer, Mock," I said. "You look like you're dressed for history."

She smiled without much warmth. And we looked at each other. That meant, I suppose, that she was thinking terrible thoughts and suppressing them. Not a word. Why had we thought to come? Comfort for the traveler but not for the embattled local friend knee-deep in home-grown manure? I wanted to get up and apologize for contaminating their sweet once-upon-a-time.

"I've got to get back to the customers," Mock said, wearily, I thought, and began to push back from the table. "Look"—and her face was pretty distressed, I'll give her that. "You know we—you're our friends. *You* know. But—" She looked over her shoulder, but if she needed moral support her husband was nowhere in sight. "See—I don't know if you—did you know Mike's been working for us? Mike Taverner?"

I was caught with my beer halfway to my mouth. "What does he do?" Reflex chatter. As if it mattered.

"Oh, a lot of different things. He's a good all-around—you know, carpentry. Electrical stuff. He's—he—uh, he hasn't been drinking for a long time now, and he's been just—super. Super."

So, I guess, if he was super, we couldn't be. There was not enough room in the state of superness for all of us at the same time. I don't think I said that out loud, but I can't be sure. Carolyn didn't look at Mock, only stared across the room with her eyes narrowed. By good luck, nobody stared back.

"Ben," Mock said, I don't know why to me—I couldn't see my own face. She finally rose; she seemed alarmingly tall. "I don't like to take sides. It's all awful, I'm sure it's been ghastly for you. But I've seen Mike, he's such a sweet helpless man under the sort of—I mean, you know, he sometimes seems to swagger a little, maybe, but it's just the way he is with us, I don't think—well, he's not too comfortable with people like us at first, and he used to be very contemptuous about our—you know"—she took them in with a single head movement—"the clientele.

But he's gotten to be quite indispensable, and he's—well, he's just been finished by this, that's all. He is ruined. His little girl. I understand he's drinking again and who can blame him, so I—"

I was tempted to say, "My little boy."

But "Mock," my wife said with shaky dignity. "I'm touched that you're devoted to your—to Mike Taverner. That's very feeling of you. But I'm not sure why you have to choose up like this. I don't quite—"

"Carolyn, don't make it hard, okay? You might not understand, from where you are. I just feel you people have —you've lost less. And you started with more. You know? Of course you have to protect him, but I hate to tell you, a lot of folks seem to feel this way too, they think—" She cast her round blue eyes upward. She was one of those people who retained the looks, I suspect, of their childhoods—this was her Exasperated Child.

"Whatever they think, they have a nerve being so sure they—"

"Carolyn," I said. "Honey. You don't want to do this."

She looked at me as if I'd just walked in. Sometimes one of us seemed to be in shock—it came suddenly, and then lifted just as fast. *Oh, it's you. And we're still here.* "You're right," she said. "Thank you. I don't." Her lips went taut.

I was sloshing the beer around in my mug the way you jiggle your foot when you're impatient; a little went over the edge, onto the wooden table. We stared at the splash as if it was a public indiscretion. Mock reached down, not with a napkin but with the hem of her perfectly white apron, the lace edge, sighing, and dabbed it dry.

My workshop stank. Closed-in air, sour ashes, something dead in the wall like wet cardboard, niggling, rancid. If I died suddenly, this was how it would be caught looking, slipshod, tools abandoned on the workbench, since I'm not one of those housekeepers who tenderly wipe and hang everything up. My figures hulked around like orphans, only half alive out in this fetid air. Only I knew what they needed to be finished.

All the times I've come out here as urgent as a lover climbing to his mistress's bed . . . I've never known why artists have reputations for sitting in cafés, drinking and gabbing, when we're all work obsessives. Even I, who seem to hang with people more than many, who came to this glorious green Hyland half for aloneness and half for community—even I had to make myself stop work to go to bed sometimes, so I could get up at a decent hour to feed my kids.

One misstep and he'd be eating jail food forever. Gluey eggs, gray French toast. Enough to make my gorge rise. We did not have him for that. We did not raise him to go off into captivity at the height of his strength with his wits intact and his body barely used. I could get very sentimental at every pleasure he'd never have, every country he'd never visit—no Seine, no Prado, no Trevi Fountain.

There was forgiveness, even in the courts, for passion. There was a little leeway, so I was instructed, for excess, bad judgment, uncontrollable instinct. But could we trust it, the jury of judges? Would they throw a good life after a wasted one? I saw that key chain of Jacob's, with Martha's bikini top flapping, doing a coy turn, acquiescent, provocative. So what, though? He was a man with a club, in the end, that's what the jury would see. Imagine this man, then, bashing her into that good night because she got under his skin and itched a little.

Panos said there were no statistics on the matter, but maybe half the parents he knew of would call the cops on their kids. Which means half would not. A matter for the *I Ching*, perhaps, or the confessional. A lot of times, of course, he said, you never knew what a parent understood and turned away from; they don't go around proclaiming it. Even with drugs, even when the kid is stealing the gold out of his grandmother's teeth . . . it's like children protecting parents who abuse them, they'll lie and go on taking it rather than give them up. He told me this because I asked.

A defense lawyer, you know, is not just a prosecutor turned inside out. He tends, by practice and maybe by temperament, toward a little compassion for his felon. He looks toward the whole damn merciful mess he works up like someone staring into the tea leaves, assembling a life, its reasons, its remorses. I thought Panos would like Jacob to go free. Was this transference? Was it that I thought he wanted his batting average, wins and losses, undiminished?

I doodled in my poor neglected sketchbook, I crosshatched and shaded, making Jacob. I'd done him so often in my sketches I could outline his face in my sleep, I knew the little hooks and turns the pen took to make him recognizable. There's a fine line between a portrait and a caricature, how far you push the uniqueness of each feature. Advance, retreat, correct, revise. Less neck, more forehead. His nose is not that pointy. Thinner cheeks these days. All this takes thirty seconds. When it works, it's a wonder. I had a likeness of him, now, under my hands.

I fed chunks to the woodstove and stood with my hands out, empty; passed them over it the way magicians do across the top hat and the dove flies out. The things that almost happen in your life but don't, by a fast flick of good luck. If you've ever driven a car, you've almost died. You've almost killed. Plus the things you've come close to wreaking on your own beloved kids, in anger. Instantly repented. Accidents, bad temper, unreconcilable dreams—like another fine line between the portrait and the caricature. How can he give his life for a single action? I've seen the state penitentiary, concertina wire around it like something in a war zone.

Well, I'd had my children, I'd had my career and even my petty successes. I wished I could go for him. I'd do it, too, I wouldn't hesitate. Who would? A new kind of plea bargain.

I seem to have put my head back and dozed. What if, what if. Nobody saw him do it. Okay. A quiet day on Poor Farm Road. Dark like the crosshatch in my sketchbook. He was honest with us, certainly. He was his own prosecutor. If he hadn't admitted it, would we have known for sure or just gone on suspecting? If he'd kept his mouth shut, or shrugged and said, "I don't know, I left her there"? And I had killed the evidence before I had a chance to think twice. I had left him some maneuvering room.

I did a subway sleep with my head bobbing. Saw a policeman bend over a body and lay on it, like a blanket, a drawing or maybe it was a photo, of a skeleton. Bones supple because they were canvas, a costume, something like that. I couldn't tell who the corpse was, even what sex it was, but I felt it was Jacob, the way you do in dreams. The policeman was tender. He covered it up gently and it lay out on a fast highway under a blanket of bones that glowed in the dark. Cars went around it without slowing down. I woke up knowing what we would do. I could feel the whole thing in my hands like something solid, with a shape to it. It was all visible to me in the good work light. If I couldn't go *for* him, I could chip a little at the possibility of his going. I could nick a corner here, build up an edge there. Work at it. Dare to. And if they took me in the end, all the better, maybe they wouldn't take him. Fathers and mothers died pushing their children out of the way of cars. Whose body was that, under the blanket of bones?

In the end someone would have to be forgiven, either Jacob for what he had done, or me for having done nothing. I'd rather—no contest, I thought, no contest at all—spend my forgiveness on him.

JUDITH

JUDITH'S PIANO TEACHER MADE HER WRITE SOME OF HER OWN MUSIC. SHE liked to be good at the things she did, and she was undone by harmony. Now she was recopying it so that at least it would be neat, her dismal little song that reminded her of kindergarten. She sat at the piano breathing hard with the effort of hating it so much.

"You weren't there," her father said suddenly from across the room. He said it firmly, his voice husky.

Judith said, "Excuse me?"

Jacob had been crossing the room on the way to the stairs. He stopped short. "Say again."

"You weren't even there. You had that argument and you walked away from her mad. You left her with the car and the keys. So you don't know *what* happened when she was out on the road there alone."

Her brother was silent for a long minute. "I didn't—"

"Then you reconsidered and you came back. And you

found her and you just panicked. Isn't this possible? Listen: So you drove home in a total fog and then you took off for Cambridge to get away. To think. Because you knew of course you'd have to be a suspect."

She heard the kind of "ttkk" her brother made, pulling his tongue across the roof of his mouth, when he was considering. "The car? Why would I bring the car home and leave without it?"

Her father was thinking, too. They were making something, Judith saw, their eyes bright with inspiration, bent over it like a shared project at the worktable. They were cozy. Her dad leaned forward, stretching, past his knees—she could just see him over her music. He cracked his knuckles and sat back up. "So no one could find you. You can always trace somebody with a car. But if you really had to get away—I mean, you were *terrified.* Who wouldn't be?" He looked pleased. The missing piece.

"God, Dad." Jacob breathed so hard he puffed out his lips, made a long *wheew* sound. "Do you really think this would—it's too simple. It seems too easy."

Her father went to where Jacob was standing dumbfounded, just standing where he'd been stopped and maybe saved crossing the room, and hid him in his arms. He was large enough to hide almost anybody. They had never been this loving when Jacob was just Jacob, annoying and disobedient. He was surely ready to obey now. It was disgusting how eager he was.

Judith held her breath. If she breathed in, the room would stink with falsehood. She wasn't sure what that would smell like, but she covered her nose and mouth with one hand and closed her eyes against all of them. If they knew she was there, they didn't care.

"Dad," her brother said finally. "Somebody saw me. There was a witness, remember, who waved to us when we were stuck by the fence, he asked if we needed help and we said no. And I don't know how many others saw us."

"You don't have to remember any witnesses, Jake. It's a quiet road."

"Oh, come on."

Her father gave a sort of Jack Nicholson grin, a little wild but also a little charming. "One word against another."

"One of them is an accused murderer."

"You say. Stranger things have happened, an accused murderer could actually tell the truth. Anyway, who knows who the other one might be? Could be somebody angry, who wants to help convict someone. A friend of the girl's family. That's not much to hang a whole case on." He sounded so enthusiastic the whole scheme had the feel of a game he was playing for pure pleasure. "Or —look, so he saw you. You aren't denying you were there, you were stuck, right? But that's not—you know, that's not *murder.* Panos told me first thing, he said, 'Murder is just an assault without a witness,' something like that. What do they have that shows you actually doing anything?"

"The car. The jack."

"Clean. Gone."

"Are you sure about the car? How do you know they don't have—like, you know, if there were any bloodstains left in there? Maybe they have a dog that can sniff for them or a test or something, who knows—"

Her father paused. "Well, I don't. I'm pretty sure, but I don't know, I guess it depends on how precise and profound—how profound the search is. I was incredibly careful, though. The whole trunk is—rearranged. As for the jack—" He put his head in his hands for a minute, he seemed to be resting from a large effort and who could blame him. "Oh, Jake, I've told you. Forget that. It's long gone. Trust me. Self-destructed. As if it never was."

"Self-destructed, huh." Jacob smiled his most ingratiating grin. "Should I not ask?" This was the same brother who wouldn't talk to them before he came home, not a word, not a glance, only anger? So simple, Judith thought. All of it, the dead Martha, Jacob screaming and swinging, coming at her in the half dark, connecting with a terrible sound, steel against bone, all of it was now pronounced long gone. If a tree falls in the forest and nobody hears (that was her favorite thing to think about) . . . but, Judith protested, but, but, but, even if the tree's on the ground unnoticed, the girl's still dead. Whether anybody heard her scream or not.

Judith had to hold on to the sides of the piano bench to keep quiet. She had argued with herself more than once by now that she wasn't the household police. If she wanted to be disgusted by eavesdropping or wholesale lying, or tampering with weapons, even, she'd have to take care of it herself. Was this the kind of thing that made people run away? The idea had always appalled her, but she was beginning to be able to imagine getting as far from them as she could. Not yet, but soon . . .

It was a little scary to think that way, because maybe eventually she might be able to understand suicide, too. So far, only Jacob fit any of the allowable categories for suicide: Did something too horrible to live with, something that can't be taken back or made better. Guilt, Physical Pain, and The World Too Unbearable were the only three comprehensible motives she could find. Death of a Loved One, like a child, maybe that too, or of a lover, like Romeo and Juliet, but she didn't think so. (She allowed that, never having been in love, or even near, she might have no right to an opinion.) He deserved to kill himself. At least, if he did that he could prove his honest sorrow. Otherwise—he was doubly guilty if he lived, and her father was worse. She saw the smile, slightly mischievous, slightly menacing, altogether unfamiliar, that he'd shown while he spun out their foolproof lie. Whenever Snappy caught a bird or a squirrel or even a little lizard, she made a strange sound in her throat, a plea, almost. It was odd, excited and frightened at the same time. A quaking noise. That was what he'd looked like, in some funny way. She had no words for it; she had no name, right now, for her father.

BEN

IF PANOS HAD KNOWN JACOB HE'D HAVE FOUND HIS STORY AT LEAST A little bit suspicious—silences, imploring glances at me, lapses of what looked like concentration but was, I could tell, conscience rising in his throat like a pill that wouldn't go down. (Or, if not conscience, then confusion—he hadn't had very long to live with the revised story. Or both.) I think Panos probably assumed this was a young kid, scared of the whole situation, just in out of the cold of his stunned silence, and shy in front of a lawyer: if he was nervous, who could blame him?

It was a little surprising that he didn't want to examine Jacob alone. Maybe it was kindness, to keep him relaxed. Maybe it yielded more to see us together; or it was willful. In any event, Panos did not know Jacob. Therefore, he listened hard while his assistant—a very earnest and nun-like young woman in dark clothes and pearls, with tar-nished blond hair, named Mag Trottier—diligently wrote down everything he said and taped it, too, for backup. Panos interrupted as little as possible but he had some questions. Only once did I really worry about my son. It was the part that was soft, the one plank that sagged, an imagined action between two real ones. "Tell me, Jacob, what was going through your mind when you left her alone with the car? Were you going for help or were you angry or—" What was it they called that in court, feeding the witness? Leading. He was leading him toward some plausible possibilities. (Did that mean he didn't think he had any of his own?)

Jacob looked at me fast as the lick of a cat. "Take your time," I wanted to say. *"Imagine."* That's all I was doing, imagining. It wasn't any harder for me to see the new story than the old one. I suppose it was harder for him.

"I was just mad," he finally said, almost inaudibly. It was probably pretty close to the truth of what he really had been feeling. "I was—I didn't want to do anything I'd regret."

Maybe a little too close? But Panos took that. It seemed extremely honest, I suppose: admit you might almost be tempted to do violence, but you were still, shaky or otherwise, in control.

"And what did you do when you walked away? How long were you gone?" The questions thickened, the possibilities for error mounted up. Jesus. Why didn't he see anybody pass him on the road when he trudged off? He walked a little, he said, then went off onto the margin of the woods, off the road. In the snow? It's thinner in there. Why the woods? He didn't want to meet anybody, and in case she came after him, he didn't want to be found. Did you see anybody? No, but he was so angry he wouldn't have noticed, he wasn't tuned in to things like traffic.

"Would anyone come forward who had seen him?" I asked, forgetting for a minute that he had never been there.

"He doesn't sound very seeable," Panos said noncommittally. "How far did you go?"

Within sight of the first houses where Bottom Street meets Poor Farm Road—he could see their lights, which would just have been coming on.

"And why did you turn around and go back?"

"Because I felt better. I talked to myself about our argument and I convinced myself we had some more things to say to each other. So I just hurried on back."

"And how long do you think all this took?"

"Half an hour maybe. Maybe more, less, I'm not good at that."

So he found her. I prayed he guessed right about where in relation to the car tracks, because they did have those, I was sure. They probably had photographs. Could there be some tiny little giveaway too small to be accounted for? The panic on his face as he told it was sincere. No way anyone could separate out one kind of terror from another.

"No weapon around?" Panos asked.

"I didn't see one. But it was dark and I was—I was really scared."

"Where were the car keys?"

"In the trunk. The trunk lock, I mean." Oh Christ, a shadow that remained from the real story. Because he'd gone looking for the jack.

"That's not where you left them?"

"I don't know," Jacob said. "I can't swear where they were. I guess in the ignition, I don't know why they'd have been anyplace else."

But he didn't ask about the jack, whether there was one, or anything about the trunk. No weapon, after all, had declared itself. It could have been anything, a rock, a pipe, something the murderer took with him. I thought about the Jack-in-the-Box innocently folded into its red case. Had I screwed up in some unimaginable way, given the police lab any easy answers?

For now I wasn't saying anything.

"How," Panos asked, with an inscrutable glance at Mag Trottier, who was bent over the tape machine with the gravity of a surgeon over a deep incision—"how did you get the car out when it had been stuck in the snow?"

But in this version, praise the Lord, the utter paralysis of the car hadn't played the same part it played in Jacob's story. (Had the witness seen the car up on the jack, that was the question. We might not know until it was too late.) Jacob shrugged. "I had to get out of there. I just gunned it and went."

"Why did you go home?"

He paused and I could see the fast calculation. "I had to get some money."

"Nobody saw you come in?"

"Nobody saw me. My parents weren't home yet. I don't know where my sister was."

Bad move, I thought. We'd have to cover for that somehow. I couldn't think this fast—wet footprints? Anything else missing from his room? Where would Judith have been? (Napping instead of practicing the piano? That was all too plausible!) A light sweat flushed my forehead with cool, like a chill.

"You took the chance of running into all those people?"

"I figured if my mom's car was there I might not go in. But she's never that early. The others—I just took a chance. My dad's usually in his workshop around then and that's not in the house, it's up the road a little, behind the garage. And I thought if I saw Judith I could—just tell her something. Anything. You know." He shrugged. "She pretty much believes everything I say."

If it seemed peculiar that Jacob had moved through Hyland as if it were a deserted town that afternoon, seeing no one and hardly being seen, Panos didn't say. But I realized suddenly that being invisible might be just as much a problem as it was a solution—you couldn't provide any alternatives. It left you naked, in a manner of speaking. I hated making Panos into a sucker, it made me queasy. I hated for our lying to take personal advantage.

Panos sat back, closed his eyes, held his hands out in front of his chin the way kids make a church and steeple with their fingers. "All right, Jacob," he said finally. "What if I said it was pretty clear you did it, you hit her with something and then took off."

I don't know if we gasped out loud. "But I—" Jacob's face had turned that terrifying red in one quick flush. I felt like I was underwater, out of air.

"Just say—I'm being the prosecution now—it's just as likely you're the one who smashed her up, how can you prove you didn't? 'Nobody saw' works both ways, you know."

"But," Jacob began again. I was holding myself back with my fingernails deep in my thighs, on the outside beside the chair where they were invisible. He gave me the look of the drowning.

"Don't answer that!" Panos said, very loud, and he held up his hand like a traffic cop. "Remember, Jacob, you don't have to answer that question. *They* have to answer it. They have to prove something on you, you do *not* have to prove the opposite."

"But what are alibis for?" I asked. I think my blood pressure was coming back down a little.

"Alibis help plenty. But they rarely win cases. They're another form of hearsay—you know, your friend, your mother, you can always get somebody to help you out by saying you were all just sitting around watching the Celtics, eating pretzels. That's better than nothing, but it's soft. It's soggy." He pushed at the air with two fingers. It yielded. "Those cases still have to be won or lost on their merits and there'd better be more solid evidence somewhere down the line."

"So this is good?" Jacob asked, looking truly innocent for the first time that morning.

"This is—better maybe. None of it is exactly what I'd call good." He sighed. "Good is never having to set foot in this office to begin with, or in that bloody courtroom. Good is—you know—dying in bed. And for you, buddy, not for a long long time." He smiled at Jacob sadly. "Which reminds me—Mrs. Reiser? Pardon me—*Dr.* Reiser? May I ask where she's spending the morning today?"

The implication, of course, was clear—did she have something more important to do than come here to discuss her son's defense?

We hesitated, both of us. Possibilities whirled by like the numbers on a wheel of fortune.

Jacob said she had the flu, before I could find a better, subtler explanation. She was feeling lousy and she said she wouldn't be much help, he went on. I wished he'd stop. Panos made a little note and smiled with his cards close to his chest. That smile made me feel like a defendant before a prosecutor.

I asked if he was entitled to a list of their witnesses. He was friendly enough with the D.A.'s office, he said, so that he'd have no trouble with that.

Jacob was silent and terribly pale. I took a deep breath and asked what kind of case we had.

Panos shrugged. Mag Trottier looked miserable, but I was to discover that she always looked miserable, as if being trapped in a room with a possible felon was distasteful to her and not of her own choosing. She reminded me of my cousin Frannie, who went to Wellesley when I was twenty or so, all done up in clothes designed not to catch the eye but to give instead a message about stability, about wifely appropriateness, as if she were a good solid banister you could clutch and lean on, rising. A professional good girl. I had such contempt for good girls, Jesus. I thought about Martha for a minute, how she hated Jacob for being nice to her. But I got to grow out of that dumb Baudelairean dream, given time enough and Carolyn's sweet patience. (And, for symmetry, Frannie, who married her Harvard man as planned, had gone a little wild herself later when the perfect marriage soured and she sowed a few late oats and did a couple of utterly inappropriate things it must have given her uncorseted soul some pleasure to contemplate.)

Panos brought me back. "I think we've got a few things to worry about. But I'll tell you—if they don't have a lot more than a couple of folks going by in cars when you're not in the act, right in their headlights—"

Jacob blinked as if the lights were picking him out right now.

"I think they might not have a case at all. Not to say this is going to be so easy. I've got to get some reliable word on their forensics. But—"

We had given him the bricks, I suppose, and now he had to build an edifice, assemble it carefully so it would stand up no matter how it was battered. He already looked preoccupied, drifting off from us, or rather, walking purposefully in his own direction, taking them to be inspected in better light. I didn't know how excited I should have expected Panos to be. I think I was waiting for the Mediterranean in him to turn noisy and congratulatory when the story was delivered in this stripped-down form, exonerating Jacob. But his forehead stayed contracted, his lips closed almost prissily while he worked out his own problems with it and made quick little notes on his pad, as if this weren't our business. He was like Wendell, I suppose they're all the same: he didn't need to be bothered with my fancy construction, he didn't want too many soft facts to play around with. *Does he believe it?* Carolyn would want to know. *Does it matter if he does?*

We were already at the door when Panos put a hand on Jacob's arm. "Jake, I'm slow sometimes. I told you—getting old. Let me ask you a little something right here."

Jacob looked terrified; his fair skin was like a thermometer, the red kept rising in his cheeks like mercury climbing with heat.

"I'm just curious. What were the two of you fighting about? Why were you so mad?" Panos hit himself a glancing blow to the forehead. "I can't believe I let all this go right by."

He was being disingenuous, thinking he'd catch Jacob off-guard. I'd have put money on it. Motive is not something you forget to inquire about.

My son smiled; hesitated; smiled some more, sheepish. "She was pregnant, for one thing."

Panos's face darkened with surprise. He smiled, too, as if they had a little joke between them. "I think we need to go sit down again, kiddo, just for a minute. This sounds kind of serious." He took Jacob by the arm and turned him around gently.

Jacob didn't wait to sit down. "I think it was somebody else's, though. At least she said it was."

Panos looked ready to break out of there and run around the block with excitement.

"This is good, Panos?" I asked him.

"This is very good, friend. This is the best news I've heard all day. You think this baby belonged to somebody else. Why?"

He shrugged. "The way she told me. I could—sort of—I believed her."

"You know who? Christ Jesus. Or can you guess?"

Jacob shook his head.

Panos let out a whoop like a drunken football fan and made a thumbs-up sign. "You're sure. And it couldn't have been yours?"

"Well, what do you mean? Do you mean, were we—you know—"

"Right. *You know.*"

Jacob sighed. "Well, sure we were. Like. But she told me this was somebody else's."

"But, Jacob. Kid. What does 'she told me' mean? She could have told you that for a whole lot of reasons. Wanting to tell the truth might have been pretty far down her list." He flung over the page he'd filled earlier and scrawled more emphatic notes to himself in the sloppy hand of a doctor writing a prescription. "The first thing we've got to do is go to the medical examiner and get a DNA report. Sheeesh. This could make us or break us."

That's not all that could break us, I thought. What would he say —more than "Sheesh," I bet—if he knew I was a liar, a tamperer, a fraud? And if I testified to all this, I'd be a perjurer to boot. A certain numbness had begun to set in, I thought, or I'd be a quivering puddle at the mere thought of the headlines, not to mention the jail cell. I suppose this was what resolution felt like: your principles stiffen you beyond mere feeling. It was instructive, and it was lonely.

I prayed I had made nothing worse except—too late to pray for this—my marriage. Carolyn wouldn't speak to me that morning before we left to see Panos. She sat in her robe looking into the mystic steam of her coffee, silent as my wooden man. I had told her what we were going to do. I had promised her it was going to work. She had not said a single word. I don't know if she was cursing us all the way out the door or wishing us luck. It wasn't fair, I thought, for Panos to hold her absence against us as if she were a witness who'd refused to testify, but he'd be right if he thought it signified. It signified. I wish I could have thought it didn't.

Back in the car, headed through traffic toward the Queen City Bridge and then out onto the open highway, Jacob was silent. "You okay?" I asked him. The radio wasn't on, we had a lot of dead air in there with us.

He shrugged.

I didn't want to push—that heavy-handedness Tony Berger warned me about. God knows he had enough to be depressed about. But this was sullen, this slouch. "Jake?"

Just a flicker of eyebrow, not very responsive. He was

way down under his cap; he seemed to be hidden under it. (The cap was the first thing he reclaimed when they gave back his belongings; he'd punched it up, lovingly, into the shape of a beret.)

"How do you think it went?"

Long pause. I mean long. I was about to ask again.

"Did he like it, you mean?"

"What do—"

"Or did I like it."

"Like what?"

He turned to me finally, his whole slumped body. "Your story."

"Well, Jesus. Yes, my story, I guess. Our story."

He looked away and I could see his eyes were full. "Yours."

"Jacob." I wanted to stop the car. If I hadn't had a pickup on my right flank I'd have pulled off the road. "Jacob, look at me."

He sniffed, but it was arrogance, not tears. It was his old fuck-you, teenage sniff. It was his Don't-tell-me-what-to-do-please.

"Do you not want to save yourself?"

"Hey, look, exactly who's saving me here?"

"I'll ask you again, okay? Don't be a child, Jake. Do you want to save yourself? Or do you want to cast yourself on the mercy of strangers? Because they're going to take one look at you, a strong, confident male with a—terrible temper—*provable*—and they'll see pictures of this frail blond girl with her head—"

"She wasn't frail."

I smiled. "Sustained. All right, she wasn't frail, she was a ball-breaker. But they can't see that, it doesn't show up in the bloody photograph. And even if it did—just what do you expect they'll do? These are not people who love you."

"All right, I know," he said, very impatient. "I've already heard this." He made it sound like we were arguing about breaking curfew.

"Jacob, you know what I'm suggesting? I want to be clear about this, okay? All I'm suggesting is that we save your life first and later on we can worry about your soul. Is that too much of an intrusion on your—what is it, your space? Tell me if it is."

He closed his eyes. "I don't know, Dad. I'm sorry. I don't know what. Of course I'm grateful." Tonelessly. He slid down in the seat and put his feet up on the dash. His sneakers left a huge fog of dusty prints. "Just let me sleep now, okay? I'm so tired, jeez, you can't imagine how tired I am."

We took the mountains, those wide, banked curves where the highway flowed like a river. Speed. The air sucking at the car as it coasted down Curry Mountain, so strong that if I opened the window the noise would overwhelm us. Goddamn, I thought, holding on. I am no Abraham. I will not sacrifice my son on the altar of any power that asks for him. I am no hero of the spirit like Abraham. He might have been the father of his people but—blasphemy—he was no proper father of his son. Who's out there to be trusted? Who can promise us a ram in the thicket of the law?

Jacob had turned his head away toward the window. He kept it there till we were home in the slush of our driveway. Then, before I had even turned off the ignition, he was out the door and gone.

CAROLYN

THEY WERE BEING SUBPOENAED, IN LANGUAGE THAT INVITED NO REPLY except submission, to appear at the courthouse in Howe to answer questions. The grand jury wanted them.

Wendell, who'd come over to watch a football game on television and, Carolyn thought, to check up, almost wistfully, on their dealings with Panos, explained the grand jury system in such detail that Carolyn lost the point somewhere along the way. It was worse than hearing football made simple. "In cities," Wendell said, "the juries are sitting all the time. Up here there's so little to do, they're off as much as they're on." He winked. "Isn't that why we live here?"

She got up and began to prepare a tray of snacks, as if this were the All-American household: potato chips, tortilla chips, beer. All she needed to know about the grand jury, that magisterial name that made her think of twelfth-century England, was that, called, you had to go. No trial itself, it existed to decide whether there ought to *be* a trial. "This is to protect the defendant," Wendell insisted, stretching his legs in front of him, casual, though the defendant didn't sound very well protected to her: he'd have no lawyer, there was no judge, each of them would be allowed to hear no one's testimony but their own. They could challenge none of it. Protection?

("The way it really works," Panos told them in the voice he used for the self-evident, "is the prosecutor gets what he wants. Simple. Or she—Mag here reminds me she's going to be a prosecutor one of these days if she gets lucky. Not my idea of luck. I'd never have guessed she liked red meat that much, but . . . Anyway. He, she, whatever, only presents cases that'll work. That's what you have to understand. If they don't work, if the grand jury no-bills someone, you can believe he didn't want to go to trial with it in the first place. He's grateful, he's off the hook on a lousy case. If it's a good case, you better believe they'll indict. I'm not being cynical, children. This is what happens.")

Jacob had joined the men on the couch in the den. He seemed to be trying to be the ordinary boy who sat in the kind of household that provided these snacks with the ballgame. He reached for a beer. "If the court says I'm an adult." He smiled. Nobody restrained him. He looked more mature than he had before all this. The contours of his face were changing, but very subtly, the planes hardening. In spite of how thin he was, this had nothing to do with thinness, he had something almost like the beginning of lines beside his nose. He was too young for the action of gravity. But innocence rounds the cheeks and experience hollows it; also, she thought angrily, bad food. It was more, though: it was a loss of something in his eyes, an avidity, an openness to take in anything you put before him, that ravenous gaze. The unguarded look of a boy who didn't have much to dissimulate. Of course he had tried to look cool, even look jaded in the presence of his parents. Chiefly, that was a matter of hooding, half closing, the eyes, if not actually rolling them heavenward. But there was no weariness, no bitterness in that, that was only his uniform, his allegiance, and he put it on and took it off like his jacket. She missed his insolence now; it had been all style, no substance. Now what she thought she saw was the dregs of the self-protectiveness that had kept him mute until he came home, and was still keeping him silent. A desperate absence of welcome. Innocence was lost to him. Was it guilt, then—double guilt, the way Ben was compounding it—or was it fear that kept him aloof?

They drove into Howe in perfect ear-splitting silence. Jacob didn't come; they couldn't make him appear, and they couldn't hold it against him. (Who says they won't, she wondered. Do they report who speaks and who doesn't speak?) Carolyn wished she could have said to him, Now. I want to know about the postcards. How did you do that? *Why?* Was that your dream of flight or was it just to mislead us, a hunk of steak to the dogs? Red herring, rather. But she suspected he wouldn't answer. He might be talking now but that didn't exactly mean he was seething with confidences. The day was heartlessly bright, it looked as if it ought to be warm in that sun, but it was twenty degrees below freezing. They filed into the quaint courthouse and were seated in the hall outside the closed door of the jury room. Panos was around somewhere, seeing to details of the procedure they couldn't keep track of. Mag, whose smile looked as if it were part of her job description, assured them he'd be there to cheer them on, to answer questions if they wanted to come out and check on something before they committed themselves to it, to debrief them after they'd had their turn. Mag herself made a rather dry adviser: be brief, be cool, don't try to play the emotional games everyone imagines trials are made of. No one will be impressed in there. They're running, fast, through the facts of one case after another, they have big books of times, dates, and documents, and they don't particularly want to engage with anyone. (In a case like this, laden as it was? Was she being naïve?)

This sweet building, with its reverently restored paint and its long windows behind their quilted shades that kept winter on the other side, was nothing like the teeming city courts—it was so genteel it was like a historical mock-up, a stage set in which nothing real could happen . . .

But then the strange part started. Gently they were called, one by one, as if their own privacy were being honored, and it was like the discreetness with which patients were taken in for a medical procedure. She felt as if they were at the hospital, not in a court of law. The throbbing of the lights, the hushed, considerate voices of the people who told them where to sit, where to get Styrofoam cups of coffee out of a machine, who called Fran Conklin first, all of it spoke of danger the way the hospital did—as if health were in question and not punishment.

Who could guess what they were asking, now that Panos had swept away Wendell's reassurances with a laugh. The district attorney's office would have its ducks in a row; there was no way there would fail to be an indictment. Panos had heard a rumor they weren't going after a capital crime. If that was true, he promised to take them out for a drink when the long day was over.

They watched Fran Conklin coming out. He nodded and turned his head away. A cop will not be sympathetic in the courthouse—it made sense, she thought, it probably made more sense than being strained and friendly, like political enemies who go for the jugular, then smile and put away drinks together in the Senate lounge.

They—*they* was a round blond woman in pale lavender with matching shoes as if she were going to a party—gestured Ben to the door. It was not the double swinging door of a courtroom, it was just a room with hard chairs lined up in rows like a classroom, and a scuffed little table in front.

By now Mag had disappeared in search of Panos; she was alone out there. She felt like one of her own patients waiting for a doctor to come out and say, "Mercy has been granted." She was the doctor behind the door who knew more than she wanted to about the illness, its bleak prognosis, the pain it had yet to exact.

Panos appeared out of nowhere. He was nearly jolly with excitement here on his own turf. "So?" he asked her.

"So?" Carolyn repeated.

"They said what and you said what."

"I haven't been in there yet. It's been the police chief and now Ben. Aren't you supposed to be out here to help us through if we're having a problem?"

"Here I am," he answered, mock-innocent. "Have there been any problems?"

"You have fun at these things?" Carolyn asked irritably. "Am I supposed to be enjoying myself?"

"Carolyn, come on. This is routine. A little something you have to get through. We could have waived this thing and gone right into the trial and it wouldn't have made any difference. We do our work later. I told you not to sweat it."

She looked disgusted. "Since it's my only son's only life being discussed in there, I suppose I'll sweat it if I want to."

"Suit yourself. I just hope Ben looks cooler than you do. You don't want to get them aroused, do you?"

Ben probably looked plenty cool, she thought angrily, but you wouldn't want to hook him up to a lie detector just now. How ever in the wide world was she going to manage to plead ignorance, to insist on such omissions, such distortions? How were they going to present a solid front when it could all crumble at a touch and fall in around them? He was right, his story was plausible. But it felt terribly laundered, somehow. It felt convenient. Last night before bed she had asked him, "Do you have misgivings about this, Ben? This monster you've strung together with spit and string—"

"If he needed an organ of yours," he had asked, unlacing his sneakers, "would you give it to him? Would you be frightened?"

"Of course I would. Yes and yes."

He pulled a sneaker off and looked at a hole in his sock. "All right, then, sweetheart. Yes and yes. You understand me."

She sat looking straight ahead now, ignoring Panos. Ben emerged then, red-faced, enraged, and sat down so hard the bench quavered. The woman in lavender, soft-voiced, appeared behind him. Her eyes were wide as if she'd seen something alarming. "Mrs. Reiser, I'm afraid we'll have to ask you to come back on Friday morning. We took longer than we expected and we won't have time to examine you today." The medical event again. The woman smiled and smiled as if it hurt her. "We don't sit tomorrow, but Friday at ten. You can be here?"

"Fine," Carolyn said, smiling herself. They were so casual you'd think she was postponing an appointment at the hairdresser. "That's fine. No problem." She was looking at Ben sidelong. What had he done? Good God. The blond woman looked as if she were afraid of him, she kept darting her eyes at him as if he might do something sudden and dangerous. Had he turned over the table? Accused them? "Benny?" she asked quietly.

Ben had leaned over and was embracing her hard, histrionically. "Screw them," he said, hugging tight. "Fuck the bunch of them." The news people were arriving finally with their cameras. "Right," Ben said, standing, turning his chest to them defiantly as if daring them to shoot. They shot their flashbulbs. "I didn't testify and I won't testify and you can print any damn thing you want to."

"You didn't testify?" Panos repeated, his eyes boggling. He looked like a man in a cartoon.

"They've got these stupid questions, some of them I can't answer and some are none of their damn business. I couldn't qualify a thing, I couldn't explain or enlarge or—"

"Oh Christ, Ben, why didn't you tell me what you were going to do?" Panos hissed. The three reporters were in the way. "What the hell did you think you were protecting in there? Jesus." He pulled on his lapels as if he were trying to lengthen them and paced up and back in front of the bench.

"There's got to be some protection, there's immunity, some kind of privilege so the state can't make you snitch on your own flesh and blood," Ben said to the reporters, two young men and a woman. "There's such a thing as the Fifth Amendment, you know. Ask my lawyer."

The photographer for the Howe *Record* poked his old-fashioned camera in front of Carolyn. She put one arm around Ben, the other around Panos and, grateful to be held up, stretched her mouth across doubt and astonishment, across reason and wishful thinking. Privilege? Immunity? Panos had mentioned no such things. He had advised the most reticent honesty they could summon. No tricks. She smiled so ingratiatingly she half expected the reporter to say, "Come on, Mrs. Reiser, you expect us to believe that?"

"Okay, Ben, we've got to talk," Panos said angrily. "The jury's done in there, come on into the room here and let's get a few things straightened out."

"Don't talk to me that way, Panos. I'm paying you, remember, not the other way around."

"Oh, buddy," Panos said, recoiling, "this has nothing to do with who's paying anybody anything, goddamn it. This is trying to keep your stubborn hide out of prison. If it's not too late." He pushed the door open and they went inside.

BEN

"THERE IS NO PRIVILEGE OF THE KIND YOU'RE CLAIMING," HE TOLD ME, and he told it to me very gruffly. "Did I need to be out there to whisper in your ear as you went in? Did I?" He sounded like my mother when she got ready to shake me by the shoulders. "How could you do this without any consultation whatsoever? They let you come out of there. I told you to come out and ask if you had questions."

"I didn't have any questions. Find me some privilege," I said.

"Fuck you, find me some privilege. What, make something up?" He was rushing around in circles. "This state, and most states, let me tell you, do not honor parent-child privilege the way they honor husband-wife. There is no such thing even if you think it might be convenient. *Find me some privilege.*"

"Don't sound so goddamn contemptuous. I don't think

this is the way lawyers are supposed to talk to their clients, Panos."

"Yeah? Well, most clients listen to their lawyers when they talk to them, Ben. You don't treat me like your lawyer, I don't treat you like my goddamn client."

"This rudeness, I suppose, is a form of concern. It's for my own good."

"Fuck rudeness. Amy Vanderbilt isn't going to do you any good in a court of law, sir. You don't take this seriously, that's your trouble. You really don't, you're incredible. You're not like any client I've had. You think you can make the rules and everyone will fall in line behind you."

"Oh," I said, "I'd like to believe that! You've never had anyone second-guess you? Go their own way under questioning? You maintain iron discipline?"

"Not with such utter, absolute, total disregard of the consequences, buddy. Do you know what you're asking for?"

I did not.

"You're asking to go to jail for contempt, for starters. You may be asking *me* to go to jail for contempt, and I'm doing no such thing for you, thank you. You're raising suspicions about your son, your beloved boy, by playing fast and loose with the grand jury. Enough for you? Why do you think you can play with this thing any way you want to? How strong do you think your will is?"

"Well," I said, "try me. Plenty of people bend the system and twist it and make it do their bidding. The bastards in Congress who get out of dirty deals clean. Ollie North, what about him. The drug pushers who go in and come right out practically the same day. The plea bargainers. Why can't you—"

"You're daydreaming, sonny," Panos said to me roughly. "Your son's in a different category and you know it, or if you don't you'd better figure it out. Your son is up on murder one, maybe, or maybe a little better—if we're lucky, I mean very lucky, manslaughter—and he's not going to get treated like a congressman or a fucking army general in a uniform full of hash. The best you're going to be able to hope for at this rate is that you two can share a bloody jail cell. Can't you see it, *People* magazine'll come and do a story on you—roommates behind bars. Jesus."

"The problem," I said to him quite calmly, "is that I have a principle here and I'm not trading it for a plea bargain or out of fear of the jury or anything else your system wants to come up with. So I'll go to jail. Worse things could happen."

"Worse things might," Panos said. He was so angry he couldn't even come near me, he kept walking around the periphery of the chairs that were set up as if for a lecture or a concert or something routine. "And the principle is what? I think I missed that part."

"I don't bargain for my son, and I don't help them convict him. That's what I told them. I gave them a statement of principle. Not that I have a single thing to hide, but why should I help them clamp the shackles on his wrists? Let them find out what they need to know without my help as a witness."

"Don't you have anything to say that would help him? I thought you were satisfied with his story."

I stared into the darkness that had begun to surround everything the way light surrounded it before. I don't know why I didn't just lie for him, I'd have attracted a hell of a lot less attention if I'd said *I don't know, I don't know, I don't know.* But the way they came at me, the whole bitter assumption that I'd help them along . . . I prayed to God I hadn't done something to doom him accidentally. "Nothing," I said. "He didn't do it and he's explained what happened. But I won't lead them to any of it, that's not for me to do. You said so yourself."

"I said you don't have to solve it for them. I didn't say you could kick them in the butt."

"He's responsible for what he did and didn't do. He can account for it."

Panos seemed surprised. "He is, but you're not."

"No, you don't understand," I said again. "You still don't. He did what he did and I didn't have anything to do with it but to accept it when he told me about it. Now it's time for me to do something and I'm doing it: I'm refusing. They're trying to get me to second-guess him, they're going to trick me into giving some kind of conflicting evidence and I won't play that game with them. I'm not going to help them take him from me. If there was any more I could do, you'd better believe I'd do that, too."

"Take him from you? You just said he's on his own. So, is he or isn't he yours, as you put it?"

"Whatever. That's for me to decide, I guess. All I can do now is just keep saying, No help from me."

"But you're playing with them, Ben. I see you showboating for the sake of your own ego. If you've got a problem taking orders from a constituted authority—"

"Why is it playing? I'm as serious as I know how to get. If they convict him, let it be without my help. I thought you lawyers were always saying, like when you defend some god-awful hardened case, some foul guilty unrepentant bastard, Let them do their job. That's what everybody says to Carolyn when she asks how you can work for some of the sleazes who come through your door. How many times have I heard it: If they can't figure out how to convict somebody, whatever he did, then the state's failed in its responsibility. Well, why doesn't a father get as much chance to say that as a defense lawyer gets?"

"A purist," Panos said with the disgust I'd expect from one of them. His or theirs, he *is* one of them, his head is full of *procedure,* and I'll forget it at my peril. No respect, only anger at the inconvenience of having to figure out how to handle me. "A purist," he said again. The insult of it. "One of those existentialist heroes you read about in college . . ."

Me: "Okay, a purist. I don't know about who you read in college. But yes, I think parents ought to be purists, at the very least. Keep their hands in their pockets and their mouths tight shut. Without apology."

My father once said an interesting thing to me. He was not one of those doctrinaire Old Testament types, in spite of the number of hours he spent decked out in his ritual artifacts praying, and he may have been unconflicted about everything, crystal clear in his expectations and his own performance, but there was justice in all his dealings. And once, when I was in some kind of trouble—my friend Mike and I had committed some sin in school, I don't remember what, but it had caught my teacher's eye and she had demanded a parental visit—he came back from his hour in my classroom disgusted by the behavior of Mike's father. Or maybe it was his mother, or both. Whoever was there for him. They lay right down in front of the teacher, he reported to me, thoroughly bemused by the treachery of it. They nodded at her and they agreed to all their son's bad habits, they even enlarged on them with examples of their own! So the schoolteachers are the authorities, he said. So they have the power. So? Why do these American parents run out on their children? They just sell them out so they can please any stranger who has a complaint about them! I'll deal with my son at home, thank you, I have the right to do that, but when I'm in public with you . . . I'll tell you something, Benny, he said. Maybe I shouldn't try to improve on what Moses heard, but I always thought there should be an eleventh commandment.

I was stunned at his faithfulness. I wasn't even sure he was right, I of all people was ready to allow that under certain circumstances somebody besides my father deserved to have at me. But you can imagine I was grateful. What commandment? I asked.

Honor thy children, he said to me. I haven't forgotten it. I probably got the back of his hand or had something I liked taken away from me for a while, locked up in his closet that actually had a key that he kept hidden (I knew exactly where: in his top drawer under his socks and handkerchiefs). I'm not saying his methods of punishment were original or enlightened. But the thing is, he took care of it privately. Out there in the enemy world, even if he didn't believe my perjured version of the event, it was the most basic point of pride with him to be my shield and my defender. Everything else was somebody else's business. To aid and abet my punishers would have been to ask his blood to flow backward in his veins. "It is," I can hear him saying, *"unnatural."*

Now I could argue the other side of that, say that's a kind of tribalism. That's how those poor suckers got done in in the Bible story where Jacob's daughter Dinah is raped and to avenge her honor her brothers end up laying waste to a whole regiment of innocent men who are the rapist's retainers: a really gory preemptive strike. Family devotion run amok. But my father, no warrior, seemed to be motivated by a humble man's simplest understanding of the obligations of parental love. He was talking defense, which is passive, which lives as a principle; he was not talking offense, which calls for action. That was something I could understand. Non-violent resistance.

So, I thought, I am only being his son now. I am only honoring the father, finally, who honored his children. I see, of course, why I had such a hard time walking away on my own two feet—it was too late to be as unconflicted about all this as Herschl Reiser. But it was not too late to close my eyes and see him nodding approval as he rarely did when he was alive and I was that boy who needed so much defending.

JUDITH

One of them showed up in school right at the entrance to her classroom. Somehow he had gotten permission, she couldn't believe it, to track her down and humiliate her in view of everyone. "Can I just talk to you for a minute, Judy?" he'd asked confidentially, very cute, young, eager-looking, in khakis and sneakers, the sort of person she'd love to talk to otherwise. But she could see his camera dangling half out of sight. "No," she answered without even looking at him and shouldered past him and went into the room. He made it sound as if he really wanted to talk to her, but she knew already from the pushy, nosy reporters who'd flooded right over them that it wasn't her he wanted but something from her that he could sell to strangers. She walked to the rear, facing the bulletin board, and stood fussing with nothing, pretending to be busy, praying he'd be gone when she turned around. Her hands shook. Of course they all whispered, why shouldn't they? If it had been somebody else, tracked down and caught, she'd be whispering, too.

How many seventh-graders were on the Boston evening news? ("Made" the news, Celeste called it. Some accomplishment.) Their faces were probably known now, and their "story," in other cities, too, all across New England. Maybe across America. *Lurid* was the word her mother used. It sounded like a chicken's neck being wrung. She imagined a whole scene around it: "Don't bring me that bird until it's completely lurid," the mother says, and the daughter twists her wrists in opposite directions, feels the snap, and the neck hangs loose.

She had been at Celeste's house for Celeste's birthday party, a chancy event only intermittently fun because she was a stranger to them all, warily waiting for someone to accuse her of something of which she was not guilty. When they did slambooks (a curse under the best of conditions), she found herself holding her breath. Someone called her Most Serious and two girls said Nicest. They weren't honest but they were kind. When the evening had wound down and the gift wrap was sufficiently trampled into the den rug, Celeste's father offered to drive her home. He was taking Lori up the road past Judith's house—her parents' car was in the shop—so he'd drop her on the way. He was especially cheerful when she was around these days, whistling, joking, trying to jolly a smile out of her.

Lori was going on about which animals belonged in the rodent family and which were unfairly included—how did they ever get on such a subject? Even as Celeste's father drew into the last long mean curve, Judith could see an odd flickering from the hill on the left, where her house sat far back, invisible from the road. It looked like a blinking neon sign, its light thrown high and then low and high again. Lori was still chattering when they turned into the driveway (minks were not rodents, but squirrels were) and Mr. Charters braked with a bump. "Jesus!" he said. "Holy Jesus Christ!" In the middle of the lawn, near the old well, stood a tall figure with its arms outstretched. It was clothed in flame.

Judith gasped. It was strangely beautiful—beautifully strange—like something you might come upon at sea or on a mountaintop, anyplace far from home, where things can be huge and out of scale. She'd seen a movie once in which a ship's mast caught fire from some incredible commotion in the sky, and it throbbed with light just like this. Its orange tongues licked wildly out into the dark and sparks flew off and blinked out or fell into the snow. Some of them took off in an updraft as if they were going to join the stars. It was nothing like a blaze in the stove or the fireplace, but a whole different element, serious and spectacular, a vast hole in the dark, in a nimbus of something like sunlight. "It's a goddamn cross!" Mr. Charters said in a kind of whisper, the way you might talk about a miracle. "I don't believe it. The bastards!"

They parked a good distance back and Judith leaped from the car. Celeste's father was calling after her not to go near it. But she was running for the house, because none of them had seen it, no one was outside with it. It must have just happened, maybe just a few minutes ago, or they'd surely have noticed the wanton light going on and off. She jerked open the door and shouted. Apparently it was supposed to be frightening—Mr. Charters had called the people who did it *bastards*—but she couldn't resist thinking the tower of light was glorious, like something struck into flaming grandeur by nature. That, she knew, was called an Act of God. After so much that was mundane, and so much innuendo, the muttering under the surface, this was extraordinary. It was huge and clear, God talking from the mountain: *Thou shalt not kill.* It was Ezekiel seeing the burning wheels—her father had read her that story. "Stay far back from there," he called now, breathing hard. "That thing's going to fall over soon."

When they had watched it for a while—she was so mesmerized she could have stayed there all night—her father announced that he was calling the police, "whatever their attitude," and turned to go inside. Celeste's father kept saying, "I'm so sorry, God, this is terrible, this is like—Birmingham or Mississippi or something." Then her father found the papers nailed to the front door. "Goddamn, it's Martin Luther time!" She thought he said it with relish. Martin Luther—did he mean Martin Luther King? He had crosses burned for him, didn't he?

Her mother was silent and shivering. Judith put her arm around her waist. "It's okay, Mom," she murmured. "It isn't actually hurting anybody."

The pages were a petition, Xeroxed, that claimed to bear 493 names. RESCIND JACOB REISER BAIL! It insisted that his presence in the community constituted a menace, that his behavior was dangerous and unpredictable, and that his parents also be jailed for their criminal behavior. "He has been identified for a long time as a community menace," it finished. "We the undersigned do not want him loose in our town."

Jacob leaned down as his father, standing in the flaring light, completed the text in a mockingly grand voice. He picked up a handful of snow and balled it in his palms, his breath growing ragged, his face contorted. He aimed the snowball at the fire. It passed right through and hit the wood with a moist slap, like fruit smashing open. He made a dozen balls, whirling and bending, rising and throwing, and most of them sailed right through the flame and expired futilely in the darkness. "So I'm a dog, right? Now I'm a dog, and they want me tied up." Judith thought of the little yellow dog he had flung stones at the way he was throwing snowballs now. "Everything's connected," her father always said. "What goes around comes around." She had never understood even vaguely what that meant.

She wanted to see him repent. She wanted to see him

make a dash for the burning body of the cross and try to throw himself into the fire. Of course somebody would save him—one of their parents would grab his arm and soothe him: Jacob, don't be foolish, come inside now. But she wanted to see him accept his guilt for at least an instant, and bleed for it. Or burn.

Around the bottom of the cross the snow had become a puddle. In the morning, or later, after the ashes had cooled, there would be an icy ring there. Ice was what her brother made her think of, not fire. Ice was what he deserved.

She stood herself beside him and whispered, in a voice she barely recognized, "I wish they *would* take back your bail. I wish I didn't have to see you." She turned to her mother, who looked alarmed. Tears had begun to rise into her throat and stop it up. She hadn't known she was going to say these things. "I wish he was dead!" she shouted, and she flung herself, her whole weight, against him. Off guard, Jacob stumbled backward and landed with a crunch. It was almost comic, the way his legs rose up acrobatically. Then there was nothing for her to do but take off running, her boots piercing noisily through the skin of ice that sealed the snow. It was so exhausting to pull her feet out of each hole that she knew she wasn't going anywhere. Shards of frozen snow were sharp as glass around her ankles. But if he'd heard her it was good enough. She didn't want a brother anymore. She wanted to wake up in the morning and not have to see his insolent face that was ruined for her and ruined everything else and made them all into freaks. From far across the lawn—the huge lawn that had spooked Martha, that made her think he was rich—the cross began to buckle with a sound like sluicing water. It poured down slowly, just slipped to the ground almost reluctantly as if it had to rip itself free, and she saw her family standing together in a ring around it, taken back into darkness, all the light quenched. Only their shins were lit, ankle to knee, with the dying fire. Judith stood with her own legs in the broken snow, her toes beginning to ache with the cold. White smoke rose, fierce as flame itself, urgently. It climbed straight up, higher than the cross had been. The bastards who did this could probably see it from their lawns, if they were out in the darkness looking.

CAROLYN

WATER SEEMED TO BE THE ONLY MEDIUM IN WHICH SHE FELT comfortable these days—it was either a primitive salve of redemption, that coating of pure transparency, or simply warm, supple, undemanding. In the bathtub she watched sharp little waves rise around her knees like a lake in rough weather. When she'd been to visit her parents in Hilton Head they'd taken her to the edge of the Atlantic, a soft long brushy walk along the coast. They had pointed out fastnesses of the Confederacy out there, islands that had held munitions stores, inlets where Southern ships had moored. What were they doing there, Ira and Bea Miller, mixed up with the Confederacy?

Then again, what was she doing, not to mention Ben, son of the pious Herschl, buried in his skullcap and tallis, living here a few miles down the road from where William James had spent his summers. They were an hour or so from Emerson's house, and Bronson Alcott's failed farm, and all the rest of the great WASP fathers, descendants of the Mathers, the Wigglesworths, those Old Testament scourges. Her house, hers and Ben's, had an amplitude and purity of design that her poor Old Country ancestors had never dared dream of: they lived like landlords. It wasn't exactly hers, that knowledge lurked out of sight always, but she didn't know what it meant—only that she hadn't been born here like Celene, had merely chosen it? She hadn't been born to her parents either, they had chosen her—what did all this signify? That choice is inferior to chance? Surely you could be born where you didn't belong, not to mention to parents who didn't need or want you. She put her head back so far, contemplating, that the hair at her neck drew the warm soapy water up into itself like a dry towel.

There was a timid scuffling at the door, which she always closed with a hard rubber wedge but didn't lock when she was bathing, in case someone needed access fast. Judith put her head in and was instantly hazed over with steam. "Can I talk to you?" she asked in a tiny voice that seemed to expect nothing, and pulled her sweater around her waif-like, as if the bathroom were not warm as soup.

It was the lying, she said. It was the assault on her sense of reality, though she didn't call it that. Carolyn watched distress bring out every incipient twitch and tremor of uncertainty in Judith, who looked as if her limbs might detach and fly off around her. She looked so queasy she must be nauseous. Her eyes were pink.

She spoke very deliberately, as if she'd been practicing. "He is *lying*. He is completely changing the truth of what happened, Mom. How can you let him do that?"

It was not a good moment for Carolyn to be naked and off her feet. Judith looked levelly at her face, ignoring the rest of her, long and pale under water that was slightly bluish, like the milk she'd first fed her daughter.

"Tell me what you mean, Jude." She knew exactly what Jude meant.

"What do you mean, tell you. They're acting like—first Daddy buries that—thing. That horrible thing he *killed* her with." Judith's eyes were full and when she moved they overflowed. Water water everywhere, Carolyn thought, so loose she felt as if she'd been drinking. Her daughter's face was drenched, her upper lip sweated with tears. "Now they plan this whole story—I was sitting right in there, in the room with them, and they just ignored me. Like it didn't matter that I could hear all this stuff, and they were planning how to—just—how to *lie* completely—about what actually happened! You heard Jacob, you know what happened." She was a beautiful girl, Carolyn thought abstractly—it was a new way to see her, across this distance that had sprung up like mist between her and every other thing. (Thing? she thought. Judith a thing?) And what difference did it make that she was beautiful. What did beauty have to do with anything?

"Are you going to do what Daddy did? Not talk to those jury people?" She narrowed her eyes as if she was trying to look comic strip mean. "Or are you going to just lie when you go there?"

She had nothing to say, she had no plans. She lay there dissolving, her cells softening into the water, her fingertips withering as if she were in a time-lapse film, becoming a crone in minutes. Sleepy she was, barely able to concentrate. "Jude—people don't go to court to necessarily tell the truth about everything that happened." It was an effort to say anything at all, let alone the right thing. "They go to defend themselves the best they can and if anyone can prove that what happened was—"

"Just because that's what people *do*—just because they might get away with it—" She looked desperate to flee. From where she lay, Carolyn could see the top of Judith's head repeated in the mirror, her fine light cap of hair. Twice trapped. Her hands kept rising in front of her as if she were lifting something she couldn't get off the ground. "How can you just plan to go and lie like that? I thought Daddy was the only one who lied." She had begun to cry noisily, punishingly, the way she used to when her big brother did something unfair which she wanted to advertise. "You let Daddy convince you. It's disgusting." Now she cast her glance down the whole of Carolyn, from the hair she had stacked messily on the top of her head with a barrette, slowly the length of her fair unprotected body, to the two pink feet that stuck up like something growing awkwardly out of the water. "And nobody cares what I think. I'm just a stupid little kid, is all. Nobody even cares if I go *tell.*"

Carolyn sat up slowly as if she were in pain. The water broke and fell back down. She was shiny, polished like Ben's best wood. Was that what was upsetting Judith, that they hadn't considered her a player at all? Was she insulted that the plot didn't include her? "What do you mean, 'tell'?" She wasn't alarmed, only surprised.

Judith looked as if she were scratching her way up out of some place where she couldn't breathe. She stretched her neck tight, as if to find some open air, then wiped her face viciously with the back of her hand. "Figure it out," she shouted and, bolting, tried to slam the door behind her. But the little rubber wedge, loose on the floor like a hockey puck, caught and held, and the door stopped halfway open, jammed there. Cold air poured in as if it were a crosscurrent of water. It chilled Carolyn like a judgment.

Drying off, she decided what she'd say to Judith. She'd remind her that even the court makes distinctions. There was something called "sudden passion arising from adequate cause"—so Panos had instructed as he walked them through the inventory of defenses—and even if they knew all the facts, they would not find Jacob a simple murderer, using that standard. Why, then, could they not use the same compassionate standard themselves? They knew Jacob, they had heard his pained admission, and things had advanced in such a way that they were going to have to be his arbiters, not a jury box full of strangers. Even the strangers would come to the same conclusion, that he had had his agony already. "Please," she was going to say, "don't feel guilty for wanting him to be free to go on with his life, after all the horror he's already felt. The disgust at himself. The fear. He didn't plan to do this damage. Please go on loving him."

Warm in her robe, she started for Judith's room across the dark hallway, but Judith called out to her, a disembodied voice. "What if it was me? Mom? What if I was the one who somebody killed?" She must be sitting in the blackness, her back against the wall; she must have been crouched there, waiting for her mother to come out of the steamy bathroom.

Carolyn stopped. The question raised every fine hair on her neck like wind. Judith, for God's sake. "What if you were the one who killed somebody?"

There was a long pause. Judith breathed stickily into it, the way she sounded when she'd been crying and her nose ran. "I wouldn't!" she insisted in a small shocked voice. "No way! I couldn't ever do anything so horrible."

Here was the difference between them, then, however smart and well-intentioned her daughter might be: she was a child and there was so much she couldn't imagine. "Never say never, darling. Do you think Jacob thought he could do what he did?" Carolyn raised her voice into the dark. "That's the hard part, Judith. Someday—"

"Don't tell me 'someday,' I can't stand when you say 'someday'!" She sounded like a child again.

Carolyn sighed heavily. "Oh, Jude, why can't I say 'someday'? It's too early for you to know some things. You're not supposed to know them, or even believe them when you hear. I'm just beginning to learn some of them myself." That was the big surprise, the deepest, the last.

Twelve or thirteen was a good age for virtue and evil. At her age they were—unseemly. Jacob must feel that, too. Nothing that can't happen. Happen to happen.

She grappled her hand across the wall, crawling with her fingertips, and threw on the light the way she'd toss a pail of water, in one douse, without a warning. Its brightness astonished her. Judith, caught in the flash of cold light, leaped up from her corner and fled.

Jacob used to say the Blood Drawing sounded like a lottery or a raffle where they fished your name out of a bowl. Twice a year a large white truck would pull up to the door of the Congregational Church basement very early, and out would come roomfuls of equipment—cots, enamel tables for work stations, endless yards of tubing, stacks of heavy plastic bags that puddled up like pools of water, tape, stickers—and the nurses set it up as quickly and efficiently as a field hospital in a war that kept on moving. Well, no wonder they had it down—when it came to town it was as thrilling as the circus, but the staff that rode around with the truck, east to west, north to south and back again, assembled it every day of the year minus weekends.

Carolyn had signed on months ago as one of the two doctors of the day. The grand jury didn't meet again until tomorrow. She saw no reason not to go now.

Not true. She saw reasons and they offended her.

Ben had been on the news last night—radio only; thank God Howe was too small for a TV station—and he had surely been on the CB gossip channel. Grand jury proceedings were secret, but he'd made his pronouncements to the press. And yes, the D.A. had said, indeed we are, we're going to hold him in contempt. Annie Dineen had called, and half a dozen others, to ask what the hell he thought he was doing. Wendell had come over in person to sit in the kitchen and be grave and censorious.

"Too bad about them," Carolyn said. "I have a life to

lead. The town has its needs, too, you know. It doesn't just revolve around us and our problems." Lying in the bathtub, she had finally thought (and then pulled herself out of the water and stood as still as the shaman spattering everywhere), It is up to me whether this thing kills all of us or only some of us. Kills me. Kills Judith. Maybe it was time for some emotional triage.

"They've probably replaced you," Ben suggested. She was having an early breakfast and he was watching it with a sickened face.

"I'll deal with that when I get there." Biting into an English muffin sharply, the way she'd snap thread.

"It could be embarrassing."

She looked hard at him. He slept in a sweatshirt and sweatpants in this season, gray and a little raggedy. "Look who's talking." She drank her coffee contemplatively. He reminded her of the Pillsbury Doughboy. "Anyway, I've already been embarrassed plenty. That's not the worst thing."

She shrugged into her white hospital coat before she left the house. Ordinarily she'd have waited till she was at the church, but it felt so good, it smelled so familiar, smelled of her real life, pungent and scratchy with cleanliness, its pockets deep enough for a stethoscope and many small useful objects, that she couldn't wait. She put her winter coat on over it. "I'll either be back in fifteen minutes with a black eye or I'll be all day." She left him standing in the doorway waiting, she was sure, for a call from her other life, from Panos, who would still be angry.

Amazing that there'd be people lined up at the door to give away their blood, exactly the way they queued up for bargains at the biannual rummage sale. It was all ritual, it was altruism laced with peer—well, not pressure exactly. Expectation, maybe. Duty. Staying a part of things, paying your social dues. This didn't work half so well in big cities; it was what Hyland did best.

She parked around on the far side, away from the crowd that was already assembling, and went in the back entrance. Most of the faces she saw were the circuit-riding nurses'; none of them looked at her with particular interest. One, a woman with a voice like an emery board, Jerry, had worked with her a dozen times before. She was a high-colored redhead who looked as if she might take a nip or two to get through. She said a warm hello, innocent. Carolyn was so happy to see her that her eyes filled. She was setting up the leather chaises that had replaced the cots that had made the whole enterprise look a little like a Victorian hospital ward. They looked like a good place for a nap.

"Hey, doc, how're things?" Jerry asked.

A sick joke, Carolyn thought. "They've been better, Jerry. How've you been? How's your daughter?"

"Ah, you always remember. You're so sweet!" So she got to hear about Jerry's daughter's wisdom teeth, an involved saga with a terrible price tag attached, and the experience of unbearable pain. Carolyn delivered coos of sympathy; nobody's troubles should be mocked because they didn't measure up on the grief meter. But, then, they shouldn't all have to share the word *pain;* there ought to be different words for kinds and degrees of pain, she thought, like the Eskimos' twenty-four kinds of snow.

The local volunteer in charge of the day came in hastily with her clipboard, saw Carolyn, and stopped short. Minette Schact was a pretty, small-featured woman in an autumn-colored plaid skirt and vest. She was the kind of decent, organized citizen whose heels never wore down and whose stockings didn't run, the kind you wanted in charge of your campaign. She looked ripe for judgment of women with unruly sons.

"I hope you have me on your roster, Minette," Carolyn said mildly, without flinching. "I've been on since fall."

Minette looked flustered under her neat dark curls. Clearly she'd have liked to produce a superior just then, at whom she could thrust the problem. "Well, we have Dr. Rafferty and—uh, Dr. Caldwell—"

"But you can always use a third," she said amiably. "Or if one of them would like to be relieved—" She was not going to plead. Doctors were supposed to be the authorities of the day here.

That was when she discovered the power of the negative to neutralize opposition: the more Minette wanted to forbid her taking part, the less she could do so. Because, she supposed, feelings ran so high against her, all these good people could do was swallow them back down, or else they'd have to acknowledge them in public, they the state prizewinners among blood donors, a town replete with holders, even repeat holders, of the gallon-club pin shaped like a drop of blood. Minette fell back as if she'd been physically threatened.

There was never actually a lot for the doctors to do, but the state said they had to be in attendance. The nurses took pressures, temperatures, pricked fingers and pressed cotton against the nick, suspended blood samples in little vials and watched to see how they performed. She did less: asked questions anyone could have managed, about illness and travel—not many sojourners to Mozambique or Mayanmar at risk in Hyland. She was an extra, though, today; she would spell the finger-prickers, she'd dismiss them to have a smoke or a snack. She could hold on to some warm live flesh, old times, and they'd be happy with time off.

Drs. Rafferty and Caldwell (George and Scott, one ancient and hard-of-hearing, the other so brand-new he looked like a college boy) were polite but bewildered. "Carolyn!" Rafferty said too loudly, opening his eyes wide in case they weren't working right again. "They didn't tell me you were on. I rather thought you'd—" He stopped himself. They were in the rackety wooden hallway near the coatracks.

"I've taken a leave, George," she said, nearly out of

breath with the effort it took to sound casual, "but, you know, I'm not officially off the staff. So I consider this still my obligation."

There were clots of people staring, she knew, of course she knew, and some of them she was sure would keep their distance—if only nobody emptied a bag of blood on her, or called her some terrible name out loud. She remembered the cheerful white-haired nurse who had ambushed her with scurrilous suggestions about what to do with Jacob.

"Look, Carolyn," the old man said in a carrying voice. "I think you're getting a bum rap, I hope you know that." She wanted to shush him, good intentions and all. "I mean, let's wait for the courts to sort things out. That's what they're for, dear, aren't they?" His aristocratic, nasal voice was querulous.

"Thanks, George," she said, and touched his arm. "I'm grateful."

"Well, a lot of people are rooting for you, you know, only they tend to be, ah—rather the more quiet part of the population. Discreet. But I trust you know that."

She supposed she did; she suspected Dr. Rafferty thought only the college-educated should have the vote. Better guard against the arrogance of the martyred, she told herself. Better guard against ingratitude—but gratitude was so wearying it was like walking with a limp, all the other emotions out of alignment.

There were no crises, at least not visibly. Someone whose name, according to his clipboard, was Monte Fitz had extended his hand to her, then taken it back, said "Excuse me" rather politely, and left her station without saying why. But when blood was about to be drawn there could be many reasons. She would not put herself and Jacob at the center of everything.

She saw some heads incline toward one another and no one emerge from the group to sit beside her, arm extended for the pressure cuff. On the other hand, a decent number of women and some men who'd come over from the piano factory in a group presented themselves with the look of challenge on them. She blushed. Somehow they must have caucused on her behalf; they seemed to have opted for a policy of decency. "Hey, Dr. Reiser," they tended to say. "You doing all right?" The women's variations were gentler; she even stopped feeling the need to smile and nod at the question. They were performing for their neighbors. She couldn't guess why they did it or what it cost them.

One dark young woman with a very fair baby on her back stood waiting to speak to her. She took all the space in front of Carolyn's table, ostentatiously, flaunting her presence. Carolyn dismissed the man she'd been interviewing (who wanted to know if a trip to Tangiers put him on the "no" list. "Depends on what you were doing there," she told him bluntly, smiling a little. He didn't smile back). The young woman leaned down and delivered her message. "I know Jacob and Jacob could not do a thing like what they're saying he did. I could tell them that for you if you want."

"You're a friend of his?" she asked, a thoroughly stupid question. "From—?"

"We used to—hang out together. You know—go out, sort of?" Her baby clutched at her hair and pulled it straight down, hard, the way you'd signal a bus driver to stop. She was just a girl, though that baby rode between her shoulders. Probably a senior—dropped out to produce that gorgeous angel-haired child. Another girlfriend they hadn't known about. "He's a good, good person?" she insisted with the improvisatory air of someone who had barely known him. "And I want to wish you strength." The word was capitalized—she took herself very seriously. Carolyn, embarrassed, thanked her and asked her baby's name.

"Gypsy," she answered, unsmiling. "She's a sixties baby, you know? She's going to grow up free—like, no shoes and no haircuts and stuff? I don't even think I'm going to send her to school, that's a trip I wouldn't wish on anybody, let alone my own flesh and blood." She hitched the baby up a little and turned away. "Tell him hello from Deanna, okay? Tell him I love him. Strength." She gave a V sign and Gypsy lunged for her fingers with a happy gypsy shout.

Business was a little slow (though not, she noticed, for Rafferty and Caldwell). She closed her eyes for a minute behind her hand. The strain of feeling as if a tide of onlookers was standing just out of her line of vision all the time exhausted her but she only felt it when she stopped. "Doctor, get a doctor over here!" she heard and pulled up out of her daydream.

A large young man—she could see this as she approached at a run—had gone under. He had crumbled just as he'd stood up minus his pint of blood; now he lay like a huge log between the frail white enamel legs of a nurse's table. This tended to happen mostly to men. (Because women were used to the sight of blood? Because men's macho cool put a strain on them? Who could say?) A couple of the male staff carried him behind a screen and she went through the usual routine—pressure, investigation of head and bones, smelling salts—while the small tide of busy noise rolled on unabated outside. Rafferty and Caldwell had been turned back. So she was a doctor after all, if only in a pinch.

The young man, in the dark green uniform of a local oil company, was freckled and fleshy, and his eyes opening very slowly against the light were starry wet. She smiled at him without condescension. He was only a few years older than Jacob. "You're okay. You still feel dizzy?"

He closed his eyes again. "Wheew, that's embarrassing."

"Oh, you'd be surprised how often that happens. You big guys seem to have the most trouble somehow."

He laughed. "The harder they fall. Thing is, I shouldn't have looked at the bag where the blood was going. Yech, I couldn't believe that stuff was coming out of me." He was still pale, his freckles dark against his cheeks. His blue eyes were pretty as a starlet's. "Jeez, it looked like a pound of beef liver. I hate beef liver!"

"You *could* believe it, that's the problem." She had a little paperwork to do, to document the fact that nothing had happened. As she went through the questions, he began to look her over carefully.

"Hey, aren't you that guy's mother?"

She signed her name, angrily, with a histrionic tail on it. "Who's 'that guy'?"

"You know—the one that killed the girl?" He had a look of amazement, maybe even delight, on his broad pleasant face.

"I'm the mother of the guy they think might have killed the girl. There's a big difference." They were so matter-of-fact about it that she was almost amused. The boy looked as if he might like to get her autograph.

"I'm going to give you to a nurse now. You going to be all right?"

He nodded. A healthy young pink had returned to his face. Only his hairline was damp. "You think he did it?" he asked shyly. He shrugged, embarrassed to specify the "it." "You know."

She looked at him a long time. "Let them give you a lot of liquid, okay? Two or three of those little cups of orange juice. A couple of sandwiches. And some cookies, too. You need your energy." She ducked out from behind the screen and called Jerry to come and get him. There must have been a hundred people in the room, little groups that held for a minute or two and went into motion independently and regrouped again, like a hive. And what it produced, a freezerful of aid for strangers, was for the most part sweet.

But she saw, suddenly, superimposed on the scene like

a double exposure, her sister, Nina, looking off into the deep distance of Montana, holding a one-way conversation with that uncritical scenery, the shadowy mountains that never asked questions. Not social. Not congenial. Every country needs its own kind of French Foreign Legion, she thought gratefully. For emergencies, for time off. For despair.

At about two, Terry Taverner came in. She was a small round woman who seemed to be composed of a set of concentric circles—even her hair was a series of small, tightly rolled curls. Carolyn remembered her from the bank where she'd worked for years, and then from—was it the Sears catalogue store or the chicken fry? Someplace where she stood behind a counter, making change and small talk. It was hard to associate her with her sexy slender daughter, but then who knew what she'd looked like before the terrible relaxation of marriage set in? She was probably younger than she seemed. She wore a bright blue parka, belted, and short boots trimmed with dead-looking fur; she had the uncharismatic look of the average aging Hyland wife, not the stylish suburban kind, but the true local, serviceable, a little tired, slightly hostile to any glamour that wasn't sent by Hollywood and then, at the end of the evening, safely withdrawn. Though she was someone who would never have found a way to be conspicuous had she not fallen victim, she seemed to part the way, now, as she moved through the crowd—people made room for her. Rude as children, they stared from her to Carolyn, boldly, and back again. "Oh, watch out," somebody murmured, cruelly or kindly or only voyeuristically. Carolyn turned her face away.

When there was a lull in activity—people came to her in clumps—she pushed back her chair and walked out of the social hall to the ladies' room to throw cool water on her face and be alone for a few minutes, to unclench. She was not surprised when she came out of her stall and found Terry Taverner washing her hands. Carolyn saw her first in the mirror, her smallish unsentimental eyes, her hair a drab toss of curls like wood shavings. Tragedy, she thought with a start, did not make everyone look like Dame Judith Anderson.

Carolyn sighed.

Terry Taverner's eyes flared as if they were coals she'd blown on, and then banked.

Carolyn's second sigh was not helpless but full of effort. "Mrs. Taverner?" She added the question mark for respect, for humility.

Martha's mother had still not turned to her. It was very strange to address the face in the mirror; it was like talking to a TV set. Maybe it gave the woman a feeling of distance; maybe even of not being there.

"I've wanted to come to talk to you."

She was going to get nothing back.

"Please," she found herself saying, though she wasn't sure what she was asking for. "This has been—for me, for us, too—the hardest time in our whole lives. I want to—" Her voice sounded too damn *careful.*

Terry Taverner was looking at her scornfully, taking in the long white uniform coat, the hair, in its blond rinse. She had the tense, narrow curls of a recent permanent. Somehow, Carolyn thought, her own waves had been opened up luxuriously, and their relaxation seemed to spell money, fancy learning, a hundred immeasurables of ambition and accomplishment. "Advantages," people would call them who didn't have them. Hair could say that, though this wasn't the moment to rehearse the reasons. No room for history in this dim, fluorescent, deodorant-tinged air.

"We're—we're probably going to lose our son," she said quietly, and hot tears gathered in the corners of her eyes. Could she really dare to instruct this woman in their shared tragedy? "I've spent a thousand hours not sleeping, thinking about Martha. I just want you to know. It won't change things, but if you could—"

"What?" Mrs. Taverner spoke her first words harshly. "If I could *what?*"

Carolyn shrugged. "I don't know." She reached out for the frame of the stall door and held it gratefully. "If you could think of us as—" What? "Human? As parents—a family, I mean, who's also—so—helpless?"

For a minute she thought Terry Taverner might nod, might even embrace her, the way she'd dreamed this scene. Absolution in the living room of the Taverners' house was what she'd prayed for; she'd run it behind her eyes a hundred times, shared tears, pooled grief, sweet reminiscence (and then hadn't dared go ask for it). But the woman stood for a minute in total suspension and then said contemptuously, "What do you have to be helpless about, you tell me that. You made him who he is, nobody else did it. He's crazy and he's out walking the streets like a sane person!" Mrs. Taverner had finally turned toward her and backed up nearly to the wall where the paper towels hung in their silvery case, as if Carolyn might be about to attack her. "People keep telling us all kinds of stuff your sweet little son used to do. My husband thinks we ought to sue you for all you're worth for not keeping that freak on a leash."

Carolyn took the words like claw marks. Her whole face stung. What did she mean, what were people saying about Jacob?

She let Terry Taverner tell her again that she thought she owned the world. Fine, she owned the world—she listened with a small smile that probably looked arrogant, but, like a mask, it held her firm against disintegration.

"She was alive in the morning when I said goodbye to her. You're a doctor, you think about this, where she is now." She put her hand on her stomach, which must hurt at the thought. "You know, her friends went up the cemetery, they put everything up there she loved—her music box is there, and their pictures, they put the pictures right in with her, in the coffin, all around. They didn't even ask us, they just got her makeup kit and her bracelets and a little gold dog with holes for all her earrings, and planted them all around, it looks just like the top of her dresser except there's snow on it. But it isn't going to bring my little girl back, and nothing you say's going to get any pity out of me." She shook her head and tears flew off her face like rain.

Oh, the things your little girl did! Carolyn thought. She didn't deserve to be where she was—how could she be under the snow? But your little innocent had a life you can't imagine either. And some of it you knew. Some of it the whole town knew. "I'm not asking you for pity, I'm saying—"

"You better take a good look at that kid of yours because he's going to end up there, too. They aren't going to let him get away with what he did to her. If we got to go to the Supreme Court, he won't get away with it, and I'm going to cheer when they pull the lever. You got a nerve asking me for one single thing. You saw that cross? That's what people think about you and your son. You're just lucky my husband never came up there to your place with a shotgun."

This all sounded so familiar that Carolyn didn't know if she had heard it already in the back of her mind or if it was just cliché. Movie talk. What could come out of this experience that hadn't been said before? The words surrounded her in a haze but they didn't touch her. They echoed like the badly written lines in an old melodrama. But surely this was no time for literary objections! You shouldn't need a good writer to talk about your grief, or make you ingratiating, or easy to pity. *You are callous,* she thought. *You are inhumane.* But no, something would get through to her. Not this but something would. She was a hard case but she was not callous. Callous people felt nothing. She felt some things. Particular things, not predictable. *Please. Something.*

She was looking for a word to say that she could actually utter, something that met her standards, but the door opened, amazing it hadn't happened sooner, and two old ladies came in slowly, carrying their coats. They had identical blued hair and the sad segmented jaws of ventriloquists' dummies, and Terry Taverner took the moment of distraction to disappear without an exit line. Carolyn, trembling, lowered her face to the cold-water tap and when she had soaked it long enough to shiver, she walked out herself and got her coat and went home.

Halloween. Jacob must have been nine. Maybe ten. The yearly rituals blended together, leaped out of order in her memory. She didn't know why this Halloween came back to her just then as she ducked behind the wheel and started the car. A tinge of fire smoke in the air? Someone going by in a cape, yes, she saw the sweep of tweed out of the corner of her eye, someone across the street headed for the library. It was the year he won the contest —"Most Imaginative"—in the Town Hall for his Sherlock Holmes costume. (Any idea that got her out of the need to run up a little fox on her sewing machine, or a simple horse complete with movable ears and a feed bag, was a winner for her. Later, bless her, Annie Dineen took care of the task for Judith: she made fabulous concoctions, elaborate, imaginative, daunting. "It's okay, hon," Annie would say cheerfully, pulling the pins out of the cancan dancer's hem, piling up the fruit on Carmen Miranda's head. "I couldn't get a medical degree, believe me. Give me a cadaver to sew up and I'm out of here.")

So that year Jacob put on a voluminous checkered cape Ben used to wear as a joke when he was an art student. (He'd never thrown it away because he kept everything to use in his sculptures—she used to tell people he kept his mother's salamis in the safe-deposit box.) Jacob found a wonderful mahogany pipe with a perilous swoop in it and a tremendous bowl in which he could have burned a whole branch. Somewhere he discovered a dark cap with earflaps and then all he needed was a magnifying glass—that he borrowed from the Oxford English Dictionary, which provided a good solid lens to help penetrate its clotted pages.

The children had walked in a wide circle while their parents stood back out of the way, a raggedy line of miniature animals and tangible concepts—the Statue of Liberty, Recycling—some very serious, others clowning and dancing. The mothers who'd slaved over their two-tone jersey cats and beaded tutus were furious when Jacob won the judging. They suggested that two prizes be given, one for "made" costumes and one for "(merely) assembled." He was jubilant in victory. "Brains!" he kept saying, and walked around in his idea of a spy's urgent stoop. "You don't have to make anything, you just have to be *clever.*"

Carolyn had wished the poor kids didn't have to compete. A defeated bride sobbed in a corner. "When I came in here before, I thought I was the most *beautiful!*" Her mother looked as if she was going to cry with her. The little girl in the veil, with a train that kept getting stepped on, was slight and blond and had tiny fidgety feet in white ballet slippers—she could have been, might have been Martha. She was somebody's lovely little girl anyway, already learning the rudiments of the up-and-down contest between brains and beauty—somebody should have assured her she'd get her own back eventually—about being chosen and passed over, about the ways, sometimes, people ought not to be judged but simply left alone to feel good. After the march, the roomful of kids ate doughnuts and bobbed for apples—it ought to have been enough.

They, Jacob and the rest of them, had always won too much. Always, she, Carolyn Miller, was the last child standing at the end of the spelling bee, or Jacob prevailed in the Mathtasks contest, or Ben's painting, so long ago, was chosen to hang in the school lobby, Judith's vaults took first in the gymnastics competition, all of them hardworking but always geared toward success. Weren't there mothers back there behind the kids who never made it, hissing "Unfair! It's always the same ones! We protest!"? None of it was given easily, but they knew how to take it—a minority habit that, to go for it. Even knowing how to work hard—it added up to ease, the way some people's investments added up to riches. And looked like privilege, somehow. *Terry Taverner staring at her, small-eyed, in the bathroom mirror. Her daughter—somebody's daughter—in her miniature bridal gown, never beautiful enough.* Wasn't merit just another privilege, if you didn't have it?

Judith was at the piano when she came in, sitting unnaturally straight. All she did was pad across the keys making dissonance, very quiet, very earnest and defiant. Blocky chords made of impossible combinations, pianissimo. The notes rubbed up against each other and grated. A statement, a series of statements.

She tried to see the house the way Terry Taverner would see it. It was the informality, not the pretentiousness, of the furniture that would bewilder and disgust her, and the arrangements of the pictures, so many pictures, huge splats of color everywhere and not much of it recognizable either: not people or scenery, the things paintings are usually about. As for knickknacks—did they, in fact, own anything you'd call a knickknack? The arty casualness, the refusal to invest in good furniture except for the few antiques from a rough, not an elegant, period (the blanket chest, the heavy corner cabinet, a dull battered Puritan blue). The worn Orientals. The books. Martha told Jacob that only Jewish people had that many books.

And no gilded artifacts. One more proof of the wantonness of their class. Show-offs. Nonbelievers.

Judith made an ugly sweep up the keyboard and back down again, heavily, with the side of her hand.

Carolyn wanted to go to her and say, "I will not fail you," but she wasn't sure what the opposite of failure might be.

Maggie Dormer called, on behalf of some of the members of Carolyn's chorus. ("Informal, this is," she said firmly. "This isn't official, you understand.") The Curry Mountain Chorus was a mixed group, from a couple of college girls all the way up through Dot Weyerhauser, who, at eighty-two, still possessed a celestial, unwavering alto. They were passionate about Bach and Brahms and worked hard at their scales. Last year before the Christmas Cantata they even invited an exchange student to help them with their German diction—but in general you didn't need a pedigree to belong. Carolyn sang alto, sometimes tenor if they needed her. These days she missed them terribly.

"We were thinking of having a sort of meeting," Maggie told Carolyn vigorously, the way she urged the chorus to practice their parts at home. "I don't know if you want to come or not. We're a little alarmed by some of the—oh, Carolyn, some of the talk has been—well, Henry called it incendiary." (Henry, her husband, was a gentle man in spite of a bass voice that was an alarming instrument in ordinary speech.) "And now that they've done that horrible—" She couldn't say it. "Truly incendiary." The group she had in mind appeared to include the core of the town music lovers, who turned out enthusiastically for chamber music in summer. If you looked down on the concert crowd from the balcony of the Meeting House, you saw a good bit of white hair, fine labels, a whole inventory of Birkenstocks; a solid contingent, clearly, from the Episcopal and Unitarian churches.

"Maggie," Carolyn had said. "A meeting to do what? How can you—"

"We can make sure there's some reason afoot out there. Henry says, and I'm afraid he's right—there's a lot of demonizing going on."

"But you're not going to change that." It felt peculiar to be arguing for incivility.

"Look, dear. Jacob hasn't had his day in court yet. We can at least remind people that you all deserve some consideration. Some human consideration." Carolyn thanked Maggie but said she didn't think they'd come, though she was touched. They'd be campaigning, she thought, if they went.

Ben picked up the *Bugler* from the front step where the newsgirl had thrown it with her admirable sidearm. When he got to the Letters to the Editor he spread it out on the table. There were two letters about them, one the petition they'd found nailed to the front door, the Edict, Ben called it, pleading that Jacob's bail be rescinded, and signed (though not on the page) by 493 members of the community. The other deplored "terrorist tactics borrowed from the bad habits of the most notorious extremists"—the act was unnamed—which, it said, were a humiliating blot on the name of the town of Hyland. "We live in a democracy and the cost of democracy is that sometimes justice is slow in its fulfillment, and even then may be full of surprises. We cannot be vigilantes who decide what the outcome should be and act upon it. For shame!" Carolyn heard Tony Berger's militant voice, and recognized that, in addition to his wife, Celene, and Wendell and Steph, the four others who had signed the letter were teachers in the district; they weren't actually people she knew, but their names were familiar. Most readers of the paper, of course, would sooner side with the 493 "ordinary" citizens than with the teachers, who might be suspected of driving Volvos and having progressive ideas.

Though that wasn't fair: this was not as simple as class. She thought about Mock Frazier down at the Inn. She thought of a dozen others, nice white-bread people, who had proclaimed their decent skepticism. God bless Tony anyhow, she thought. He was no fair-weather friend.

And there was an editorial, too: "People are entitled to feel whatever they need to feel after a horrific event like a murder," the editor chided, "but it is the test of a state and a people that they can overcome their passions and let justice take whatever course it may. Brutal threats and scare tactics do nothing to restore a sense of peace and order to our town at the very point when those are the things we need most." It was all so impersonal—every time anyone invoked Democracy, she wanted to hit something. Democracy the bitter medicine. Democracy the postponer of vicious blood gratification, the long, wearying process. The name of the Accused was a hole in the language, a gaping silence. Well, of course, better to make him faceless and emblematic than Jacob Reiser with an address and a phone number, or out come the cross burners and the finger pointers, true enough. Terry Taverner would probably agree with her, that was the funny part—she, too, would feel roughed up by such abstraction every time it turned somebody's eyes away from Martha, her particular girl, her flesh-and-blood child, gone. Democracy awaited all of them with its leveling touch. Cold comfort.

Carolyn leaned her elbows on the spread-out sheets and rested her head on her palms.

One last try. "You will not let him tell the truth and Panos can ask for—"

"What can he ask for? A short sentence? Manslaughter? A little leniency around the edges? You think this is a haircut—'Just take a tiny bit off here, leave the rest alone'?"

She ignored him. "Even—maybe—probation. Maybe they'd let him go free under some kind of psychiatric supervision. If he told it just the way he told us, how could you doubt him? Sometimes if you tell your story sympathetically enough—"

"Right. That or twenty years. He's got one life, Carolyn. *One life.*" He said it like a threat.

"So did she, Ben. Didn't she?" It seemed impossible that she could manage to sound abject before both Terry Taverner and her husband.

"Just take the Fifth. It's clean, it's legal, it's neutral. You won't be lying."

"The Fifth is about yourself. What about when they ask about Jacob. That's what's gotten you in trouble."

"You only know what *you* know, that's the point. If you're silent, you don't lie, you don't tell the truth. You sit in the middle and wait. Like Zen. Stasis. Perfection."

"You're going to be the Zen master of the Grieves County Jail."

He smiled and a tense peace radiated from his face. "A Jewish Zen master. Well, I surely won't be the first."

Around ten o'clock, when she walked downstairs wrapped in her robe, Ben was in the kitchen making English-muffin pizzas. Jacob had his home-tutoring notebook open, his elbows on the paper, eyes closed, drowsing. ("You could be on death row," he'd said, not amused, "waiting for your last meal, and they'd still be drilling you on equations and asking you to find Bosnia-Herzegovina on the goddamn map.")

"Where's Judith?"

Ben looked up from the cheese slicer innocently. "Judith doesn't seem to favor our company these days. I think she's boycotting us." He said this neutrally, which amounted, she thought, to smugness.

She shivered. "Jake, put a little more wood in, will you? I'm just out of the shower." She sat down, angry. "You haven't given any thought to why that might be?"

Jacob had reached into the woodstove with the iron

tongs to prod a piece of wood that was hiding in a back corner. All Carolyn could see was his face and shoulders as he leaned in. She saw his eyes widen before she heard his howl. He leaped back as if he'd been flung, and flailed his arm in the air wildly, flaming like a flag. "Jake! Here! Jake!" Ben hurled himself at the arm and surrounded it with his chest, and dragged him to the sink to plunge it under a burst of cold water. Jacob was gasping, "Ah! Ah! Ah!" as if in ecstasy.

She was up and tearing at the remains of his blackened sleeve, but she couldn't tell if it was glued to his skin or only soaking wet. "Break off a piece of aloe," she commanded Ben, who ran to the windowsill and cracked off a fat oozing end of the succulent plant, spiny and charmless in its pot. Carolyn had managed to push back the sleeve very carefully, a centimeter at a time, to be sure it wasn't fused to Jacob's flesh. She spread a huge slick of colorless grease on the blistering skin, trying to keep her fingers light, and thought of the burning cross. The threat, the warning. Fire *wanted* him.

"We're going to the hospital," she said in a voice they couldn't argue with. "Let me get into some clothes. This needs some real medication fast." When she came downstairs, Jacob was in his jacket, his right arm out, his face as white and damp as a cut potato. "Oh, honey." She ran her hand across his forehead. "It'll feel a lot better soon, I promise you." She put her arms around him, careful to stay away from the burned side, then opened the front door onto a medicinal chill.

The Professional Building was dark except for the red lights that glowed above the emergency exits like hot cinders. When she turned the lock to her office and switched on the light she felt as if she'd never left it. The yellow-and-green flowered cushions in the waiting room looked a little more worn than she'd ever noticed, and Karen—what a thoughtful friend—had taken the plants out of their wicker holders to minister to them at home.

Otherwise, it was Before, and she felt elation rise in her like adrenaline.

"Okay, come on in here, let me get this cleaned up properly, and we'll put some cooling stuff on it. We've got to be careful about infection." She bent over him her strenuous attention, and her fingers moved, gratefully, to do what they understood so well, the fine balance of hand and mind that she was lucky enough to live with. "Wait a second." She leaned into the corner where she kept a tape machine-radio stocked with children's music to distract the criers. She clicked it to FM and fiddled with the dial until she found some familiar rush of noise. "Hammer, cool," Jacob said. "Okay, leave it right there."

She worked at his arm, at the soft underside, slowly and carefully. So many small innocent bodies had passed under her hands in here, appendixes prodded, bones set, phlegmy chests listened to. She held Jacob in her sight, but her mind flooded: little boys with sheepdog bangs and knobby shoulders, girls with curls softer than the cotton balls in the jar. Meek ones who gazed at her like spaniels, and feisty ones, wrigglers, hysterics, kids who brought out words their mothers didn't know they knew. "Pediatricians have to have a sentimental streak," her favorite professor, Timonelli, had told her once. "I'm shameless," he'd said, though he was a tough enough bastard with them. "I'm not sure how I ever got past my own pacifier and security blanket—just a fellow baby at heart, looking out for my own kind." They loved to hear him say that; he was a hulking man with a large pocked face, an inquisitive nose, and furiously tangled dark hair, about as far from the tenderness of his baby self as any man they knew. But he could whisper. "That's why you've got to be tough about what you do with them. No room for error with those kiddos. Punish yourselves, so they won't have to be punished."

The bandages were as clean as blank paper, though they wouldn't stay that way ten minutes. "Does it hurt?"

she asked Jacob, and as he shook his head—"Still numb"—she saw again how honest-looking he was, how the distance between his eyes, the set of his chin, all of it was mysteriously spaced to make you trust him, such tiny increments of angle and arrangement. (Wasn't Mickey Mouse designed to look like a baby—she'd read this somewhere—to make us go soft at the sight of him, his head huge, his ears set low? She seemed especially susceptible.) Every child who'd been up on this examining table rumpling the paper, kicking her feet, looking over his shoulder for his mother, alive and needy—and the mother needy as the child—was watching her. God, she missed it! The room was full of faces, hovering, a children's picture where the faces hide in the trees, invisible. Jacob was one child, only one. Martha was one, that little girl with visible ribs and tiny nubby breasts, and the blondest eyebrows over cloudless blue eyes. (How sentimental can we be, Timonelli? she pleaded. Where do you draw the line?) Judith was another one, just another child, neither better nor worse than any other, nor more valuable or less—what did those words mean before *privilege* set in? Judith long-legged, fair but not fairy-blond like Martha. So many ways to be fair. How Judith always shrieked when her mother gave her a shot—she'd finally handed her on to whichever nurse was working: let her hate the nurse instead.

Had Martha screamed at the moment of—impact, wasn't it? Annihilation. She saw Judith's fragile ear where it was lapped with short soft hair, that ear she used to whisper into endlessly when Judith was little and loved pretend secrets. (Though what if she didn't have a Judith? Could she only feel for Martha because she had a similar girl-child, blond and clinging?) Judith would hoist herself up to giggle into her mother's ear, overcome with nothing to say, just the need to keep the game going. And the incredibly smooth temple beside the ear, fragile as eggshell, faintly lined with one blue thread. Growing up is all a matter of toughening, hardening from eggshell to leather. And then softening again, later. Dissolving. What is it *for*, she asked now—felt it, didn't ask it in words. Why save them, Timonelli? Why keep them from pain, after all? How could she save one who was already gone? What could she give?

Well, it was indecent, maybe, to need a daughter to make her feel the loss, but there it was—she did. She had a daughter. She had a son. All she could do was give away his safety.

She could step out of the way and leave him out there in the open, to the mercies of other people's parents. He wouldn't be alone, his father would be with him. Judith would be with her, then. There would be a line between them, indelible.

She felt a sudden peculiar falling inside her, like dominoes tumbling down, keeling over in a slow heap, inevitable. Their collapse went on for a long minute and then stopped, as if they'd come to the last, they'd leaned against the bottom one and it gave and the whole fluid collapse was finished.

It would be the end of them. Wasn't Martha under the snow the end of the Taverners? Wouldn't this be worse? Jacob smiled at her, finally relieved, and gestured at his arm. "Can I get out of doing my schoolwork now?"

She took him into her own arms again, smiling back. Once the motion in her chest had stopped, she was cold, still, inside. Finished. I'm leaving you, she thought, my best darling boy, I'm abandoning you to yourself. It was facing-up time, and if he came through it—but she couldn't get herself even to think the words, she was too dwarfed by the size of it all—he wouldn't be her boy anymore, or his father's, either. She had told Terry Taverner they were going to lose their son; she knew the woman hadn't believed her.

It was as if he had thrown her to the ground and put his foot on her chest and she had decided to stop fighting and try to lie still. She would close her eyes and let the snow fall on her face, and when it melted, it would be tears.

Ben had not come with her. She walked out of the grand jury room straight to Panos. He was sitting on the bench beside Mag, waiting, popping his knuckles. There were a few other people at the other end of the hall, a very fat woman in turquoise and her snappy-looking lawyer, deep in conversation. Carolyn gestured to Panos and Mag to move and they made room for her on the bench.

"How'd it go, trouper?" She imagined Panos kidding with his sons in a house crammed with too much furniture, too many people, all of it smelling like the kitchen. He never liked to sound uptown.

She covered her mouth with her palm for a minute, as if that might keep her from having to speak. It was a habit Ben laughed at, as if main force could keep the words in. "Well, I guess I told them the truth."

Panos laughed. "Thank God somebody's sane over here. So he didn't convince you to go belly-up alongside him. Well, what can I say. Good."

"That isn't what I mean. I mean that Ben and Jacob haven't been telling you the truth, Panos. I can't believe you haven't known that."

The silence was thick. He waited her out.

"There's a different—oh God, I don't know what you're going to do about this, Panos."

"What *I'm* going to do. Hmmh." He narrowed his eyes at her. "Go on, then," he said sternly. "I don't like suspense." He sounded angry at her, as if she was trying to be difficult. He and Mag exchanged impatient glances.

She was weak, her whole upper body was almost impossible to hold up. "Can we talk about this somewhere else? This is very hard, it sort of—doesn't lend itself to, you know, hallway chat. And here come the guys."

The news photographers were bearing down on them.

She always had the feeling they stood somewhere out of sight with their stopwatches and then, at a given moment, like an invading army, descended. They hated the secrecy of the grand jury but they could at least catch the retreat of the principals, the more anguished the better. Carolyn restrained herself. Lights flared at her back. They found a deserted conference room, more plastic chairs, more fluorescence—the Law seemed to proceed in a hard-edged world. It was worse than the hospital.

She told him Jacob's version, with intermissions for silence in which she stifled tears. (They had cried enough, all of them, she thought irritably, and it changed not one damn thing. But it took too much energy to resist.) She told him how Ben had made a few significant changes, not very many, just enough. "Did you really believe that story? Didn't it seem awfully—strange?" she asked him, but Panos only grunted in reply. "Keep going," he said. "And the weapon? That car jack you said he used? Do you know where it went to?"

"You don't want to hear."

"Maybe I need to."

"It won't surface, I promise you. But I'm not going to say."

"Did you ever see it?"

She shook her head.

"Then it's hearsay. Be grateful for small favors." Panos had broken out into a sweat; his swarthy forehead looked like Ben's after a four-mile run. It was an accomplishment, she thought dimly, to have shaken Panos Demaris so.

"You can't be forced to testify against your husband in a court of law. Would it help you to know that?"

She smiled. "Does that extend to discussions with your defense attorney?"

"As you will. I just don't want it coming back to haunt me and make me look sloppy. If you don't care what happens to you, I care what happens to me."

She nodded. "Fair enough." Then silence.

"Jesus." He looked, quite suddenly, exhausted. "Do you realize everything you said in there is indelible? Do you know, roughly, what that means?"

She nodded. Very roughly. She didn't know anything one way or the other.

"You couldn't have consulted with me first? God, you're just like he is, you're independent operators, both of you. I don't know what the hell you're paying me for, if you want to know. My counsel doesn't exactly come cheap, but you don't ask, you don't discuss, the two of you just call me in to clean up the messes you make." He looked a little awed. Mag just stared. "Carolyn, I don't even know if I can stay on this case now. We've got a lot of hard thinking to do." The "we" meant Panos and Mag; she had had all the say she was going to.

"What do you mean?" She saw that Mag's head was in her hands, dramatically, as if this were her own calamity. What did you buy of these people, anyway?

He took the kind of deep breath, huge, she made patients take when she was listening for rales. "There are questions of ethics involved, my friend, if you know your client's lying. If he's asking you to suppress what you know. This is the kind of conundrum you just love, isn't it? 'Do you have to believe your client's innocent?' "—he did that in a mean, high, mocking voice. "All that blah-blah of yours. Well, now. Look what you've done to bring it to a head. If I know—"

"You don't know anything, Panos. You weren't there. And neither of us has the first bit of proof, it's just our word, one—parent—against the other. You said before it was a lousy case for the prosecution and it still is. So it's a lousy case for the defense now, too."

Panos closed his eyes in exasperation. "You're going to be out there by yourself, Carolyn, if they want to keep their story. If we're pleading not guilty and you come in with manslaughter, sudden passion, whatever, you'll be hung out there to dry all by yourself."

Mag had picked her head up and begun doodling savagely on a yellow pad. Her obsessive circles, so thick they dented the paper, felt like a fingernail on a blackboard.

"Or he will." She didn't feel as tough as she sounded.

"If I tell his story in there, I won't be there to help you. You're going over to the prosecution, you realize."

She supposed she did, without having thought of it that way. "If you accuse me of lying, then I look vindictive. I look like a witch-mother trying to put my son in jail. Will anybody believe I'd do that without a reason?"

"Or crazy. Don't forget crazy. You could look nuts. You could look out to get your husband however you can—*there's* a reason, and not an uncommon one either, you know. Baby, if I say what I could say I can make you look like Medea." He slashed his throat with his hand.

She was out of replies. Let them call her crazy, then, small price. Let them find Jacob sane and innocent, she'd have told what was true. *Medea?*

"God, you're as stubborn as he is," Panos said without admiration.

"Oh, I'm worse." She contemplated the matter. "Ben gets mad and he digs in, he shouts a lot, but then he cools down fast, no grudges. He gets it out of his system, and the stubbornness, too. But me." She thought about herself, locked up, her sense of propriety once she had proof. "Me, I do a slow burn but then I stay mad forever. I never thought about it, quite. But I'm really not very forgiving, Panos. Or changeable." Her eyes filled at the truth of it. "I'm—I've got a lock on a lot of things. Facts. You can get to me with facts. They set hard as stone for me." Her sister used to tell her that every chance she got. Her sister flowed like water and she crystallized like rock.

"Your husband sounds very Greek to me. Mediterranean. Lots of quick flare-ups and—*ffft,* the air is cleared. Cleansed. Thunderstorms. We used to call my father

Stormy. My father put his foot down so hard one time he smashed the front stoop in half. My brother took a Polaroid and gave it to him and he thought it was so funny he framed it." He looked too hard at her. "Did you tell Ben what you were going to do?"

"Not yet."

"You're going to?"

She laughed at the preposterousness of withholding it. "I can't think of a way not to."

"Christ," Panos said. "All I can say is I hope he doesn't have his son's temper or I'll worry about you."

That was probably meant to be black humor. "Worry. He doesn't have his son's temper, his son has his." He had done the best he could with that anger of his, she knew. But what can you ask of a person but that he know he has a problem, and then that he try to control it? Hadn't he hauled himself to therapists like someone with a painful invisible illness, hadn't he done everything but stifle his mouth with a gag? Well, was he responsible for what was left if he sometimes failed at it? Or for what was forever perceptible under the surface? Children tasted what their parents swallowed.

"I think Ben always expected the kids to be like him—you know, to *get it,* sort of. Not to feel threatened. The way he'd flare up and then die down fast. Only they could never see anything except the anger part. But you know," she went on, contemplative. "I may be worse for them than he is. A punisher isn't any better than a—a swatter who can give you a smack and then laugh over it and hug you hard." Was she romanticizing? Or was it the combination that was lethal, his leap of fury, her hasty, cauterizing constriction? Both of them doing the best they could do, but oil on water maybe. Maybe Jacob was the inevitable flame. "Anyway," she said, returning with a little embarrassed smile, "the point is, I did it. In there. It's done. The tale is told."

"What, exactly, did you tell them?"

She looked around, panicked. The sign on the half-open door said *Jury Room.* This was where they'd sit, or one just like it, small and plain, lit only by their own concentration. "Mag, do you think you could find me a soda in one of those machines out there? Anything at all, just wet and cold." She reached into her bag for some change. How many diversions would she need to keep from breaking down? She would pinch herself raw before she would break down like a child in here.

Mag rose slowly, obediently. She didn't take the quarters. "That's okay, we'll put it on the bill."

"You're stalling," Panos told her.

"The whole confession he made."

"Admission. That wasn't a confession. Okay. How much of it?"

"Everything, I said."

"Pregnancy?"

"I told you, everything."

"So you even gave them a terrific motive. You ever read that *American Tragedy* book? About the guy and the girl and the rowboat?"

"But this wasn't his, he isn't—wasn't—"

"Jealousy, then. Just as good. Superb, even. What did you think you'd accomplish for Jacob, handing them such a good reason on a goddamn platter?"

Mag put a diet Coke in front of her, its cold sides glistening.

"But what really happened—"

"Carolyn, *screw* what really happened! What's it going to take for you to get this? 'The truth' in a courtroom is just a construction of effects. It's *theater.* There is no such thing as simple truth, as long as its presentation can be shaped, or perverted, or invented, even. Not the facts, mind you. I'm talking presentation. Either side can skew the way things appear, and how they appear is all that matters."

"You're describing public relations. You're describing an ad campaign."

"Correct. I am." He took a swig of her soda and made a face. "God, it leaves wax in your mouth. My tongue feels like the goddamn kitchen floor." He wiped his lips with the back of his hand. "This means we have a bunch of different elements to play with—Jacob's personality, if he testifies. Your husband's attitude if we can get him to condescend to speak about his beloved son in public. The girl's reputation, which will not, I guarantee you, for all your Girl Scout theatrics to redress and do penance and all that—will not survive this trial. A girl, no matter how innocent-looking, who's screwing one guy and having some other guy's kid is not made for sainthood in a courtroom, I can promise you that if I promise no other thing." He looked hard at her. "Don't crumble on me, Carolyn. You've done what you've done and you're going to see out the consequences of it. 'He's so crude.' I can hear you going home and saying that to Ben. 'Oh, he's so gross, he hasn't got a single compassionate cell in his body.' " He got up and skulked around the table. "Shit, Carolyn. I don't want to see your kid convicted, but if you wanted to make my job impossible, you did a terrific opening number." He danced a little soft-shoe. "Applause from the D.A. He ought to send you roses."

She sat perfectly still, taking the assault. This was why she hadn't come to him first. "It's absolute, Panos, why I did this. That's why I didn't come asking your permission. I didn't want it. This isn't one of your courtroom strategies." She had told Judith there were no absolutes at her age, that they were a luxury. There seemed to be no one she hadn't lied to.

He laughed. "Oh, tell me about it. You and your wildcatter husband. You and your saintly goddamn absolutes. I want to tell you, you're more selfish than you can begin to realize, both of you. You'll see what a bare little thing your principles are. You want him to face the consequences, he'll have a few to face and then some. And it'll be too late to call back a single word."

Driving home alone, around the lake, past the old graveyard, out into the open stretches of straight road, she felt her eyes mist over. It was hard to see, caught in such a downpour of anger. Now Panos was furious, too, though his fury was rational and contained and she couldn't blame him for it—the man was doing his duty. Nobody spared her, though. Was it inherited or learned, what Ben and Jacob had in common? There seemed to be a genetic disposition to so many incalculable things—hyperactivity, they were learning. Short attention span. Shyness. Why not wrath? Choler, centuries ago when they thought it was a physical quality.

She tended to think of Jacob cowed by his father, shouting back, or holding on in strained silence but terrified at the quick. Ben towering over Jacob, though it had been years since he could do that: they were eye to eye now. Saw Ben's captive creature. Father and son, she could imagine them, tearing at something that looked like a huge fruit that they held between them, veined and fleshy, running with juices. They were sharing it, eating from opposite sides, but it never seemed to get any smaller. She had seen them that way, she realized, after one of their conflagrations, head-to-head, a ceremony of rage over some petty infraction. What was it—oh, Jacob had borrowed a sweatshirt, Ben's favorite, it was from the Boston Museum, a Matisse on the front and someone else on the back, Braque maybe—and had ruined it, stained it or ripped it or something. Nothing. After an evening of watching them, hearing them, she had seen them in her sleep, eating that fruit. It had stayed with her all day, sickening as a rancid taste in the mouth. What a peculiar image it was: two children with their faces smeared, and she the irritated mother coming after them with a wet washrag, coming at them like a witch, a hag breaking in on their pleasure, and both of them shrieking.

BEN

"WAIT HERE," I SAID TO HER. "YOU WAIT RIGHT HERE."

And I went to get him. I had to pull him, objecting, out of his bed, where he was lying in the dark with his bandaged arm out of the blankets and that endless music on, the screeching and wailing of boys looking for trouble. "Come hear what your mother's done," I said. "She's done it, boy, and it isn't going to come undone." I pulled him down the cold hall toward our room, his hand inside mine, pulling back, trying to tear away. The windows were so steamed up with the cold there seemed to be smoke billowing outside.

She testified in the morning and then she vanished. God knows where she went; I never did find out. I made supper for the kids and wondered if I ought to report her missing. There *is* catastrophe, even if it would seem like a bad joke today. People drive off the road into Derby Lake. They get sick without warning. They even get murdered.

But she came in around ten and didn't look at us and went to bed. I followed her up the stairs and waited while she undressed in the bathroom—first time since I've known her. And then I had to hear it.

I was afraid of this. I didn't trust her, I thought it, every time she sat there at the table nursing a mood, she was getting herself ready for this. She never wanted to save him. From the very first minute when I saw the way her hands opened and closed, opened and closed as the words sank in, she was never going to forgive him.

"Tell him," I said. I stood in the doorway but I pushed him into the bedroom so that he was out in the middle of the floor like an animal. I had both of them terrified, trembling, but it was her own doing. You have a choice in these matters. Whatever's handed you, goddamn it, you can shape it at least a little bit. You can try.

"Because she was a person, too," she said, as if the rest should be self-evident. "That's all. I love you and want to protect you, but her parents loved her and wanted to protect her, too." She was crying as she said this, very quietly and evenly like a rhythm under the words, and the more she cried the more I wanted to shake her, to get her to face what she was doing to us. "Do you think your life is the only one that's ruined? Ben? Sometimes you act like Martha's parents are just—an irritation. An inconvenience. And Martha—" She flung her hands out in a parody of impatience. It wasn't fair to be simplified that way.

Jacob just stood and took it in. He didn't even frown, his face was perfectly still. What do you think when the mother who gave you life puts her hands around your neck and squeezes? Children are abandoned at so many different points along the way, from birth onward. But a baby, you know, is only a theoretical person. When he's rejected it isn't really rejection, it's only circumstances, his mother's life can't take him in and hold him. A million reasons but they're not his reason, they're not his fault, they're not *him.* Carolyn was given away like that, but I don't think she's ever felt *discarded.* But what is Jacob thinking standing there, whose whole self, everything he's been for seventeen years, everything, isn't enough to make him valuable? She knows him better than anyone but she will not save him.

"Every tug of the rope," she said with her eyes closed, "made me more sure I had to do this. Benny, you'd do well to stop. When you get me to remember him as my baby, my boy, my darling, that only tightens the other end, why don't you understand that? Martha was *their* baby, *their* girl, *their* darling. Don't you hear me?"

"Why don't you let her parents worry about her. Are they worrying about him?"

Jacob looked from one of us to the other.

She pulled into herself like a turtle. I watched her shrink up, her legs pulled under her, her shoulders folded in somehow. "Jacob," she said. I had to strain to hear her. "Jacob, can you understand that at all?"

"You're asking a hell of a lot of him," I objected, "if you expect your own kid to understand that you betrayed him. You mean *forgive?*"

"It's not betraying, Dad," my son said to me. "I sort of know what she means." Why did he look as if he was afraid of me? Both of them stared as if I were the criminal here. "What if somebody did that to me? Accident or not." He shrugged as if it was simple. "I don't think that's —I can understand that. Everybody needs defending. Martha—it's too late, but I can see that. Martha could use some defending." His eyes were wet. They were the color of a certain kind of rock I love; wet, they were deeper blue-gray, the way the stones at the pond get dark when you splash them. Those beautiful eyes, neither hers nor mine.

She got off the bed and put her arms around him and he laid his head on her shoulder the way he did when he was half his age. He was comforting her. I went weak in the knees, I was seeing the grand jury ranged around in that empty room, its eyes on me, the unforgiving women with their steely-gray hair, steely eyes, flinty souls that I swear have never dared a moment's honest fury, the righteous young housewife with her little smile of amiable doubt, the man who twitched his keys as he spoke to me, a nervous twitch like sleigh bells in the distance, he flicked them with his thumb. The very round man, banded with fat lines like a baby, who asked me some nasty questions about the car, clever questions, smiling the whole time. "The Fifth Amendment is for criminals," he said, and the man from the D.A.'s office told him he couldn't say that. "No comments, please. No intimidation. This is a fact-finding body while Mr. Reiser's in here. You can talk about what you think later." Fact-finding maybe, but they didn't find any on me. None. "I'm looking for intent," the fat man said. "I want to find intent." He didn't know what he was talking about. "Fine," said the D.A. "You look as hard as you want to for whatever you like, but you do it with the facts. Please." My wife went to those people and gave him to them. Just handed him over.

"Are you asking to be punished?" I asked Jacob. "Is that what you think you deserve?" Jesus, punishment enough by now, everybody's lives in shards at our feet. What more does he have to give?

No answer from him, but Carolyn said, "All right, Ben," with a long-suffering kind of patience I found deeply insulting. "I understand why you did what you did. Believe me, I do." This felt like a sop, to keep me at bay. "But I'm not talking about the way you see this. I'm talking about the way *I* see it." They closed ranks again, her arms tight around his narrow back. He was limp, struggled over this way.

"Jacob, Jacob," I heard her say—she was wearing one

of those sexless sack nightgowns, the Granny kind, that was a whole wide meadow of daisies, orange and yellow. "How could I have doubted you for a minute? Who did I think you were?"

PART 3

JUDITH

In some parts of Houston the traffic rages and snarls and really gives the city a bad name. The freeways flow like lava rushing down a mountainside night and day. You know that if you stop in front of them you'll be buried. One corner, two ordinary streets right in front of the Galleria, where the whole world shops, has so many lanes and green turning arrows appearing and vanishing that I think it would be easier to walk across the ocean than navigate from one side of the street to the other on foot.

But there are gentler places. We live on a quiet green street. We have a yard where our cat hassles the squirrels in peace and sits on the fence in the sun. We grow egg-plants and arugula and better tomatoes than we did in New Hampshire. But the zucchini won't live—impossible to imagine, since we never used to be able to give them away fast enough. Something lethal gets them here and makes them rot in the buggy hard-sweating air of early summer, or there aren't enough bees to communicate between the plants and spread what my father calls their sexual honey.

Sometimes I sit in the yard under a giant lacy pecan tree reading a book, and I feel myself being happy and I don't know what to do. A long time ago we were sentenced to sadness, my family, and so when I remember I am eaten up with what is left of guilt. I think I may have to pay for this later, when I've stopped remembering altogether.

My mother says I am paying for it now. She accuses me of keeping my distance from everyone and everything. I do, but I think I would, no matter what. Boys have always been disgusting, nothing new in that. They have their uses, but up close they're all still babies—me! me! me!—and they have a wicked grasp. The ones who aren't dangerous are ridiculous. They do me the greatest favor by keeping at a distance. And friends—I never had a lot of friends at one time, and I never will. And I found that the ones you have—my best friend was Celeste Charters, who was fun when I was much younger and it wasn't so hard to understand me—they can't follow you into your deepest trouble and help when things get complicated. Nobody can, much. My own mother ought to know me that well, at least. I think I am just like her—she was never what you'd call sloppy with feeling. Not to the eye, at least.

My brother, Jacob, too. I think I shy away from him a little, in case he does anything strange. Not that I expect him to hurt me, I can't imagine that. I'm not sure I can say what I expect. But I treat him a little too politely, like—I don't know, a visitor, I guess. One of those exchange students you don't want to offend because you don't know the customs of their country.

And worse, how is he supposed to trust anyone when he can't trust himself. If I were Jacob I'd be afraid of breaking things that had gotten into my hands. Then I'd be afraid of not coming clean. And he's like my father there.

Nobody comes clean much in this world, I've decided that. Everybody slips and slides around each other once you start looking at them hard, and they get what they want if they're good enough at it. I can see how my family, although I love them, is a mess of threats and surrenders and regrets and things they won't say to each other, and maybe they always were. My family and half the kids I know, their families, too.

But here's the thing: we are in this other place now, this *city* that is larger than the whole state I was born in, a few times larger—and you may believe it or not believe it but the whole question for all of us in this different place, when we first came, was what matters and what does not matter, and who we were and who we are now, today. As time goes on, even those questions have mostly dropped away—you'd have to be obsessed to keep going on about them here. We are who we have become, and that's all there is to say about it.

When I first started school in Houston I didn't think I should hide it. Why did you move here? someone would ask me innocently. Mostly I wouldn't say, but finally, if somebody was getting to be a really good friend, I would answer, Well, you see, my brother killed somebody—and I'd get a strong stare and a long silence and then they'd say a word or two to show surprise or else they'd change the subject immediately, before that could even register. I was going to an "arts" high school for my dancing that gathered up what my father called "odd lots and broken sizes"—not only kids who were talented but those who couldn't fit into the sane, square, ordinary schools. Together we made a lot of noise and color—you could call us dramatic—and I suppose that kind of place can absorb a lot of irregularity.

Everyone seemed to come from a colorful family in

which something crucial had gone wrong: there were ordinary divorces, but there were also more complicated ones. For example: My friend Mark's father became a woman, no joke, and when she came to see him star in *Amadeus* he introduced her as his "second mother." She —he?—was a tall, big-boned woman, but very good-looking, with dramatically flared cheekbones and a smooth chest showing above the top button of her blouse. Only her voice seemed to come from the old history she was trying to change. Her voice was too deep even to be sultry and it came as a nasty shock. But Mark seemed less upset than you might imagine. I don't know what he went through getting there, but when he introduced her to us it didn't show. Also, a girl I don't know, in the art department, had her whole family kidnapped off a boat in the Gulf of Mexico, somehow because of drugs, and she hasn't heard a word from them for about three months. The F.B.I. is looking for them. Imagine.

So you can see that I didn't really get very much attention from anyone when I unveiled my own secret.

I personally found this a relief because, frankly, for years no one thought much about anything in our family except my brother, and I had come to the point where the whole thing was very—well, it was *unreal.* That's the best way I can describe it. I got to where I wasn't sure I believed anything had happened, the way a word stops making sense if you say it too often. And in a way I felt bad about that. You feel terrible, even while you're relieved, when you stop thinking about the dead. But probably, to be honest, even Martha's parents will come to a point someday where they don't think about her all the time, and then they'll feel awful, as if they've failed her.

My father, for example, went to jail for about six months because he would not testify against Jacob to the grand jury. They put him in the county jail, but it wasn't exactly what it sounds like, it was this little cinder-block building in the middle of the cornfields. Just below it was a lovely arched stone bridge over a narrow brook, or maybe it was even a small river, that sounded like a person breathing hard. I guess they couldn't hear it inside because the windows were so totally sealed. But they could see it. It was a very strange and peaceful place for a jail. The first time I went to see him, I remember, by the time his appeals had gone from one court to another, up and up, and he finally lost, it was late summer. He and my mother had not said a single word—not one—since the day she talked to the grand jury. Later, in the trial, of course, she did the same thing, and so did I, and all of it was in the newspapers and even on TV, they couldn't get enough of the "Family Feud." But by then I was used to it.

My mother said it was pride on both sides, but neither one of them would move out of the house, they just planned never to be in the same room at the same time. This could get pretty ridiculous sometimes, like the kind of play where people keep opening up the door on the person they least want to see, but mostly it proved to me that you could get used to anything in this world. Frankly, I had nothing I wanted to say to my father, either. I thought he loved Jacob too much and everyone else—everyone and Truth with a capital T—too little. I kept wanting to ask him why he cared so little about what happened to me while he twisted up reality for my brother. But I was afraid to ask.

And sometimes I wasn't even sure if what he did was the best thing for Jacob. I would have said, No lies for me, thank you, and let them punish me in return for feeling clean and honest. At least I think I would, to the best of my ability to know. Jacob never said a word (not that I would have asked him). On this score, he's like an amnesia victim. But we don't talk much these days about anything except things that don't mean much to either one of us.

Strangely, after a while I wasn't angry at Jacob anymore. At least I don't think I was—he was too sad now.

That was how he paid. I could see that he was still a kid, sort of. At least not an adult. More like someone who stops growing. And I almost thought there was a little something the matter with him—he had had a terrible shock and it was like I could excuse him if all his "moral faculties" weren't quite working. (That's what the prosecutor called them in the trial—it took a little figuring out what he meant, believe me. I had some questions about his moral faculties before the shock, but they always stayed questions.) The thing is, I expected more of my father. My father *chose.*

Of course, when it came time for me to go visit my dad, my mother wouldn't help, so it was my brother who drove me down. By then I was thinking in headlines, we were like a show-business family, and this one was too bizarre: ACCUSED MURDERER DRIVES SIS TO VISIT JAILED FATHER! I had gotten to where I translated everything into that breathless nonsensical shorthand: KILLER TEEN'S SISTER HAS TROUBLE CONCENTRATING, HANDS IN HOMEWORK LATE; RECEIVES FIRST "F."

REISER SISTER FIGHTS OFF CLASSMATE, INJURES ATTACKER IN PLAYGROUND SCUFFLE.

ALLEGED MURDER KIN REPORTS LOCKER VANDALISM; DOOR SMASHED, BELONGINGS SCATTERED.

One of the things that kept me going when people were being mean to me was that this friend of the family—of my mother's, really—Annie Dineen, kept saying, "If you can get through this, you'll be very strong," and "This will make you ironclad." Though I'm not so sure ironclad is exactly what I had in mind for myself. But I hung on, put my head down and let them do what they wanted with me. The *I* went somewhere else, is what I mean. Don't ask me where. Inside, I guess, out of sight.

So Jacob the killer teen drove me to the jail, into the hills north of Howe, down the most shadowy curving roads. He sat outside sleeping in the car—he slept a lot those days, that was probably the only time he didn't have to remember that he had a murder trial ahead of him—while I went in, because he was under indictment and you lose a lot of rights that way. Visiting a jail is one of them, but just as well, I think. You don't have to rush things, and it might be your future in there. To make things even weirder, of course, I didn't particularly want to see my dad, and I suspected he didn't want to see me. But, even though we didn't speak at home, there we were and there was this horrible glass between us. That just broke me up. Right up the road from God's sweet green fields I was staring through this glass full of the fingerprints of total strangers, other sad families who spread out their fingers in desperation, and I was supposed to whisper to him by telephone! That was when it began to be very hard to *feel* how the awful thing that Jacob did one winter day could lead to *this*. I thought, I don't understand anything about what people do or why or how they deserve to be made to pay for it. Are there criminals, or criminals' loved ones, who can keep all the cause and effect together in their heads and suffer when they're supposed to be suffering, and then feel thoroughly punished, the way you feel clean after a hard shower, and go home pure, and "put it behind them"?

My father was brought out to me with these much rougher-looking men, or at least poorer-looking. (They had done things, he told me, like pass bad checks, beat people up, steal cars, nothing that serious. But one had supposedly abused a very little child, not his own but his girlfriend's, had flung it against a wall and burned it with a cigarette and maybe even sexually molested it. I never saw him, they had him in separate confinement for his own protection.) My father's beard was gone, his hair was cut like a marine, he was wearing sloppy gray sort of pajama things, and—this was what got to me the worst, I think, even more than the beard, which was hard enough because I don't think I had ever seen his bare face, his chin and the soft places around his mouth and neck and all—but he had on one of those bracelets they attach to your wrist in the hospital, like he was a piece of something anonymous in a warehouse and they had to keep track of him officially. Like, *asking* him his name would hardly be reliable, they had to staple it on so it could only be cut off by some special tool they have. My father inventoried like a dress that could get stolen except for the plastic tag. They had every inch of the place under surveillance—you could see the little blue TV screens in this sort of *war* room, and you kept hearing heavy doors buzzing open and closing, opening and closing.

All of it was too much for me, I could only cry and cry. I felt like a baby. At one point the guard (who wasn't too thrilled having a kid in there in the first place, without "adult supervision") almost put me out, but I made myself stop for a minute till he left me alone. Annie Dineen was right, I was getting tough.

About my father: I didn't approve of what he did, not so much the keeping quiet that got him put in here for "contempt," but making up that lie that his jailers didn't even know anything about, to cover up Jacob's actions, and his own, too. But *this* was unfair. This was inhuman. He deserved more dignity than pajamas and a computerized ID. He looked like someone else entirely without his beard, and young. Or sort of young and old both, a little lined and tired, but much less forceful, less—aggressive. The skin that hadn't been seen in the light for, I don't know, maybe twenty years, was so pale, like a girl's, and fragile-looking. I wished I could put my arms around my father. (Later I could, he graduated to what they called "contact" visits, and he was allowed to work on the prison farm, which he liked a lot. He got dirt under his nails pulling carrots and onions, and he managed to work on some of the farm machinery because he was good at that kind of tinkering. His new skin turned red, then tanned and hardened up and pretty soon he didn't look so much like a punished dog.) It wasn't so bad, really, it was like a regular job, only you couldn't come home at night to sleep. Somehow it looked to me as if they all got used to being there together. People adapt, he told me. They make the best of it. Some of them I like a lot, he said. They've learned the wrong way to solve their problems maybe, but some of them are pretty bright a few layers down, and they're greater menaces to themselves than to anyone else.

When I came home my mother wouldn't ask a word about our visits, but I always told her anyway. I said, "Please, Mom, start figuring out how you're going to forgive him when he comes home, he's so lonely." He didn't even have Jacob to talk to, the Jacob he was in jail for. Because I was only a teenager and we're supposed to be completely unyielding, I think she expected more stubbornness out of me, and maybe more anger than forgiveness. But it made me sort of humble—I could almost understand how he had worked his way to his perjury for Jacob. Crimes of too much love couldn't be the same as crimes of indifference or hard-heartedness—I think that's how my mother finally came around. Someone—a rabbi in Buffalo—wrote to us and said, number one, when Jonah was angry at God for killing the little gourd plant that gave him shade in the desert—this was after he finished with the whale and ended up parched instead!—God told him he had no right to be angry: You didn't raise it and love it as I did, He said. Meaning, I think, you can't pass judgment on what *I* feel like. No one can know what love and caring feel like to anyone else, and what lengths they will go to for that love. And two, he told my father that Jewish law lets parents keep silent against their children. The law of your country is what you have to obey in the end, he said, but, "Mr. Reiser," he wrote him very respectfully, "you should know your impulse is a natural one that is sanctified by thousands of years of spiritual decency." He didn't say anything to my mother about justice or loving someone else's child as your own. I thought he should have mentioned that and praised her, too.

Anyway, no matter what happened, even if I disagreed with him, my father was my father, and I had been loving him all my life. It wasn't possible for me not to care about him. Is this good, is it bad? Whatever the answer, I don't see quite as much choice in the matter as I thought there was.

And my father taught me his favorite word that year while he was still in county jail—*irony*. It was a little hard to get your hands on what it meant, and when it was exactly right to use it, but still I had a lot of chances to think about it and try to apply it right, and it also came in handy when I was reading. First of all, I think I just liked the sound of the word, the way it sort of flowed over your tongue like something wet. But better, the whole idea of it was useful because you could see how often two opposite things seemed to be happening at once, or two feelings needed to be held at the same time, but they were in conflict with each other, or worse, they were both right! It was better than *weird* or *confusing* or any other word I could think of. I thought, if irony was water, we'd be drowning in it. If irony was food, we'd never be hungry again.

What we went through while the lawyers' files got thicker and thicker, and the rumors of interviews all around town thickened up also—our lawyer Mr. Demaris tried to talk to them, but they all said no—was waiting more than a year for a trial. But maybe that was just as well: everyone's anger wore out. I think that's what happened, anyway—our own attitudes just softened up. If you're at all sensitive, you can't stay stiff with fury forever. My father came home from the county jail to see that Jacob and my mother weren't at each other's throat, that Jacob refused to see her as his great Betrayer. When my father was gone, whether I like to say it or not, it was actually easier to spend time talking. Everything shifts around a little when someone's missing. It isn't that you fill up the hole, but you rearrange yourselves, sort of.

Plus, all of us were together more than we'd been in the past, because there was this chill, you know, almost everywhere else besides home. (That's a good irony: to be punished by loneliness and to turn to each other almost gladly.) Because Jacob was not exactly safe in the streets of Hyland. When people have burned a cross on your lawn and shouted nasty words at you in the street, you don't tend to want to hang out all over town, eating pizza and strolling down Main Street like Mr. Teenage New Hampshire. Someone wrote *Jailbird* on the side of the car in yellow paint when it was parked at the A & P and when we got it off you could see where it had taken a little of the paint with it, there was a ghostly word on the fender that will probably be there forever.

Mother finally began volunteering some time at a clinic in Howe under another name. That was the price of her free service, she told them—she could work as Dr. Joanna Miller (her middle name and her maiden name) and no one would say a single word about who she was. But it hurt me to see her—she almost went in disguise, so that she wouldn't be recognized from those "Family Feud" stories in the papers. She wore her hair in a prissy bun, the kind you can stick a pencil in, and she got these big headlight glasses. (She even considered dyeing her hair brown, but I pleaded with her not to, and I guess she was relieved when I convinced her that was going too far.) But she said it was worth it to work even if she had trouble answering to her own name. I only hoped no one would "unmask" her; that would have been a horrible way to reward her for putting in long days with sick children for no pay at all.

The first day she went to work I thought, *What has happened to my life?* It was almost funny—first my father has most of his hair taken away from him, like Samson, and now my mother is becoming someone else I can hardly recognize, right before my eyes! This was the moment, I thought, for me to put on a really short leather skirt and a tight sweater and try to become somebody else myself. If I wanted to, this was the time. But all I could manage was longer, looser clothes that hid every bit of me, and boots to meet my skirt hems, plus as much neglect of my hair as I could get away with—I stopped cutting it, it just got sloppier and grimmer-looking by the day. We were all in hiding one way or the other, and the worst of it was that all we wished was that we could go to sleep and wake up on the other side of IT. The trial was IT, everything was Before or After IT, when our real lives might begin again. Or might not. But at least we'd know.

The trial took place in a town called Savoy, as far from Hyland as they could get and still be in the same jurisdiction, because our lawyer, Mr. Demaris, proved that Jacob couldn't get a fair hearing where everyone was so sure what had happened and threatened him left and right. We stayed in a motel where we played a lot of cards at night for want of anyplace else to go; a policewoman sat outside our room just in case. "There are these ad hoc revenge seekers," Mr. Demaris explained, "and it never hurts to be prudent." He talked that way. He made me smile.

During the day we pretty much played out our old parts even though by now we were a little different from what we had been at the beginning. There was "the accusing mother," "the denying father"—Daddy was not refusing this time, he said he'd made his point and now it was time to get Jacob his freedom, but he managed somehow to make himself very wimpy and un*int*eresting, so that people must have wondered "What was the big deal?" about testifying in the first place. And there was "the hushed and respectful son" in one more disguise, a new gray suit with a striped tie. (When we were alone he liked to hold the tie up over his head like a noose and stick his tongue out and bug out his eyes, and I was supposed to shriek and say, "Jacob, they'll see you!" But I wouldn't do that anymore. I'm not sure my sense of humor was improved by any of this.) I suppose this isn't unusual—Jacob on the witness stand was also incredibly bland. Just pure *vanilla.* He and Daddy must have practiced being dweebs together. It was like, you put on the suit, the uniform of decency, and all your weird and special intenseness—*whoosh!*—gets wiped away. Otherwise, you'll scare people and they'll believe the worst.

And I was supposed to wear this large white collar, I guess to make me look too young to lie—and I got to say "Yes" eight times and "No" fourteen, and then repeat, in mincing little baby-steps, question and answer, question and answer, what I remembered Jacob told us. It's a very tiring way to tell a story. Also, as it turns out, it isn't like the movies, the witness stand is not a place where you'd want to tell much of a new story, anyway. The tension in the courtroom is terrible, like a stage only worse, your heart beats fast from the minute you get near it, and you don't want to forget your lines or say anything that hasn't been planned. I practiced in front of the mirror. Mother wouldn't help. She said, "You don't need a drama coach. Just say what happened. Be fresh and simple—and don't forget, you're not trying to convict him!" But you have to remember that all of us were *witnesses,* except for Jacob, who was the only one who was allowed to sit there through the whole thing. All of us were walked in and walked out again by the bailiff practically in chains, so none of us saw the whole thing. After all that waiting, I thought it was pretty funny how we were off in another room, busy missing it.

But here's the most frustrating thing: all this was on TV and we couldn't watch. Just like a real show, only much much longer, and without commercials. The whole crazy drama was coming out of everybody's television set from the minute the judge banged his gavel to open up the day to the minute he shut it down. It's a whole new idea and for some reason, even though New Hampshire wasn't first about much besides Presidential primaries, they decided to do it this way. They used to have people sketching in the courtroom, Mr. Demaris said—you couldn't even take a camera behind those doors. And then all of a sudden they've got their crews and their snaky wires and everybody's, like, very self-conscious in case they accidentally get on camera. He kept going on about it. "I'm surprised they don't have those cards they hold up that say 'Applause.' " My father said all that meant was "Is it good for my client?" Who knows who it was good for, except the folks with nothing better to do who sat around all day watching like it was just another soap. I heard there were people who were arguing about who they liked and who they didn't trust, and whether they thought Jacob was *handsome*, and putting money into pools about whether he was going to "win" or "lose," whatever that meant. I thought the least they could do was pay us star salaries.

Anyway, the camera didn't bother the important people much, the witnesses, it just sat still and stared—what made me extra nervous, which I didn't need, was somehow knowing that the whole state was in there with us, thinking their thoughts, full of opinions but not actually knowing anything. I mean, the courtroom was kind of small, not a big one like in the movies. I think there was only room for about twenty-five people in the spectator section, and those were pretty much all loyal friends of both sides who came up from Hyland. But nobody else who got to see, while they flipped channels between Exercise and Cooking, had anything much to gain or lose—watching it was a game. It was creepy.

And we were the only ones in the whole state and out over its borders a long way who cared about it but were missing it! When we asked Mr. Demaris if we could watch —I mean, there it was, we had a TV in our motel room like anybody else—he said, "Look, don't do it, okay? Not while the trial is on. We don't need any complications."

I asked him why not. I was learning to speak up a little.

"Figure it out. You guys are witnesses." He was a little impatient, I think. Frankly, I didn't know what difference it made, as if anyone would change their testimony at the last minute because of what they saw. "You don't have to contaminate yourselves that way. In this state we tend to have a lot of trust. We don't sequester juries very readily and we don't lock up our witnesses, we've always just asked people to refrain from reading the newspaper or watching the news. So now there's this new technology that's not really intended for you. Whether I like it or not, this thing is not for the players, it's for the audience. And you're not the audience. Don't take advantage." He gave my father a very harsh look when he said that: he didn't trust him. It meant, I know you have a way of making your own rules. I guess he could imagine Daddy sneaking off to get a glimpse of the forbidden proceedings, sort of like an alcoholic taking a quick nip. "Just don't," Mr. Demaris warned him. "Prudence, for once. You'll find it a heady experience."

But later. Later it was legal. Mr. Demaris gave the tapes to my father and he carried them in gingerly, like something that would explode if he dropped it. We sat down around the television set and there was no way to do that without thinking of all the easy innocent hours we spent over the years watching the Celtics or Masterpiece Theatre or Saturday Night Live, and my mother sighed and put her head back with her eyes closed. It was like she was saying a prayer. At first she hadn't wanted to watch, she said it had all been too much the first time around, why did we have to do this to ourselves?

"It's been done," Daddy said to her. "It's part of reality now. It's *out there.*"

"Where's 'out there'?" she asked him. "You just don't want anybody else to know anything you don't know."

But I think he was right: everybody else had seen us, friends and strangers. Until I saw what we looked like, I kept feeling they could see me behind my back.

Martha's parents were very emotional, just like we expected. Her mother kept breaking down and having to wait until she could continue, and her father was so eager to answer he was always starting to talk before the questions were out. He looked sort of like an intelligent rodent in a suit and tie, like a character in a children's book that they made into the animal he most resembled. Even the prosecutor had to try to keep him calmed down. My dad said it was "contrived," but I didn't see why it would have to be, even after all this time. I thought about Jonah's gourd and how to be generous about the love others had for their creations. I tried to imagine how I'd feel if they finally got around to a trial over the murder of someone I loved, like him—I put my father in Martha's place, although that was just about impossible—and I didn't have any trouble imagining how horrible that would feel and how I'd have to "struggle for composure," the way the newspapers say it. But who knows? I've gotten very cynical, along with the generosity. They sort of alternate in me now. So I don't believe everything I hear, like, there's always a little itch of doubt. But why would her parents have to fake a single tear—if mine could lie, why couldn't hers do anything they wanted to? I'm not *that* cynical.

The witnesses we had been most afraid of were her friends like Tina Guy and her cousin Donna who back in Hyland had called Jacob "dangerous." But of course they weren't allowed to talk like that. I knew they'd like to accuse him of shoplifting. Borrowing a car once without permission, before he had a license. Drinking under-age and just enough grass to make him normal. Everybody admitted they "experimented" with different kinds of pills and even some cocaine. But they all did it, for years they did it, so Jacob didn't seem worse than anybody else. His own friend Jackie had said in school, and it came back to me in a whisper, that when they were at Whalom Park, the amusement park, Jacob threw firecrackers off the Ferris wheel that theoretically could have hit somebody, and he had some fights at the bowling alley, but always in groups. I said Big deal when I heard this—is this heavy crime? Donna tried to say from the witness stand that Jacob once had a fight with Martha at a party and he threatened to "make her sorry" for flirting with someone. He pulled her head back by her hair and yelled in her face. Mostly, she said he brought an "air of danger" along with him. (I knew what that meant—how he seemed to be dreaming of danger, worse than shoplifting and firecrackers, even if he wasn't committing it.) But Mr. Demaris objected—what did this have to do with the crime he was accused of here, today? Jacob Reiser is not on trial, he said, for "an air of danger." Later, he made fun of the whole "air" idea. "Did he smell of gunpowder?" he asked the jury. "Do you think you could smell him coming?"

The worst part that I can remember was that Jackie went on the stand because he was with Jacob just before Jacob picked up Martha at work on that very day, and they did a lot of talking. Jacob was "agitated," he said, a word that was so much beyond his vocabulary you could tell he'd been helped a little. He said Jacob had told him that Martha drove him so wild that if she ever two-timed him he didn't know what he would do, he didn't think he could control himself. Mr. Demaris made him agree that Jacob never said what he'd do, he didn't "specify." So it was like, wow, what a confession.

Jackie also claimed Jacob had complained—this was all on the way to the ice-cream shop!—that Martha had "a certain part of his anatomy in a vise," and he couldn't get it loose. "Would you like to specify the particular part?" Jackie was a big, short-haired boy whose neck, in a crew-neck sweater, looked like a football player's. He blushed and the courtroom "tittered." (Newspaper words. I love them.) It didn't seem like a courtroom that tittered much, so the laugh sounded good for the defense. It was amazing how little "hard" evidence they had that Jacob was any more of a menace than most teenage boys. (Mr. Demaris always talked about hard and soft, as if you could feel the testimony in your hands, and touch its texture. Well, maybe a lawyer can.)

So he made it sound like Jacob was more a neighborhood pain in the neck, a "ruffian," or even just a "would-be ruffian," than a cold-blooded killer who should have been off the streets. And most of that the defense kept out —it was gossip, not evidence. There was only one serious witness—the others, if there really were any, never panned out. "In a small town like this," my mother said suddenly—it was the first thing anybody had said in a long time and I was shocked by her voice out of the half dark—"people will do that. They get afraid of committing themselves in public, though they'll have plenty to say behind their hands." The one brave witness had seen the two of them stopped by the side of the road, a Mr. Gellhorn, who worked in an insurance firm in Howe and was driving home on Poor Farm Road just at twilight, and he could only say they were standing beside the car talking —nothing suspicious about that. No, he didn't think they had anything in their hands, but it was hard to see if you weren't looking. They might have been arguing, but he couldn't honestly pretend to know, it was just a quick glimpse. He had slowed and shouted to them to ask if they needed help and they waved him off—"Both of them?" "I don't remember"—and that was that. No, Martha had not looked desperate, particularly. He had shrugged at the prosecution, who clearly wished for more, and said, "Sorry."

The forensics testimony was garbled. Mr. Demaris knew that already because he had gotten reports on it, but he was still ecstatic. (These lawyers already know so much when they come into the courtroom. Mr. Demaris said surprise witnesses only show up in the doorway in bad movies, and everybody gasps, and then you know they're going to hear the real truth.) I remember how he kissed Mag Trottier and danced around the room with her; she had predicted that they had nothing good, and in a case that is only "circumstantial," she said you needed really clear physical evidence. (Mr. Demaris called it "hot props.")

Now, on the tube, somebody said "the couple"—Jacob and Martha—had used the cabin that afternoon, there was lots of proof of "recent use." But no one had denied that; they couldn't make anything out of it. And too much time had elapsed before the police impounded the car—they admitted it "might have been" tampered with; it might not. It was suspicious that Daddy had looked in the trunk before the police came with their warrant, but in itself they couldn't make that prove anything. (They tried to show that it was "intent to suppress suspicious evidence," but Mr. Demaris asked "what guilt, specifically, a father's concern would express if the contents were left untouched.") I suppose you could say my father got lucky, because the inspection of the inside of the car was "inconclusive." The evidence in the trunk was impossible to read, a lot of old sawdust mashed around—they couldn't tell how long it had been there—and a tarp and a lot of hunks of wood lying loose. There were fibers from some kind of carpet, but in general it was such a mess they couldn't tell much—the evidence was "not suggestive." They could demonstrate, with hairs and bits of thread, that Martha had sat in the front seat. But that was no big deal, no one was denying that.

They found a jack, a little baby one, all neatly folded up in a box, but the only fingerprints on it were my father's and some that must have belonged to whoever owned it before he did—they certainly weren't Jacob's. He had never fixed a flat in his life. It was amazing what Mr. Demaris thought of: they had a guy from the Southside Garage come in to say he had gone out once on a rainy night to jack up the car for Jacob. (I remember

Jacob heard it from my father for that. Daddy made him pay for it—he wanted to have him pay double, but Mother said that wasn't fair, what you can't do you can't do, and you shouldn't have to be punished twice for it. Daddy said he just didn't want to get wet, and can and can't had nothing to do with it.)

A lot of people testified about Jacob's sainthood. Friends of the family, the Bergers, Annie, a few nice people from around town, one very classy woman Jacob worked for one summer cutting brush around her house, and Nat the school-bus driver, who said he was usually polite, even if he was always late and noisy. "School buses are terrible places," he told the jury very seriously, like they were a social blight or something, but "As boys on school buses go, I'd say he was a very good one."

Then it was my turn. There I was, dressed about five years younger than I was, looking a little less than real. They kept asking me to speak up and now I could see why—how could I have known my voice sounded like it was coming out of my shoes? And it was mortifying, I looked so stunned you'd have thought I was just waking up from a coma. Honestly, I didn't know I was that scared. But even if I gave a great Hollywood performance, it wouldn't have mattered: me they dismissed. It was clear, somehow, that I was my mother's "object." I would say whatever she did, I was "under her power," so nothing I said proved anything one way or the other. The lawyer was insulting just under the surface, very soothing and patronizing as if he was talking to a four-year-old. I might as well have stayed home. It made me so furious—I'm afraid I sulked more than I should have if I wanted to prove I wasn't a kid. Mother told me I did fine, but I know I was just the baby again.

So we sat there—this was over days, you know. A whole trial without a word missing cuts into your time worse than anything, and bad enough it did that once in real time, here we were captives a second time around, of our own free will! I couldn't believe so many strangers had cared enough to watch the whole thing. We had our munchies while we watched. Sometimes we ate a whole meal; the sound of chewing, swallowing (my father is the noisiest drinker), sort of punctuated the cast of characters, which by now everyone had turned into. The camera didn't really move around like it would in a movie or a good TV program, but it did all feel like a play sometimes. Dinner theater.

Then one night after we had cleared the dishes and pushed the little TV tables away, my mother came on. (She was, technically, a prosecution witness, but she refused to have anything to do with the "state team." She just went to say her piece but would not, as she put it, fraternize.) She was wearing her soft blue dress, it was one that I loved and I helped her pick it—not severe, not sexy, just a nice sort of dress that didn't give you any ideas about her whatsoever. Her voice the newspaper called "soft and regretful," which was pretty accurate. My father was sitting on the couch and my mother was right next to him, they were not quite touching. She wasn't even watching, she kept her eyes closed, but Daddy was so tense he looked like he was going to fall on the floor.

And I was very proud of her. Every time the prosecutor tried to get her to say something, she'd raise her hand and move it in that soothing way that says, "Patience, patience," as if to a child—I know the movement from my whole life, I'm sure she practices it a lot in her work when terrified mothers are throwing too many symptoms and stories of how-it-happened at her at one time, just "There, there, easy now, we'll get it all in good time." And she will not be hurried. As she talked about what Jacob had confessed, it just seemed a sad, unplanned, accidental act, a boy's mistake. All her own anger seemed to have seeped away, or to have washed away like old blood. Someone wrote in the paper that she seemed "defeated," but I don't think that's the right word. All that was left seemed to be sadness.

Somewhere along the way I saw that my father, there on the couch beside her, had turned to my mother and was staring at her, not at her flat image out there in front of him. He would do that awhile, and she'd keep her eyes closed, just listening to her own voice going over this terrible ground, and then he'd switch back to the set, and his lips would move a little but I couldn't hear any words. Then he'd look back at her again, the real, solid woman in her purple bathrobe with the television light flickering high and low over her face. She looked totally different and yet wasn't—and was—and I thought how we had all dragged through so much together and I still couldn't dare guess what he was thinking about her. If deep down he respected her or hated her for what she was saying, or if he could even understand it. Was he, like, trying to lay one image on the other and see if they really matched? Or guess what she felt when he looked at her that way, he seemed so astonished and hurt and familiar and far away, right there at her side?

The next night, though, in a different mood, I guess, he called out, "Hit it, hit it!"

"What?" Me.

"You've got the remote. Back it up."

"To where?"

"To where she starts that—"

"Jesus, Ben," my mother said and sat straight up. "Isn't once enough?"

"What, don't you like hearing yourself say that about your son?"

"Oh, please."

The stupid laughter of *Love Connection* flooded the screen while I waited for my orders: a gross man with a headful of vain blond hair was telling the world how his date came downstairs to meet him looking "sort of like a dog who fell into a blow dryer" and the audience was howling, cheering him on. The date had to sit there and laugh with them.

"To where you said you sometimes worried about him."

"Ben, please," Mother said to him quietly. On the screen she looked drugged with the pain of all this, you could tell her mouth was dry, and she was sitting tight, as if it hurt to move. He was still on her, I thought, like an anxious dog, and she was aloof, alone—a cool, quiet cat. He still didn't understand.

"Why don't you leave her alone, Daddy?"

He shot me a look, about as surprised as I was, and settled down again. It was the beer, I told myself. He had lined up a couple of bottles on the floor beside the couch, like other people's fathers. Like if you tried hard enough you could pretend this was a football game.

So this was what all those strangers were seeing when they probed for motives, the attorneys for both sides, trying to straighten out what happened and why. It was enough to make you dizzy. And it *was* just like the soaps, I could sort of see it: Why would this woman condemn her own son? How could parents try to cancel each other's stories out that way? Mother had thought Mr. Demaris would tell the jury that it was Marital Hell that did it, a fight to the death over the body of their child. But how would he prove such a thing? They weren't one of those famously miserable couples, nobody would come in and testify that she hated him so much she'd lie about a hideous thing like this just to make him suffer. None of their friends would say what would have to be said.

Mr. Demaris's questions were terrible. "Tell us what you saw when you attended the body of Martha Taverner in the emergency room." That shook my mother, anyone could see that, like he'd struck her in some sore part of her own body. She had been through this once already, there she *was*, and she had read the news stories about herself (the "blonde," how she was "pale but determined," "cool and unshakable"), but it didn't seem to be less of a shock at this distance, even if you were braced for it. How did she get along with her son? She loved him, of course, loved him tremendously. He made her go on with that—how gentle she thought he could be in certain situations. How kind, how unviolent. Troubled and in need of attention, but basically a superb boy.

Then I suppose he got where he was trying to go: to what she knew about Jacob's sex life. How she felt when she heard Martha was his girlfriend.

"Not good," she admitted.

"Why 'not good'?"

"Well . . . remember she was already—I was hearing this in the context that . . . she was already dead."

"Why 'not good'?"

"Because—well—I didn't think—wouldn't have thought"—the tangle of tenses was awful, and this was so cruel because it was all past tense already and he knew it! "I'd have had trouble imagining they'd do well together."

"Because?"

"Because she was—"

"Wasn't it that her background was different from Jacob's? Her class, one might say?"

Of course he was warned off that line of questioning—everybody knows that's called leading the witness—but I guess Mr. Demaris always knew exactly what he was doing and he wasn't much fun to have on the other side: he was smirching Martha and my mother all at the same time. And you can never take anything back, even if the judge says "Disregard that" to the jury and gets angry with the lawyer. Lawyers can twist things up so badly, and give them shadings.

What Mr. Demaris told instead of the Story of Marital Hell was much weirder. He basically said: A family is a mystery. There is vengeance here, and darkness, there is an unhappy woman who saw, actually confronted *in the flesh*, a dead girl her son knew better than she ever realized. She was a doctor, she was used to controlling everything. Maybe, like a lot of the surgeons you read about, she even had a bit of an "ego problem." And she couldn't deal with it, he said. She and her son had been very close while he was growing up. And now her boy had this intimate relationship, this totally secret "liaison," and with an "unacceptable" girl, and it was very, very upsetting to her. Possibly she even knew about the pregnancy. And so . . . and I think he let the innuendos sort of fall, almost gently: there was nothing *she* could do about this relationship, so she had to imagine *him* hurting her, annihilating her (his word!) . . . she had to imagine him removing her from his life, like an alien thing, an enemy. He made it seem like she enjoyed this fantasy. She needed it. She wanted to make it be true. In some kinky way he never quite said it made her happy, as if she imagined Jacob did it for her. But that was the feeling you had to have. It was amazing to me how not saying certain things could make you surer than sure you'd heard them.

Mother went absolutely white when she heard what Mr. Demaris said about her. She said it was too sick to listen to. "I thought he threatened to make me sound like Medea," she said, "but I think I came across as Jocasta instead." (I didn't know what she meant at the time, but believe me, I've learned.)

And one more thing. My mother wasn't only disgusted by the sick imagination of the defense. ("Oh," she kept insisting, "Panos doesn't *believe* that," and I think she was trying to sound merry, only her voice kept shaking. "You can see he'd say whatever would hold together long enough to get through this.") But what he did to Martha's name was even worse. "This is the part I'll never forgive him for," she cried out when she heard his speech to the jury, his closing argument. "I can take care of myself, thank you, but this is the lowest blow. You can do what you have to to help your client, but this is beneath contempt. The bastard. The newspapers didn't get the half of it." She covered her eyes and was quiet for a long, long time.

Although Mr. Demaris had told my father that killing the dead again could be very dangerous and could really antagonize the jury, he had also told him it would be "positively criminal" to let it go by. I guess he just had a different stopping point from Mother's: he did what he thought he could get away with. So he waved the lab reports of the DNA test that showed that Martha was having somebody else's baby while she stole off to "the love nest" she and Jacob kept "deep in the woods." (I thought the newspapers did just fine: they were foaming at the mouth with this stuff.)

"God," Daddy said, pulling the beer bottle away from his lips to shout, "he looks like Joe McCarthy with a fistful of lists of Commies!" I don't know who loved it more, Daddy or Mr. Demaris. Well, Jacob had gotten to see it when it was actually happening right there in the courtroom. He had to stay all sober and upright, but I'll bet he wanted to poke his finger down his throat.

"Why," Mr. D. asked the jury, "why should you assume she was killed by her disappointed lover? She was two-timing *both* of them, this boy over here"—and there was Jacob with his head modestly bowed—"and the poor father of her child, who could just as easily have stalked the lovers that afternoon and taken out his jealous rage on the girl who had been unfaithful to him as well. He could have confronted her—think about it—just as soon as Jacob abandoned her. There she stood, by the side of the deserted road, miserable, waiting for Jacob to return and forgive her, and who should she see approaching her but —and here, of course, the trail turns cold." That was true: the police didn't have a clue about who the father was. (But there *was* a father. It was the hardest evidence they had. There *was* a father, Daddy kept reminding Mother—he isn't inventing this just for the occasion.) Can you imagine someone crawling out, though, to take credit? Even the gossips lay low through this one. Maybe they believed he'd come and get them, too! (And then I'll bet there were some sickos who must have thought Mother did it, or had it done. God knows, Mr. Demaris gave her the motive.)

The line the papers liked best, and repeated and repeated till it got really old, was: *"This is a story full of fire and ice, of inflamed love and fierce coldness. A winter story."*

Daddy suggested an Academy Award for Best Acting Job by an Attorney. He talked about Mr. Demaris as if he'd written a masterpiece, building up suspense, pausing at just the right instants, leading the jury along to the feeling they were coming to their own conclusions. Mother looked at him impatiently, but—I think there's a word, "indulgently"? In a strange way, both of them sitting there in the half light together while Mr. Demaris was spinning out this complicated invention about Jacob and Martha, about *them*—I could see how this was theirs. Just when they should have despised each other—how ironic—they were very married.

I pushed the power button and the trial was over.

And the jury was hung.

Then we did it again for a different jury, the whole thing a second time with all the same lines over again like a play that's been running too long. My mother kept hoping that my father would let Jacob change his plea to guilty, or plea-bargain for manslaughter, but he was not about to crumble. And he won his gamble: the jury was hung again. Talk about anticlimax. It seemed as if everybody everywhere thought Jacob was guilty, *knew* it, even, but there wasn't enough legally satisfactory evidence besides "hearsay"—at least one honorable person on each jury just couldn't convict him. After all this, that was the amazing thing: that all it took was one man or woman, somebody very strong or very stubborn.

It turned out to be two on the first jury and one on the second, but they never said anything very clear or interesting about what they were thinking. *Doubt,* that was all they could say. *We kept wondering. It seemed so strange, you sort of believed everybody and then you didn't believe them. Back and forth. It took a long time.* Great, I thought, that really says it. Not that I wasn't happy, you know, but there was something very disappointing about it: all the thinking that went into this, and all the crying and cursing and confusion, and this is what comes out. Mag Trottier said this wasn't the time to care—she and her boss would study the little bit the jury said, because they could always learn more about what worked and what didn't, but we shouldn't worry about it at all. Just snap our fingers, I guess. I wonder if she really thought we could do that.

We had to restrain my father from sending roses to the holdouts. "Enough," Mr. Demaris said. "Enough, Ben. Let it alone. Justice is impersonal. And jurors have their own hidden reasons. Especially when they're deadlocked, you'd better assume there was somebody in there who heard things his own way. (Excuse me, Mag: his or hers.) You want to ponder why, you'll have to talk to their psychiatrist. It's just—things resonate unpredictably. Consider it a gift you don't need to reciprocate."

When we finally got home we found a noose made out of clothesline dangling from our biggest maple tree, compliments of the cross-burning brigade (led, we all suspected, by Martha's father and who could blame him, really, he had so few ways to express his anger and humiliation). Pounded into the tree on a piece of wood was a sign that protested in blood-red paint "The Wrong People Got Hung." It made me want to cry for everyone.

Mr. Taverner was so angry and humiliated before, we were all afraid to think what might happen now that it looked like the law had given his daughter's murderer more rights than she had. That was when we knew we had to find another place to live. All those good years gone, and no one "victorious." And Mr. Demaris agreed, which frightened us even more. He agreed, and told us not to dawdle more than we had to. This convinced us that he thought there was some justice in the Taverners' anger, or if not justice exactly, then, as my mom said, more sticking power in anger than there was in sorrow.

"Go get yourselves a life," he told us with a kind of a crooked smile that showed he understood how strange our lives must have been all this time. And how let down we all were by this "victory." How nobody felt much of anything one way or another except that it was over, and how hard it would be to just pick up where our lives left off years ago. We were walking around in circles, and the worst thing was to wonder how many ex-friends would dwindle back into friendliness now. Who needed them? Your life isn't elastic, it doesn't just snap and pull back into its old shape. "Go someplace big where nobody knows where the hell New Hampshire is. I mean that." Mr. Demaris took us out to dinner after the trial (on our money, Daddy said) and repeated, "Go someplace you never even imagined in your wildest dreams you'd live. Go where you can leave the albatross at the state line."

The first thing I noticed about Houston was that it didn't have any cowboys, at least not at the airport. No big hats, no bolo ties, surely no horses. Nobody looked like a country singer.

"What did you expect," my brother said. "You're crazy. This is a *business* town."

That meant there were milling crowds dressed more or less alike, in business suits, men and women, all of them looking as if they'd gladly sell you something. There may have been a lot more hair, or hair*do,* on some of the women, blond, puffed and turned up, than I was used to.

They opened their mouths wide when they talked and sort of hit their *r*'s hard and round, which was nothing like New Hampshire. New Hampshire kept its mouth closed as if, open, the cold might get in. While we waited for the baggage handlers to deliver up Snappy in her cage, I listened to two little girls complaining to their mother that their brother was *fotting* with them. I remember that this awed me.

But that was all that seemed peculiar and I had to concentrate even to hear that. I had to stare. I suppose I was expecting some kind of border, maybe even a passport control like the time we went to England. Not really, but inside me. What did *a new life* mean, anyway? A different language, not just a tilted vowel or two, a different sound when you struck the air. I thought of us as refugees. I don't think I knew the word *refugee* when we came; I was almost fifteen. That's not a child's word. But this year I've seen how many there are out there, for all kinds of reasons. My school, like I said, specializes in them: kids escaping from bad divorces, hurtful families, from the suburbs with their awful standards for what's acceptable, from the cruelties of other kids if you're a little off-center. And wanting to be some kind of artist—my father used to tell me that before I ever knew what he meant: how you grow up lonely if you see angels dance on the head of a pin. Now that I want to *be* one of the angels myself, I really know what he means.

When I think of Hyland, something rises in my throat, maybe fear, maybe . . . I don't know what, exactly. It's a shame when you can't look back with simple sweet memories, but I suppose I'm glad at least we're banished together.

My father had driven ahead with a carful of wooden people to keep him company. He didn't have a lot of new work—he had gotten very little done since that day two and a half years before in January when Jacob rearranged everything—and he kept saying he was out of the "sculpture business" forever. But he arranged the old ones lovingly in the station wagon, some in crates, some just propped up and strapped in. They looked out the window like friends and protectors. It must have been weird to be someone on the street in a little town in Tennessee or Alabama and walk past our car while he was inside a restaurant eating lunch, and have this crowd look out at you without a word, serene and slightly larger than life. Surely more permanent. When the sun hits the shaman's eyes just right, they can ignite paper.

He called when he found a house for us. A nice ordinary house, he promised. "You won't find a single adjective to apply to it. It's the kind of house that destroys adjectives." The "garden of friends" was stashed in a locked shed, out of sight. ("There are no basements down here. Or attics, either. It seems to be a rule of thumb that they don't ever seem to have basements and palm trees in the same place.")

He said he had driven practically straight through—slept one night in a rest stop and another in a motel off on a hillside away from the highway, where it seemed safe for "the guys" to spend the night in the car. I wanted to tell him I couldn't imagine anyone stealing a wooden shaman with glass eyes or a dog on wheels. But he wouldn't have been convinced; he'd have said, "There are crazier people than I am out there." So I pictured a trucker looking over his shoulder for witnesses, then stealing off with a piece of polished ash in the shape of a naked woman in boots and holding a purse, hiding it in his refrigerated van between his stacked-up crates of broccoli.

When we got there finally, to our new house—it was a sort of bungalow, long and flat and odd compared to our beautiful square high old farmhouse—the first thing I wanted to see was the sculptures. I peeked in the window of the shed and it was a relief to find them huddled in there like people told to wait patiently who were making the best of it. They were my other family, and it mattered to me that we had all made this trip, like a long sea voyage, only accomplished unbelievably in the wink of an eye between takeoff and landing. (At least my father had had a chance to change climates slowly, to get used to different trees and highway signs and names of supermarkets and television channels. He could get a little *accustomed.)* How could I pretend I wasn't curious to see what would come next. The difference between being alive and, oh, poor Martha, being not-alive, was nothing but having what-comes-next to look forward to. I could walk to the corner and back and see what the other houses looked like, and the Houston grass and flowers, which might not be the same as I grew up with. Curiosity. Who cares about dying for any other reason?

BEN

THE PUNISHMENT IS EXILE.

Did you know that the Bible talks about Cities of Refuge, where you can go if you have killed someone accidentally? They are for the blameless, who are endangered nonetheless. They are the only places that are officially off-limits for the seekers of revenge. Safe cities.

The damage you may do yourself is not forbidden.

There are some beautiful buildings here, but my buildings have always been mountains. Still, there's green. It's a fecund place, nastily moist sometimes but otherwise benign and surprisingly sweet. No snow, my grief. Cold, hard freezes even, but nothing beautiful to take the place of what disappears in winter.

The power of positive thinking: This is not an escape. It's a continuation.

Everything I've hated about cities shields us here—so I was right about them. There are 1,924,763 people within the city limits and only four of them know about my son and Martha Taverner. Everyone we've met seems to have left some kind of life behind, even the natives: a husband, a wife, a profession, a city of origin. So in our case it's a little more dire, our history, but no one knows us well enough yet to care that much. Or they have trouble imagining, even if they believe it. The kids have an expression—"location situation"—that means, as far as I can tell, "You had to be there."

What continues the connection with Jacob's guilt?

Almost nothing. Legally nothing. He was set free by the state to go in peace. He can vote. He can carry arms. If he's crazy, in another fifteen years he can run for President.

Does that seem unfair?

Not really.

Do you feel guilty?

Yes. Really.

There is a whole new sky here, I'm not sure it's the same one I've looked at all my life. Gaudy at sunset, flamboyant as hell, lit red, often, at night by—refinery fires? Particles of deadly chemicals hanging snagged in the moisture? Sometimes the air smells of coffee, vaguely burnt, and sometimes of a greasy indeterminate. Often, suddenly, of flowers, as if a powdered woman has walked by out of view.

The magnolia trees are self-possessed, cool, glossy: domineering beauties. Everything about them is slick and huge—their leaves, their seed cones like hand grenades, with red seeds lined up so carefully inside. Their soft flowers more like skin than skin. I wish I could make one, but they're already made.

Women walk down the street near my house, Mexican women followed by many small children, with one long braid down their backs. Sometimes one will carry her laundry on her head. I think about Hyland, how the keeper of the Hometown Laundromat and Quality Dry Cleaners would goggle at the sight.

Always the sense of sleaze just held back at the edges —money and malls, class and power at the center, NUDE GIRLS NUDE off at the margins. There's a lot of that, but there's a lot of not-that, too. In Hyland you need permission of the zoning board to put up a sign for lettuce and fresh eggs.

Mostly it's like every other place, though—mail delivery, traffic helicopters, gas stations, cemeteries, bus stops, streetlights, green-long yellow-red. It all flows on. No matter what you've done, or not done, it flows on. Maybe if you've lived here all your life this is your small town. One cemetery is full of people with streets named after them.

Carolyn's hospital has a staff two-thirds the population of Hyland. She parks half a mile away.

I work in hard metals with welding tools now, goggles, a mask, a concrete floor to quash the sparks—my pieces have an edge, I think, a not-nice quality: not so friendly— in a warehouse that used to be full of cotton batting, Ex-Lax, and garden tools. Or so I've been told.

What it comes down to is, the worse our history the more we had to stay together—only *we* knew all the parts, good and bad, even if we added them up differently. People were surprised, I think: Don't families fly apart after "tragedies"? Indeed they do. Or might. But who can ever tell? Panos was amazed, I know; Annie Dineen wasn't, she's an optimist where people she loves are concerned. But who would have understood us if we'd gone out into a world of strangers? We were cripples with congruent wounds.

This is not sentiment. It's realism.

CAROLYN

ONE NIGHT SHE CAME TO BEN IN THEIR GROUND-FLOOR BEDROOM—IT WAS a low wooden house, nothing like New England, and shady because shade is at a premium in semi-tropical light—and said she thought they needed another baby.

This was an astonishment to someone who had not thought about babies since Judith's car seat had gone into the recesses of the attic. He quizzed her very carefully. Aside from impediments like age, could her state of mind support the idea of beginning again? Had she not fought a tumultuous battle with herself, with him, over responsibility, blame, the outcome of love and concern?

Just so. "I have. Of course. So have you." She smiled. There was a crazy way they'd say that in New Hampshire that made no sense at all: "So haven't you." But they said it, anyway.

Jacob was not particularly thriving, although he was holding his own. He was learning to drive a forklift for a cement company, which was not what they'd have predicted for him, but he seemed to be resting his mind, disengaged from anything that had consequences. He seemed stunned, that was probably the way to think of him. He would not get angry—mild irritation seemed about as much as he would show. A kind of hopeless acceptance of slights, piques, impediments. What, she wondered, was that costing him? Worse, where was he hiding it? She didn't believe psychology was simply the physics of the coiled spring, but now and then she would sneak a hard look and worry that he might, if he kept on being so good, one morning take a shotgun to them all. But he was clean, given the temptations out there. (Seemed clean. Who could say.) He was shy, constrained, conservative, like someone who'd been terribly sick. One of these days he would get his own apartment, but apparently not yet. She wished she could ask if he was afraid—he ought to be if he wasn't—but she asked him nothing. He had begun to run every day, to play basketball, to groom his body, which must have seemed innocent to him, and pliable. He didn't talk much.

And Judith. It was the first time she had ever really worried about Judith. Even at the height—or maybe it was the depth—of the confusions over Jacob and how to go on together, she hadn't exactly felt anxious about her, Judith's instincts were so right, so very pure and young in their extremity. Now, though, she was growing unsentimental with alarming speed. All she showed at home was an I've-seen-it-all contemptuousness. It wasn't making her bold, exactly—Judith would never be a Nina, a bad girl, an acter-outer. But she was too repelled by everyone to make friends, and her judgments were not kind: they were babies or deadheads or clingers or talentless clones; they wore too much denim or too much black. What are you saving yourself for, Carolyn asked her, but she got no answer. Only her dance seemed worth the effort, and if it made her ambitious and not too nice in competition, *tant pis.* (A good French student, like her mother.) She was surely the up-and-coming star of the dance department, and her dance instructors loved her long legs, her flexibility. They loved her will. Carolyn did not—it frightened her.

She had one fierce child now and one mild one. But they had changed places. Ben said it was all in flux. She's a teenager, Carolyn, this is ordinary nastiness. Temporary. Typical. Children do not easily exchange hearts.

Given their particular history, she thought she could be excused her fears; she couldn't survive another set of mysteries. What in the world did *ordinary* hide? She did not have a child left that she could trust.

She couldn't explain about wanting a baby, really. When they'd decided to go on, it was a decision, not default. She thought, we're stuck with life. Otherwise, to be consistent, didn't they need to put their heads in the oven, or drive off a cliff? Her sister had called and told her, "Carolyn, listen. There's a moment that comes. If you've had trouble it comes—I don't know about the others, I don't actually know many of the others—and you can choose. In the end, it's alarmingly simple. I wish I'd known it earlier." It was what she had told Jacob when he first came home: Don't do it to yourself. Others will be glad to do it for you, to you, if they want to. Don't *help* them. She seemed to like to have advice for Carolyn; she called often. She had surely changed hearts with someone.

"I don't know why," Carolyn said again. It was a little like the way they'd made love after Ben's mother died (finally, right after the first trial, as if, there in her nursing home where the television blared on about this murder, that murder, she'd been lingering to hear the outcome. It was the only time Ben had been grateful that she didn't have the faintest clue about what was happening to her beyond lunch, beyond sleep). They'd done that defiantly, that raw dance of the flesh, to go on, to celebrate. Like Kaddish, Ben said, like the mourner's prayer that praises and will not blame or grieve.

"If we're going on, we're going on," she said to him. She shrugged. "Or else why bother to try to be—what? Resilient?"

"You want to put your money where your mouth is," Ben suggested.

She laughed. "That's as indiscreet a way to say it as anyone could have come up with!"

"What will a child think who gets made as a counterbalance to all this?" (And what, he wondered, would the Taverners think if word got back to them?)

She didn't know. Her parents had chosen her, not simply and naturally but with forethought and courage. There was nothing wrong with choosing against loss—it was the best you could do, in fact. Also, she threw in, this baby would open its eyes on the wide Texas sky as a native. "We need one soul among us," she said, and began the elaborate unbuttoning of her wine-colored Victorian blouse with its high neck and voluminous sleeves, "that will feel at home here." She sighed. "One of us who wasn't shown the gate under a flaming sword."

"And the gate opened into Texas. Who'd have expected?" Ben, sad and happy, wondered if they could really devote a soul to the future that way. He wondered if their very genes hadn't been scarred by fear and repentance. But what did you ever know about anyone you brought into the world? What could luck or love or so-called knowledge guarantee? Even knowing what he knew, wouldn't he be father to Jacob again, and to everything Jacob had done?

"Amen," he said, trying to believe. "Girl or boy, we'll name it Sisyphus." And leaned in to help her with her buttons.

* * *

But it didn't happen. Ben, relieved, decided it was the Revenge of the Feminists, Carolyn's friends who didn't think you should try to solve old problems with a new baby. She said, "You mean my ambivalence." Maybe.

Probably it was age. That was her doctor's opinion. (Could she really be forty-four?) "That's a borderline, you know. You should have started a little earlier."

"Hardly," she answered him dryly. He didn't know her past; thought she was just another woman panicked at mid-life who wanted one more chance to walk around the park with the young mothers pushing strollers, cheating age, while her husband had his mid-life crisis some other way (probably involving a woman as young as these primiparas). "Why don't you wait a little and enjoy being a grandma?" She shuddered, but he thought it was only disappointment.

Ben did not tell her, because there were a lot of things he didn't tell her anymore, that it was no surprise to him—the potency of his contribution to the child was dissipated in weariness. In lack of conviction, somehow. She had not, apparently, convinced him that another life was what they needed, to complement the troubled ones they already had in their charge. A fresh chance. A clean slate. But every slate was murky with their parentage, their defeats, even the waning of their desperation. Your apparatus could work fine but sperm needed an optimistic spirit to make them swim as hard as they had to, and he'd fallen, his spirit had fallen, like a winded runner, and knocked the breath out of him.

They were in a canoe, a large one, all four of them, paddling down the bayou toward the silvered towers of the city. It was an odd excursion—you could rent a boat and cruise inside a deep wide gully with tangles of green and bushes full of small pale flowers that covered the steep sides. Large fish bumped the prow almost companionably as if in greeting. Birds with carrying voices flew over their heads; there were feeding boxes for wood ducks along the route, nailed into the trees like mailboxes. Not many people did this trip—no one thought of Houston as a city with a river.

What was strangest about it, though, was just that hiddenness—you couldn't hear them from here, but very close, up at street level and through the thin woods, were the busiest streets, clogged with good shiny cars. Trailing their fingers in the water here, they weren't that far from Macy's and Neiman-Marcus! A cardinal skittered from branch to branch, an arrow of red like the emphatic slash of a pen. Carolyn laughed. "Listen!" she said. There was the faint airplane-engine roar, continuous as a ground bass. "Leaf blowers!" The woods they passed below were solidly green, just beginning to turn—Houston's hardwoods made meek overtures to fall—and over the ridge and out of sight somebody's yardman was herding piles of the first-fallen leaves from a driveway, polluting the air.

Carolyn leaned against a wicker backrest that came with the canoe. She looked, Ben taunted, like bloody Cleopatra. Though the bayou didn't look much like the Nile.

It was the kids who were pulling hard, shooting them down the little sluices, navigating around a herd of rocks that suddenly appeared like the tan backs of horses. "One of these days," Ben said, "we'll get it together and drive down to Big Bend for the real thing." For now, though, it was sufficiently entertaining to know they were here in this slice of valley below the visible Houston, in pure country—fake pure country.

They coasted east at a good clip toward the extravagant skyline, its faceted mirror-skins and fanciful silhouettes, Gothic, Mayan, Unnamable, listening not to the sound of tires but to the genuine sweet lap of water against the side of the canoe. "It sounds so—*wet!*" Judith said. "I haven't heard anything really wet in this town but rain." Judith, part of the dancer's subculture now, wore her eyes made up to be seen in the last row; her hair was much shorter than Jacob's, with a blond little rat's tail down her back.

"One of these days," Carolyn had repeated to herself about Big Bend, which was rumored to be the ultimate big sky, the place where the cowboy movies live behind the eye, pure geometries of purple and green and yellow and orange, and that—"one of these days"—was what the capsule of grief was filled with as it broke under her tongue. *Winners again!* Mike and Terry Taverner would say. The Taverners rode with her everywhere now, they commented on what would be her luck, her husband's and children's luck, until they died. All they had lost, the Taverners had said whenever the chance came up, was some time, some money, some respect, their house, nothing real. *Not true, not true.* But they were all here, all of them, she couldn't deny it. However battered, they could still say "one of these days," and that was a slash of joy she felt, no pretending otherwise, when the sun came down on the bayou like a handful of pale gold coins flung on the ripply water. "Jacob, look!" Judith called, and they both reached over the side for a fistful of glitter at the same time, tipping them perilously, laughing. As the boat poked forward, the coins scattered and rearranged themselves like a gambler's treasure under an impatient hand. Joy was another privilege she was stuck with. Unsanctioned, regrettable, it swept right over her and made her turn her eyes away, like too much light.